CROWN OF CROWNS DUOLOGY

Crown of Crowns

Godly Sins

CROWN OF CROWNS

DUOLOGY

Crown of Crowns
&
Godly Sins

CLARA LOVEMAN

ISBN: 978-1-8380623-6-1
First Edition: June 2021

For Charlie

CONTENTS

CROWN OF CROWNS

GODLY SINS

CROWN OF CROWNS

CR⊕WN
⊕F
CR⊕WNS

CLARA LOVEMAN

ill they punish me for being here?

I was far from where I was supposed to be, far from NordHaven, my home. I must have looked strange to the commoners. They were casual in lightweight clothing, while I walked among them wrapped head to toe in heavy blue garb. Gaard's brutal sun had me stopping to wipe sweat from my brow, the sound of my heartbeat thrashing in my ears.

"No time to stop," Roki said, looking back at me. "I have so much to show you."

I smiled at his eagerness. "I'm coming."

Of course, I would have followed Roki anywhere. I had already followed him from the safety of my home and into the rabble of the city. I would have followed Roki to the Surrvul Desert and beyond. This boy was something new, something exciting that I'd never expected to find.

"Just up ahead," he called back. "We're almost in the square."

I paused another second to adjust my headscarf. I had it

wrapped around my neck but also covering my nose and mouth. I looked like one of the Ava-Surrvul, the desert people who lived in sand huts. As I adjusted the scarf, someone bumped into me, and my sunglasses slipped off. "Oof," I said. I looked back and saw my four Protectors appear out of nowhere and surge into action like rabid machines out for blood.

Their mechanical hulls were shaped like human chests. Their legs were clunky metal limbs, and their arms were fully plated in bulletproof steel. They strode forward as a group, intent on the poor man who had bumped into me. Exactly what did they plan on doing with him? I held my breath.

"I'm sorry," the man said. He spoke with a commoner's accent. He was disheveled, wearing loose rags and a pair of weathered sandals.

The mechanized Protectors were almost upon him. I wanted to scream, "Leave the man alone!" But I had frozen, rooted to the spot.

Thankfully, Roki whisked ahead of me and stuck out his hand. "No," he said, and to my disbelief, the Protectors stopped, reversing back into the crowd and fixing their lifeless machine eyes on me.

"How did you do that?" I asked, gaping at Roki.

He shrugged. "Protectors may be controlling, the steel arm of justice and authority for all of Geniverd, but don't forget, Kaelyn, they are still machines. They're just robots. We made them, not the other way around. And because they are machines, they are programmable."

I blinked up at him, letting my head fall back, and crossed my arms. I was in ever-increasing awe of the man who had swept me off my feet. Roki was witty, charismatic, mysterious. "You fascinate me," I said.

He had a grin that conveyed secret knowledge. "You

haven't seen anything yet." Roki took me by my hand. "Come, I want to show you more. More, Kaelyn. There's so much more!"

I let him guide me through the throngs of commoners in the historic district of the city. It was all so foreign to me, even though these were *my* people, the Ava-Gaard. I was fifteen years old, and yet I had never been among them. Not like this. Never had I struggled through crowds while sweat burned my eyes and so many shouting voices threatened to deafen me. I could feel my heart thudding in my chest, could hear blood rushing through my ears. This was the thrill I had been waiting for my whole life. It felt like everything I'd ever known—my dull existence inside the halls of NordHaven, my family, my friends—was all a monotonous blur up until this moment.

Still, I was quivery, my mind racing. What would Mama and Papa do if they knew where I was?

He must have sensed my trepidation. "I know you're nervous," he said, still leading me by my hand. "You've never pushed through a swarm of Ava-Gaard while they breathe in your face and step on your nice leather boots. This is a change for you."

I glanced awkwardly at my boots as if I'd just seen them for the first time. How much was there that I didn't know? Roki had only agreed to take me here after I'd begged him for days and promised to wear a disguise. He'd said my parents would never allow any of this, but because I'd been stubborn about it, he let me join him for part of the morning. I was thrilled to pieces to be among the people I might be honored to serve one day. But now ... even my disguise wasn't right. I was the only person in the market with polished leather boots—with boots that weren't scuffed or dirty or covered in muck.

Roki loved it here. He was like a kid let loose in one of

Gaard's annual carnivals, and I stumbled behind him, giggling. His energy was contagious. I was bubbling over with excitement as we navigated through narrow streets packed with people, their skin tanned by the sun, their black hair somewhat lightened from long hours outside. No one paid me any attention. No one knew who I was. Only Roki knew what was in my blood, and he didn't care. I was sure he liked me for who I was.

"Here," he said. "Isn't it marvelous?"

We had stopped in a crowded square. Everywhere I looked, people were selling fruit and vegetables from makeshift stalls that had been erected in front of the regular businesses—chic cafés, modern restaurants, and stores that sold expensive clothing and futuristic home decor.

"What are they doing?" I asked Roki. "Why are they selling fruit? Look, there's a wooden stall with a man selling fish. Are those live fish? What is this place?"

Roki laughed as if I had asked him the dumbest question in the world. "It's a market," he said. "You really don't know what a market is?"

I shook my head, feeling stupid. "No," I told him, pressing my lips together tightly. "It looks old fashioned."

"It is!" said Roki, so unabashedly happy that he grabbed a peach from the nearest stall and tossed it to me. "Look."

I caught it and gasped. "What is this?" The peach was cold and hard in my hands and had none of the fuzz the fruit is known for. "It's fake," I said, baffled. "Why are people buying fake fruit?"

Roki let out a deep, satisfying sigh, his countenance glowing. His chest was out, chin high, and even though he was right next to me, he seemed to take up all the space, like he owned the ground we walked on. Something cocky about him. Was he trying to prove something to me? That was just another thing that drew me to him. Roki's unpredictability and charm had kept me coming back to him for the past two weeks. I couldn't get enough. I didn't think I ever would.

"It's Market Reenactment Day." He spoke boisterously. "I can't believe you've never heard of it. Your parents are the ones who permit—I might add, *rarely* permit—the common folk in Gaard to hold this event. It's the same story everywhere in the world. You see, hundreds of years ago, people all across Geniverd set up markets to sell goods: fruit from the lush forests of Shondur, fish caught by the brave fishermen of Nurlie Island, herbal cactus extracts from the Surrvul Desert. They sold it all!"

I was surprised to hear of my parents' role, as they'd never talked about market reenactment. Were they hiding something from me, or was I too protected?

I peered up at Roki, sucking in a quick breath. "But not anymore," I stuttered, putting the fake peach back into its basket.

Roki hung his head. "No," he said, "not anymore. Markets existed before the great plague that wiped out nearly half the population, before the rise of technology. It was a simpler time. A warring time, perhaps, but simpler. Now, monthly food rations are delivered by Protectors. The food is healthy, don't get me wrong. It's just that we've lost the way."

I was stunned. How did I not know so much about my people, yet in a few years, I might be expected to govern them? Why was I being shielded from them?

Roki sighed and shook his head, looking nostalgic. "Life used to be hard," he told me. "Hard but simple. Things used to matter. Now, instead of a hardworking population of farmers, businesspeople, bankers, construction workers, fruit sellers, all we have is robots. Human beings used to work for something, Kaelyn; we used to do something. Now big, clunky

9

Protectors do all the hard work that we should be doing. The machines toil in the fields, deliver our meals, take care of our infrastructure, build our hospitals. They even work in our hospitals, doing medical jobs that humans used to do."

I stared at Roki for a second. I had always thought him to be wise beyond his years, but now he was talking as if he had been around so many years ago to see these markets, as he called them. He spoke of the technological rise as though he had lived through it. There was such experience in his soft eyes, such knowledge. He was only sixteen years old!

"This market," Roki continued, "is a picture of the old life. In truth, I think people love this day so much because it makes them feel like they have a purpose. I think that people want it to go back to the way it was, before they got lazy and complacent and jobless, shuffling through poverty while clans of rich people lord over the entire planet with inherited empires of —" Roki stopped and looked at me. "Sorry," he said. "I didn't mean ..."

"I know." I gave him a smile. "Don't worry about it. I like it here. I like seeing all this old stuff. It gives me a sense of our heritage. Maybe you're right, Roki. Maybe the world is too easy."

I had to agree with Roki. What he was saying made sense. I knew more about wealth and boredom than I cared to admit, and now that Roki had brought me to the market, I saw the world opening before my eyes. Somewhere along the way, something had gone wrong, and this was the result. Less than one percent of the population had everything they could ever want and were still bored out of their minds, while the rest were just as bored, only they didn't have the money or means to do anything about it.

"I'm glad you like it here," he said. "I was skeptical about bringing you. I know it's rare for you to leave your gilded cage, as I like to call it. I'm glad to share your first outside experience with you."

I told him, "I wouldn't want to share it with anyone else."

We smiled at each other then, a hint of something dangerous in the air between us. I thought he wanted to reach out and touch my cheek, maybe kiss me. My body heated at the thought of it. Instead, Roki bit down on his lip.

"Come," he said, quickly dismissing the sudden tension. He took me by my hand and led me deeper into the market. "We have to hurry. We only have a few minutes before the Protectors take you back. There's one more thing I want to show you."

It was a park, but inside the park were women with round bellies and small strollers, pushing the strollers with one hand while they held their tummies and laughed with their friends.

"What is this?" I asked Roki. I didn't understand.

"They're pretending to be pregnant," he said. "It reminds people of how we used to only have natural births, back before the clan leaders imposed strict regulations on how women are allowed to bring life into the world. This display reminds us of a happier time, when people were free and the world was natural."

I gave Roki a weird look. I wondered what more freedom would mean for the world order. I'd never appreciated these ancient things or considered them as an alternative. What would it be like to actually be pregnant? But Roki was also talking about these things again like he knew them firsthand. I thought, *That's just how mature he is. Roki knows his history better than me. He is more sophisticated than some grown men I know! Of course I'm attracted to him.*

Then again, I had been attracted to Roki since the night we first met, since the very first time I laid eyes on him, at a ball thrown by an Ava-Nurlie noblewoman in honor of my parents' successful leadership. Roki had bought his way in somehow. He had introduced himself, telling me, "You have the saddest yet most stunning eyes I have ever seen. They portray a longing that can never be fulfilled. I feel drawn to you. Perhaps because your eyes say what I feel about our world."

Yeah, that had unnerved me. He had seen me for who I was. Just me, plain and simple. Not an heiress, not a potential queen, not a rung on some political ladder, just Kaelyn. I had been obsessed with Roki ever since.

"... and that was the reasoning behind artificial births," Roki was saying.

"Huh?" I realized I had been daydreaming and missed most of what he had said. I felt heat radiating from my face. While he was talking, I had been fantasizing about our previous dates, the cute things he had said to me the night we met, and how he had lifted me high and spun me in the air outside the noblewoman's mansion. I couldn't help it. Roki had been so romantic!

"I was explaining how Decens-Lenitas, our mighty moral code, put an end to natural births in favor of lab babies. Our rulers say that it's avoiding natural births that enables the gene editing that has eliminated cancer, allergies, and all but infectious diseases. Still, it's one of the things I wish hadn't changed, because pregnancy used to be a pleasant experience for many people." He narrowed his eyes at me and smirked. "Wait a minute. You were daydreaming!"

I was still blushing. "A little," I said. "I still can't believe you're with me. There are so many other girls to choose from. Can ... can I ask you why?"

He smiled and said, "There are no other girls. That's why. There's only you, Kaelyn. When we met, I saw a rebellious young girl with a sullen spirit in need of some much-needed happiness. I saw your soul, and I wanted to be a part of it."

I had to turn from Roki before my emotions boiled over and I started to cry. My cheeks were so hot they could have been sunburned. For so long I had lived in a bubble of bland nothingness, and now here was Roki, making me feel so alive, so overwhelmed with emotion!

"We should get you back to NordHaven," he said. "I don't want your parents to be upset with you before the big ceremony for your brother."

"You're right," I said. "Thank you for bringing me here. It was a relief after all the time I've been imprisoned at home. I hope we can come here again. I've never been happier than I am right now with you. To be honest, Roki, I don't think I can go back to the way things used to be."

"I feel the same," he said with a smile. "Don't worry, Kaelyn. We have all the time in the universe to be together."

* * *

I WAS HAVING separation anxiety even before I got home. I wanted to be with Roki so much. I missed him fiercely. Pushing open my front door, I could have sworn I smelled him in the foyer of our house. Could I have been so obsessed with Roki that I was now smelling him when he wasn't around? Then again, I had lingered during our parting hug in the square, with my face nuzzled against him. Perhaps his scent still clung to my clothes: earthy, herbal fresh, slightly smoky, faintly toffee sweet. I'd have to put off having them laundered for a few days.

Mama was descending the grand staircase into the foyer with a judgmental look on her face. Even when she was displeased with me, I held my mother in high regard. I vener-

13

ated the long hours she put in chairing Gaard's council meetings. I admired her statuesque figure, now emphasized by her long olive-green velvet gown, and mirroring the shapely vases of roses flanking the heavy oak doors of NordHaven.

"Enjoy your morning?" she asked.

"It was nice," I said. I didn't want to lie, but I also didn't want to admit that I had spent the morning frolicking with the man of my dreams. Even if she suspected I'd been with Roki, I doubted she knew exactly where we'd been, considering Roki's control over the Protectors.

I tried to shift the conversation. "Where's Papa?"

"Getting our things into the flyrarc." Then Mama gave me that unimpressed motherly stare. "Where's your boyfriend?"

There was a touch of sarcasm in her voice that I didn't like. Mama irked me when it came to Roki. She had forbidden me from seeing him at first, accusing me of bringing shame to our family. Then she had restricted our time together. I had invited him over for dinner, hoping Mama and Papa would get to know Roki and like him as much as I did, but that wasn't what had happened. My parents had stepped out of the room during the meal, and I had overheard Papa telling her, "Don't worry, dear. Kaelyn will come to her senses soon enough, and we'll be rid of the lowborn scoundrel." The worst part was that Roki had heard it too.

Enough was enough. I said to Mama, "And so what if he is my boyfriend? Would it be so bad for me to date an ordinary boy from Nurlie?"

"Oh, honey," Mama said, shaking her head sadly. "You are the daughter of Gaard-Ma and Gaard-Elder. Have you forgotten that? As the highest-ranking family of Gaard, we are bound to the moral code of Decens-Lenitas. We are role models. We must marry people who are like us. I'm sorry, Kaelyn, but you simply cannot be with someone who doesn't share our moral code. Why not someone of royal blood from another clan? What about Jaken or his brother, Zawne?"

I was frustrated and angry at having this conversation over and over.

"I don't want to be with Jaken or Zawne," I said. "I want to be with Roki." I stomped my foot, not caring how childish I must have looked. "I don't care where he's from or if he doesn't agree with Decens-Lenitas. What does it mean, anyway, our moral code? Roki has a love for all things living. So what if he doesn't belong to a royal line? I know he would put his family first. And who cares if he doesn't believe in lab babies and if he prefers natural births?"

Mama gasped at this. "Family? I had no idea you two were getting so serious." She stood up straight and said in a domineering tone, "You are not to see him anymore. He believes in natural births? Is he mad?"

"He's perfect," I said. My composure was flaking apart. I was so angry with Mama. I spoke without thinking and didn't care if it got me into trouble. "Roki has my feelings in mind. He took me into the heart of the city today, to the Historical District, where I saw the market reenactment. He did it so I could escape this stuffy place and all your stuffy rules. I don't want this to be my life!"

Mama's eyes were wide. She looked mortified.

I kept on in anger. "You've never done that for me, taken me out into the city. Not with a chance of your face being on the news." I made quotation marks in the air and said, "Headline: 'Gaard-Ma seen with civilians.'" And I scoffed, "No, not with your precious reputation to uphold. You'd never go to where I went today, walking in the street with the people. We are supposed to adhere to the moral code, but why does the moral code need to make us so ... so lofty! We should be able to love who we want, go where we want, and do what we want. I hate being trapped in this system!"

A thousand emotions were passing across Mama's face. As she stood before me, frozen, I wondered what she was thinking, what she was feeling. I hadn't meant to denounce Decens-Lenitas. I believed wholly in its teachings. The moral code encompassed many things. For example, love for all living things, strength of mind, recognition of the class system and the monarchy, obedience to the Protectors, and outlawry of pregnancies in favor of lab-conceived and lab-grown babies. I just didn't understand why virtue meant being a snob.

"Kaelyn," Mama said. She appeared to have composed herself, though I could see a ferocious heat burning underneath her pinched smile. "In time you will come to understand that life is not easy. We must make sacrifices for the greater good, for the good of Gaard and for all of Geniverd. We clan leaders must maintain appearances and marry into other clans with hopes of ascending the throne. The more virtuous in the laws of Decens-Lenitas you are, the higher your chance of being promoted to king or queen. It's why Raad, now that he has completed his Aska training, is much closer to reaching the throne."

I couldn't have cared less about the throne. I was proud of my brother, Raad, and I loved him. Askas were considered to be highly skilled at Decens-Lenitas and at fighting, and so were highly esteemed. A few of them who weren't heirs were allowed to become engineers after their training, to oversee design blueprints for Protectors. Raad was brave and strong and wise for completing the brutal training, yet I didn't see what it had to do with Roki. I asked, "Are you upset with me because I haven't lived up to Raad? I'm not as virtuous or as brave as him. Is that why you torture me like this?"

"Honey ..." She shook her head. "Of course, no. I love you

16

both very much. I just don't want you to waste your life. Look at what happens to those who don't follow our moral code. They become Gurnots. Have you not heard the reports about terrorism, about the anarchist Gurnots lashing out across the territories, lighting fires from here to Lodden in an attempt to sabotage the monarchy? I've even heard they are stealing dangerous weapons from the Protectors! These people are treacherous, Kaelyn. I don't want your angst to become something volatile."

"Angst!" I was in a huff all over again. "I have no angst. There are six clans on six continents, Mama. There are eighteen blood-born heirs and heiresses, plus their spouses. That's thirty-six choices for the crown. Let one of them have it. Let Raad have it. We all know my brother deserves to rule over Geniverd. Why can't you just let me live my life and be with Roki? Not all ordinary people turn into Gurnots. Look at Lordin. She's an ordinary girl from Gaard, and she's world famous for being one of the most wholesome, kindhearted, moral people in the world."

"Lordin is an exception," Mama said. "She got very lucky. And we're not talking about Lordin; we are talking about you. The coronation ceremony will be upon us in just over three years, and either you and your husband, or Raad and his wife, will replace us as Gaard's clan leaders. One of you might be chosen as king or queen. I just want you to make the right decision for your future."

She slid her fingers into silky leather gloves, signaling she was ready to leave. "Now hurry up and change. We need to head to the capital for your brother's ceremony."

"I can look after my own future," I said. "And I'm not going to Raad's homecoming ceremony."

I felt silly and selfish as I said this. Raad was my brother. He had just spent the last two years in the most dangerous

17

conditions in Geniverd for his Aska training. Trekking through the Surrvul wasteland, brutal physical training in Lodden, swimming with sharks and fighting leopards. I wanted to see him, to celebrate his triumph and his transformation now that he was a skilled Aska warrior, yet I wanted to see Roki more. I wanted to gaze into the flecks of gold and brown in his dazzling silver-gray eyes, which complemented his skin. I wanted him to hold me.

"Does that mean you're firm in your decision?" Mama had her arms crossed, that bleak look on her face.

"Yes. I want to stay home. I can see Raad tomorrow when he gets home. I don't need to be flaunted before Jaken and Zawne just so you can try to sell me like fruit at the market."

Talking about the market again had Mama shaking her head. "Okay. Cool down, Kaelyn. We can discuss this when your father and I get back from the ceremony tomorrow. You're disappointing your brother by not being there. Think about that while you're with your boyfriend. I hope he's more important than your family." And with that, Mama flounced past me and out the front door.

At that moment, I desperately wanted to launch the towering vases of roses at the awaiting flyarc, but instead, I stormed off to my sleeping quarters, getting there just in time to see the vehicle zipping past the window, rising high into the sky.

2

*R*ight after Mama and Papa had left, I called Roki and invited him over. Sometime later my visin beeped in my ear for the tenth time. I tapped the top of my wrist, and the device produced a projection in front of me, a translucent screen in the air. It was Mama calling again. I tapped my wrist and the projection died. "I'm busy," I said sulkily, as if she could hear me.

I checked the time. It was nearly four. I had been brooding in my bed for over two hours! Roki was supposed to be at NordHaven any minute.

I launched myself out of bed and ran to my dressing room, where I fumbled with gown after gown until there was a pile of fabric in the middle of the floor. I finally chose a summery viridian dress and combed my hair quickly in the mirror. I smiled remembering the time Roki had said my extended eyeliner and long carbon-black lashes complemented my upturned eyes. My visin beeped again, and Roki's voice was in my ear.

"Hey. I'm out front."

"Coming!" I shouted by accident. I was so nervous I could hardly control my voice. This was our first chance to be alone, completely alone, without Mama or Papa around to spy on us. I had butterflies in my stomach. I had already forgotten about the argument in the foyer. I smoothed my dress and ran to greet Roki.

He was outside, leaning against the marble balustrade, handsome as always, in a casual jacket, his hair wild. "Wow," he said. "I never get tired of seeing your amber eyes. They're so beautiful."

Ten seconds in, and I was already blushing. "You're too sweet," I said. "Really, too sweet."

Roki extended his hand to me. "Take a walk?"

I took his hand, and Roki led me around our impressive estate and into the garden. Bees hovered above the flower beds, and butterflies fluttered merrily beside the cobblestone path. It was peaceful here, and I was happy in Roki's presence. The garden smelled sweet, like honeysuckle after a morning rain. I couldn't tell if it was naturally coming from the flowers or if it was the day's smell generated by the atmospheric bubble around NordHaven.

As we walked, Roki asked me, "Do you feel guilty about not going to your brother's homecoming ceremony?"

"A little," I said, feeling a sudden shame in my heart, "but there was no way I could have sat in the flyrarc with Mama for two hours after our argument. Raad will survive a day without seeing me. After all, he is an Aska now. He's supposed to have hardened his mind, soul, and body. He can survive one more day without his sister."

"True," Roki said. "Askas are the fiercest warriors in all of Geniverd." He hesitated, looking into a bed of roses. "But what happened with Gaard-Ma? I hope it wasn't an argument about me."

20

"It was and it wasn't," I said. It was a little embarrassing to tell Roki I had screamed at my mother, "He's perfect!" Instead, I said, "It was more of the same, the same argument we've been having a lot lately. You know, about the expectations my parents have for me to become clan leader, even to become queen. I'm just so tired of it, Roki. People think I'm set for life because of who I am. Mama tells me I should be excited about all the prospects I have, about all the potential suitors. All I want to do is hide under my bed. There must be more to life. There must be more than ceremonies and extravagant balls and fancy retreats all over Geniverd."

I knew by Roki's gentle expression that he understood what I was saying. Roki always got me. It was like he was tuned in to my frequency. He raised his bushy eyebrows and let me go on ranting.

"Mama's just mad because I'm not as good as Raad," I said. "She's also scared that if Gaard doesn't produce a king or queen soon, our family will be deposed, demoted to simple folk. Oh gosh, the horror! Mama always talks about how our lineage is cursed. It's a ridiculous thought. We aren't cursed just because I reject the path I'm supposed to follow."

"Why do you think that is?" Roki asked, back to admiring the roses. "Why do you reject what's expected of the First Daughter of Gaard?"

"Maybe I don't want to be the First Daughter of Gaard." I hung my head. Roki was trying to be sweet by asking me how I felt about everything, about my life, but it was just making me depressed. "I hate how Mama wants to sell me off to the Shondur Clan like I'm a tool for trading. She wants me to marry Jaken or Zawne so that I'm in a better position to be chosen at the coronation in three years."

"Of course she'd want you to marry a prince." Roki raised

his eyebrow. "It's been nearly forty years since the last coronation. Wow."

"Yes," I said. "A little over three years until the Crown of Crowns swoops down from the sky and lands on the head of the chosen one. Papa told me stories about the last coronation. He said it had been amazing to watch. He said that the bird had soared from the sky, seemingly from no place at all, and landed on the heirs of Shondur. They were made queen and king instantly. That was thirty-seven years ago."

A quirky smile came to Roki's lips. "I do wonder where that bird comes from. It's a real mystery," he said. Then he plucked a rose from the flower bed and gave it to me. "Here, a beautiful rose for a beautiful girl."

I smiled, twirled the rose in my fingers, and said, "I prefer to be with you. I don't want to marry Jaken or Zawne."

"I don't want you to either."

"And who knows?" I said with a sudden burst of energy. "Maybe if you divulge your intentions to Mama and Papa, and we are officially together when the time of the ceremony comes, the Crown of Crowns will land on your head. Can you imagine it, Roki, you and me as king and queen? We could make the kingdom a better place. We could make Geniverd better for the common man, try to loosen the stranglehold the upper class has over society, and make Decens-Lenitas more accessible for everyone. Think about it, Roki."

Roki laughed somewhat sadly. "If only that could be. Let's try not to think about it. Gaard-Ma and Gaard-Elder would never allow our official union."

"In that case," I said, giving Roki a playful look, "I'll marry another clan head and take you for my secret lover."

"Your lover!"

"Sure. Why not? Mama told me a story once about a woman who was promised to marry an heir—I can't remember which one. Anyway, the promise was revoked at the last minute, and the woman felt horribly scorned. Then the heir became king. He took the woman as his one and only mistress, loving her more fiercely than he loved his own wife, the queen. Then, um … Shoot, I forget the rest."

I stopped and scratched my eyebrow. It was hard to remember all the details. Mama had told me the story so long ago. In my brief confusion, Roki watched me with a smile. He was always so courteous.

"Oh," I said, "that's right. What happened was the Gaard-Ma at the time needed the mistress's help. See, the mistress had a huge influence over the king, more so than the queen did. Gaard-Ma beseeched the mistress to sway the king's mind over some land acquisitions he was trying to make near Cara. He wanted to steamroller farmlands and absorb them into Cara. He wanted to make the world's capital even bigger while displacing hundreds of Gaard farmers.

"The mistress refused Gaard-Ma's request. She claimed the king needed that land and there was nothing anyone could do about it. Well, Gaard-Ma was known for her vengeance. All Gaard-Mas are. She started a rumor among the upper class. She denounced the mistress as a harlot and a thief, a traitor to the king and a schemer against all the people of Geniverd. After the rumor spread throughout the kingdom, the king had no choice but to banish his beloved mistress. She was forced to live in the bitter highlands in the north of Gaard. Her climb to the top ended in misery."

Roki gave me a puzzled look. "Are you saying you want to have me as your lover just so you can banish me?"

"No!" I latched onto him, bucking against his chest. "I just thought the story related to our talk. I could never banish you, Roki! Not from my life, not from my heart."

He stroked my head as I hugged him fiercely. I liked the

23

feeling of his fingers in my hair and his warm chest against my body. I could smell his sweet aroma; it was more powerful than the honeysuckle scent that permeated the air around us in the garden. I never wanted the scent of him to go away.

"That's a good fantasy you have for us," Roki said, "but let's focus on today. Okay? Let's enjoy our time together." We stood, and he took me by the hand. "Let's walk some more."

WE STROLLED through the gardens of NordHaven for what felt like years, trailing alongside the artificial creek with the backs of our hands touching as if we both wanted to hold hands but were too shy. We walked beneath the artificial apple trees and laughed together, strolled below the canopy of fake leaves and vines, and across the wooden lovers' bridge. The scents changed as we walked. I realized for the first time how much of my home was fake: the leaves, the low-hanging apples, the shifting scents wafting down from the atmospheric bubble. It was sunny and warm inside the grounds. I wondered if it was raining outside, if people were huddled under awnings in the city and shivering from the cold.

Roki and I walked until our legs got sore. Then we sat on the edge of the big marble pool Papa had built nearly forty years ago, when he had become clan leader of Gaard. There were fish in the pool, little blue ones swimming in circles and big yellow ones with bulging eyes, sucking the film off the bottom.

"So much simpler to be a fish," I said. "There are no fish heirs, no king or queen ruling over all the other fish, no Aska training or moral code to uphold. Yes, I think I would like to be a fish."

"Me too," Roki said. "It never ceases to amaze me how much in sync we are. It's like we share the same mind."

"Isn't that a scary thought!" I told him. "Can you imagine sharing your mind with someone else, someone living inside your brain, inside your skin? I can't. I prefer you just the way you are, our thoughts intertwined, and our fingers too."

He squeezed my hand and I squeezed back. It was so nice in the sun, the fish darting around our feet in the water. The Protectors were out of sight. There was no one around.

Still, my thoughts drifted. "Maybe I would be better off training with the Grucken than getting married off to a stranger," I said. "He is the guardian of Decens-Lenitas, after all, the most respected person aside from the king and queen. Oh, and aside from Lordin. She might be the most respected person in the world. And she trained with the Grucken!"

"The Grucken only accepts one intern per year," Roki said. "But I know he would select you. I've heard all he does is look in an applicant's eyes. He knows just from their eyes if they are the one to be trained. I'm sure he would take one look at your pretty amber eyes and know immediately. You'd be the next Lordin."

"I wish," I said. "She's not even an heir. I wonder who she'll marry. Surely someone important. Surely one of the clan heirs will take her for themselves to gain a better position for the seat of power, to be king. Her moral code is higher than anyone's. Plus she is loved by everyone in Geniverd. They watch every move she makes on their visins. She's the most popular person on this planet."

"I know," he said dryly. "I've seen it. They look at the girl like she's a goddess. But is she really? Be careful who you idolize, Kaelyn. People are different in their souls."

I frowned at him. "Now you sound like Mama. Soon you're going to be warning me about the dangers of natural birth, how I need to freeze my eggs at the clinic, how I need to prepare what genes I want edited in my baby, and insisting I get all my vaccines so I don't die of a superbug. Or worse, soon you'll be warning me of the dangers of the Gurnots!"

"I'd never," he said, so seriously I furrowed my brows at him.

"You don't side with those ... those Gurnots, do you?" I asked.

"Eh." Roki shrugged. "They aren't that bad."

"They're terrorists!" I almost shouted. "They're fire starters! Haven't you seen the news reports? They burned down another seaside estate this week. It was lucky the estate had just emptied for the season, or people could have died."

"Maybe," Roki said, his tone a little too relaxed for the topic of death. "Or maybe it was intentionally like that. They may seem like terrorists to you, Kaelyn, but to others, they represent change. Change for the people of Geniverd. I know the Nurlie Islanders support them. A lot of people do. Much of the world views Decens-Lenitas as an oppressive moral standard. They want to be rid of it. They are tired of this lopsided rule, these rich families who inherit power and then pass the power along. Nobody even knows where their power and wealth came from anymore!"

"What about the wars?" I asked. I could hardly believe what Roki was saying. "Aside from the Gurnots stirring up trouble, there haven't been major conflicts in two hundred years, because of our moral standards. Would you see people die?"

"No way." Roki looked at me, his eyes powerful in a way I hadn't noticed before. I thought they could make me do anything. He seemed so serious. "Gurnots are against classism, which is promoted by Decens-Lenitas. I hate the idea of hurting people. That's why I think we need change, so people don't get hurt. Maybe you'll be the one to do it once you're queen."

I sighed. "Sure, with you as my mistress."

We laughed. We held hands. We kicked our feet in the pool, and soon the sun was getting low.

I said to Roki, "We should go inside and dry our feet."

He smiled. "Whatever you say, Kaelyn."

* * *

I LED him past the sitting rooms, the kitchen, down the long hallway and up the back stairwell to the second floor.

"I've never been up here," Roki said as we walked. "We've always stayed downstairs, in the dining room or in the parlor, where your parents could keep their eyes on us. Where are we going?"

"You'll see," I said. My heart was hammering in my chest. I was more nervous than ever as we neared my room. It seemed like the right thing to do and the right time to do it. Me and Roki, alone in my bedroom. I'd never known a boy I felt so strongly about. For that matter, I'd never had a boy in my room. Everything felt so … fated.

I pulled him through the threshold and stopped, turned to look into his eyes.

Roki made a loud gulp as he looked around. "We're in your bedroom."

"I'll get some towels to dry our feet," I told him, only half aware our feet were already dry.

I went into the adjoining washroom and came back with two fluffy white towels. Roki was seated on the edge of my bed. He looked out of place. Everything in my room was colorful, blue sheets and blue drapes, cute outfits hanging on hooks in the smaller closet, and makeup scattered on my vanity. I wondered how long it had been since Roki last ventured into a girl's room. I wondered if he ever had. It seemed unlikely to me that such a handsome character hadn't, even if he was still so young.

"Here." I passed him a towel.

"Thanks," he said with a laugh, "but my feet are already dry."

I looked at mine and burst out laughing, mostly from awkwardness. "Mine too," I said.

And that was when something happened, something powerful and indescribable. We both stopped laughing and regarded one another. The air thickened. Heat rose from an unknown place and overtook me. He parted his lips to speak, then stopped. Magnetism was drawing me to him, my hand to the flaxen scruff on his chin. It was soft, inviting. I said, "Roki …" and he shushed me with his finger to my lips.

Now his hand was at my cheek, caressing my skin. I thought, *This is it. It's what I've been waiting—no, yearning for!*

"Can you feel it?" Roki said, his voice low and deep.

I nodded, swallowed dryly. "Yes."

He was leaning toward me. I could hear his shallow breaths. I touched his chest through his shirt, felt the hard contours of his pecs, ran my fingers down his sculpted abs. I was in awe of his perfect body. His eyes pierced mine and then glanced at my lips, as my fingers slowly rolled over the stubble on his chin and jawline. His lips were getting closer. Electricity prickled through me, and I leaned in to meet him—

"Kaelyn! Kaelyn, where are you?"

I jolted in surprise, pulled away from Roki just as my lips brushed against his. "Is that my brother?"

Raad's voice sounded again, booming through my open doorway. "Kaelyn, are you here?" His footsteps thundered and shook the house as he searched for me.

I looked at Roki. "He shouldn't be here until tomorrow. I … I …"

But our moment had passed. Roki's panic was clear on his face. He looked scared, like he had been caught doing something he shouldn't have been doing.

I touched his knee. "Don't worry. Raad's my brother. It's okay if he sees us together. We've done nothing wrong."

Before I could say more, Raad exploded into my room. "Kaelyn," he said, short of breath and totally wild. He looked different than I remembered. He was grown, burly, menacing. The Aska training had turned my brother into a fierce man.

"Yes, brother. I'm here. What is it? Why do you look so panicked? Shouldn't you be at the—?"

"It's Mama," he said, and the blood drained from my face. "Something terrible has happened."

Instinct maybe, or maybe the strip of mourning sackcloth wrapped around Raad's left bicep—either way, I knew what he was going to say. I could feel it, could see the devastation in my brother's tanned face. Already tears were welling in my eyes. I fumbled for Roki's hand but couldn't find it.

Raad took ten huge steps into the room and knelt in front of me. The tragedy was clear in his eyes, and I didn't want to see it. I gawked around the room but couldn't find Roki. He had vanished. But to where? And how?

Raad took my hands in his. I thought he was crying, but how could that be possible for an Aska warrior? Only something truly horrific could make an Aska cry.

"Kaelyn …" Raad was sobbing into my hands. "Mama's dead."

That was when I fainted.

3

I was alone in the darkness of my apartment, a stack of unread books and tea beside my sofa. The visin embedded in my wrist was emitting a projection, a square holographic screen in front of me. I was crying softly. It was the hundredth, maybe two hundredth time I had watched the video in the past year. It always made me cry. There was something so final about seeing the mausoleum Raad had helped construct, the polished white stone seeming to swallow her casket as the funeral procession carried Mama's remains into the structure.

Then there were the faces I recognized in the news footage. I was there, veiled in black and crying. Always crying. And there was Papa, hardly able to keep his composure. Raad was inside the mausoleum with Mama's casket. The other clan leaders were outside, dressed in their own ritualistic funeral attire. Ava-Shondur in leather, Ava-Surrvul in dark green fur, Ava-Krug in white garments, Ava-Nurlie in full-length purple and gold silk, and Ava-Lodden in elaborate sisal.

The only person missing was Roki. It made me mad when

I remembered he hadn't come. He had avoided Mama's funeral just as he had avoided me. The night of her death, Roki had sent me a message on my visin: *Sorry for disappearing so quickly. Everything okay? I miss you.*

I had typed a handful of responses, but none felt appropriate. I had just lost my mother. I was in shock, broken, wounded, and grief-stricken beyond belief. And I was angry because in my time of need, when I had fainted and then sobbed heavily in Raad's arms, Roki hadn't been there to console me. Poof, gone like a ghost. And he had never come back.

I turned off the video of Mama's funeral and flicked through the news channels on my visin. There were reports about a new species of fish found off the Nurlie coast. Another volcanic eruption had devastated Lodden, and three Aska trainees had perished trying to save the residents of a small village there. Gurnots had ambushed a tanker and stolen nearly sixty gallons of high-grade flyrarc fuel, yet the Protectors couldn't find where they had stashed it. Three more fires in one of Surrvul's wealthiest neighborhoods, huge properties burned to the ground—the authorities were beginning to suspect a single individual, perhaps one specialized team of Gurnots. And Lordin and Zawne's wedding had just been announced.

I stopped on the channel showing Lordin and Zawne, took a sip of tea, and turned up the volume. They were quite the match. Lordin was highly esteemed and adored by all the people of Geniverd. Zawne was a prince.

The newscaster's voice came loud in my ear: "The dashing couple, after dating publicly for the past eight months, have finally announced their engagement. These lovebirds have been spotted flaunting their affection on all six continents, and now finally they are to be wed. What could this mean for the upcoming coronation? Could Lordin and Zawne be the next king and queen?"

I hoped so. They were the ideal couple. Lordin did enough volunteer work to put anyone to shame, and Zawne was the son of the current king and queen. They were all anyone had talked about lately—Lordin this and Zawne that.

"Have you seen the footage of them together on the beach in Surrvul?"

"Have you heard what Lordin did for the orphans in Gaard?"

"Have you seen the way they look at each other?"

"Have you seen the secret footage of their first date? They made a song together and sang so beautifully. They're truly in love!"

I adored them like the rest of the world, especially Lordin, a lowborn girl from Gaard who now had a shot at the throne. Lordin gave the people hope, real hope. She promised them a better future by potentially rising to queendom. I agreed with a lot of her reform ideas. I particularly liked Lordin's idea about giving some of the Protectors' jobs back to the people, reducing how much we rely on machines, if not just to give thousands of people some sense of purpose in their lives. However, this line of thought reminded me of Roki, and I tried to ignore it.

The only thing that irked me was how quickly the news of Mama's death had gone away and been replaced by the unconventional lovers. Mama had been poisoned, and they had never found her killer. She had writhed in horrible pain and died before Raad's homecoming ceremony could be concluded, right there on the floor in front of all those clan leaders and nobles. The fact that it had been swept under the rug so quickly upset me.

I endlessly replayed the events of that day in my head.

What had Mama wanted to say when she called me? Why hadn't I picked up? Why had I reacted so defiantly? Had she been right about Roki? If I'd been with her, could I have saved her? At the very least, if I'd swallowed my pride and resisted my craving for Roki, I'd have gone to the homecoming and been on better terms with her before her sudden death. I had thought we'd have more time together. Time to compromise. Time to mend our differences. Time for her to attend my wedding if I was to get married one day. And so her death didn't seem real. Every time someone visited NordHaven, my heart reflexively jumped at the thought it was Mama coming home.

It was only after the ritualistic one-month mourning period that I truly grieved. The heartache got worse as the visits, flowers, and cards from all over Geniverd diminished. How could she be gone, forever and ever?

I turned off my visin and stared into the darkness. It was going to be one of those introspective nights, I could tell. I was already dwelling on the past. I was wondering why Roki hadn't reached out to me after that initial message the night of Gaard-Ma's death. Sure, I had ignored him that one time, but I had been grieving! I had been angry with myself! My last conversation with Mama had been a fight, a silly rebellion. I had chosen Roki over my family, and I could never take it back. I hated myself for it and couldn't stand to talk to him right away. I had thought, *If I don't have Mama anymore, I don't deserve to have Roki either.* I had gambled with family and love, and I had lost both.

Then time had moved forward, and Roki had never tried to reach me again. I had hoped to hear from him once my emotions had cooled off a bit, but he never contacted me. I lost faith in him. I had been so sure he was the one for me. I still felt sometimes like he was, still smelled his scent on my clothes or when I walked into a room. I had been willing to profess my undying feelings for Roki and risk my family's obsession with public image to be with him, and he had never contacted me again.

Eventually, I didn't want him to. His silence justified my contempt. But I never stopped thinking about Roki. Obviously, I was still thinking about him a year later as I sat alone in my apartment, drinking fine tea by myself.

* * *

THE NEXT MORNING, I showed up to the office with a slight headache. It was nice to go to work. I had purpose here. It was my foundation, GMAF, Gaard-Ma Foundation, the organization I had set up in the capital city to keep Mama's memory alive. We were doing good work with orphans, wildlife preservation, women's shelters, education in rural areas, and other sensitive social issues. We were trying to regain some semblance of social purpose with the "normal" people, who happened to make up most of the world's population. They needed work, better lives, and some way to feel like they belonged. With so many Protectors buzzing around and not enough work for everyone, it was no wonder there was so much social divergence going on.

"Good morning, Kaelyn," Tissa said as I entered the space we rented in the bustling downtown. She was sitting at the table with paperwork splayed across it and a half-eaten granola bar in her hand.

"Morning," I said. "Is that your breakfast?"

"You know how I am," Tissa said. "Too busy to stop and eat. I can't help it. We've been getting so much work these past few weeks. Just this morning we received an aid request from Lodden. Apparently, they need more than just the Askas to assist after the vicious volcano two days ago. I'm going over the bankroll to see if we can move some funds around and pay for extra aid workers. I'm wondering if we should pause the construction of the new school in the secluded Butri province of Krug. That way, the construction workers can relocate to Lodden."

"No," I said, sitting down at the table with Tissa. "If money is a problem, I can ask Papa for more funding. I don't want to, but I can. We can also make some emergency calls for money if we need to. But that school is important. We should pay trained aid workers to go to Lodden and leave the construction workers in Krug."

"All right," Tissa said. "That sounds good to me. We sure are lucky to have Gaard-Elder to help support us. He's been so generous since you started this foundation. I'm proud to be working here with you. I know Nnati is too."

I smiled—both at Tissa's kindness and at the thought of my father. "I think Papa needed to be a part of this as much as I did," I told Tissa. "We were both so distraught after Mama's passing. Papa was worse off than I was. It was like he had died, like his soul was empty without her around." I sighed, pushed some loose papers around distractedly. "I can't blame him for it. Times were tough. We were all depressed. It was GMAF that pulled us out of the slump. When I told Papa about my idea to start this foundation, he perked up for the first time since Mama's funeral."

I paused to chuckle, thinking back on the day. His reaction was priceless. "It could be good," Papa had said to me. "You can pursue a charitable career in advocacy while at the same time keeping your mama's memory alive. Not to mention that what you're talking about—a foundation for helping the lower-class citizens, using Decens-Lenitas—can help advance your own status as a well-versed woman of the moral code. It

CLARA LOVEMAN

brings you closer to the throne. Perhaps we can involve the Grucken somehow, get it publicized. Any funding you need, I'll provide. I'll help you move to the capital city. I'll help you with all my business connections. Anything you need for this endeavor, daughter, I will help with."

Tissa must have known I needed a friend-to-friend therapy session. She listened attentively as I said, "I remember the sparkle in his eyes. It was exactly what Papa needed. He helped me with the research, with finding this space for our office, with hiring you and Nnati, and with getting us noticed by the public. At the same time, he made sure I had private tutors to help me finish my studies. And now look at us, Tissa. We have daily requests coming in for our assistance!"

She gave me a coy smile as she produced a letter from her pile of papers. "Not only requests for our assistance," Tissa said. "You'll never guess who this is from."

"Who?" I nearly jumped out of my chair.

"You're not going to guess?" She waved the letter teasingly. "Come on, Kaelyn. You're going to freak out when you find out."

My mind was racing. We had gotten a lot of attention recently from potential donors. A manufacturer from Surrvul called Veeln-Co, the company that built and distributed visins, had approached us about partnering for an ad campaign meant to raise awareness about workplace harassment and workplace safety. I wondered if the letter was from them.

"Is it Veeln-Co?" I asked. I was on the edge of my seat.

"Even better." Tissa was grinning fiendishly. I marveled at how adorable she was. She and Nnati were old friends from Nurlie. Nnati was only a few years older than Tissa, who was closer in age to me. Being in such a metropolitan city, the capital of Geniverd, I liked all the different faces, light and dark eyes, and complexions.

"Tell me!" I said. "Please, Tissa, tell me."

"See for yourself."

She handed me the letter, and I screamed when I saw whose name was on it. "No way!" I leaped out of my chair, doing a celebratory dance even though my head throbbed. "Is it real? Did you read it?"

"I was waiting for you," Tissa said, enjoying my excitement. "For you and Nnati. I think we should all be here to see what Lordin has sent to us in the letter."

That was when Nnati walked into the room. "Did someone say Lordin sent us a letter?" He looked nearly as excited as me. He readjusted his glasses with a huge smile on his face, glancing between Tissa and me. "Well, are we going to open it?"

"Yeah we are!"

I didn't even use the letter opener. I clawed the thing open with my nails and pulled it out, then read it aloud.

"'Dear Kaelyn, I am writing to you on behalf of myself and my partner, Prince Zawne, regarding your foundation, GMAF. We have been following your work closely—how you have been building new schools, quietly campaigning in the capital for social change among the lower classes, beseeching the clan heirs for their support in using Decens-Lenitas for the betterment of the people, assisting in natural disasters, and organizing wildlife protective services. And honestly, we are amazed at what you have accomplished. We are beyond impressed. I must say, Kaelyn, as the First Daughter of Gaard, you have gone above and beyond your station to help the people of this great continent, and indeed the world. Prince Zawne and I would like to invite you to Sud Cottage for dinner. We have a proposal for you. We hope to see you tonight at six p.m. sharp. Yours truly, Lordin.'"

The three of us were speechless. I placed the letter gently

on the table and looked at my friends. "What do you think?" I asked.

Nnati nearly screamed, "You need to buy a new dress and get your Gaard butt over to Sud Cottage tonight! That's what I think!"

"Me too," Tissa said. "This is such an incredible opportunity. Lordin—I mean, Lordin! We have watched her on our visins since she was a little girl working with the rural farmers of Gaard because she wanted to help others. This is the girl the whole world watched blossom into a beautiful young woman with a kind heart. Lordin, who was courted by the most eligible bachelor in Geniverd, and then tamed him. This is the person we are talking about, Kaelyn. We're talking about *the* Lordin. It's sure to be one heck of a proposal."

My legs bounced restlessly under the table. I was excited, nervous, intrigued, scared—all the emotions at once. "What kind of proposal do you think it is?"

Nnati considered my question as he rubbed his chin, clean-shaven and professional in a bow tie, as always. "Lordin said she has been following GMAF's work, and we all know the kind of humane causes she supports and projects she runs. It must be a merger or a funding campaign. Maybe she wants to help us reach more people. Our views are basically the same as hers. We both want to help make a better world."

Then Tissa's face lit up, and she leaned over the table. "Do you think Prince Jaken will be there too?"

I laughed, seeing the heat in Tissa's face at the mention of Prince Zawne's older brother. "I'm not sure, Tiss. Maybe."

Tissa settled into her seat, and a dreamy look dulled her face. Tissa was a girl born under the most common of situations in the most common of places, and maybe that was why she had a deep reverence for the princes of Geniverd. When her eyelids fluttered and she sighed at the thought of Prince

Jaken, I knew it wouldn't have mattered which prince we were talking about. Sometimes I thought she was attracted to the royalty more than the people themselves.

"I know Jaken is married," Tissa said. "Even so, I'd love to go on a date with him. Just one date, nothing serious, no physical contact. He's just so handsome. I just want him to treat me like a princess for one day. Just one."

Nnati raised his hand. His smile was devious. "I'd also like a date with Prince Jaken," he said, "but can mine have touching?"

We all laughed. "Nnati," I said, "you're such a dog!" But I didn't mean it. Nnati was great, playful, classy. Hiring him and Tissa had been the best thing to happen to me since moving to the capital and starting GMAF. I loved them both like family. Well, I saw them more often than my own family. I didn't know what I would have done without Nnati and Tissa. I didn't feel like royalty when I was with them. They made me feel like just another person, like another normal citizen of Gaard. It was, in a way, a vacation from my pampered life back in NordHaven.

"But in all seriousness," Nnati said, deepening his voice and raising an eyebrow, "I like the idea of working with Lordin, and at the same time, I don't. It will be great if she agrees to work with us on our terms, but I don't want to get too tangled up in the upper-class workings of Decens-Lenitas. My pardons, Kaelyn, I know it's your foundation and your rules. It's just the whole paradox of the more 'esteemed' points of the moral code upsets me. I don't want to start helping the upper-class people. You built this foundation for the commoners, for the wildlife, and to keep your mama's memory alive."

"I understand," I said, "but I don't think it will be a problem. I, like everyone else in Geniverd, have been following Lordin's work for years. Even though she is now marrying

Prince Zawne, her dedication to the homeless, the needy, the lost children, it hasn't changed. Her programs are still running. Perhaps she wants to join forces."

I stopped, a sudden look of bewilderment in my eyes. "Could ...?" I licked my lips nervously. "Could it be that Lordin wants to pass the torch? She may become queen next year." I blinked at Tissa, totally shocked by my revelation. "This could be huge!"

Tissa and Nnati beamed at me.

"You better get ready," Nnati said. "Take the day off, Kaelyn. Pick out your dress. It better be a cute one. You have a date with Lordin and Zawne tonight."

* * *

I WAS SWEATING in the courtyard of Sud Cottage that night, not only because of its grandeur—though it was only a quarter of the size of NordHaven—but because of my nervousness at meeting Lordin. I, like so many others, had revered her for so long. Now I was moments away from finally meeting her.

The door swung open, and Prince Zawne stood in the threshold. We had met before as younger people. Not much about him had changed. He still had a handsome smile, a full head of hair, smooth bronze skin, and a certain warmth about him. Zawne was just like the man I constantly saw on my visin, the man in love with Lordin.

"Welcome," he said. "Lordin is waiting in the parlor for us. She is a touch tired. I guess she didn't sleep well last night. But come in. Our home is your home."

"Thank you, Zawne," I said as I followed him into the foyer. He was polite, and I liked that about him.

As we moved through the hall, he made small talk to make me feel more comfortable. Maybe he had noticed how nervous I was. "Sud Cottage is not so grand as VondRust Palace, where I grew up," he said, "but it is cozy. Lordin and I love living here. Because there aren't a zillion rooms, we feel more connected, closer to each other at all times."

"That's nice," I said, recalling the tour of VondRust that his brother, Jaken, had kindly given me just before I'd moved into the lavish apartment in its grounds, provided for me by the king and the queen. It was their principal residence and administrative headquarters with at least ten music rooms, fifty grand ballrooms, twenty-six kitchens, and hundreds of offices and meeting rooms for councillors and other important people. "It's such an honor to be invited here. Congratulations on your engagement!"

"Thanks. We're thrilled," Zawne said. "How about you? Are you seeing anyone?"

"Nope. I've got too much on my plate right now with the company."

Zawne talked about being with Lordin as though it was all he cared about in life. I found myself a touch jealous that I didn't have that same love. And like so many times over the past year, I found myself thinking about Roki. I wondered where he was. I wondered if he had found somebody new.

Inside the parlor, Lordin lay on a large, plush sofa with her eyes half-shut. I was surprised when she perked up at my entrance, shone her bright white teeth at me, and said, "Welcome, Kaelyn. I am so glad you could come."

"Me too," I told her. Then I bit my lip hesitantly and said, "You're even more stunning in person," feeling an instant wash of embarrassment after I said it. But it was true. With her strong jaw, pointed chin and big blue eyes, Lordin was as cute as a button. No wonder Zawne was crazy about her!

"I appreciate you saying so," she said. "Please, Kaelyn, take a seat."

Lordin gestured to a chair across from her sofa, and I sat down. Zawne sat down beside Lordin, and I smiled as she slithered into the nook of his armpit and nuzzled her head against his chest. It looked cozy there. I thought for sure she would fall asleep.

"Are you all right?" I asked. Lordin looked fatigued beyond reason. I noticed her eyelids were a touch red, as if she'd been crying.

"Yes, I am quite all right. Sorry, Kaelyn, I just didn't get enough sleep last night." Lordin spoke with heavy eyelids, purring into Zawne's side like a cat. "But you, dear." She smiled. "You are beautiful, a true daughter of Gaard."

Now I was the one blushing. Could she mean it, that I was beautiful? Had Lordin never looked in the mirror?

"We should get to business," I said, suddenly awkward and clumsy. "You sent a letter saying you have a proposition for me. What is it?"

Lordin tried to speak but was arrested by a long yawn. Zawne answered in her stead.

"We have been watching what you're doing with GMAF," he said. "And truth be told, we love it. We love it a lot. With Lordin's new position as my betrothed ..." He squeezed her thigh, so intimately that it made me blush.

"Sorry." Zawne cleared his throat. "With Lordin as my wife-to-be, the fact is we may be raised to the status of king and queen. There is also a chance that I will become the next clan leader of Shondur. If that happens at the coronation next year, Lordin and I must relocate out of the capital and back to my native land."

I could already feel where this was going. I was anxious. Could they really want me to ...?

"We need someone strong, capable, and upholding of Decens-Lenitas to take over Lordin's charitable works,"

Zawne explained. "As the head of your own foundation, with your high-profile lineage and the fact that you're unwed and, sorry to say it, have a low chance of being queen, we want you to begin transitioning Lordin's beloved projects over to GMAF. This means a ton more funding, more manpower, a bigger office, more responsibility, and more ways you can change Geniverd for the better."

"Yes," Lordin said, sounding so weak I was surprised she had the energy to speak, "my work must continue. It is imperative that you take over from me as the lead on all my charity projects and volunteer organizations. I want this very badly, Kaelyn. It is important to me that you make the decision now. I need to see you're committed to helping the people. Only then can I ..." She licked her lips and choked back emotion. Something was definitely bothering her, something other than lack of sleep. "Only then can I rest well tonight," she finished.

Whatever bothered Lordin had no effect on Zawne. He was all smiles, caressing Lordin's back, stroking her hair. He loved her so much!

"I say yes!" I declared, way too loudly. I was nervous and had lost control of my voice. It cracked as I said, "I mean, that would be acceptable, Lordin. I really appreciate the opportunity and your trust in me. As the most beloved woman in the kingdom—and the most visinized—your belief means a lot to me. Really, it does."

"I'm glad," she said. "I feel that our interpretation of Decens-Lenitas is the same. I feel, Kaelyn, that we are of the same heart, the same cloth."

I couldn't believe what Lordin was saying. She and I, of the same cloth? Could it be true? And the whole time, Zawne was petting Lordin and smiling at me. Was I in a dream?

"We need you to sign the papers right away," Zawne said. "I've prepared the necessary documents to transfer ownership, funds, and other technical details from Lordin's private work over to you." He gestured to a small stack of papers on the table between us. "Will you sign them?"

I beamed widely. "Do you have a pen?"

* * *

"It went well," I said to Tissa. We were in the office the morning after I had accepted Lordin's offer, going through the insane amount of paperwork that had flooded in overnight. "Lordin was different in person. She was tired. Like, really tired. It made me wonder if something more hadn't been going on behind the scenes."

"Like what?" Tissa asked.

I crinkled my nose. "I'm not sure. It was just a gut feeling, you know? Something felt off."

"But how was Zawne? Is he as handsome in person as he is on the—?"

I rolled my eyes at Tissa. "I can't answer that, not with the way he and Lordin were totally in love with each other. It would be inappropriate of me to call Zawne handsome ... which he was!"

She giggled. "I knew it!"

"Seriously," I said, "Zawne and Lordin are the most lovey-dovey duo I have ever met. At one point, after I had signed all the documents, Lordin fell asleep, and Zawne quietly told me about their first date. It was so magical!"

"Magical how?" Tissa asked. She had forgotten all about her work. "Tell me. I must know!"

I straightened up. "Okay, here's the deal. Zawne told me they first met at Prince Jaken's homecoming ceremony, two years ago, after his Aska training. Zawne was in the crowd, and Lordin came out on stage with the Grucken. He told me how beautiful she had looked to him, speaking into the microphone, congratulating the bold warriors on their hard years of struggle and training. Lordin was showering the warriors with praise, telling them all how proud Geniverd was of them. But all that Zawne could concentrate on were the blue oceans in her eyes."

I sighed, getting soft at my own telling of Zawne's story. "Once Lordin got off the stage, Zawne scrambled through the crowd, looking for her. He completely ignored the throngs of young women and heiresses keen on trying to seduce him and found Lordin on the other side of the room. He was out of breath when he got to her. Zawne pulled her aside and said, 'I know this is inappropriate. You might not even know who I am, so I apologize. But your beauty has arrested me. I must see more of you, Lordin. Can we meet?'"

I was giggling now. "Isn't that great, Tiss? It was love at first sight. Obviously, Lordin agreed to the date, but they kept it secret. They met at Lithern Shrine in the Grucken's training complex early one morning. Zawne arrived in his blue steel flyrarc like an action hero. Lordin made him tea. They lingered around Lithern Shrine all day and were in love before nightfall. They continued to see each other in secret for over a year."

"That's kind of hot," Tissa said, getting all flustered. "I wish I could have a secret romance … Well, any romance would do. A secret romance with a rich prince would do better."

"You will have your time," I assured her. "Your day is coming. Actually, I wanted to mention something to you about my brother, Raad. Maybe if—"

"Be careful, Tiss." Nnati entered the room and cut me off. "You could find yourself on the throne!"

Tissa and I winked at each other. I'd save that conversation for another time. I knew that Tissa would absolutely gush if I told her my brother was interested in a date with her.

Later that evening, when I was alone in my apartment, my mind returned to Lordin's moist eyes and her sunken body. I turned my visin on and flicked to the celebrity channel, hoping to catch a glimpse of her looking more cheerful. I flipped onto the news channel for a moment first and saw that there had been another fire, this time a huge inferno that had swallowed some nobleman's nine-story castle in the northern Lodden mountains, where he and his family went skiing in the winter. The fire was so strong it had melted the stones and left a brown spot in the snow, but somehow there were no casualties at all. The reports on the news were starting to call the arsonist "the Gurnot Dragon."

I finally reached the celebrity channel and gasped at what I saw on the screen.

Lordin has been found dead on a walkway near Sud Cottage, where she lived with Prince Zawne. There are reports that she was decapitated with a cleaver.

4

$\mathcal{I}$ was still in shock at the funeral a month later. It was hard to comprehend that Lordin was dead. I had watched her for so many years on the visin, then finally been invited into her home and embraced as a friend, only to have her gone the next day. I had spent the last month in shock. The only thing that had kept me sane was focusing on the overload of work that she had passed on to me. It made me wonder, *Did Lordin know she was going to die?*

"Bad way to go, huh?" Nnati asked. He stood to my left, Tissa on my right. We were watching the crowd of mourners cry as everyone readied themselves for the traditional Gaard burial. We were to walk Lordin's remains one mile to her ultimate resting place on land acquired by VondRust Palace on Zawne's behalf.

"Yeah," Tissa said. "I can't believe someone cut her head off. It's just so …"

"It's brutal," I said. "The way she was killed makes me sick. And what's with the groundskeeper who told the police a swarm of bees had killed Lordin? That's really weird."

I sighed and gave my head a shake. "Anyway, Lordin's a martyr now. The people of Geniverd are furious, especially here in Gaard. She's been elevated far beyond what she was in life. I've heard the Gurnots are cycling rumors through the capital that Lordin was killed by the upper class to stop her from meddling with Decens-Lenitas. I mean, she was highly versed in the teachings, but I know she opposed some of the more controversial aspects regarding the monarchy. The rumors have sparked outrage. I know that there was some serious division between the classes before, but this has incited some real trouble. Have you guys seen the riots?"

"Yeah," Tissa said. "People are throwing themselves from roofs. They're marching in the streets and demanding justice. The higher-ups still won't give out any information on who killed Lordin, or why."

"They should," Nnati said with a peculiar edge in his voice. "I was never one of Lordin's followers, but she was still a human being, and people deserve answers. I'll be the first to admit she seemed genuinely benevolent, like she really helped people. It's not right to cover up what happened. Why won't they tell us anything?"

"I don't know," I said. "That sort of thing is way beyond the station of a mere heiress. Papa hasn't said anything to me about it."

"It's suspicious," Nnati said. "And it's causing problems. I've heard the Surrvul are vying for the throne now. Word on the street is that they have six heirs going to the coronation next year. They're hoping to steal the seat. It's been two hundred years since the last Surrvul rulers, and they're peeved about it. It's funny, actually, maybe even ironic, that the richest continent is the most desperate for the throne."

Tissa nodded in agreement. "With Veeln-Co in their territory, Surrvul has enough money to fund a war."

48

"Hush," I snapped, not meaning to. I hated hearing about wars. I hated hearing about how viciously Lordin had been killed. What kind of monster could harm such a perfectly radiant being? And what would happen now at the coronation? Poor Zawne. He must have been in tatters.

"Sorry." I hung my head. "I'm just upset—maybe because I had thought I could never be as morally upright as Lordin; then she came into my life and showed me I could try. She trusted me." I sighed, fighting back tears. "Then someone cut her head off! She handed me the torch and died the next day. Who's going to change the world now?"

Tissa and Nnati remained quiet, sullen. The mood was bleak. Thousands of mourners talked in quiet whispers all around us. We had all come to bid Lordin a final farewell, people from every continent. It was one of the greatest pilgrimages Geniverd had ever seen. I had known she was popular and loved, but this was crazy. It seemed like the whole world had come to say goodbye.

"Death is a thief," I said. "It steals hopes, dreams, experiences. Death is the robber of life, happiness, family. Death takes everything and gives nothing. Death is the most unjust sentence ever passed."

* * *

THE PROCESSION BEGAN. We joined in the thousands of people marching slowly through the fields of Lordin's mother's estate. Lordin was to be cremated and placed inside a newly constructed mausoleum.

As we marched, drummers beat on their drums, and the Ava-Gaard sang out in painful bellows. Nnati and Tissa joined in as best they could, since they were Ava-Nurlie and didn't know the words. I belted out the words as loud as I could, danced the dance of the dead, and surrendered my body, swaying to the beating of the drum as we marched through the field. By dancing, the Ava-Gaard promised Lordin a peaceful rest with our ancestors in the afterlife.

We danced and chanted and marched all the way to the cremation site, to the mausoleum Raad had helped construct, since he was the soon-to-be clan leader. He had been practicing the duties, and he stood near the front of the crowd, wearing full Gaard-Elder garb. It made my heart swell to see my brother looking so regal.

And I wasn't the only one. Tissa couldn't keep her eyes off Raad. Or was she looking at Zawne? The two men stood beside each other, roughly the same age. Zawne was thinner beside Raad. He had suffered a month of grief, and it showed in his baggy clothing, his dark eyes, his sunken cheeks. Zawne looked half-dead. I supposed he was less alive without Lordin, his shining light.

Zawne stepped forward onto the podium and took the microphone in his hands. The hundreds of P2 camera drones buzzed around him like locusts, transmitting the tragic event to the whole kingdom. Zawne didn't seem to mind. He was probably used to them in his life of royalty and fame. It made me glad to be away from that boring life, constantly swarmed by cameras and press. Before Zawne spoke, he turned to look at a veiled woman standing alone at the back of the stage. Lordin's mother, I guessed. Her skin glowed the same pale white as Lordin's had, the porcelain complexion so rare for an Ava-Gaard.

"I'd like to recite a poem," Zawne said, his voice shattered by loss. "I loved Lordin more than words can describe, and I have written this poem to try to commemorate her. Maybe in death she will hear my words."

The crowd melted. I could feel them soften and whisper. Who could blame them? Zawne was the perfect model of a bereaved lover. Even Tissa said, "He's so romantic. I wish I had a man like him."

Zawne cleared his throat, then read his poem from a scrap of paper. "My love. Our love. I thought I knew what living was.

"Until I met you.

"Through the fog. I couldn't see. Every breath I took.

"You saw.

"Every smile or frown.

"You foresaw.

"I soared. We soared. I saw the birds for the first time and learned their songs.

"Heard their vivid tales, their blitheness, their misery.

"I saw all people beneath the surface.

"I was free. We were free. Our trees stand tall in the quiet of the night.

"Quiet to the untrained ear.

"Innumerable stars shine. Buzzing, purring, humming, rumbling, hissing.

"Thick gray clouds pour.

"Our branches and leaves sway. The winds are strong and cold.

"I never yield. We never yield. The darkness around us is perfectly lit.

"The abyss, a heavy universe.

"This season is a mirage. All seasons are none. We are forever one.

"I rest with you.

"Geniverd rests with you."

Zawne bowed his head, and a respectful silence permeated

the gathered thousands. I had tears in my eyes. So did Tissa. Even Nnati had to wipe his cheeks. The poem was beautiful. Lordin deserved it.

Once the moment of silence was over, Zawne looked back at the crowd and said, "I have one more thing to say. Without Lordin, my life is worthless. I've spoken with the Grucken, and he agreed it would be a good idea for me to strengthen my inner soul and find a new purpose through becoming an Aska. I'm not doing this for publicity. I'm doing this for Lordin, so that she may be proud of me in the afterlife."

Zawne paused, waiting to hear reactions in the crowd. People were gasping and chatting among themselves. I heard Nnati say, "He'll never make it. My left foot says he drops out after the first day."

Zawne went on. "My brother, Prince Jaken, believes I have the strength to make it through. My parents, the king and queen, are also supportive, and I know Lordin, if she's looking down upon me from some ethereal plane, is also behind me. I want to thank the people of Geniverd for coming on this solemn day to mourn the bright life of our beloved Lordin. Goodbye."

Zawne passed the microphone over to the Grucken and retreated to the back of the stage. He gave the veiled woman, Lordin's mother, a brief glance, then hugged his brother. I watched him shake Raad's hand. Then Zawne was gone and the Grucken was speaking.

"Geniverd," the Grucken said, "thank you for coming. I'll keep this short. A child of Decens-Lenitas is committed to ashes on this day, and it is too sorrowful for speeches. I will say only that Lordin has not truly died. She has merely transcended her body and mind and all things physical. Lordin is still with you in your hearts, in the souls of every living creature in Geniverd. And Geniverd will never forget. Farewell, Lordin."

The men of Gaard boomed, "Gaard to Gaard."

And then the women said, "Breast to breast."

* * *

MY FRIENDS and I spent the night at NordHaven. Papa had gone to bed early after three glasses of wine, and the hour was late. I sat on the sofa next to Nnati so that Raad and Tissa were forced to sit on the opposite sofa together. The room smelled of fresh daisies, of spring and renewal. After living so long in the city, I had forgotten what it was like to live inside the bubble of NordHaven, surrounded by pleasant smells and perfect weather. Tissa looked more comfortable here than I was. She looked quite at home on the plush sofa next to Raad in his royal vestments.

"Have you considered seeing anyone since you moved to the city, Kaelyn?" Tissa asked me. The talk had turned to dating.

I immediately flushed. "No way! How could I have time for a boyfriend with all the work we've been doing?" Then I scoffed at her, trying to get the spotlight off me. "Isn't this an inappropriate time to be talking about dating, Tiss?"

"It's the perfect time," Raad said. He was sitting rather snugly against my friend. "With all the death surrounding us, we deserve a bit of happiness. We all deserve special people in our lives. It's what Mama would have wanted. Besides, Kaelyn, we both need to be married by next year for the coronation ceremony."

I rumpled my nose. "And what if I'm not?"

"Then you won't ascend to queen. If I'm chosen for king,

you'll have to become a solitary leader of the Gaard Clan. You'll have men chasing you like crazy!"

I sighed, sagging deep into the cushions on the sofa. "I don't want any of the other heirs. There's only one man I really want."

My words came out too fast without me thinking and suddenly everyone in the room was staring at me.

"Who?" Nnati asked. "Who is the one man you want? I can't believe it. Kaelyn has a crush!"

Even Raad was grinning at me. I noticed his fingers getting awfully close to where Tissa's hand rested on the sofa.

"I … He's no one … He's just …" I sighed, defeated. I couldn't lie to my friends. "Fine," I said. "His name is Roki, and we were, dare I say it, on the fringes of love."

Tissa was bug eyed. "When? Where? How? Spill the beans, Kaelyn!"

"It was over a year ago," I told them, "before Mama's passing. We spent every day together. I had never felt so in sync with anyone before. I was sure we could have ruled the world together. I may have wanted to become queen if I had Roki as my king. He was amazing."

"So it wasn't just an infatuation," Tissa said. "It was intense."

"Yeah." I nodded. "It was emotionally powerful. We were bonded. But then Mama died. I couldn't bear to see him in the state I was in. Then, well … we drifted apart."

Nnati was grinning mischievously. "So," he said, "drift back together. Why don't you reach out to him, explain that your heart was broken and now you're ready to date again? Things happen; life happens. It doesn't mean you can't get back together."

I blinked at Nnati, totally dumbfounded by his totally perfect rationale. I suddenly wanted to ditch my friends, run to my bedroom, and try to call Roki on my visin. Did I still have his number? Could I bear to hear his voice again? Would he even still want me?

"You're thinking about it," Nnati said slyly. "I can see the gears turning in your head. Just do it, Kaelyn. Life's too short. We could all be killed by a superbug at any minute."

I laughed. Nnati was cheering me up with his typically grim demeanor, talking about superbugs as if there had even been one in the last five hundred years. I was also cheered to see Raad and Tissa giggling in their own little bubble across the room, their fingers entwined. She really did look right at home.

"But enough about you, Kaelyn," Nnati said, dramatically flipping his wrist. "Let's talk about me. I need a man too. Now that Zawne's single, maybe he'll come play for my team. What do you think?"

Raad answered for me. "I think Zawne is currently on his way to Gaard's southern coast. By tomorrow night he will be paddling two hundred miles across stormy, shark-infested waters. If he doesn't get sucked into a whirlpool or eaten by a giant squid, he will be trekking through a merciless wasteland for the next eight months. After that he'll have serious training in Lodden for nearly one and a half years. I think dating is the furthest thing from his mind right now."

"Right," Nnati said, pouting his lips. "Do you think he'll make it through?"

Raad thought seriously about this, his eyebrows furrowing. "I think he has what he needs to get through it," he said. "If Zawne can embrace the pain of Lordin's death, draw strength from it, and let the pain and hurt guide him, then yes. Yes, I believe he can make it."

We all quieted then. I'm sure we were picturing a grief-stricken Zawne shirtless and sweaty in the desert, trudging along with dull resolve, battling leopards with the anger from Lordin's death. I could see by Nnati's raised eyebrows he liked the idea. As for me, I felt sad for Zawne. He had adored Lordin, made a home with her. Now Zawne was alone with himself and the wilderness. His only company would be the other lost souls desperate for purpose, and the hungry vultures circling above.

5

I was immersed in a sea of white arum lilies, my body buoyant on the current. I ducked below the canopy of white-spotted green leaves and swam among their impossibly long stalks. The petals brushed me softly, sublimely. Their musky scent filled my nostrils. I was alive, floating in a flowery paradise.

A new scent came to me: earthy, herbal. It was a sweet fragrance accompanied by a presence, a construct of pistils, a thousand flower eyes. It was a hot gaze that made my body shake, and I came to a stop amid the field of lilies. I felt naked here, bare and contrite. The large orange petals were reaching out for me. I let them brush against my skin, the flowery presence making me feel secure, filaments blown about me on a sudden breeze. I lifted my face, and there he was.

Roki in the flesh. The scene changed, and we were two bare souls in the field of arum lilies. He had a smile on his face. I realized I was crying, solid in my body. We were hugging. My tears streaked down his bare chest, slithered between his abs.

"What do you want, Roki?" I said against him. He held me tightly and allowed me to weep before I leaped back in anger. "Why are you here now?"

"Because I love you, Kaelyn. I need you to come back to me."

Roki's words were honest in this sacred dreamscape. I hadn't realized how much I had longed to hear his voice. It was like honey. I wanted to drown in it.

But I was still angry! So much time had passed without him to comfort me. "Why should I love you?" I demanded. "Why should I return to your embrace? You left me, Roki. In my hour of need, you were nowhere to be found!"

He took the brunt of my anger. He seemed to understand it and shook his head sadly. "I never left you. I've been here all along. I can't let go. By the world, I have tried. Yet your spirit lingers in my mind, in my being. I need you."

I hated how much I wanted to shrug off my anger and kiss him as if we had never parted. His words were sweet, yet they held no meaning for me.

"Where were you?" I asked. "When I was sad, beaten, crushed, and powerless, where were you? I was certain my grief would swallow me alive, and you weren't there to console me. I was hopeless. I had betrayed my mother for you, and in my time of need, you were gone."

He lowered his face close to mine. Roki, so handsome, so strong. How could I fight him? I was supposed to hate him, yet I wanted to touch him. My legs buckled, and I dropped to my knees.

He knelt beside me and pleaded, "Please, Kaelyn. You must believe that I was right there with you in your days of misery. I sobbed with you. I shared your pain and tried to comfort your soul. Maybe you felt me, smelled me. I was there. I could hear your mind, hear your thoughts of anger, and sense your grief. I respected your pain and your frustration, and kept my distance. I wanted so badly to stay away and let you grow on your own. You deserve a full life without me to drag you down. But now …" Roki paused, swept his hand across my moist cheek. "But now I've heard you. I've listened to your heart and understood that you need me. I will be here from now on. I'm here, Kaelyn. I'm yours."

I had no words. I was so confused. Roki lifted my chin delicately. His fingers, his touch—they were perfect. "I love you," he said. And in his eyes was truth.

I caved, closed my eyes, and reached with my lips …

* * *

"Roki!" I screamed into my empty room. I sat upright in bed, sweating and hot.

"Just a dream …"

I was disappointed and more than a bit confused. The dream had been so vivid, so real. Even Roki's scent continued to linger. It seemed like the universe was trying to tell me something. Did I need Roki back in my life?

I shook my head, trying to shake the dream from my system. It felt insane that he would appear to me in my mind on today of all days. I hadn't seen Roki for three years. I hadn't been back in NordHaven since Lordin's funeral two years ago. Yet there I was, in my old bedroom, my brother married to my best friend the previous night, and Roki's ghost was playing midnight tricks in my head. I already knew it was going to be a strange day. I could feel it in the air.

The service had been splendid. Tissa and Raad exchanged Gaard-Nurlie vows, and the massed crowd went nuts. Nurlie was happy because their chances of having an Ava-Nurlie queen were exceptional with Tissa's marriage to my brother.

Gaard was happy because they adored Raad and figured he was sure to be picked by the Crown of Crowns. But Surrvul was displeased. They craved the throne with dangerous ambition. I was beginning to wonder what any of it meant for the common folk. What did the coronation mean for the people?

"Morning, newlyweds," I said as I entered the kitchen. Raad and Tissa were eating breakfast. The whispers of new lovers permeated the space.

"Morning, sister," Raad said. "Did you sleep well?"

"Yes," I told him, moving to the platter of strawberries on the counter. "Did you?"

"Hardly," Raad said, and he and Tissa erupted in secret giggles.

I was happy to see them like this. The past year had seen a lot of courting, a lot of travel back and forth between the capital and NordHaven. Now Tissa and Raad were finally wed. They were radiant together. I felt ashamed for being a touch sad that Nnati and I would soon fly back to the capital in our flyrarc while Tissa remained in NordHaven. She deserved some rest after the hard work she had put in over the past two years at the foundation. But for me, it felt like the end of an era. I could only hope everything would turn out well in the end.

"I have to talk to you about something," Raad said while chewing his eggs. "It's quite a serious something…" He looked to Tissa. "Do you mind, wife? It really is rather private."

"Of course." Tissa bowed to Raad in the humble fashion of an Ava-Gaard wife. Then she came to me and kissed my cheek, squeezed my arm. "We're sisters now for real. You'll never get rid of me now, Kaelyn."

I laughed and said, "I'd never dream of it," and Tissa went into the hall and left Raad and me alone.

"What is it?" I asked him. He was squirming uncomfortably.

"As you know, sister, Prince Zawne had his homecoming two days ago. He survived the brutal trial of Aska training and made it home in one piece."

"I do know," I said. "I watched the ceremony on my visin. Zawne looks ..." I bit my lip. "Improved."

Raad flashed his teeth. "You mean he looks hotter, more muscular, tanned, and totally kissable?"

"No!" But my protest was useless. It was all true. Zawne had become a hunk from his two years of training. He had transformed from a prince into ... well, into a man.

"It's encouraging that you feel that way," Raad said, "because nearly two years ago I made a pact with Zawne's brother. I'm sure you're aware of the trade conundrum between Gaard and Shondur right now. People are scared that once the Shondur-born king and queen step down and a different clan takes the reins, the already shaky trade deal between our continents will crumble, and chaos will erupt."

"I've heard reports," I said, not at all liking where Raad was steering the conversation.

"Good. It's something you should be concerned about as the heiress to Gaard. I am. Papa is. Jaken too. It's why Jaken and I made the pact. We want to keep the balance between our prosperous domains. The best way to do this is through marriage. Since Jaken married a high-class lady from Krug to keep that alliance strong, Zawne is the only way. And you are the only daughter of Gaard. Get what I'm saying?"

My mouth opened and closed like a fish's. I had no words. Raad wanted me to marry Prince Zawne. Was he crazy? Zawne was Lordin's ex-fiancé. Might as well be her widower. Their bond was legendary. I could never fill such shoes.

"Are you serious?" I asked. "You're acting like Mama, trying to sell me off to a stranger."

"Don't be silly," Raad said, still chomping away at his eggs. "Zawne isn't a stranger. You're acquainted. I can tell by your reaction to his new physique that you're attracted to him. What's the issue?"

"I barely even know him!" I was irate. Sure, we had met, but I didn't *know* him. "And I could never replace Lordin. She put her entire faith in me, gifted me the prosperous foundation I have now. Who knows where GMAF would be if it wasn't for Lordin? For me to marry her living fiancé would be … it would be treachery!"

"Nonsense," Raad said. "People move on. It's necessary. It's also one of the things you learn during Aska training, that the world continues to spin without you when you're gone, that people continue with their lives. Zawne surely learned the same thing through his ordeal in the desert and in Lodden. I'm sure he will be happy at the thought of keeping our kingdom intact. I doubt he will have any qualms about marrying you, sister."

"You don't understand!" I protested. "Lordin and Zawne were truly in love. *Love* love, Raad. Love times a thousand! And the people. Oh, the people loved them as a couple. I'll be a new face and an utter disappointment next to Lordin."

"Don't sell yourself short, sister. You are …" Raad squirmed. "Pretty. And men desire you. I have no less than twelve requests for your hand in marriage from the noble families in Gaard alone. You're a hot ticket."

"I don't want to be a ticket," I said. "I want to be loved. Can you imagine what the people would say about me dating Lordin's Prince Zawne?"

He looked at me incredulously. "Zawne was never Lordin's to keep, and Lordin wasn't even of noble birth, and … she isn't even here anymore! Why are we even talking about her?"

It wasn't the idea of dating Zawne that provoked me the most. It was the feeling that I would be betraying Lordin and the sanctity of their relationship in Geniverd's eyes. Didn't he understand what Lordin meant to people, what she represented? What she'd always represent?

I knew Raad's mind was made up and there was no talking him out of it. So I changed tack. "He worshipped the ground she walked on, Raad. She owned him. I also don't think Zawne will ever love anyone as much."

"None of that matters," he said, waving his right hand dismissively.

"He might not even want me," I said. "How could any man want to marry me before he knows me? It's absurd."

"It's strategic," Raad said bluntly. The business of taking on more and more Elder duties had hardened Raad, made him deathly serious when he needed to be. "It's for the people and for our family. Mama would have wanted this for you."

"Still, you're asking me to marry someone I hardly know before the coronation, which is in three weeks." I was thinking of Roki now, the dream that had molested me in my sleep. I wanted to see him again, but he was gone. Maybe it was time to move on.

Raad said, "Zawne will love you in time. That's how these things work. He intends to marry you, if you're also interested in him, and he'd like to meet with you as soon as possible. Please don't be selfish, Kaelyn. The Ava-Gaard need you to be strong for them. There's more at play here than love and affection. Your feelings may have to suffer, and I am sorry for this."

"I hate you." I crossed my arms and frowned. "And I also love you, so I can't be mad. I know what could happen if the trade agreement falls flat. More expensive food for Shondur from our farmers, more expensive leather and gems for us. There could even be a currency collapse. It would be chaos. And this is on top of all the other madness going on right now. People are suffering, more and more every day, it seems, and they don't need another reason to suffer."

Raad nodded. "Exactly. This is for the good of Geniverd."

I conceded. I always felt timid and weak before Raad, and this morning was no exception. "Fine," I said. "I'll go on one date. One! If there is no connection between Zawne and me, then there's nothing I can do."

Raad wiped egg slop off his lips. "I knew you'd understand." He smiled at me. "And I know you'll do what's right, both for your heart and for Gaard. We are the leaders of this society, and we must be role models. We must be moral. We must uphold Decens-Lenitas."

* * *

IT WAS a pretext for us elitists, Decens-Lenitas. It always had been. It was a tool used to keep those on top firmly placed above the rest, to give those beneath something to aspire to. It had good roots, but over time, these roots had been forgotten, corrupted, then rotted into something ugly. I wanted to break that cycle. I wanted to make our moral code moral again. I saw nothing moral in the suffering of millions while a small portion of privileged people dictated the fate of the world from atop their castle ramparts—the ones not burned down yet by the Gurnot the news had titled "the Dragon." And for what? Most of the rich and the clan leaders were so bloated with the wealth of the world, all they could do for entertainment was play their game, fighting for the crown, for more power. They'd forgotten about the rest of the world.

I thought, *If I'm ever to become queen, that's what I'll do. I'll fix it all. I'll fix everything.* It was a reason to make the date with Zawne go well.

Nnati and I were in the flyrarc on our way back to the capital when I told him about it. "The part I can't believe is that Zawne wants to marry me. Me, over all the other girls in Geniverd."

"Why not?" Nnati screwed up his face. "You're gorgeous, well connected, smart, virtuous. Everyone wants to marry you."

I rolled my eyes. Compliments never sounded real coming from Nnati. He was like a second brother to me; he had to be nice. "You're just saying that," I said. "I've struggled with Decens-Lenitas my whole life. I'll never be as respectable as Lordin was. I'll never be as beautiful."

Nnati fixed his eyes on me. It was an angry look, like he wanted to scream at me. "Are you joking? You can't be serious, Kaelyn. Do you even own a mirror? Men stumble just to look at you when we walk in the street. They smash face-first into signs, trip off the sidewalk, crane their necks in their flyrarcs. You're gorgeous, Kaelyn. And as for being humble, being a good servant for the Decens-Lenitas fanatics—well, who cares? Lordin's just a myth now. You're real and virtuous in a meaningful way. Anyone can see that."

I thought, *Roki saw that. He saw it when no one else could.*

"Thank you," I said, feeling silly. Twice already today I had been judged as stubborn for ignoring my looks. I supposed it could have been true. Roki had liked me. Zawne was interested in seeing me. Maybe I wasn't a ghoul after all.

I swallowed my doubts and said to Nnati, "Do you remember the guy I talked about the last time we were at NordHaven? Roki?"

Nnati nodded. "I do."

"Okay. Well, do you think that by dating Prince Zawne, I would be betraying him? It's just ... I know it was three years ago, but I still feel connected to him somehow. Do you think I've waited long enough?"

Nnati stared at me like I was crazy. "Um, yeah," he said. "Kaelyn, you waited for him through your prime teen years. He never showed. You're eighteen now. You're a woman, and the coronation is in three weeks. You did all you could for that boy, and he left you high and dry. Go on the date with Zawne tomorrow and see how you feel. If it's good, move ahead. Move on. You deserve it."

"Thanks," I said, but I didn't feel like I deserved anything. I'd never be able to ignore the fact that I had left Mama with cruel words instead of love before she died. It would gnaw at me for the rest of my life.

"And Gaard deserves it," Nnati went on. "The Ava-Gaard deserve you at your best if you're to be their leader, maybe even their queen."

"Oh, come on," I said. "Now you're the one being silly. The Crown of Crowns will never pick me. Not even if I marry Zawne. Over the years, several eligible heirs have either trained with the Grucken or become Askas. All I have is the foundation."

"That might be all you need," Nnati said, "your kindness and your heart—oh, and the marriage to Zawne. Just remember, Kaelyn, marry in haste and repent at leisure. Keep the kingdom in mind on your date, but also follow your feelings. You'll know what to do."

* * *

I THOUGHT it was crazy that we hadn't even talked first, Zawne and I. Raad and Jaken had been the orchestrators of our little date. They had even decided on my apartment as the venue, which seemed a bit too intimate for my liking. I reasoned that it may have been improper to meet there, but I didn't want to be caught in a public place with Zawne, in case nothing came out of the meetup. The main VondRust Palace buildings were also risky, since too many people could see us. And so there I was, standing at the threshold of my apartment while lightning flashed across the black sky and Zawne stood on the stoop, smiling, rain washing his handsome face. Thunder rolled in an ominous boom as he said, "May I come in?"

"Of course." I gestured him inside. "Get out of the rain. How rude of me."

As I closed the door, I whispered to myself, "Just one date. Be strong, Kaelyn."

I had thought throughout my childhood that Mama and Papa would marry me off to a foreign heir. I had never imagined that when the day came, my brother would have a hand in it. And I never imagined that the man would be Zawne. When one of the Gaard councillors once suggested to me that Zawne and I would be a good fit, I had instantly rejected the theory. I was fifteen, and I thought we were too different. He seemed extroverted and cheerful, whereas I gloried in my solitude. If it had to be a prince, Jaken was much more to my liking. But so much had changed since then. Jaken and Raad had gotten married, and Zawne was now an Aska. I found myself asking: Did Zawne really want me, or was he going along with it just because it was expected of him?

On the plus side, the potential marriage could also be the answer to my anxieties about Roki's invisible pull. I wondered if it was because I thought about him so much that I was starting to dream about him. It was time to cut the cord. All this thinking only made me restless, and Zawne was shaking the water from his hair like a dog. "What was that?" he asked.

"Nothing," I said. "It must have been the wind. I have the fireplace roaring," I told him. "Let's go into the sitting room and get you warm." I gulped, seeing his wet shirt clinging to his muscles. "You're soaked."

I led the way, modest yet alluring in the silk dress I had chosen to wear. A slit in the skirt showed off the sheen of my calves, and I could feel Zawne's eyes fixating on them as he followed me into the sitting room.

"Are you cold?" I asked.

"No, not really. I swam and paddled for weeks through the frigid waters off the coast of Surrvul. I spent half a year with no shelter in the wasteland. It's a hot nightmare during the day but a cold and miserable place by night. I've stopped being cold."

"Oh." I didn't know what to say. I knew the Aska training was tough; people were killed by beasts and ravaged by the elements. I tried to sympathize with Zawne by saying, "Raad never talked about his time out there. You make it sound like a harsh and unforgiving wild."

"It is." Zawne took off his wet shirt and hung it on a peg above the fireplace to dry. His skin was moist, body chiseled like a sculpture of an ancient warrior. He had scars on his ribs and on his chest.

"Are those claw marks?" I asked.

"Huh?" Zawne inspected himself, looked at the scars on his right pec as if he had forgotten they were there. "Yeah," he said, "but I don't know which scar is from which leopard. I battled two of them. Or was it three? It happened so fast. My apologies, but my memory is fuzzy."

I had a vision of Zawne on a hot desert while three leopards circled him, snarling, baring their teeth. "No one thought

68

you would make it," I said, not meaning to be blunt. "But you did. You battled leopards, survived the wild, trained in Lodden, and came back a changed man."

"Only three days ago," he said, with a dazed look in his eye. "It is strange being back." Even though Zawne had been a pampered prince all his life, he seemed somewhat uncomfortable on the dainty sofa in my living room, surrounded by frilly throw pillows. He probably never saw a pillow during his Aska training. It made me appreciate what I had. I understood how fortunate I was, especially compared to the rest of Geniverd.

"I'm curious about one thing," I said. "Why was your first order of business to have a date with me?"

I wanted to cut through the formalities right away, no mucking around. I needed to know Zawne's intentions before we proceeded. He had had a reputation in college, bedding girls by the dozen, playing the field, and never settling down. I was sure Lordin had changed him for the better. But without Lordin, after being pummeled by the Aska training, who was Zawne now? Who was the muscled man bent in front of my fireplace, drying himself by the fire as if still in the wild?

"Can I be honest?" he asked. His eyes were dark and mysterious.

I gulped and nodded.

"Good," he said, "because if we are to be man and wife, we should begin with honesty. I don't know you well, Kaelyn, and you don't know me, but Lordin trusted you, and that makes you my number one choice for a wife. You're also beautiful, one of the most breathtaking women I have ever seen in my life. I caught myself thinking of you on occasion while I labored in Lodden. I would be at the watering hole, wondering to myself, 'Where is Kaelyn right now? I wonder what she's wearing.'"

I blushed. Surely he was lying. He could not have been thinking about me in Lodden!

"There is also the power of our alliance to consider," Zawne said, casting his gaze into the fire and glowering. "I hate the idea of arranged marriages. I really do. I would prefer people marry for love rather than power. Yet it is my responsibility to lead. That is what it means to be an Aska and an heir. I must be a leader of men. With the coronation ceremony only three weeks away, I must cast aside foolish pride and seek a wife. I must at least attempt the throne."

Zawne's honorable words were making me feel guilty. All I wanted was to follow my heart, while he was willing to sacrifice his personal feelings for the good of the people. I found myself thinking, *Of course Lordin loved him. He's selfless. He's a hero.*

My mouth moved without consulting my brain. "If the future of Gaard is at stake, I should also attempt the throne. I have a vision for this kingdom, and I would like to see it realized. It's taken your bravery to rouse my own. Yet all the same, I cannot marry a man if there is no chance of love. I refuse to be an emotional outcast in a loveless marriage."

"I understand," he said. Then Zawne smiled for the first time. In the glow of the fire, he was rugged and tanned, sultry, like a romantic lumberjack. And so defined! His muscles were hard and rippled as he moved. I wanted to touch them ... just a little.

"If that's the case," he said, "then I better make you love me tonight. I'm talking about here and now, Kaelyn, for the sake of Geniverd. Just give me the night to make you see that we can be lovers."

I gave him a warm smile and said, "I'd like that," meaning it sincerely. It was kind of what I had planned, anyway—one date to see if love was possible, then shirk my usual timidity and dive headfirst into a relationship for once in my life. He was rugged, handsome, and apparently caring. If Lordin could love Zawne, why couldn't I?

"Do we have a deal?" he asked through his grin.

I nodded. "Yes, Zawne, we have a deal."

"Great!" He rubbed his hands together. "This is going to be a perfect union. Mama and Papa will be so proud."

Zawne stood up, brushed his hands on his pants, and stepped closer to me. He was so tall. I had to tilt my head to look in his eyes. "You'll see," he said. "I will be a great husband. I can protect you, love you, care for you. I can be an ear, a friend, a partner. It will be fantastic. Lordin always used to say …" He trailed off. He must have seen the subtle crinkle in my brow at the mention of her name. Of course, he would always think fondly of Lordin, but this was our first date. I preferred not to talk about Zawne's true love. I didn't want to picture Lordin rolling in her grave as her fiancé tried to seduce me.

"It's all right," I said, moving away from Zawne and plunking myself down on the sofa, crossing my legs. "You mourn her still, I'm sure. But it's something we can get past. My wise brother told me yesterday how it's all part of life. I never expect you to forget Lordin, but while you're with me, could we at least not talk about her?"

"Of course." He bowed to me. "My apologies, Kaelyn. Please forgive me."

His seriousness made me giggle. When he bowed, his abs were more defined, water droplets weaving through his coarse body hairs. "You are forgiven," I said. But he was more than forgiven. I already liked Zawne a lot. His muscles, his charm, his determined soul. In that moment, I wanted them all to be mine.

* * *

WE WEREN'T EVEN HUNGRY. At least, neither of us admitted to being hungry. I poured two glasses of wine, and we curled closely together on the loveseat in front of the fireplace, listening to the wood crackling, to the rain pelting the rooftop.

"This is a nice place," he said. "It's nice company."

We clinked glasses and drank. "It's a bit lonely here by myself," I admitted. "Sometimes I have bad nights."

Zawne swished wine around in his mouth, swallowed, and said in a husky voice, "Sud Cottage is like a graveyard. So silent and creepy. I feel like a dead man walking through it. Maybe when we get married, we can move in together. We'll have a much bigger place, of course."

"Who said we're getting married?" I asked, gasping and pretending to be offended. "I haven't agreed yet."

Zawne got closer to me, looked straight in my face. "Yes, you have. I can see it in your eyes. I can feel it in your body language. You've already agreed to be my wife."

"Maybe," I said, and immediately averted my eyes. Zawne was intimidating with his lips two inches from mine. Not in a bad way. Mostly because his breath was sweet. His manly scent was invigorating. If we stared into each other's eyes for too long, I feared that I would ...

No! I told myself. *Not yet. You're a respectable woman. You are the daughter of Gaard-Ma. Control yourself!*

I took a gulp of wine and began to hum nervously. Zawne chuckled. I half heard him say, "I always suspected you were timid."

But I interjected, blurting out in a panic, "Tell me about Lodden!"

He eased back in the sofa and scrunched his face. "There's not much to tell that you don't already know. Lodden's horrendous. Earthquakes, the most recent volcano, tiny tremors daily. The people who live there are almost completely disconnected from the rest of the world. They refuse to pack up and go someplace else. Instead, their lives revolve around building and rebuilding. They live in squalor, in the mud, in small houses built of volcanic rock. What you may not know is that Lodden is the last place in Geniverd where the people still worship false gods. It's why they stay. They once claimed to be in everlasting servitude to Gomorogha, the fire god who lives in the volcano."

"Wow," I said. "That's news to me. Someone told me once about how the world used to be very different, about how …" I trailed off, wondering if Roki was on a date too, huddled in the rain with some cute girl he had found in another noble's mansion.

"You all right?" Zawne asked.

"Yeah, sorry. Tell me more."

"That's pretty much it," he said. "My friends died. I battled leopards and furious temperatures. I allowed my pain to encapsulate me, to numb me and guide me forward. It was how I survived the harshness of it all. In the end, my pain led me to you."

His last words caught my breath in my throat. I choked on my wine. Could Zawne seriously be this romantic to me? I still wasn't convinced. His words were so pretty, so flattering. I had to be sure he wasn't playing me for a fool, trying to put the moves on me and then call the engagement off tomorrow morning. I was all too aware of the ladies' man Zawne had once been. I needed to be certain he was committed to me before I opened my heart, that the loss of Lordin hadn't made Zawne revert into a primal beast.

"You talk the talk," I said once I had finished choking on my wine, "but can you walk the walk?"

Zawne smirked. "Why don't we find out?" And he slithered close to me.

"No," I said, knocking the cocky smirk off his face. "That's not what I mean. What I'm trying to say is that you have been sweet and seductive with me all night, but will you follow through? I need to know your intentions are pure before this goes any further. I need you to give your word to the king and queen that we are to be wed. Only then will I open my heart to you."

I felt childish saying this, but it needed to be said. I could never give myself up so easily.

I had expected Zawne to crumble at my ultimatum, give up and go home or find another girl to be with, who was easier than me. I was shocked when he put his glass of wine down on the table and said, "I'll do you one better."

I didn't have time to react. Zawne had touched his wrist to activate his visin. He swiped this way and that, then directed the holographic screen at himself and made sure I wasn't in the shot. "Get ready to look happy," he said to me. Then he hit the livestream button.

"Hello, citizens of Geniverd. It's Prince Zawne here, streaming live to the entire world, all six continents on all four billion active visins. Some of you may know that I am now an Aska warrior. What you may not know is that I'm engaged to be married."

Zawne paused for dramatic effect while I freaked out next to him, mouth dry, eyes wide, heart palpitating. I couldn't believe it!

"That's right," he said to the projection. "I'm getting married to Kaelyn of Gaard. We will be wed just in time for the coronation."

Then he maneuvered his visin's screen, showing four billion people the dumb expression on my face. He put his arm around me and pulled me close. "Here she is, my bride-to-be. Everyone, meet my new wife."

I guessed I had my answer.

6

_E_verything happened faster than I could have anticipated. Before Zawne's livestream had ended, my visin was bleeping in my ear. Then Raad was screaming at me, "You got engaged in less than four hours? Did he even bed you yet?" His face was huge on the screen, as if he could open his mouth and swallow me.

"Whoa," I said. "Back off from the camera. You look like an angry giant."

"Sorry." Raad moved back. He was grinning triumphantly. "I'm so proud of you, sister. Finally, with three weeks before the coronation, Gaard has a fighting chance at the crown!"

"Calm down," I said. "I don't think I'm going to be queen."

"I'm just glad you listened to my advice," Raad said. "Queen or not, you agreed to marry Zawne for the sake of the Ava-Gaard and Geniverd as a whole. That really says something about you, Kaelyn. You're growing up." Then he paused. "Or maybe I'm wrong. Maybe you only agreed because he's smoking hot."

Raad doubled over laughing, and that was when Tissa

shoved herself into the frame of his visin. "Kaelyn, congratulations! Now we just have to find a man for Nnati! All three of us are going to reach such fabulous heights, Kaelyn. It will be like nothing we have ever imagined."

"Maybe," I told her. "Oh, and speaking of Nnati, he's calling me. Sorry, guys, got to go."

I ended the call and answered Nnati. Beside me, Zawne was being congratulated by noble after noble. His visin was ringing nonstop.

"You did it!" Nnati screamed. He sat in the darkness of his apartment, wearing pajamas. "How does it feel? What happened? Was he sweet? Was he gentle? Did you like it?"

Beside me, Zawne's laughter was insatiable. "Is that your friend?" Zawne asked. "He's funny! We'll have to invite him for dinner." Then he got up and began to pace the room. His features darkened, and I thought whatever call he had picked up on his visin was business related.

"We just talked," I told Nnati. "It was nice. I think I can do this. I really think I can. I feel like I'm evolving, Nnati. I feel like I've transformed from the bored, unruly girl sulking around NordHaven as a teenager into a woman who has a chance to make change in the world. I feel like I'm truly becoming a woman for our people."

"I'm happy for you, Kaelyn. This is great. Uh ... but your picture is all over the news. It's not a good one either. You look surprised and a little scared. They are playing Zawne's live feed on a loop. Questions are already being raised, comparisons between you and a certain dead fiancée. Brace yourself."

"I will," I said. I had already thought this might happen. The people still loved Lordin, and to some, I would seem like a shoddy replacement.

"Anyway." Nnati eased back into the shadows of his room

and yawned. "I should go to bed. I'm sure you're not done answering calls. I'm happy for you. I hope you made the right decision."

I glanced at Zawne, pacing before the fireplace and yammering into his visin.

I said to Nnati, "I hope so too."

* * *

I LET Zawne sleep in my bed. It felt right, and it was worth every second. I felt complete when I nestled into his arms and drifted to sleep. I felt content.

And this was where things took a strange turn. I was sinking into slumber, head full of fluff, body heavy, when everything changed. My limbs started to tingle, but I couldn't open my eyes to look. I couldn't move a single muscle. I felt electrified, fuzzy with little vibrations like a thousand electric raindrops.

Then I was floating out of my body. I could see again—see myself, Zawne snoring gently beside me. I passed right through my ceiling and caught a glimpse of the capital, with all its bright lights and the flyrarcs zipping between skyscrapers. Still I ascended, pulled upward by some supreme force into the clouds, into the atmosphere. I could see the whole continent of Gaard like a pancake on the water. But I rose higher still. I rocketed into space at a thousand miles a second, through plumes of pink and purple space dust, galaxies of a billion twinkling stars. I zoomed through the cosmos faster and faster until it all became a blur and ...

I was in a void. My soul had been sucked right through the endlessness of space and into a place of nothingness. The floor was white and solid, but it looked like mist. All around me was endless and blank, yet above flowed a sky of peach clouds. It was tranquil and oddly euphoric. I wasn't even panicked. In the back of my head, I thought, *This is a dream ... yet it's not.*

"Queen Kaelyn, so nice of you to come."

"Who said that?" I whirled around. There was no one there.

"I did," the voice said. It seemed to boom from all around me. "You can call me Riedel."

Then another voice, a woman's, soft and sublime. "And you can call me Hanchell."

I gawked in every direction, but no one was there. "Where are you?" I said. "I can't see anyone."

"Settle down," Riedel said with great authority in his voice. "Be still and concentrate. You won't be able to see us with your human eyes. You'll have to use your other senses."

"Okay ..."

I closed my eyes and strained every muscle in my body, but nothing happened. Then I focused on listening. I listened, and when I did, I could hear the leagues of silence like subtle vibrations. It occurred to me my senses were enhanced in this spectral void. I took a deep breath and felt the air beyond my fingers. Every particle spoke to me, showed its existence. When I opened my eyes again, the air before me was shimmering. There were two shapes of light and motion. They were constructs of sound and spectral energy. Riedel was on the left—I could smell his manly, cedarwood scent—and Hanchell was on the right. I could also smell Hanchell's rosy odor, sweet and relaxing. Both were distinct to me now that I had focused my mind.

"Good," Riedel said.

"Very good," Hanchell echoed. "You can see that we are here, but you cannot see our true forms. No human can see the true forms of the Crown of Crowns. Only the Min can do that."

"I ...Who? What? Huh?" I blinked, confused and thrown off guard. The Crown of Crowns was a bird. That was what Papa had always told me. And what was a Min? Where in the world was I?

"It's understandable," Hanchell said in her delicate voice. "Humans are often shocked and awed by this place. It's called Shiol, by the way."

"It's like another dimension?"

"Kind of," Riedel said. "It's more of a spirit dimension. We are spirits, as are the Min. Only the Min may travel freely between spirit realm and human realm."

I kept blinking. I had no idea what Riedel was talking about. It was so strange watching their intangible shapes of light wriggle and sparkle before me.

"This is where we choreograph events in Geniverd and the other civilizations," Hanchell explained. "Right now you are in a protective bubble. The other spirits can't interact with you unless we allow it. Don't be afraid."

"I'm not," I said, which was strange, because I should have been terrified.

"Good," Riedel said. "There is no time for fear. We have brought you here for a very important reason, Kaelyn. It is our practice to inform the new kings and queens of Geniverd of their positions before the coronation."

"Wait." I pinched the bridge of my nose, trying to digest all this information. "You're telling me Zawne and I will be king and queen? What about the bird Papa used to tell me about? If you are the Crown of Crowns ..."

"Yes," Hanchell said, answering my thought. "We take turns being the bird. It was Riedel last time, so I will be the bird in three weeks."

Riedel groaned. I could tell from his shifting light pattern that he was disgruntled. "I like being the bird," he said. "But fine, you can do it this time."

"This is all really crazy," I said. "No one is going to believe this!"

"We should hope not," both spirits said at once.

Then Hanchell said, "Kaelyn, you are forbidden to tell anyone about Shiol or our existence. We refer to this as the Great Secret. If you reveal the Great Secret to anyone, you and whoever you tell will die."

"Oh ..." My heart fell, but I supposed it made sense. People couldn't know there were spirits in an ethereal realm, pulling the strings down on Geniverd.

"It does make sense," Riedel said. "And yes, we can read your thoughts. But none of that matters. What matters, Kaelyn, is that we have chosen you and Zawne to be the next rulers. You two have a lot of work to do together. We need strong humans to lead Geniverd. Out of all the eligible minds and hearts we have searched, yours were the best. We were thrilled last night when your engagement was announced. We scanned your worthiness and couldn't believe it—leagues above the rest!"

I was more stunned by this revelation than by any of the supernatural stuff. "How is that possible?" I asked.

"We do not make mistakes, human," Hanchell said, very sweetly. "Your heart is the one we need."

"And Zawne's," Riedel added.

I thought Hanchell's light form smiled as she said, "But mostly yours. The truth is, Kaelyn, you are a strong and capable woman. We feel comfortable with the fate of Geniverd in your small human hands. We will help you, of course. You will need to see us five nights a week during your reign as queen, to be made aware of current events. This will exhaust you. Visiting Shiol takes a toll on the human body, but you will learn to cope."

"First you must decide if you want to be queen," Riedel said. "We shouldn't talk too much of your duties until you've decided to take the throne with Zawne by your side. But you must make the decision by tomorrow night."

"Why is it my decision to make?" I asked. "Why isn't Zawne here too?"

"It's a mercy," Hanchell said. "You see, if you say no, we have to kill you in a tragic and painful way. No humans aside from the Geniverd rulers may know the Great Secret. This way, should you not feel up to the task, only you must die. You'll be sparing Zawne's life."

"And if Zawne refuses the job?" I asked. "This seems utterly biased!"

"We're sure he won't," Riedel said. "He is a more basic human than you are. Your heart is complicated, like Lordin's was. We thought she would accept the job, but she didn't. We hope you will be different."

It hit me like a slap across the face. Lordin had been killed because she'd turned down the role as queen. But why? What would cause her to renounce the throne and be willingly butchered?

"It's true," Hanchell said sadly. She had read my thoughts. "Lordin turned down the offer to become queen. She thought Zawne didn't have what it would take to be ruler. Sad, really, the way we had to kill her."

"She's a Min now," Riedel told me. "Min are spirits that can move between our worlds. When someone who knows the Great Secret dies, they become a Min and work for us. This means we give them tasks, and then they are free to roam habitable planets, like Geniverd, and even inhabit another human's body. The only rule is that a Min may not influence people's ideas of their dead self, or ever reveal the Great Secret. If they do, they die an irreversible death."

I had so many questions, so many feelings. Two omnipotent beings were flipping my perspective of the world on its head. I stuttered, trying to ask everything at once. "So that means ... If I were a ... Does anyone else ...? What about my ...? Do you think ...?"

Hanchell laughed. "Calm, Kaelyn. All these questions will be answered in time. Firstly, yes, we do believe Zawne has what it takes to be king. And secondly, we don't seek overtly virtuous people. We instead search for pure and incorruptible hearts, like yours."

"Oh." That made me feel better. Maybe I wasn't as virtuous as Lordin was, but my intentions were certainly pure. I was more unnerved about Zawne discovering the reason for Lordin's death. I wondered how he would react, if he would turn on me or even turn on himself. I worried that he would hate Lordin for not having believed in him.

"I have another question," I said.

But Riedel cut me off before I could ask it. "Yes, your mother is at peace. But no, we cannot tell you anything more than that. The ultimate knowledge of what happens after death could alter your purpose in life."

"All right," I said. It was enough just to know Mama was at peace. "How will I get back to this place tomorrow night to give you my decision?"

Riedel said, "Spell Shiol over your heart as you lie in bed. Your ethereal self will be pulled into our mirror dimension. For now, when you awaken, you are going to hear glass shattering. Zawne will then come into the room with blood on his finger. The current king and queen will have invited you both for lunch at one p.m."

"This will prove to you that we are real," Hanchell said in

83

her soft voice. "Now go to sleep, Queen Kaelyn. Tomorrow will be a hard day for you."

With that, the light of Hanchell and Riedel faded. The clouds above churned, and my vision got fuzzy. Everything went black.

* * *

I WOKE to the sound of shattering glass. My eyes burst open and I sat upright, the memory of my time in Shiol flooding my mind. "Zawne?" I called out. "Zawne, are you all right?"

He appeared in the doorway, blood trickling down his finger. "Sorry," he said. "I cut myself on a wineglass. I'm trying not to get blood on my suit."

He looked good despite the blood, and it made me smile. I was glad we had spent the night together. Still, I was exhausted. My body was heavy, and there was an itchy burning in my eyes.

"You look beat," Zawne said, "which is weird, because you slept in quite late. It's almost noon. The only people I've ever seen sleep so late are my parents."

I wanted to say, *Because they've been visiting Shiol throughout their reign! They were being given orders on how to run the kingdom by the Crown of Crowns!* Instead, I said, "Do we have any plans today?"

"Yes," Zawne said, a little surprised. He was bandaging his finger with a roll of gauze. "How did you know? We have a lunch date with the king and queen in an hour. We're supposed to be there at one o'clock. I told them you were still asleep, and they both grinned at each other like they were in on some personal joke."

They know, I thought. *The same thing happened to them forty years ago.* "Cancel it," I said. "Your parents will understand, trust me. I have a lot of thinking to do."

And that was exactly how I proceeded to spend my day. Zawne didn't understand, and I didn't expect him to. Before he left my apartment, I probed him a bit. "Would you make a good king? ... What do you think of the current model of Decens-Lenitas? ... Would you allow me to change the world for the better? ... Could we reform the system of monarchy to better benefit the people, spreading the wealth throughout the entire population? ... Would you be up for promoting some of the older forms of tradition and society, bringing purpose back to the world and taking some of the overwhelming power away from the royal bloodlines?"

All his answers came back positive. "Anything you want, my love." His eagerness to help with my vision for Geniverd made me confident I could trust him as an ally. I was sure I would make a decision by the end of the day. I was getting more and more amped up at the thought of a new Geniverd, shaking the system to its very core!

I almost called Nnati to tell him the news, then remembered what the Crown of Crowns had said: *No humans aside from the Geniverd rulers may know the Great Secret.*

I couldn't risk telling anyone. I sat curled on my sofa and deliberated alone. Could Lordin really have thought Zawne so worthless? The thought made me bitter toward her. How could she have thrown away her life and jeopardized Zawne's chance at the throne? He had been so in love with her. Was Lordin not the woman she had seemed to be?

I forwarded all my calls from GMAF to Nnati, adding an apologetic message and informing him that we needed to double the staff immediately, but I refrained from telling him why. If I was to become queen in three weeks, the foundation would need a new boss. Someone would have to look after things while I busied myself with my royal duties and spent my nights in Shiol.

As I ate an early dinner and spun these ideas around in my head, that was when it hit me. Lordin had transferred her charitable works to me the day before she refused the Crown of Crowns. She had planned it all out. She had wanted her important work to go on but didn't want to take on the responsibility of queen, because she had thought her future husband was unfit. Instead, Lordin had entrusted me to look after things, and now I was in the same position, only I was going to make Zawne my king.

Lordin must have been blind. Zawne was the perfect man for the job. As I lay down for the night and spelled Shiol over my heart, I knew exactly what I was going to tell the Crown of Crowns.

* * *

"HELLO, QUEEN KAELYN," Riedel's powerful voice boomed. "We sense you have made your decision."

"I only have one question," I said. I was apprehensive. I needed to hear that the Crown of Crowns believed in me as much as I believed in Zawne. "How do you know I will be a good queen?"

"It won't be hard," Hanchell said. "We do most of the heavy lifting. Before we intervened hundreds of years ago in the choosing of Geniverd's rulers, men warred with each other, were killed constantly by infectious diseases, ravaged the countryside with pestilence, and even acted out genocides. They prayed to false gods and sacrificed children. It was chaos. Then we stepped in. Now everything is fine. We foresee immediate events and plan accordingly. You, Kaelyn, will be our commander in the physical world. You are here to heed our warnings and act accordingly. You are our adjudicator."

I pursed my lips and narrowed my eyes at the insubstantial light masses. "Which makes you the bosses?"

"Yes and no," Riedel said. "You can say no to us ..."

"But we wouldn't recommend it," Hanchell finished.

"Okay." I took a deep breath. I had already made my decision. The needs of Geniverd were too great for me to ignore the call to the throne. Zawne was a good man and would rise to the occasion. We would do away with the corruption, the mass boredom, the uselessness of the strife. I couldn't wait to ruffle some feathers among the clan leaders. Even if Zawne wasn't as keen as I was for change, it didn't matter. I needed to fix the class system before our world regressed into peasants and kings, like in the ancient days. I needed to fix the dwindling middle class and bring peace to the agitated sections of the world, like on restive Nurlie Island.

Also, being queen next to Zawne, waking up in a palace every morning ... it couldn't be that bad.

"I agree," I said, back straight, eyes firm. "I will be the queen."

"Excellent!" Hanchell cried. If I hadn't known better, I'd have said she was clapping.

"The next step is to inform Zawne of your decision," Riedel said. "Do it tomorrow, when you wake up. We can bring you both back the next night for a debriefing. We don't want you coming back too often, Kaelyn. You will be too exhausted to complete your duties. Rest for tomorrow, tell Zawne, then come back the next night."

I nodded. "Got it, boss."

Hanchell tittered. "You don't have to call us that. Oh, and before you leave, there is a visitor for you. It looks like you have some friends in the spirit realm."

"Who?" I asked. "Is it Mama? Is it Lordin?"

But Hanchell and Riedel had vanished. Everything was still for about three seconds. Then I sensed a different scent, a scent I knew very well. My head lifted, my chin sticking out. My eyes searched as I spun. It was a man who answered me finally, his shape forming in the distance of the vast, clouded plain.

"Kaelyn." The voice was low as it danced my name.

I choked, overwhelmed with emotion. And then my tears brimmed over. "Roki?"

$\mathcal{W}$e stared at each other for over a minute, unblinking, unflinching, utterly mute. I studied his hair, the soft handsomeness of his face, his muscular frame. Roki hadn't changed that much in three years. He was the same man I had adored before the world fell apart, back when I was an ignorant little girl.

What was he doing in Shiol?

Roki came to me, floating across the ground like a spirit. He took my hands in his and said, "I've missed you. I was looking for you just now. I saw your body lying in your bed, but you weren't in it. Your body was empty. I flew directly here and saw that the Crown of Crowns was speaking with someone. I couldn't see you inside their bubble, but I knew it was you. I signaled to them that I wished to meet with you. I told them we used to be friends."

"You were in my bedchamber?" I said, a little scandalized. "You were watching me as I slept?"

"Yes …" He made a face, probably realizing how creepy

that sounded. "But it's not weird. I do it all the time. You see, I'm not a human, Kaelyn. I'm a Min."

I gaped at Roki, speechless. I would have torn away from him, but I liked the warmth of his hands over mine. I moved my mouth, but no sound came out. How could Roki be a Min? All our time together, and he was a spirit? I had given my heart away to a spirit!

"It's tough," Roki said with a laugh. "I get it, I do. I've been alive for a long time, and I have never once told a human being what I truly am. If I let the information slip, I would suffer a final death, and the person I told would be killed. I have always expected this kind of reaction. It's great seeing it from you."

"I'm funny to you now?" I had started crying. I was mad that he was here, mad that he had lied to me about being a spirit, mad that I loved the feeling of his hands enfolding mine.

"No," he said, becoming serious. "I'm sorry. You're not funny to me. You're adorable and radiant, even now when you're crying." Roki delicately wiped the tears from my cheeks. He had always been a gentleman. "It's just, I use laughter as a medicine, you know? It's why I always jested with you, always tried to make you laugh. It felt appropriate now, in this strange moment, you here with me in the spirit realm. I just want to make things right."

"Okay ..." I sniveled, trying to hold back my tears. It was hard to stay mad at Roki. "But why now?" I said. "Why didn't you make things right before, when I needed you the most, when I was at my lowest low? If you're a spirit, you could have visited me anytime—"

"And I did!" Roki said, suddenly enveloping me in his arms. He said in my ear, "I've visited you every night since the fateful day your mama died. I sat on your bed and watched you. I walked with you through the quiet halls of NordHaven. Then I followed you to the capital. Sometimes I watched you at work. I wept tears of joy when I saw how well you were doing with the foundation. You've helped so many people climb out of poverty. You've given so many young children meaning and a future. You even helped to save all those turtles and that coral reef."

"Then why didn't you reveal yourself to me?" I demanded. My face was pressed against his chest, and I clung to his shirt for dear life, as though he might evaporate. "I could have used a friend like you. I've spent so much time wondering where you went. You could have made it easier for me!"

"I wanted to," Roki said, "but in those first days, I felt your heart and heard your thoughts. You didn't want to talk to me. You blamed me in part for the way it had ended between you and your mama. You had chosen me over your own family, and then death came like a wrecking ball to demolish your emotions. It would have been wrong of me to go against your wishes."

I tore away from him, feeling dumb for crying like a child. "You could have tried," I said, hardening my expression. "It would have been nice knowing that you did everything within your power to see me again. Instead, you abandoned me. You left me alone."

Roki pouted, stepped back, and hung his head. "I stayed by your side. I followed you into your dreams. I let my scent linger in your room. I know it feels like I deserted you, but I didn't. I never lost my feelings. I never forgot about you. Instead, I let you grieve. I gave you the space I thought you needed. I didn't want to ruin your life by getting you mixed up with a Min."

"I wouldn't have cared if you were a space alien!" I launched myself forward, pulled Roki's arms around me, and hugged him fiercely. "But I forgive you. I understand now you were doing what you thought was right. It's the reason I was so crazy about you, because your soul is pure." Then I laughed. "I guess it has to be. All you have is a soul!"

Roki smiled and pushed me gently away, looked down into my eyes. I knew right then I would believe anything he said. His eyes sparkled with sincerity. "I know you've changed," he said. "You're not the same naive girl who followed me, laughing, through the fake market. You've gotten stronger over these last three years. You've become wise and selfless. You've become a woman. You've also gotten engaged, so I know we can't be together like we used to be ..."

"Not necessarily," I said, hating myself as I said it, as I began to scheme in my brain. "It's true, I am engaged to Zawne. We are set to be king and queen in three weeks. It doesn't mean I can't have you for a friend. It would mean a lot to have you around. You know, giving me moral support, telling me jokes, letting me confide in you. It will be frustrating not being able to talk about Shiol with any of my human friends."

Roki brightened. He had an air of mischief about him, the same excitable energy I remembered. "I would agree to that!" he said. And right then I knew my life was about to change. Nothing could be simple anymore. Roki was back. This time, I knew he was back for good.

* * *

ROKI WAS RUBBING his hands together. "Let's start right now," he said. "Let's forget all the other stuff and start over. How can I be of service, my queen? What do you want to know about Shiol or about Min? I'll answer anything."

I thought about it for a second, stroking my chin. Then I said, "Tell me everything."

Roki was biting his lip, trying to contain his excitement. I now believed everything he had told me, about how he had watched over me, about how he had only wanted what was best for me. It made me think of him as my watcher, as my guardian. I wasn't mad anymore.

Roki said, "I'll start with where we are: Shiol." He waved his arms like a magician, and the emptiness of the void rippled and changed. I suddenly saw in the distance a land unlike any on Geniverd. There were tower spires of gold, cities nestled in the clouds, odd gaseous auras moving freely throughout the mystical empire, humans flying as if they were birds. It looked peaceful and divine, the radiant sun shining over the other-worldly civilization.

"Wow …" I had no other words.

"It's just a fragment," Roki said, and waved his hand. The vision faded, and we were back in the endless void. "Where we are now is like a meeting hall the Crown of Crowns uses to parley with various monarchs. But that, what I just showed you, is the space Min call home when they aren't out on missions or goofing around in other realms."

"There were so many," I said. "How can there be so many? Geniverd only has four billion people. And what were those weird electric auras I saw floating around?"

Roki laughed. He hunkered down on the ground and smiled up at me. "One thing at a time, Kaelyn. The universe is bigger than you think. There are worlds, dimensions, planets. There is more than just human life, and the Crown of Crowns presides over it all. They use Min as their servants of order. We keep the scales balanced in these different worlds. We all have assignments, and for the past five hundred years, I have been assigned to Geniverd. It was where I was born, died, and became a Min. But that's a story for another day."

My jaw had hit the floor some time ago. I felt woozy, overwhelmed by all the information. I kept picturing the Shiol city, the magnificent structures unlike anything I'd ever seen. Who had built such a place? How long had these spirits been pulling the universe's infinite strings? Could Geniverd evolve into such a futuristic place one day?

"As for the auras," Roki said with a smile, "those are Min without bodies. Like I said, we're just spirits. Most Min don't have a special upbringing. Some are created in Shiol, some on other planets, and some are born to other Min. Yet each Min has the ability to possess a life-form within his or her zone of assignment. In simple terms, we take over bodies and use them to do our jobs. We need them to infiltrate governments, become authority figures, influence the masses to keep civilization from imploding. In truth, most of the successful people on Geniverd are Min: the athletes, celebrities, serial killers, businesspeople. There are no restrictions on what we can do, and some Min have a mean streak. Some of the worst Min like to murder because they enjoy the way it feels."

I was appalled. "And the host doesn't know what's going on, that they're being used as a tool for evil?"

"No," Roki said. "And yes, it sickens me too. Yet this is the way of the universe. The host's mind cannot know what's going on. They have no idea they're being controlled by a Min. The Min quashes fear, trepidation, anxiety. The Min makes them almost superhuman."

Then Roki chuckled. "But it's not all bad. We also use humans for fun. For example, when I inhabit the body of a human, I can feel despair, joy, love, anger, euphoria, and physical pain. The human senses become heightened. Oh, and the human still lives inside their body. They just take a back seat, like a passenger in the back of their mind." He saw my skeptical expression and assured me, "I never kill them. That would be cruel."

Then he went on, saying, "Sound, sight, hearing, smell." He gave me a look. "Touch. These sensations all become enhanced. Colors are brighter. Smells are more pungent. I find myself pausing for five minutes every time I pass a bakery. But touch is the big one. I can feel the air like it's water. I can feel the blood flowing underneath my human skin. And women ... don't get me started. When we hug, it's like we're—"

"Stop," I said. "I don't want to hear about the women you've been ... hugging over the past five hundred years."

"Sorry." Roki shifted awkwardly. "In truth, that was just physical stuff. I prefer deeply emotional connections. And in terms of minds, I have never interacted with a mind like yours. Never. You don't accept something without questioning it first, even if it sounds like the greatest opportunity in the world. You genuinely care about the consequences and everyone's welfare. Those other women were just bodies. You are both."

"Oh," I said, but stopped it there. I didn't want to start flirting. Roki and I had only become friends again five minutes ago, and I already felt like I was betraying Zawne. I tried to change the subject. "How have you kept your body for so long? What's the person on the inside doing? I know you said they don't know they've been possessed, but what's going on with them?"

"Ah," Roki said, nodding. "This is where things get complicated. See, a Min can possess a body either for a brief period or for the full course of the body's life. It depends on the assignment. My supersecret mission means that I am in this body for the next eighty years at minimum. The man inside is kind of dormant, at rest."

"That's like murder," I said. "It's like a mental murder."

"The man was dying when I possessed him," Roki said. "He had been infected by a pathogen and would have been dead within the hour. If anything, I saved him."

"Oh." Again Roki had twisted my judgment around and made me feel stupid. He hadn't killed the man. He had saved him. The man was getting to live it up with a Min for eighty years. I was more concerned that someone had been about to die because of a pathogen. I'd thought we were beyond such casualties. If there was one good thing about our society, it was that our medicine was top of the line.

"You're not stupid," Roki said. "And yes, I can read your thoughts. Sorry about that. I'll try not to. But really, you're not dumb. You're worried and kindhearted. I can already see that your core values haven't changed in three years. You're the same girl I fell for. It's no wonder the Crown of Crowns picked you over the other heirs. I've eavesdropped on their thoughts and can tell you this. Half of them are evil, a quarter are hubristic, and a quarter only want the throne because it's expected of them. Ninety-nine percent are just bored and looking for something to do. They think ascending the throne will give their restless lives some entertainment. You know how they are. These people have so much wealth and influence that life is borderline meaningless. But you, Kaelyn, you are driven by love and social justice. You are more righteous than them all."

"Thanks," I said. It was no use arguing anymore. I had heard this same thing from a dozen people in the last week. I was just going to shut up and start accepting that yes, perhaps I was fit to be queen.

"Speaking of queens," Roki said, "we'd better get you to

sleep. You need to be well rested for tomorrow. You've got a busy day ahead of you, I'm sure."

"But I want to know more," I cried. "I'm not ready to go! Tell me more, Roki. Please."

"Fine," he conceded. "One more question. Then you need to get some rest."

I thought long and hard, mostly because I was distracted by Roki's soft lips curled into a smile. Then it came to me.

"Mama," I said. "Please, Roki, tell me who poisoned Mama."

Roki's face drained of color. He took one of my hands in his and said, "I'm sorry, I don't know. Min don't pay too much attention to murders in Geniverd. I asked around, but no one could tell me. And I was with you when it happened."

Now I was sad. I didn't want to think about Mama's suffering because of some rival leader's wrath. It made me want to unleash a wrath of my own!

"You're tough in your thoughts," Roki said, teasing me like old times. "Now get some sleep, Kaelyn. We will talk more later."

"When?"

Roki flashed his perfectly white teeth. "When you wake up." He waved his hand in front of me, hypnotizing me deep into a slumber.

* * *

IT FELT like I had slept for a whole week. I dozed dreamlessly in a black nothing. When I finally awoke, it was to the sight of Roki's bright eyes blinking at me.

"Good afternoon," he said softly.

Roki was kneeling at my bedside. I groggily reached up and caressed his face.

"Afternoon?" I immediately took my hand back. I was in

the real world again. I couldn't touch Roki without betraying Zawne. I had to keep this as a friendship, a very close friendship.

"Yes," he said. "It's already noon. And don't stress about it. We've done nothing inappropriate."

Before I could respond, Roki vanished into thin air. At the exact same moment, Zawne walked into my room.

"Sorry to barge in like this," he said, "but I've been calling you on your visin all morning. Are you all right?"

"Yes," I said, finding it hard to sit up straight. I was incredibly tired from my time in Shiol. "I must have slept in again. All the excitement has got me fatigued."

"That's understandable," he said. Zawne crossed my bedroom in four brisk steps, leaned over, and planted a kiss on my lips. He pulled back just enough to look in my eyes. "I've been missing that."

I needed more. The talk with Roki, the fact I was to be married—it had a fire burning inside me. "Again," I said, then grasped the nape of Zawne's neck and pulled him close. Our lips touched, then our warm tongues swished and pressed and tugged; I was lost in it. I knew then that Zawne and I could rule the world.

"That was unexpected," Zawne said as he sat on the edge of my bed, panting. "You're fiery for such a sleepy woman."

"I guess I needed the affection," I said, which was true.

Zawne gave me a smile. "You'll always have mine."

I wondered if that was true. Would we always be so close and loving? I felt ashamed all over again for allowing Roki back into my life.

Zawne said, "I'm going to have a quick shower, my love," and he went into the bathroom. The second he closed the door, Roki was right back at my bedside, and I was lost in his eyes and his wild hair, his cut jaw. I was pulled between two worlds!

"How did you do that?" I asked, trying to keep my voice low.

Roki grinned, devilish in the way he silently teased me. "Every Min has heightened senses and extrasensory powers. I can detect moods, changes in temperature, slight fluctuations in air molecules. It means I can sense when someone is coming. I can even sense what they are going to do. It's how I knew Raad was about to barge into your room with bad news that day. It was why I left, to let you and your brother mourn together."

"Wow," I said. "That's amazing. It must be so great to be a Min. No wonder Lordin gave up her human form."

"That's not all," Roki said. "We each have one special ability. It comes with the package when you're transformed. Mine is that I can mask presences. For example, I could mask my presence, and you would forget I was here. I can mask smells, feelings, even entire ideas. It's incredible."

I gawked at Roki. "All these you can do ... and you choose to visit me."

"You've sold yourself short for too long," Roki told me. "I'm happy to see you're coming into your own. You're turning into a splendid woman, Kaelyn. I'm eager to see what the next forty years of your rule have in store."

I opened my mouth to speak, but the bathroom door was opening. Roki vanished and out came Zawne, naked but for the towel wrapped around his waist. He was wet, bearded, and delicious. I suddenly felt like a very bad person, like a little girl and not at all like a queen. I motioned to him. "Come here. Sit close to me."

Zawne smirked. "I thought you might say that."

As he sauntered over to me, I remembered there was

something important to tell him. My strange new obsession with his body would have to wait.

He sat on the bed, stretched one arm over me, and said, "So, now what?"

"Now we have to talk." It made me feel bad that his expression went slack. Zawne had had something else on his mind. The silly man would have to wait.

He sat up straight, suddenly a bit edgy. "Talk about what?"

I remembered what the Crown of Crowns had said about Zawne being a simpler person than me. There was no way he would deny the offer to be king. So I spat it out.

"Zawne, you and I are the chosen ones. We're going to be king and queen."

His expression remained unchanged. His eyes were locked on mine, but there was no emotion. Was this part of his Aska training, to be as cold as ice when he needed to be?

"Could you repeat that?"

"We're chosen," I said. "We are *the* chosen. The Crown of Crowns came to me—well, sucked me into their dimension. I know the Crown of Crowns is a bird, and they are a bird— well, they take turns. Anyway, they told me we would be selected as the next king and queen."

I told him everything from beginning to end, every rule and every crazy new universal truth I had learned over the past forty-eight hours. I even snuck in some of the stuff Roki had told me. When all was said and done, I sat panting on the bed, and Zawne stood by the window, the afternoon light slashing across his rock-hard abs.

"I always had a feeling," he said distantly, as if talking to himself. "I always knew there was something strange about my parents. They slept so often, and always like they were dead or in comas. They even had rules about not being disturbed. Whenever I woke with a nightmare, I just crawled into bed with my brother."

"So ..." I gulped. This was the moment of truth. "So, do you agree to rule Geniverd with me?"

Zawne stared seriously out the window. It was one of the things that was totally in contrast to Roki. Where Roki was a charismatic jokester, Zawne could be stiff and severe. Yet it was one of the reasons I was so attracted to him.

"I agree," he said. "I agree in the name of Shondur and in the name of Geniverd, for my parents and for the people." Zawne turned to me, a smile finally breaking through. "If I had said no, would you have been killed?"

"Yes. I was quite nervous. We both would have been killed."

"Not to worry," Zawne said, swooping across the room to sit with me on the bed. "We will survive, prosper, and rule with compassion and courage. We will face this trial together as man and wife. When do we go to Shiol?"

In that moment, I was proud to be Zawne's fiancée. I wondered if Roki was watching me. I wondered if he was there in the room, listening to my thoughts. Was Roki jealous?

* * *

THE FOLLOWING EVENING, as Zawne and I lay down to sleep after a busy day of wedding planning—our wedding was to be held the day before the coronation—we both spelled Shiol over our hearts. Seconds later we were being zipped through the eternal cosmos.

"What a ride!" Zawne said as we materialized into the Crown of Crowns' bubble. "The gaseous bursts of space, the huge planets, the interdimensional tear into a pocket of the universe. I could get used to that!"

"I already am," I said, laughing. "It's amazing how fast the human brain adjusts to a new experience. This was my third time, and it didn't even faze me."

"And it never will again," came Riedel's voice. I had to concentrate and reach out with my senses to see his twinkling form standing beside Hanchell.

"I can't believe it," Zawne said. "You are built of light. This is amazing."

I supposed Zawne didn't need to focus to see Riedel and Hanchell. He was an Aska. His training would never leave him. Still, it made me feel inferior. Zawne was already better at this than I was.

"I see you've made your decision together," Hanchell said. She sounded pleased.

"Yes." Zawne took a bold step forward. "I agree to your proposal, Crown of Crowns. I agree to become king of Geniverd."

"Good for you," Riedel said. His voice was an earthy boom, perhaps to try to put Zawne in his human place. "But there are things we must go over before we proceed. This will be our last meeting before the coronation, so you must understand all the rules before you leave here today."

"Got it." Zawne folded his hands and stepped back. I touched his arm, trying to show some solidarity between us, but Zawne was at attention, as if he were listening to his squad leader.

"The first rule is that you must come here to Shiol five nights a week," Riedel said. "We suggest you take shifts, split up your time here. That way one of you is not constantly tired."

"When you come to Shiol," Hanchell said, "you will be given our recommendations on how to adjudicate the following day's council meetings. You will be ruling over disputes and issues between two or more clans. These are important, and we highly suggest that you adhere to our recommendations."

"But we don't have to?" I asked.

"No," Hanchell said. "You don't have to, but no one in hundreds of years has ever gone against us. We suggest that if you wish to make the business of governing four billion people on six continents easier, you listen to what we say."

I nodded, but Zawne wasn't convinced. "Where do you get the information for your recommendations?" he asked. "How do you decide?"

"Irrelevant," Riedel boomed. His voice shook the void with authority. It left no room for debate.

"And you cannot discuss our findings with anyone," he continued. "Not with the ex-queen or ex-king. Not even with the dead! If you do, you and every person you've revealed any part of the Great Secret to will be killed brutally and painfully within the hour."

That was enough to shut Zawne up. He stood straight and didn't say a word.

"Should you need to speak with us urgently," Hanchell said, "you may take a power nap. Drift quickly here, ask for what you need, then return to Geniverd. This will wear you out, so please don't do it too often."

Good, I thought. *If I get overwhelmed, I have a place to go.* However, I could always ask Roki for his opinion. It was going to be nice having a Min at my disposal while I was queen.

"Our recommendations will also come with physical evidence for your human eyes," Riedel told us. "You may read through reports, flick through video, and listen to audio recordings here in Shiol. Then you must return to sleep and make your judgments the following day. This will be a stressful process. Ready yourselves over the coming weeks."

"One more thing," Hanchell said. She was audibly giddy.

"Whose head would you like me to land on at the coronation? I'm so excited!"

Zawne and I exchanged a glance. "I'm okay with it being Zawne," I said, smiling at him.

For once in the meeting, he smiled back. "Thank you, my queen. I appreciate it."

"It's settled!" Hanchell said. Her blob of light was agitated, sparking with excitement. "I will land on Zawne's head in two weeks' time. Now go to sleep, humans. You have a wedding and a kingdom to plan. We will see you soon."

Hanchell and Riedel fizzled out, leaving Zawne and me alone in the endless vacuum of the bubble. I kept thinking of the marvelous city just beyond the illusion. I wondered if Roki could take me there one day.

"Are you ready?" I asked Zawne.

He nodded. "We can do this, Kaelyn. We can rule together with the help of these beings."

Then he took my hand and kissed it lightly. Zawne's unexpected romantic side was always a treat, and it made me giggle. "I'll see you in the morning."

We closed our eyes and entered the blackness.

8

_I_t was two weeks of mayhem. Dress shopping with Tissa, planning the ceremony with Zawne and his royal parents, sorting out the Ava-Gaard guest list with Raad, and spending countless hours gossiping with Nnati. The toughest part was keeping my mouth shut about Shiol and the secret Min living among us. I wanted to tell someone so badly! This was where Roki came in handy; he was always around, leaving a trace of his scent like a signature to let me know he was watching. We'd talk sometimes in the space between meetings. He'd visit me on the rare days I went to the office. Roki even promised to be there at my wedding, masked somewhere at the front of the crowd. He was a good friend to me, and it sometimes hurt that he couldn't be more.

You're getting married! I had to remind myself. _You wouldn't betray Zawne. You wouldn't!_

But hadn't I already?

Tissa and I were in the dressing room before the ceremony, a space the Grucken had set aside for me at Lithern Shrine, inside his training complex. Through the walls, we could hear the intense clamor of singing voices outside, the banging drums, the wild chanting. It was a Gaard tradition that the attendees chanted and danced frantically for up to four hours before the bride revealed herself. It was meant as an enticement for her to be wed, to arouse passion for her and the groom's union in the hearts of the people before the wedding began.

We had been listening to it already for two hours when Nnati came into the room.

He stopped just inside and gaped at me. "Wow ... Kaelyn, is that you?"

I laughed. "Of course. Who else would it be?"

"You're ..." Nnati was tongue tied. I'd never seen him like this before. "You're beautiful," he said. "Your dress, your hair, your glow. I can't believe it's you."

"Thanks," Tissa said for me. "I helped with the design of the dress. It's pure white to match Zawne. I thought the diamonds and white silk were a nice touch. I also gave her a scoop neck and a sweeping train. And what about my outfit, Nnati? Being married to Raad sure has its perks. Check out the diamond necklace my hubby bought me just for his sister's wedding. Look closely—these are real diamonds embedded in the gold."

Nnati gave her a look with one eyebrow raised. "You're sure getting comfortable in your new life, huh? I suppose it's understandable. Nobody where we come from could have purchased you such a gift if they had saved all their money for forty years."

Tissa grinned, mostly to herself. She was fiddling with the necklace.

"Anyway," Nnati said, charging across the room to give me a hug. "You look amazing!" He stopped just short of me with his arms spread. "I want to hug you, but I also don't want to wrinkle the dress."

"I appreciate it," I told him bashfully. "And thanks for your kind words. They mean a lot."

Nnati blew me a cheeky kiss. "Anything for you, darling." Then he turned his attention to the window. "They're acting like lunatics out there. It's like that mad parade for the dead at Lordin's funeral. What's going on? Why do the Ava-Gaard commoners have their faces painted like birds?"

"It symbolizes the Crown of Crowns," I told Nnati. "It's meant to be good luck for Zawne and me in the upcoming coronation. It's supposed to raise our chances of being the chosen ones."

I thought, *If only they knew the truth. I wish I could tell my friends!*

"I doubt you'll need luck," Tissa said as she put the finishing touches on my dress. "You're as benevolent as they come. Your work with GMAF says it all."

I said nothing. I was afraid that if I spoke, all the truths would come spilling out. I didn't feel like accidentally getting my friends killed because I wanted to gossip.

Nnati was still peeking out the window at the crowd below. "I don't see a lot of clan leaders," he said. "No one from Surrvul or Krug. No one from Nurlie. The usual Gaard folk and some emissaries from Shondur are here, the king and queen, your Aska bro. But none of the other main players. What gives?"

"The coronation is tomorrow," I told him. "They're all busy. The clan leaders are getting their heirs ready. All the families have a thousand things to do before the coronation."

"Gotcha," he said. Then Nnati broke out laughing. "Your Gaard traditions are comical, Kaelyn. I love how enthusiastic the Ava-Gaard are. Will you and Zawne be jumping over the borehole?"

"Borehole! What borehole?"

Tissa shot Nnati a look. "They don't do that here. That's only in Nurlie, Nnati. Not even at my wedding to Raad. And honestly, it's a little diminishing for such royalty."

"What is it?" I said, ignoring Tissa's weird attitude. "Tell me. It sounds fascinating."

Nnati always loved telling stories about the solemn and archaic traditions over on the Nurlie continent. He clapped his hands together and said, "Before two people can be wed, they must jump over a borehole hand in hand. If they miss and fall into the hole, not only could they get a broken limb or a black eye, but their wedding is considered cursed. Many who fall into the borehole cancel their wedding on the spot."

"That's insane," I said. "You guys don't actually believe that, do you?"

Nnati shrugged and Tissa made a face.

"Who's to say?" Nnati said with his usual pessimistic flair. "Some couples have good marriages. Some don't. The ones who don't, they blame the borehole."

I was starting to wonder what would happen if Zawne and I were to jump over a borehole. Would we fall in and be cursed? Would we become king and queen?

"But enough of this Nurlie talk," Nnati said, coming close to me. We stood in front of the oval mirror, all three of us in the frame. "This is a happy day. Happy for you and happy for the whole of Gaard and Geniverd!"

"And your dress is finished," Tissa said, a pincushion and some thread clutched in her hand. "It's time for you to go, Kaelyn. They're chanting your name. They're cheering for their new Gaard-Ma."

Queen, I wanted to correct her.

I didn't. I smiled instead, stood between my two best friends in the most beautiful dress I could have imagined. It was my wedding day. Tears of joy spilled down my cheeks. "Thank you so much," I said. "Thank you for being my best friends. I promise we will never part, no matter what. Nothing will ever change between us!"

* * *

STANDING on the podium next to Zawne was a dream come true, a dream I had never known I had. He was handsome in a snow-white tuxedo, dashing with his hair gelled and his teeth whitened. Strong, tough, unbending, and yet he was gentle and loving. We held hands while the Grucken began the wedding ceremony. The crowd silenced. I looked out and saw Papa's face shining in the front row beside Raad and Tissa. Papa was so proud of me. Mama would have been too.

"Love prevails," I said, Zawne and I facing each other to do our wedding vows. "Ava-Gaard, we call on you all to help us to abide by Decens-Lenitas."

Then Zawne recited his Shondur verse. "Love prevails. Ava-Shondur, help us to abide by Decens-Lenitas."

And together we said, "Only love until the very end. May Mother Geniverd help us to abide by Decens-Lenitas."

"When asked to choose a human quality you both possess that you place above all else for my blessing, you chose love," the Grucken said. "Let all who've gathered here bear witness. Prince Zawne, why love?"

Zawne pasted his eyes onto mine. "When I look upon Lady Kaelyn, I see love. Her love is honest, kind, respectful, caring, and empathetic. Her love listens, shares, and has integrity."

The Grucken turned to me. "What about you, Lady Kaelyn?"

"His love is brave and does not fear pain or danger. His love is faithful, sincere, and resilient. He is love."

* * *

WE WERE MARRIED. Zawne and I kissed, and the crowd went crazy. He picked me up and whisked me offstage to the cheering of our clanspeople. He carried me all the way to our flyrarc, and we were gone, the merriment below like a rioting crowd at a music festival. Zawne put the flyrarc on autopilot, and we kissed all the way to Sud Cottage. It was romantic, dreamy, everything I could have hoped for.

He kicked the door open with me cradled in his arms in my wedding dress. We were both giggling. "Take me to the bedroom," I said. "I want to kiss my husband."

Zawne carried me through the halls of Sud Cottage as if I were weightless. It was funny, because we would only live in the cottage for one night. After tomorrow's coronation, we would be moved into VondRust Palace. It was only a brief honeymoon.

Everything was great until Zawne dumped me on the bed and I saw half-packed boxes stacked by the closet. Lordin's things had been crammed into them. Jutting from one of the boxes was a framed portrait, a picture of her wearing a diamond tiara and looking very much like a queen. It made me think, *Did I usurp her? Have I stolen Lordin's place?*

Then, *Is she watching us right now as a Min?*

9

*E*very forty years the world stopped. Four billion people held their breath as the heirs of Geniverd gathered in Coronation Square and awaited the Crown of Crowns. It was something many of us were experiencing for the first time. It was something the older generation would experience for the last.

P2 camera drones hovered above the square like silent metal hummingbirds. They were broadcasting the coronation throughout the kingdom. They were the paparazzi, technological eavesdroppers. The people were gathered below them by the thousands. Six distinctive creeds mixed in the enormous lower courtyard of Coronation Square. Anyone who owned a flyarc hovered in the sky and watched with binoculars. The sky was so full of them it looked like an invasion. The streets were packed. No one was at work.

I was on the raised podium above the masses, surrounded by a barrier of Protectors. We heirs were an island above the people, eighteen pairs kneeling in a wide circle. The air was tense. I knelt on a cushion next to Zawne and Raad, with Tissa very near to us. Directly across the square was Jaken and his wife, Kyna, representing the Ava-Shondur. To the left was Surrvul's insane cluster of heirs. They were all married to other noble Ava-Surrvul. It was a real nationalist offering, and they glared angrily at everyone else, pale faced and blue eyed. They wore bright pink hats with sawtooth points along the brims. They were kind of creepy.

The Grucken stood center stage. He wore a long robe of many colors and leaned on his jeweled staff. We were all waiting for the Crown of Crowns. Everyone was nervous except Zawne and me. The Grucken was deadly serious as he turned slowly in a circle, scrutinizing the heirs, acting as though he was judging our hearts, as if the Grucken were a Min and could hear our thoughts.

I suddenly realized how paranoid I had been growing over the past two weeks. I was seeing Min everywhere I looked. I sometimes whispered Roki's name so he would appear. I would ask him, "Roki, is that a Min?" pointing through a window in the palace residence at any person who I thought was suspicious.

"No, Kaelyn," Roki would say. "Not everyone is a Min."

But how could I know for sure?

The Grucken's words reverberated as he summoned the flight of the Crown of Crowns. He was saying, "We implore you to choose wisely from these couples offered by Geniverd, the elite, the wise, the moral. Whomever you choose will be named the Most Courageous, the Shielded Ones, the Most Supreme Majesties. They will rule unquestioned for forty years. They will lead Geniverd into the future."

The Grucken bowed his head to the current king and queen. "We thank you for your service, the Queen Emerita and the King Emeritus," he said. "Geniverd thanks you for your service. Please step down."

As per tradition, Zawne's parents rose up from the twin thrones at the far end of the square and stood nobly beside them, ready to pass over control of the kingdom. They looked happy, watching Zawne and me with subtle grins. I had to remind myself, *They already know!*

And that was when the bird appeared. The Grucken raised his jeweled staff and cried out, "The Crown of Crowns has come!" Silence washed over the crowd. The hairs on the back of my neck stood on end. It was a magical moment. Some of the heirs wore worried expressions. Lady Juni of Nurlie had her eyes shut and her arms folded over her sand-colored gown. The Surrvul heirs straightened their backs and tried to appear their most decent, their most righteous, as if Decens-Lenitas had any importance at this stage of the game.

The bird was just as Papa had described to me when I was a little girl. Its bill was straight and yellow. It had a long turquoise tail for such a tiny creature, yellow breasted with white feathers, and red sprinkles on its feet. It came streaking from the sky as if from Shiol, almost leaving a trail of color behind it. The heirs took a quick glance and then bowed their heads. No one breathed.

The crowd gasped when the bird landed on Zawne's head. There was a surge of whispers, shouts; every one of the Surrvul heirs cursed under their breaths and stood up angrily. I caught Raad's eye, and he grinned wider than I had ever seen. Tissa gave me a thumbs-up. Then the trumpets blasted. The cheers were deafening. We were in Gaard, after all, in the capital, and most of the crowd was local. The bird flapped off Zawne's head, circled the podium, then flew off into the sky.

Everything happened in a series of flashes, almost too much for me to handle. We were being ushered into the middle of the square by the Grucken, who congratulated us quietly while some of the heirs stormed off and some lingered on the fringe with big smiles, happy for us despite their loss. The Grucken said to the crowd, "May I present the Most Courageous, the Shielded Ones, Their Most Supreme Majesties, King Zawne and Queen Kaelyn of Geniverd."

The people lost their minds. Hats were thrown in the air, firecrackers, fireworks exploding above the city. Flyrarcs diffused special fuel mixtures to create spritzes of rainbow-colored exhaust overhead. Two royal clerics were draping me and Zawne in vestments of gold silk. I didn't even see who placed the gem-studded tiara on my head or the spiked crown on Zawne's. Then we were bowing to the roar of our people ... *our* people ... *my* people.

"Thank you," Zawne bellowed in his strongest voice. "We will serve Geniverd well."

I said nothing. I couldn't. My throat was tight, and I was having a slight panic attack. The Grucken led us to Zawne's parents, and hugs and handshakes were exchanged. Then we sat in the thrones while the ex-queen and the ex-king bowed to us. The King Emeritus and the Queen Emerita were bowing to me! Me, Kaelyn of Gaard! I wept tears of joy while the world worshipped me. The smell of earth and toffee filled my nose. Roki was close by, and it made me cry harder. Later I followed Zawne and the Grucken to our flyrarc with tears in my eyes.

* * *

WE LANDED at VondRust Palace to a welcoming committee of servants, Protectors, and a peculiar man who was short and balding. Greeting us with an enthusiastic smile, he said, "Congratulations," then got straight to business as we walked into the palace flanked by Protectors.

"My name is Torio, as Zawne already knows. I am the head

of the council and will be assisting with the royal transition. If you have any questions, my number is already programmed into your visins. You may call me at any time of the day or night. From this moment onward, you will be escorted everywhere beyond the palace by at least five Protectors. This is for your safety."

I was trying to take everything in. Zawne was so calm, nodding and hemming as he rubbed his chin. But it was a lot for me. I tried to keep up as Torio led us through the grand mansion that was now our home. It was such an extravagant place. Everything was furnished in velvets and golds, the ceilings stretching high, and each corridor was a massive tunnel of portraits and archaic candelabras that must have been gold. The entire palace smelled faintly sweet. It was not a flowery smell, more of a refined scent, like cherrywood or burnished copper. It was hard to define, though the smell of it was easing my panic. I wondered if the atmospheric bubble around VondRust infused a calming herb into its generated scents.

Torio talked quickly as we walked. "Your calendars are already full," he said. "You can check the schedule anytime on your visins. It's all been preprogrammed. Tomorrow you will be selecting your councillors."

"Thanks, Torio," Zawne said. They had known each other for twenty-five years. "Where are Mama and Papa? Where's Jaken? He's Shondur-Elder now, right?"

"Right," Torio said. He was articulate with his words. I could tell Torio knew his duties well and would be extremely useful in the weeks ahead. "Your parents have already left for Shondur ahead of Jaken. As you know, there are huge parties being held in all six clans. Jaken will be inaugurated as Shondur-Elder, with his wife being ushered in as Shondur-Ma. I'm afraid your parents won't be back for at least six months."

"They deserve a break," Zawne said.

I agreed with him, yet internally I was panicked. I thought, *Who's going to give me advice for the first few months if I can't talk to Zawne or Roki?*

At least Zawne was confident. He swaggered through the lavish halls beside Torio as if he had been born for the role of king. I guessed, in a way, he had been. But then again, hadn't I been raised for the role of queen?

"You'll have ten councillors," Torio said. "You may review the short list of names tonight and pick fifteen suitable candidates for interviews, then choose your final eight tomorrow afternoon. They are all eagerly waiting on standby. As for the other two councillors, you each get an independent pick. I'm sure each of you has a trusted friend you would like to make an adviser."

"I do," I said right away, thinking about Nnati. But then I remembered the foundation. It was my tribute to Mama's memory, and Lordin's dying gift to me. Who would look after it if Nnati was living in VondRust and advising me?

Torio stopped. We had been walking for five minutes through a labyrinth of hallways, and I was utterly lost. We were in a honeycomb of golden trim and red carpets. "These are your quarters," he said, gesturing to a huge open doorway. "There will be Protectors outside at all times." The Protectors who had been following us branched off and stood on either side of the doorway, silently menacing in their robotic armor. "There will also be Protectors below your windows outside. In total, there are about a hundred Protectors on the estate. They work through a hive-mind synapse system. Any sign of danger will be registered by the whole company. You've never been safer."

Except from Min, I thought.

Then Torio was bowing. "I will collect you in the morning. Get some rest, check over the files, and once more, congratulations. You are the new rulers of Geniverd. I bid you good night, Your Most Supreme Majesties."

Torio scampered off down the hall. Zawne looked at me, extended his hand, and said, "Shall we, my queen?"

I took his hand and let him pull me into the bedroom. This was it, my new life as a queen. Zawne shut the doors and carried me to the royal bed.

* * *

"SURRVUL ISN'T HAPPY," Nnati said. "They're saying the crown shouldn't stay in the same family, meaning Zawne. But really they're just peeved because they have to wait another forty years for another shot at it. People are saying they might inflate visin prices or even restrict their distribution. They could even shut them down altogether. Oh, then there are the Gurnots. They've made encrypted messages available for the public to let them know that they are watching. People are scared of what they might do."

"They won't do anything," I told Nnati. I was in the main sitting room of our royal mansion. Zawne was snoozing in the bedroom while I chatted with Nnati on my visin.

"They already have," Nnati said. "Didn't you see? There was another fire today, this time in Shondur. The authorities are saying it was the Dragon, the rogue Gurnot who keeps lighting wealthy people's estates on fire. This time it was the local retreat the ex-queen and ex-king were supposed to be staying in. Before their flyrarc could land, the entire place went up in flames, even melting the Protectors that had been stationed there, melting them into nothing but metallic jelly. Nobody has a clue how the Dragon—or Dragons for all we know—are getting away with it. Some say secret Gurnot weapons technology."

"But the Gurnots are a minor threat to the kingdom," I said. "There aren't even that many of them. Where did all this damage come from?" I stopped to think, then said, "Maybe if I make it clear to the Gurnots that I have the interest of the people in mind, they will stop the fires. I've been thinking about bringing them into the fold. Maybe I can give them an official seat of power to stop their violent activities and their burning."

An idea was percolating in Nnati's head. He stared at me on the projected screen, gears turning behind his eyeballs. "Interesting ..." he said. "I'd like to see how that turns out. Maybe if you make a statement to that effect, you can alleviate some of the fear. Maybe the fires will stop. However, to side with Gurnots would mean public outcry. Be careful, my queen. Tread lightly."

"I will," I said. "You always give me such good advice. It's actually the reason I called you. I need you, Nnati. I have one free seat on the council, and I want you in it. Could you do that for me? Could you join me in VondRust as my loyal adviser?"

Nnati gaped. He had been doing a lot of that lately. Funny how much can change in three weeks. "Is that not a title held only by royalty?" he asked. "I'm only a commoner. I have no royal blood. And what about GMAF?"

I bit my lip, smiled at Nnati, and said, "I'm going to shake things up a bit. This won't be like the last administration. I'm really going to push for change. Noble blood or not, I want you as my adviser. In fact, I want to start bringing a lot more so-called commoner blood into positions of power. This government is going to be run by the people, for the people, just like it should be. As for GMAF, we've already doubled the staff. I trust you to find a suitable replacement."

Nnati was speechless. I had to goad him. "So, what do you say? Will you help me?"

Nnati fumbled for words, trying to be my friend while at the same time trying to speak to a queen. "Yes, Kaelyn. I mean, yes, my queen. Yes, Your Most Supreme Majesty."

"Cut it out," I said. "We're alone. Can't we just be normal?"

He let out a massive sigh and sagged over himself. "I was hoping you were going to say that. I can't stand being fake, and I don't think you can either. Can we talk about something normal before bed?"

"Of course," I said, happy Nnati felt the same as I did. It would be nice to have a real friend on the inside. "What do you want to talk about?"

"How's Zawne?" he asked. "How is your relationship?"

I opened my mouth and paused. I didn't have an answer. We had been so busy the last few weeks that we hadn't had much time to be a couple. We slept in the same bed, went through the same routine, but were often very distant. I said to Nnati, "It's been a whirlwind ever since we got engaged."

"I bet," he said. "But what abou—?"

The smell of sweet toffee swirled into my nostrils, and my eyelids fluttered. Oh no! Roki was in the room! He was right beside me, masking everything except his scent.

I blurted into the visin, "Sorry, Nnati, got to go." I got a glimpse of the shock on Nnati's face as I hung up.

It was quiet, but I could feel his eyes watching me. I tried to steady my breath, my heart pounding wildly in my chest. I whispered, "Roki, are you here?"

10

*N*ordHaven couldn't hold a candle to the absurd grandeur of VondRust Palace. Our private estate within VondRust was three stories tall, had eight sleeping quarters, twelve bathrooms, several large dressing rooms, two kitchens, a tennis court, a home theater, a vast wine cellar, an indoor pool and an outdoor pool, a gym, and a sauna. Not to mention the flyarc pads on the roof for the king and queen's personal flying machines. We even had our own miniature atmospheric bubble, scenting the air, controlling the temperature, conjuring rain or sunshine at will. The place was epic. Wandering through its halls was dizzying, and I could hardly get used to it. I kept thinking, *Do I really deserve all this? Does any one person deserve such massive excess?*

Either way, it was ours. VondRust could have been a city of its own for all the various manors and structures, the guesthouses reserved for clan leaders, and the huge government building in the center of the flowery courtyard. Everything was connected via well-kept pathways. Zawne and I even had hover scooters so that we didn't have to use our royal legs.

Spoiled is what I called it. I often missed my old apartment and my daily commute to GMAF. All the people I'd known in the city were probably still living in tiny pods stacked up like bricks, and there I was, in my own subcity.

But hey, the view was nice. I stared out the window of our bedroom the morning after the coronation, admiring the mountain peaks in the distance, the snowy inclines and patches of firs. It was a tranquil scene after such chaos. I liked listening to the water run through the pipes as Zawne showered in the other room. I felt introspective.

"Morning, beautiful," came Roki's voice.

I whirled around to see Roki sitting on the edge of my bed. I felt panic rise in my chest, then remembered Roki could vanish in a split second if he needed to. "What are you doing here?" I asked. We had talked for two hours last night while Zawne slept. I felt guiltier than words could describe.

"Don't feel guilty," Roki said, reading my thoughts. "We're friends, remember?" He looked sad as he said this, as if I had shackled him, made him a prisoner of friendship when we both wanted something more.

Then Zawne yelled from the shower, "Who are you talking to?" He had turned off the water and was likely toweling himself dry.

"Nnati," I said hurriedly. "I'm on a call."

Roki was grinning at me. He loved the thrill of being bad, of being in the same room with me while my husband dried his naked body less than twenty feet away.

"I had another reason for coming," Roki said, not even bothering to hush his voice. It was like he wanted to get caught!

"What is it?"

"I'll see you tonight in Shiol. I'll also be with you all day during your council decisions. It turns out I really love watching your lips move. I love watching you, giving you a whiff of my scent but not showing myself. It thrills me. I'm obsessed with you."

Zawne emerged from the bathroom. Roki was gone. "Finished your call?"

"Yes," I said, but I didn't sound very convincing. I swallowed hard and changed the subject. "You look wet."

Dumb! Who says that?

But it was true. Zawne wore nothing but black briefs, his muscled form moist from the shower. I wanted to consume him on the spot. Let Roki watch. Let him discharge his earthy scent while I shoved my tongue in Zawne's mouth and we became lost in a frenzy of love.

It was almost as if Zawne could hear my thoughts. He strode across the room without saying a word and scooped me up. He was so rough when he wanted to be. "I don't think I got all the way clean," he said, and carried me giggling into the shower.

* * *

BREAKFAST WAS LAID out in the main dining room downstairs: fried eggs, bacon, blueberries, pancakes, strawberries, and tea.

"Wow," I said to the chef, a short fellow in a white smock. It was rare to see a human chef when so many were Protectors now. The palace must have been paying him a fortune. "How did you know what I like?"

"We know everything that will make Her Most Supreme Majesty happy," the man replied.

I looked to Zawne. "Is this how you grew up?"

"More or less," he said, casually chewing on a strip of bacon. "My mother and father were the rulers of Geniverd. Jaken and I had a ... cozy childhood."

"Cozier than mine," I said. I took a seat, and the chef left us to eat in private. There were two Protectors standing guard outside the kitchen door. Even though they were machines, they still made me uncomfortable.

"Listen," Zawne said, getting serious as he leaned over the table and found my eyes. "I have an idea. It's never been done before, but I think it could work. I grew up with my parents being constantly exhausted, and now I know why."

"Shiol," I said quietly.

"Exactly. So I was thinking that if we split up the council, call it the King's Council and the Queen's Council, we could get double the rest and double the free time. We would split the duties in half."

"That's a great idea," I said. "The only thing is that we have to"—I looked around, then said at a whisper—"follow the recommendations from our friends."

"We must," Zawne said. "That's not up for debate. But I'm sure they won't mind. It's a great idea."

It *was* a great idea. I found myself surprised by his gusto. Zawne wore the mantle of king well.

"Which subjects would you like to handle?" he asked me.

"Health," I said immediately. It was the first thing that came to mind, since Gaard, my home, was known for manufacturing medicines. I had to open my visin and check the other categories.

"Industries," I said, flicking down the list. "I'll take ecosystem, preservation, human resources."

"Great," Zawne said. "That leaves me with trade, defense, and finance."

He made for the door, stopping to kiss me on my head. "Enjoy your breakfast, Queen Kaelyn. I'm going to get ready. We have a long day ahead of us."

I ate my breakfast feeling like a happy schoolgirl. I had my macho man, my Aska warrior, my husband, and I had my confidant, my spirit boy with the charming smile who always kept me on my toes. I couldn't tell if it was Roki I smelled or a spice from my toast. Either way, I was happy.

* * *

SELECTING the councillors was easier than I had anticipated. Zawne and I sat at the head of a huge room with a domed ceiling while one by one the applicants introduced themselves. We had no trouble picking eight of them. They were all noble-born or Aska certified. Besides, it was Geniverd law to have at least one adviser from each continent on the council.

In the end, I chose an additional Surrvul councillor, a young woman by the name of Shiru. She was an heir and too young to become clan leader ahead of her many siblings. Shiru needed something to do for the next forty years, and I was happy to oblige. There was nothing worse than a clan heir with eighty years of life, all the power and cash in the world, and not a single thing to do with any of it.

Zawne chose the other extra, a stern man by the name of Aska Nikhel. He was Ava-Lodden, a rare breed in the capital. Zawne said they had met during his training.

The most enjoyable part of the whole ordeal was when we called the selected councillors into the main chamber, including Torio, who had been reinstated as Head of Courtiers, and delivered the big news.

Zawne stood up and said, "We have an announcement to make," then paused for dramatic effect. He seemed to love doing that. "We will be splitting the council into two parts, the Queen's Council and the King's Council."

Everyone gasped. Torio looked ready to faint, his jaw on

the floor. "You're sure about this, Your Most Supreme Majesties?" he asked.

"Yes," I said, standing up to take Zawne's hand. It was better that we appeared as a single unit of authority. "We have talked it over and agreed. This is for the better."

The councillors exchanged a flurry of confused glances. Then we split them into groups.

The Queen's Council consisted of Nnati, Master Widrig, Lady Katrin, Aska Nikhel, and Aska Xi.

Zawne's council consisted of Aska Stingl, Lady Shiru, Master Nokag, Aska Chu, and Aska Tatu. It was almost entirely made up of Askas.

AFTER SPENDING the entire morning and afternoon in the conference room, choosing our councillors, it was nice to attend the welcome party Torio had organized for them. Zawne and I showed up fashionably late, around six thirty. I didn't want to linger too long. I was eager to go to bed and transport myself to Shiol, where I could find out what Roki had to say. I was smelling him everywhere. I figured he was close by.

Didn't he have a job to do?

Zawne and I were seated at the head of the table, our councillors to either side of us. There were seven courses, endless bottles of wine, and lots of laughter. Lady Shiru loved to tell jokes, and everyone else seemed to appreciate her sense of humor. This made me feel confident about our decisions earlier in the day. We had to spend four days a week governing with these people for the next forty years. It was important that we all got along.

It was as Lady Shiru began to tell a joke about three Ava-

Lodden and an unfortunate goat that Zawne whispered in my ear, "I want to go to Shiol tonight."

My heart sank. He couldn't be serious. Roki was waiting for me, and I wanted him to show me more of Shiol. There was no way I could miss our meeting! I had been thinking about him all day.

"Why?" I asked.

Zawne crossed his arms and pursed his lips. "I just want to," he said, no explanation given. He was acting like a stubborn baby.

"You can't." I had to make something up quick. My heart was racing and I was sweating. "It's my turn," I told him. "We need to keep to the schedule. I'm sorry, Zawne, but I won't budge."

His face warped into a scowl. I thought he was thinking of something mean to snap at me. Why was he doing this? It seemed so unnecessary. But then something occurred to me. I realized that Lordin was a Min. She could watch us, read our thoughts, follow us as a bodiless spirit. She could also visit Zawne in his sleep. Now that I was thinking about it, Zawne had been waking up around the same time as me every day. Had he been going to Shiol in secret? Had he been seeing Lordin like I had been seeing Roki?

I boiled over with anger. It was a good thing the councillors were distracted and half-drunk. No one paid me any attention when I hissed at Zawne, "I'm going to Shiol and that's final. And I better not see you there. I know you don't have an appointment with you-know-who, so I don't know what you want to do there."

I got up in a huff, pushed my chair back too loudly, and the whole party stopped to stare at me.

"I'm going to bed," I said flatly. "Thank you all for agreeing to work with me and the king as we mend our kingdom and push forward into the new dawn, but I'm tired. Good night."

Nobody questioned me—I was the queen. They all bowed their heads, and I left Zawne at the head of the table, glaring at me as I stormed off.

* * *

THE FIRST THING I wanted to do when I got to Shiol was run my hands through Roki's silky hair and kiss him.

No!

I cringed, clenched my teeth, and squeezed my eyes tighter. I couldn't cheat on Zawne. It wasn't in my personality. But I kept thinking about Lordin. I couldn't help but wonder, was Zawne cheating on me?

All I could do was allow myself to get sleepy, sink deep into our cozy bed, and spell ...

S-H-I-O-L.

I zipped through space in my spirit body, landed in the Crown of Crowns' reception hall, and found them waiting for me beneath the cloudy, ethereal sky. They were sparkling light, the same as always. Riedel greeted me warmly enough.

"Queen Kaelyn, we're glad you've come. We have seen that you and Zawne split the duties in half. We were surprised. It's a wise move."

"You might even get some rest," Hanchell said.

I moaned, "Thanks, but it was Zawne's idea."

"We know," Hanchell said.

Riedel's laugh echoed through the void. "We know everything."

I just wanted to get the meeting over with. I wanted to see Roki. We had a lot to discuss. I wanted to ask him about Lordin, if he had seen her with Zawne. I needed to know if they were an item again. If so, it might seriously change my feelings toward Zawne. It might also open up possibilities between Roki and myself. I needed to see him!

"Can we get to it?" I said. "I have a meeting after this." I didn't mean to be blunt, but it seemed like recently I had been shedding the timid, awkward girl I used to be. I was becoming bolder. I didn't know if it was from age, stress, sleeping in bed with a man every night ... or from finding out there were entire worlds secreted just behind the fabric of our universe!

"Of course," Hanchell said. "You are a busy woman. Here, this is what's on the docket for today."

A blast of images, documents, video clips—all exploded from thin air and cycled around me. It was a lot to make sense of. All of it got sucked into the visin implant in my wrist.

"You may now access the files," Hanchell said. "Use your visin normally. It will function in Shiol, but the files will be immediately erased upon your return to the physical world. We can't have them slipping into the wrong hands."

"Okay." I was a bit excited. If there was one thing I knew how to do, it was to ignore my problems and bury myself in my work.

"One more thing," Hanchell said. Her electric form seemed to giggle. She was awfully excitable for an all-powerful spirit.

Then Hanchell's light fluctuated, and the space we were in changed. The clouds were gone, sealed off by a high ceiling. Four walls materialized, and within seconds, I found myself standing in NordHaven's study, the one Papa had always used for work.

"It's just a projection," Hanchell said. "We hope it helps you as you go through the material. Take a seat on the sofa by the fire. Relax. You have time to review the evidence."

"Thanks so much!" I said, but they had already evaporated.

* * *

I WALKED through the room in awe over how the Crown of Crowns could manifest NordHaven so accurately. It was my papa's study down to the last carpet fiber: dark, musty, more comfortable than any royal chamber at VondRust. It even smelled like old books and smoldering wood, just like Papa always programmed it to smell like. I plunked myself down on the leather sofa, felt the warmth of the hearth on my feet, and turned on my visin. It was time to get to work. I needed to absorb all the information and still have time left over for Roki ... and there were ten claims I had to go over!

At the top of the list was a request from Nurlie, asking for the Crown to stop a covert petition from Nurlie Island. The island was demanding independence from Nurlie. Over eighty thousand islanders had signed the petition, and the shadow government of the island wanted to push ahead with a referendum. The island represented forty percent of Nurlie's exports, mainly due to rich mineral resources. It was one of the few places where the mines were still operated by human workers. The Nurlie clan leaders were fearful that the shadow government might try a hostile takeover of the continent, fueled by anti-mech and anti-authority sentiments.

I scrolled down to see the Crown of Crowns' recommendation. It stated that I should side with Nurlie and put an end to the island's shadow government before it could do any damage. Then I watched some video evidence that showed the island's leaders plotting to transfer lucrative business contracts to some companies in Surrvul once they took over. This would infer a strong and dangerous relationship between Nurlie and Surrvul, not to mention total anarchy for the Nurlie continent.

I made a mental note to side with Nurlie and moved on.

Next was a breach of contract complaint from Gaard about the purchase and supply of antimicrobials. A large company based in Gaard had been providing antibiotics and antivirals to Surrvul, but Surrvul had canceled the contracts in favor of an innovative new company in Krug. Surrvul claimed their reasoning was a supply shortage. Gaard denied it. I was recommended to side with Gaard, forcing Surrvul to continue purchasing through the Gaard company.

When I read the third case, I began to see a pattern. Surrvul had lodged a complaint against Shondur. Surrvul needed phosphorus for fertilizer and the production of steel. The main source of phosphorus was in Shondur, and Surrvul claimed the Shondur government was being stingy. They wanted easier, ampler, and fairer access to the mineral. The recommendation was to rule in favor of Surrvul and force Shondur to give them what they wanted.

At this point, I made a mental note to speak with Lady Shiru and have a long discussion about what exactly the Ava-Surrvul and their rulers wanted. They seemed to be at the heart of every conflict.

I skimmed through and memorized the rest of the complaints and cases until I finally made it to the last one. I was wondering why Roki hadn't shown up yet. I had hoped he would massage my feet while I did my deliberations. A foot massage wasn't outside the realm of friendship, right?

The last case was a plea from Gaard, Lodden, Shondur, and Krug to commemorate Lordin formally. The idea irked me, and I skimmed through most of it. Basically, the Crown of Crowns recommended that I ask all clan leaders how they wanted to keep Lordin's memory alive. It made me wonder, *Why does everyone still care? She was just a woman!*

I closed my visin and sat back, glad to be done with the day's dealings. But where in the name of Geniverd was Roki?

"Roki?" I called out. I thought maybe he was waiting for me beyond the illusion of Papa's study.

I was surprised when an unfamiliar girl walked through the illusion like a phantasm and stood a few feet from me.

"Hello, Kaelyn," she said.

"Uh …" I didn't recognize this girl at all. "Who are you?"

"It's me, Lordin."

It may have been the first time in my life that my tongue had literally slithered into the back of my mouth. I gaped at her in horror. I had no words. I wanted to scream at her, "Have you been seeing my husband?" But I also wanted to wrap my arms around her and thank Lordin for all the good she had done. It was a real quandary.

"I got a new body," she said, showing no signs of reading my mind. "That's probably why you don't recognize me. I know, I'm not as cute. But hey, I'm younger. And I have all the perks of a Min. Everything I do feels a thousand times better than it used to. Life as a Min is great!"

She was bubbly, petite, still pretty even though it wasn't Lordin's original body. Maybe it was her personality that made her so attractive.

"That's great. I'm glad you're doing well." It was all I could say. I didn't have the strength to confront her. I also didn't have the strength to apologize for stealing her fiancé. I'd never felt like more of a fraud! I thought I was the queen of Geniverd. Where had my confidence gone?

Lordin hung her head and took a step closer to me. "I actually came here because I have some sad news."

Oh no, I thought. *Is she going to confess?*

"What sad news?" I asked.

"It's about Roki."

"Roki?" A thousand more questions bubbled in my head. How did she know about him? Had she been following us?

Did she know about Roki's secret visits? Was I the villain here?

Lordin said, "Yes, your friend Roki." The word *friend* sounded sarcastic. Then Lordin came up beside me, held out her wrist, and activated her visin. The holographic screen bloomed in front of us. "You'd better see for yourself."

Lordin brought up a carousel of photos on her visin. Every one of them was of Roki. But not just Roki—not even just Roki and another woman. The photos were of Roki and other women! Plural! She showed me ten photos of him kissing other girls, all the while my heart hammered madly in my chest. I was getting angrier by the second.

Lordin pointed to the last photo and said, "That was taken today. I'm sorry, Kaelyn, but Roki has been playing you. That's why he's late for your date."

I was seething mad. Lordin turned off her visin and stepped back, leaning on Papa's oak bookshelf. It was so weird to be talking to a Min in the illusion of my old house.

"I just had to tell you," she said. "But I am sorry. Min are jerks. When you live for so long—"

"Exactly how long?" I asked. I needed to know how long Roki had been messing with girls' emotions.

"Min live for a thousand years," Lordin told me, "an extra three thousand if you get promoted to Crown of Crowns. We're basically indestructible. Other Min can kill us if they try hard enough, but that's rare. The only thing that can kill us instantly is the Seeing Water."

"The what?"

"Never mind," she said. "I have to go. Roki's coming. Remember, Kaelyn, trust no one."

Lordin vanished through the hologram of Papa's study just as Roki materialized in front of me. "Who was here?" he asked, sniffing the air.

132

"Go die," I told him. I had tears streaming down my face. I clenched and unclenched my fists, pacing the room and snarling like an angry bull. I didn't know what to do. I had put so much faith in Roki. I had betrayed my husband's trust to be with him. And now ... now he was a no-good liar and a cheat!

"Why are you thinking these things?" Roki asked.

I hated that he could read my thoughts, that he answered questions before I could ask them, before I could assault him with accusations. It was rude and annoying. He was annoying! What kind of pervert would continuously read my thoughts? It was another violation of my trust!

"Get out of my head!" I told him, screaming at the top of my lungs. My face must have been smeared with mascara, and I must have looked crazy. "You're evil!" I said. "You're an evil Min, and I hate you. I'll never forgive you again. I should have trusted Mama. I should have listened to my gut. This is the last time I ever go against my family, against my morals. Yet ..." I paused, Roki looking at me as if I were the heart-breaker and not him. "I deserve this, don't I? I deserve it for my own treachery, for betraying Zawne. No honor among thieves, huh?"

"Kaelyn ..." Roki reached for me.

I slapped his hand away. "You're just a filthy spirit," I said. "Geniverd is your playground, your sick human playground. Well, I won't be your toy anymore. I'm done, Roki. Don't ever watch me at night again, you creep. Don't leave your scent like some pervert's trail around me. Don't read my mind. Don't visit me in my dreams." I closed my eyes and screamed, "Stay out of my life!"

Roki was weeping. "You have to trust me," he insisted. "Kaelyn, I love you. I would never—"

But I was done. I let my body relax and dissolved into the blackness, away from Shiol and Roki's lies.

11

I was mad at myself mostly. I was mad at myself for getting tricked. I had let it happen. I had let Roki use me. I had deceived myself into thinking he was a good spirit, a good Min, a good man—whatever he was supposed to be. I had dug my own shameful hole, and there was nothing left to do but suffer in it, drag myself through day after day with the unbearable guilt of what I had done.

Zawne noticed the change. I was gloomy, paranoid, always sniffing the air and looking around as if Roki might appear and club me over the head. It was frustrating, because I knew he could mask his presence. It came to be that every scent generated by the atmospheric bubble around the palace made me think of Roki. The smell of jasmine at sunrise, the scent of toffee in the parlor by night. I knew he could be watching me at any time. What I didn't know was what happened when you angered a Min. Could they strike back and hurt a human? Would Roki take out his anger on me?

I asked this one night during a meeting with the Crown of

Crowns. "I know Min hurt people for fun, but can they hurt royals?"

Riedel answered, "As long as a Min fulfills their obligation to us and doesn't reveal the Great Secret, they are free to do as they please. This is the covenant between Min and the Seeing Water."

Again with the Seeing Water! Just what in the name of Geniverd was the Seeing Water? The Crown of Crowns refused to give me more information about it, and I left Shiol in a bad mood—again!

Later that day, Zawne called me out for my decline in attitude. "What's gotten into you?" he asked when I woke up, staring straight into my face. "You've changed this last week. You're grumpy and depressed. Have you forgotten that you're the queen of the world?"

"I'm just tired," I said, slipping out of bed. "I'm sorry that I don't have your Aska training. I'm not as strong as you. Okay?"

Zawne said something, but I was already in the bathroom with the shower running. I stood under the hot water and cried silently. Why had I been so quick to let Roki consume me? I hated how much I missed him. I hated what I was doing to Zawne. I felt like garbage, like a piece of trash. I had betrayed my husband, my vows, and worst of all, myself.

* * *

I HARDLY TOUCHED my food at breakfast. Zawne wouldn't talk to me. He got up as soon as I entered the dining room and left without looking in my eyes. What had I done? I had destroyed both my relationships in one fell swoop.

My visin was beeping in my ear as I poked cold eggs

around with a knife. I saw it was Raad and hit ignore. I didn't feel like talking to anyone.

I got dressed, moving sluggishly through my closet. I had an important council meeting in an hour, but who cared?

I got there late. Nnati was pacing by the doors of the council chamber, waiting for me.

"Are you crazy?" he said. "You can't be late for these meetings, Kaelyn—you're the queen."

"Exactly," I snapped. "I'm the queen, and I can be late if I want."

I stopped, tears welling up in my eyes. "I'm sorry ..." I collapsed into Nnati's arms, hugged him fiercely. "I'm just so tired. I ... I'm exhausted, Nnati."

He hugged me back and whispered in my ear, "I know, I know. But you're stronger than you think, okay? You can get through this. We're only at the beginning. Give yourself some time. You'll bounce back."

"Thanks, Nnati," I said, pulling away from him and wiping my eyes. "I knew it was a good idea to have you by my side. I couldn't ask for a better adviser."

He looked awkward then, biting his lip as if he had something terrible to tell me. I couldn't take any more bad news.

"Since I am your trusted adviser," Nnati said carefully, "I want to talk to you about some recent rulings."

"Oh?"

"Yeah." He leaned in close to me so that the courtiers walking through the grand hallway couldn't hear. "This deregulation case for Gaard's main medicine manufacturer, I'm not sure we're doing the right thing."

"Why?"

"Well, we have already deregulated the sale of certain antigens twice, making it easier for the company to manipulate the market and potentially drive other manufacturers out of business."

"Oh … yes, I remember."

But I only half remembered. It was easy to forget things when the Crown of Crowns was making decisions for me, pulling the strings, sometimes without giving me good reasons. I felt like a tool. I was also starting to understand how the social system had managed to become so skewed over the past few hundred years. With the Crown of Crowns running the entire world from an alternate dimension while the kings and queens dwindled their time away in Shiol and spent their days exhausted and sucked of their energy, it was easy to see how our world had become so upended without the monarchy fully realizing it. It was as if all of Geniverd were on autopilot.

"And there's another request for a different deregulation today," Nnati continued. "This one will make it easier for the company to absorb and acquire other properties and manufacturers. Essentially, they will have a monopoly on the best antimicrobials."

Now I remembered. The councillors had argued with me over the last two deregulations, but I had stuck to the Crown of Crowns' recommendations and allowed them through.

"I think I will allow it," I told Nnati. That was the recommendation, and I planned to abide by it. I was to let the Gaard company do whatever they wanted, even if it didn't feel right in my gut.

"Seriously?" Nnati was floored. "But, Kaelyn, it's going to have serious repercussions."

"They have a delegation coming, do they not?"

Nnati nodded. "They do."

"Then let's listen to what they have to say," I told him, trying to balance logic with the Crown of Crowns' ruling. "So long as there are still manufacturers outside of Gaard, and so long as they don't raise their prices, commit to not raising the prices, and ensure the medicine remains effective and safe, I see no reason to hold them back."

Nnati shook his head. "Yes, my queen." And he opened the door and gestured me into the council chamber.

* * *

MY SEAT WAS at the head of the wide room, covered in red and gold upholstery. My councillors flanked me, Nnati to my left and Torio to my right. We were silent as the delegation from Gaard took the floor and bowed to me.

"Your Most Supreme Majesty," they said in unison.

One of the delegation members stepped in front of her colleagues. She was tiny and young, shockingly beautiful, with radiant skin and golden hair. She had my attention immediately, and the attention of every man in the room.

"Your Most Supreme Majesty," she said, curtsying, "we thank you for seeing us. Shall we get straight to business?"

I nodded. "Present your case."

"Yes, Your Most Supreme Majesty. My name is Hagan of the Ava-Gaard, and I represent VBione Corp. Our proposal is for an acquisition of a Krug-based company called Medseet. This will be the biggest absorption of another manufacturer in twenty years."

Hagan took a deep breath. The councillors were hushed and attentive. She said, "The reason this case is being brought to you, Most Courageous, is because Krug is concerned that our acquisition of Medseet will mean all of Geniverd's antimicrobials will be made by one manufacturer in Gaard. The Krug council is upset, but Medseet is eager to be bought out. The money we have offered them is substantial."

Aska Nikhel raised his hand and looked at me. "May I speak?"

"Of course."

Nikhel cleared his throat. "The problem I see with this acquisition, Your Most Supreme Majesty, is that VBione Corp would be in possession of all the highest-value medicines. They would have the largest portfolio of medicine in Geniverd. If they chose, they could limit the distribution of said medicines."

"I see your point," I said, but it was moot. I had already made my decision. I had to obey the Crown of Crowns. I wasn't about to cause problems a month into my reign just because of some company acquisition. These things happened all the time. Companies in Geniverd were in a perpetual state of consuming one another, leaving workers scrambling to find new jobs and a handful of CEOs with their pockets bursting. I needed to fix the system but not today. Not with this ruling.

"Hagan," I said, "present your rebuttal."

"You are correct, Aska Nikhel," she said. "We do have a large portfolio. However, there are other valuable medicines not owned by us. Our takeover of Medseet means we will be able to create synergies to benefit everyone. We are not restricting innovative companies in other clans, or even here in Gaard. In fact, you will see that over time these other companies will produce transformational medicines that will benefit the world. Once our acquisition of Medseet is complete, production costs will be lowered, while the extra money will go into research."

"That sounds appropriate," I said, nodding in turn to my councillors. "Yet what do you say about job losses in Krug?"

"There will not be any," Hagan said. She was very confident. "The plant in Krug will be under VBione Corp management, but the workers will stay to help us. We will continue to employ all qualified workers."

"That is acceptable," I told her. There were some hushed whispers from my councillors, but no one could openly argue with keeping jobs and advancing research. Hagan's proposition was solid.

"Your time is up," I told her. "Are there any final remarks you wish to make?"

"Yes. On behalf of VBione Corp, we would like to thank you for your time, Your Most Supreme Majesty. We urge you to think of the future, of the cooperation between Krug and Gaard. With the extra money placed into research and development, we will be even more capable of combating the ever-mutating viruses and bacteria that threaten our society. With our innovative data repository, linking with Medseet will enable fast-paced antiviral development and response time, should an outbreak occur."

"Councillors," I said, "any final thoughts before I pass judgment?"

"I don't like how powerful VBione Corp will become after this acquisition," Nnati said, defiant as always. It was nice to have someone with Nnati's commoner upbringing on the council. He always called it like it was when the noble-born council members sucked their thumbs and remained quiet. I respected Nnati for that, but it didn't mean I had to agree with him.

"Noted," I said.

Aska Xi spoke up. "I think it's a good thing. Superbugs have been a threat since the beginning of time, and our defense against them is tenuous at best. Our medicines are regulated no matter what happens here today. To have more effort put into the development of new drugs to help our citizens is an opportunity we can't ignore."

"Thank you, Xi," I said. Then I looked down at Hagan, standing patiently and with supreme confidence, as if she already knew her case was won. "I side in favor of VBione Corp," I announced. "This case is closed."

Hagan didn't whoop or smile. She simply said, "Thank you, Your Most Supreme Majesty," and walked backward from the room with her burly associates, bowing deeply.

I could feel Nnati's anger. He had his arms folded, staring straight ahead. I wanted to comfort him, to say it was the right decision and I was sorry, but Torio spoke up in his loud voice. "Next on the docket," he said, "the commemoration of Lordin. The clans would like to build a monument in the capital. People could visit, see her work, remember Lordin for—"

"Skip," I said. I didn't want to think about Lordin. I was sure Zawne was visiting her binightly in Shiol. I had resolved to speak with him about it but hadn't found the time. I'd been too upset about Roki and too busy being queen.

"Skip?" Torio sounded confused.

"Skip," I repeated. "On to the next, Torio. I'll deal with Lordin later."

* * *

ZAWNE and I ate dinner quietly that night, nothing but the sound of our knives scraping against our plates. I needed to broach the subject of Lordin without coming across accusatory. I started with something neutral.

"What do you think of the rulings?" I asked. "Do you ever consider ruling differently from what the Crown of Crowns recommends?"

"I wouldn't dare," he said, very matter-of-factly. Then Zawne did something I hadn't expected. He got up and moved around the table, hunkered down next to me, and cupped my face in his hands. It made me feel delicate, priceless, like he did still want me.

"I'm sorry we have been so stressed," he said, and kissed me on the lips. "I want us to be okay together." He kissed me again, his breath delicious, his voice raspy.

"Me too," I said. I was lost in his voice, spellbound by his beautiful eyes. It felt like forever since we had spent quality time together. I still hardly knew him, yet I was drawn to him nonetheless. I wanted to explore this draw, explore our relationship together. But I was worried about Lordin. I needed to know … was our marriage authentic?

I moved to kiss him more deeply, helpless in the moment; Zawne had already gotten up and moved toward the door. "I have to go," he was saying.

And I just blurted it out. I had to say something before it drove me to insanity. "Have you seen her?"

"Who?" His face was scrunched up.

"Lordin," I said in a mousy voice. I was fearful of provoking Zawne's wrath. I didn't want to cause any more problems than we already had, especially now that Roki was out of my life. My husband was all I had left.

Zawne's demeanor grew cold. He stomped across the dining room, grabbed a chair, and dragged it loudly across the floor, flipped it around in front of me, and sat down, leaning and glowering into my face. "I don't know," he said. "Have you seen your boyfriend, Roki?"

My heart stopped. I bumbled, "I … Roki …"

Lordin must have told him about Roki and me! No wonder Zawne had let me be depressed the last week or so. He had known the whole time.

"That's what I thought," he snarled. "And yes, I have seen Lordin. She was my fiancée before you, remember? She came to me one night after we were crowned. She told me about you and your sweetheart. She told me everything."

"We never touched!" I said, feeling humiliated. It was worse because we had touched. I had touched Roki's sweet face, held his strong hands ...

"It looks like we both have secrets," Zawne said.

I felt I needed to explain myself. Maybe if Zawne heard the truth from me, we could get past it together. Maybe we could still salvage our relationship. "Roki was my first love," I stammered. "I never knew he was a Min. He came to me around the time of the coronation, and I agreed to be his friend. But nothing else happened. He's not my sweetheart, as you say. I haven't even seen him in almost two weeks."

"Sure," Zawne scoffed. He didn't believe me.

I knew it was unfair of me to demand anything from Zawne, but I had to know if he had gotten back together with Lordin. "Are you done with me?" I asked. "I know I screwed up, so I understand if you've gone back to Lordin. Just please tell me, have you? Are you seeing her again?"

"I'm not going to answer that," Zawne said, standing up angrily and moving across the room. He stopped at the door. "You knew what had happened to Lordin this whole time, about her death, about how she had chosen to become a Min over ruling the kingdom. But you hid that from me just like you hid Roki from me. How does it feel to be kept in the dark?"

I started to cry. I had never imagined Zawne could be so icy, so heartless. Yet it was my own fault. I had lusted after two men, and now I was paying the price.

"I didn't betray you," I said, but my words came out weak. "I'm not going to see him again. I am yours, Zawne. I am only yours."

But a part of me wondered, *Am I only saying this because Roki turned out to be a scoundrel?*

Zawne saw my pain, and his anger faltered. His expression changed to one of compassion. He wasn't so heartless after all. "We will work it out," he said, his voice softer. "We are set to be king and queen for the next forty years. We will be together."

"When?" I asked. I hated how I seemed to be begging my own husband for time together.

"We'll find opportunities," he said. He sounded sad, unsure. "We're both busy between council meetings and visiting Shiol, but we will find time. We'll find a way."

Then Zawne left. I was alone, tears spilling onto my untouched meal.

* * *

I NEEDED TISSA. I had Nnati available to me every day, since he lived on the other side of VondRust in the advisers' mansion, but my sister-in-law was on the other side of Gaard, ruling the Ava-Gaard alongside my brother. It had been ages since we'd talked. One night, after a long series of council meetings, while Zawne drifted off to Shiol, I fired up my visin and called Tissa.

"So good to hear from you," she exclaimed. "It's been too long. How are things?"

"Things are things," I said. I was ready to unload. "It's a bit chaotic. Everyone in the kingdom is waiting for me to rule on Lordin's commemoration, the monument they want me to approve in the capital. It's been weeks and I'm still undecided. All I can say is that I'm glad the ex-queen and ex-king are coming home early from Shondur. They decided to live in VondRust, and they'll be back tomorrow."

"It's good to have a confidant," Tissa said, reminding me of how Roki had been just that before the betrayal. "But why are you so undecided about Lordin?"

I groaned into my visin. How could I possibly explain to Tissa that I was competing for my husband's love with a dead woman? "It's complicated," I said. "I'm just unsure what to do. I don't know if Lordin really deserves a monument. It doesn't seem very humble, if you ask me."

"No," Tissa said, "it doesn't. What does Nnati think?"

I laughed. "You know Nnati. He wonders how we can spend all that money on such a thing. He doesn't think one person deserves to be raised up so high. She was righteous and fluent in Decens-Lenitas, and people all over Geniverd looked up to her, but Nnati questions the morality of the project."

"As he would," Tissa said with a smirk. "We've always known Nnati thought Lordin was too self-righteous, using her fame to reach for the stars. Sometimes I wonder if he isn't a secret Gurnot."

"As if!" I said. "Not in a million years. Besides, Nnati has too much work to be running around with those scoundrels, setting fires and wreaking havoc. Not to mention he's loyal to me. There's no doubt about that."

Tissa nodded her agreement. "No doubt at all."

"Anyway," I said, "the clans want a monument, so I suppose I will have to build one. Really, there are too many important things I need to focus on besides Lordin. It's a relentless barrage of problems here. It seems like everyone has a grudge with everyone else. And Surrvul is always involved in one way or another."

"It's the same here, on the other side of Gaard," Tissa said. "Every day is something new. Raad and I try to deal with the problems as quickly as possible, but even with our council, decisions are tough."

We both went silent then, letting the gravity of our new appointments weigh upon us.

Then Tissa said, "By the way, I meant to introduce you to Rein and Forschi." She shifted her visin from her face to her bed, where two big dogs with puffy white coats and little black eyes sat quietly. The dogs lifted their paws and waved at me. They were adorable.

I waved back. "Hello!"

And then Tissa's face zoomed back in. "Aren't they just the cutest?" she said. "Raad had them made specifically for me. I got them yesterday. You'd never guess they aren't real, right? They are smart replicas. They understand everything I say; they can dance; they can cuddle me; they can follow complicated orders. Plus I can turn them off when they get annoying! They don't even need to use the toilet. I'm supposed to keep them clean, but I just make one of the Protectors do it for me. I really can't be bothered with cleaning anything but myself."

"Do people have real pets?" I asked.

"People do, Kaelyn, not nobles. Nobles get smart replicas. They're better than natural animals, which can be unpredictable and stinky. The last thing I need are muddy paw prints all over the new carpets in our chamber. That would be a disaster, and I simply don't have time for it."

Tissa sighed. It was as if the mere notion of a dirty carpet stressed her out. "Things were so much easier, huh," she said, "back when we worked from our office in the city. Our only concern then was helping the less fortunate. Now a whole new team is running GMAF. I'm ruling over Gaard with your brother while you try to mend the world with Nnati whispering in your ear. Things sure have changed."

"They sure have," I said. Things were tough. Even with the

Crown of Crowns' recommendations to guide me, I repeatedly had trouble making firm judgments. I worried that my council was beginning to question my indecision.

I began to ask, "How's Raa—?" but my visin bleeped in my ear. It was Torio. He had never called me so late before. My heart dropped like an anvil. What could Torio possibly have to tell me in the middle of the night?

"I'm sorry, Tiss," I said, "I've got to go. It's Torio on the other line."

She made a sad face. "Okay, I understand. Duty calls. We'll talk later. Raad is missing you."

"And I'm missing Raad. Please tell Papa I love him. Bye, Tissa. Bye, Rein and Forschi."

The dogs yipped in the background as I ended the call and picked up Torio. His face appeared on my holographic screen. He looked agitated.

"Torio, what's wrong?"

"People are dying," he said—no pause, no formalities, straight to the point. Torio didn't beat around the bush. "Twenty deaths in Nurlie since yesterday. Five deaths in Surrvul. Three deaths in Krug. It's an outbreak, Kaelyn. It's a viral illness unlike anything Geniverd has ever seen. We're hours away from a pandemic!"

"What do you mean, an outbreak? What's going on, Torio?"

I was suddenly very awake, hunched on the edge of my bed, shouting at the screen of my visin. Zawne was sprawled out behind me in la-la land, probably in Shiol with Lordin.

"It starts as a fever," Torio said. "Then it escalates into vomiting, hallucinations, and eventually death. We think it began two days ago. As of right now, there are three hundred people hospitalized."

"Why have they not received medicine?" I asked. "Tell me there's a plan, Torio. I can't have widespread disease in my first year as queen!"

Torio made a face, ran his tongue across his teeth, and said, "Well, Your Most Supreme Majesty, the sick people have indeed received antivirals. However, the ones they need—the ones that can combat this virus—are not being delivered. This is also a mutated strain. We need an antiviral to be produced."

"So," I asked, "what's the holdup?"

"We are still waiting for word from the manufacturer. You might remember it: VBione Corp."

I gasped. "Don't tell me ..."

"Yes," Torio said, a look of deep remorse on his face. "They bought out the other companies. The only other manufacturing plant that could have engineered the right vaccine or produced antivirals was Medseet. VBione Corp absorbed them after you gave them permission. They shut down the plant in Krug, pending change of ownership."

A wave of nausea swept over me. I got out of bed and stumbled through the darkness of the apartment. Had I made the wrong decision? Why had the Crown of Crowns made me rule in favor of VBione Corp?

"Is there no one else?" I asked Torio. "What of the antimicrobial producers in Gaard? There must be some way to stop this before it spreads."

"We've started to quarantine," Torio said, "but it may be too late. I'm not sure that you gauge the scope of VBione Corp's influence. They've gobbled up every large antimicrobial manufacturer across the six continents. We're relying solely on them to fix this, and they aren't delivering."

I was chewing on my lip. I had no idea what to do. How was I supposed to solve a global pandemic?

"Set up a meeting," I said to Torio. "I want everyone in my private council chamber in thirty minutes. Got it?"

"Yes, Your Most Supreme Majesty."

Torio ended the call. I paced for thirty seconds in the dark, wishing I could wake up Zawne. But no, he was flirting with his dead fiancée in Shiol. To heck with it, I could run the kingdom myself. I was the daughter of a Gaard-Ma. I had to keep her strength alive!

Then I remembered Raad. My brother was Gaard-Elder. I figured if anyone had access to the Gaard medical companies, it was him. I dialed his number on my visin while trying to get dressed in my massive dressing room.

"Kaelyn?" Raad was red eyed, half-asleep. I must have woken him. The light from his visin made him look like a ghostly silhouette. "What's going on? It's the middle of the night."

I spoke in bursts, trying to jam my legs into a pair of pants. "Disease spreading across Geniverd. Emergency. No medicine. People dead."

"Whoa," Raad said, sitting up and rubbing the sleep from his eyes. "What are you talking about? Slow down, sis."

I stopped, took a deep breath, and explained as best I could. I told Raad everything Torio had told me.

My brother gave me a look of resolve, but I could see the fear in his eyes as he said, "You need to stop this outbreak right away, before it gets out of control. Get ready for your emergency council meeting while I make some calls about VBione Corp. I've heard about their recent acquisitions, but I also heard you gave them the go-ahead. That's why I didn't make a fuss when they swallowed the last of their competitors here in Gaard. After Medseet, VBione Corp was simply too big. No one could refuse an offer from them."

I was having serious reservations about my decision regarding VBione Corp. I couldn't help but feel like I had been played for a fool. Yet it was what the Crown of Crowns had recommended. Did they have a divine plan regarding the outbreak? I needed to have a chat with Riedel and Hanchell as soon as possible. Something here didn't smell right.

I thanked Raad and ended the call.

* * *

I WAS on my personal hover scooter, zipping through the dimly lit pathway toward the government building with Protectors gliding behind me, when Raad called back.

"Any news?" I asked. There was no projection, just Raad's voice in my ear.

"Yes," he said, "and it's not good. First off, the spokesperson for VBione Corp claims they are having stability issues with the antivirals. They can't send them out, because they're not ready to be administered to humans. There is a batch undergoing testing as we speak. I don't know. It sounded fishy to me."

"Do you suspect foul play? Do you think their takeover of the industry was a precursor to the outbreak?"

"I don't know," Raad said, "but I don't like it. When I tried to figure out who the owner of VBione Corp is, I got lost in a web of fake names and addresses. There are backdoor dealings signed by twenty different people. There are mailing addresses in Surrvul, Krug, Shondur. I even found an address in Lodden that was devastated by an earthquake three years ago. It doesn't even exist anymore! Whoever owns VBione Corp has put a lot of effort into not being found."

"I don't like the sound of that," I said. "Not one bit."

"Neither do I. It seems orchestrated to me," Raad said. "I'm going over to VBione Corp with Protectors and some of my best Aska councillors straightaway. We're going to get to the bottom of this. You work on containing the infection."

"Got it," I said. I was coming up on the government building.

"And one other thing," Raad said. "I checked the news before I called. More people are dying. Five hundred people in Nurlie, fifty in Lodden, and thirty-eight in Surrvul. You need to get a message out and advise people to stay indoors. You can't let this thing spread to the capital."

* * *

TORIO GREETED me as I entered my private council chamber. "Your Most Supreme Majesty, I have requested Dr. Weintag be sent for straightaway to assist in the emergency meeting. He should be arriving shortly. Dr. Weintag is an expert in airborne infections and viral mutations."

"Excellent," I said. I took a quick look around to make sure everyone was present. All five of my councillors sat red eyed in their respective seats, waiting for me. "Let's get started," I told Torio. "We have no time to waste."

"The king?" he asked. "Shouldn't the king and his council also be here?"

"He's busy," I said, moving past Torio to take my chair. "All you've got is me. Now let's get started."

We squabbled for a few minutes over the best way to proceed. Master Widrig suggested stifling the news so we didn't cause a panic, but I quickly squashed that idea. I ordered Lady Katrin to put out a public warning for people not to go outdoors without breathing masks and to leave their homes only if there was an emergency. I had Master Widrig authorize huge overtime payments to doctors and nurses for the extra work, then had him order every able-bodied medical professional to their nearest hospital. "We need to be fully staffed and prepared," I said, "even here in the capital."

Next, Torio sent out orders to the Protectors to begin door-to-door safety checks and take any infected people straight into quarantine. Special bubbles were already being put into use all over the globe to try to contain the virus. Still, I had Aska Nikhel put out a travel ban. No flyarcs, no boats, no trains. As of that moment, travel between continents was off-limits.

And that was when Dr. Weintag entered the room. He was an older gentleman with white hair and a dusty lab coat.

"Good morning, Dr. Weintag," I said. "Please take the floor. Tell us everything you know."

Dr. Weintag cleared his throat and activated his visin. He began talking us through the images on his screen.

"We're dealing with a sudden mutated strain of the flu virus, which we're calling KS3. It's airborne. That's why we're having trouble containing it. As far as we can tell, it has spread to all continents. We now have a global pandemic. This is a red-alert situation, Your Most Supreme Majesty. Testing from the last twelve hours indicates KS3 is continuing to mutate and evolve. None of our medicines are working. Upon entering the human system, KS3 bypasses all antibodies and attacks the central nervous system, causing fever, chills, nausea, vomiting, delirium, and ultimately … death."

"What's the death toll at now?" I asked. "Someone check the damn reports!"

Master Widrig said, "Four thousand in Nurlie, eight hundred in Krug, four hundred in Surrvul, two fifty in Lodden, one hundred in Shondur, and fifty in Gaard. The capital is no longer safe."

No one even gasped. They just blinked, eyes huge, breathing shallowly. Lady Katrin said, "At this rate, the world could be gone by tomorrow night."

"Not all of it," Dr. Weintag said. "We will live, and the clan leaders, I'm sure, have already retreated to their secret underground bunkers. None of the clan leaders dare retreat to their remote lodgings or private sanctuaries, because of the Gurnot pyromaniac on the loose. The ones who will suffer seriously from this disaster are the commoners, all the people in the street who can't escape the devastation of KS3. As for you, my queen, I suggest wearing a breathing mask from this point on."

A Protector then entered the room with a box full of sterilized items. My councillors and I each put them on, then exchanged frightened looks through our masks and visors.

"We need an effective antiviral," the doctor said, "and we need it now. This is the most potent flu we've seen in our time, much like the Great Destroyer Bug, which wiped out over half our population five hundred years ago. The basic reproduction number is very high. By our calculations, over five hundred million people will be dead by next week. We have roughly forty-eight hours to put a lid on this."

"What can we do in the meantime?" Nnati asked. "How can we protect ourselves and the people?"

Dr. Weintag ran his hand through his wispy white hair. He was visibly trembling. I could understand why. This outbreak had the potential to end the world. "We need the Protectors to begin handing out antiviral sprays," he said, "breathing apparatus, gloves, sterile wipes, and even flimsy bodysuits to keep the masses relatively safe. As for the nobility, I highly suggest refraining from touching or even being in the same room with others."

"Got it," I said. Then I addressed my councillors. "From now on, all meetings will be held through visins. I want my staff barricaded in sealed rooms behind sterilized barriers. Everyone, take extra breathing masks with you when you leave and only let the Protectors into your rooms to deliver supplies."

I turned my attention to Torio, who had been listening while swiping the channels on his visin and responding to messages. "Any news of VBione Corp?" I asked.

"They claim the test batch failed. They're starting trials for another batch. They hope to have it ready within two days."

"Damn it!" I smashed my fists down on the table. "We don't have two days! I want everyone on their visins right now. I

don't care who you have to call, who you have to pay, who you
have to threaten with banishment—I want the old Medseet lab
up and running by noon today. I want every available scientist, biologist, pathogen specialist, and medical expert in that
factory working on a cure by tonight. Do you understand
me?"

"Yes, Your Most Supreme Majesty," they all said, scrambling to get to work.

I realized then that my breathing was erratic. I was all
jacked up on adrenaline. It was the intensity of the moment,
the whole world threatening to implode while my team and I
scrambled to fix it. And where was Zawne during all this? He
was hanging out in Shiol with his mistress. Maybe Lordin had
been right in assuming Zawne was unprepared to be king.

I pushed my chair back and stood up, feeling more like a
fierce queen than I would have thought possible three years—
no, three weeks ago! "And someone find out who owns
VBione Corp," I said. "I want a name within the hour!"

* * *

"I JUST DON'T GET IT," Nnati was saying over the visin. We
were both in our private quarters, waiting for the Protectors
to finish sanitizing everything and lock us inside until the KS3
scare was over. "These are profit-making companies. VBione
Corp should want to make money. Why are they being so
stubborn about getting the product to the people? They could
be making a fortune!"

"I don't get it either," I said, sagging into my couch. Zawne
had been placed in another part of the mansion under his own
quarantine. If neither of us showed signs of infection after
forty-eight hours, we would be allowed to rejoin each other. "I
just really hope they're being honest. We haven't seen this

kind of outbreak in a long time, so it's understandable if they were unprepared, what with so many people having immunity and the mandatory vaccinations. There shouldn't even be a superbug!"

"Yet there is," Nnati said with a sigh. "I feel bad. I've been joking about it for years, and now ..."

"Don't think like that," I told him. "We are going to work this out. The councillors are hard at work containing this, while Raad is investigating VBione Corp, and Dr. Weintag is helping to get the Krug medicine plant back up and running. Together we will come through."

Nnati gave me a confused look. "Where the heck is Zawne? What is the king doing in all this?"

Canoodling with Lordin, I wanted to say. But that wasn't entirely fair. Zawne was trapped in a private quarantine, just like me. I was sure he was working with his own councillors to mend the situation. "He's working tirelessly," I told Nnati. I wasn't about to start slandering the king, my husband. Not yet, anyway.

"Good," Nnati said. "I was beginning to think you were the only one ruling around here."

Just then Raad bleeped in on my visin. I told Nnati, "Got to go. Raad's calling," and switched lines.

"You have news?" I asked as my brother's sweaty face filled my screen. He looked crazed, stressed, totally frantic. I'd never seen him like this. I wondered how disheveled he would have been without the Aska training.

"A lot of news, and none of it good."

Raad wiped sweat from his brow, closed his eyes to steady himself, and then said, "Someone's out to incite global chaos. I can't tell you why. It could be because they're angry about you and Zawne taking the crown. It could be an idea that's been fermenting on one of the continents for a long time, maybe a shadow government, maybe the Gurnots. I really don't know. But listen to this, I got nowhere at the VBione Corp main factory. They have batches of the antiviral being made on the assembly line but claim they're not ready. They claim it isn't potent enough to halt the virus from spreading. They need to create an entirely new compound. I saw their scientists busy in labs, so they do appear to be working on a cure. Meanwhile, it's not ready and people are dying."

Raad sucked in a gulp of air. "And it seems like no one is in charge. Or at least, no one knows who's in charge. There are factory foremen, but the higher-ups all respond to a computer, to messages sent to their visins. I have my best techs working on triangulating the signal. However, it's being bounced off satellites. It's like we're up against a supervillain or something. I don't know what to make of it."

I didn't either. A supervillain? Why did disaster have to unfold under my watch? All I wanted was a peaceful kingdom. But no, I had maniacs unleashing viruses, polluting the planet with toxins, killing thousands. Never had I wanted to be in Zawne's embrace more than in that moment, to have him hold me and tell me everything would be all right. But I couldn't even do that. We were under quarantine for another forty-eight hours. I didn't even care about Lordin anymore. I just wanted Zawne.

I slumped into my chair. "Thank you, Raad. Will you let me know when your techs find a name? I want this person brought in for questioning and VBione Corp destroyed."

"You've got it, sister queen. But ..." Raad hesitated, lips twisted in a scowl. "But that's not all. There's more."

"Oh dear." I whacked myself in the forehead. "What is it? Give it to me straight, Raad. Things can't get much worse."

"They can," he said dourly. "They can and they have. Remember the dispute between Nurlie and the rogue

157

islanders? Well, it's elevated into rioting. The entire island is in upheaval. People have taken to the streets, burning vehicles and smashing windows. It's anarchy. They're demanding a referendum while the shadow government is gearing up for an invasion of the mainland. Nurlie is scared."

"Can't we send in Protectors?" I asked. "Can't they put a stop to the riots?"

"Maybe," Raad said, but it sounded a lot like a question. "The problem is that too many players have come onto the stage. With the KS3 virus ravaging Nurlie, all the little weasels have come out of their holes. The Gurnots have taken up arms on the mainland and on the island, inciting both sides of the conflict to all-out war. They've brought tech with them, high-end stuff that they shouldn't have. I'm talking laser clubs, proton beams, mobile incinerators. We sent a legion of Protectors to the island, and they were disabled in just a few minutes, their circuits fried by camouflaged Gurnots with laser clubs."

Raad groaned. "And don't even get me started on the fires. Whole squads of Protectors have been melted into mercury by an unknown assailant while the last few luxury retreats in Surrvul have gone up in flames, all of them belonging to clan heirs or heiresses. I know the media calls the arsonist the Dragon, and I'm starting to wonder if it isn't true, if it isn't a flesh and blood dragon."

While Raad explained, I divided my visin screen in half and turned on the news. P2 drones were recording the pandemonium in the streets of Nurlie and on the island. There were flyrarcs crashing and smoldering in buildings, waves of demonstrators waving the island's flag and throwing bricks at the barricade of Protectors, sick people dying in the streets. It was absolute carnage.

"I can't believe this," I said. "Who's responsible? Who's

given them such high-tech weapons? I thought weapons were reserved for the Askas and highest level of Battle Protectors, the P5 Protectors."

"They are," Raad said, and I could tell he was mad by the growl in his voice. "But one of my inside sources told me Surrvul's new clan leaders are funding the rebels and maybe even the Gurnots. It sounds to me like this could have been in development for a long time. It could also be an opportunistic move by the eldest of the Surrvul Clan, who took power last month. Everyone knows they want the crown with a violent passion. I wouldn't be surprised if they're trying to cause so much global turmoil that you and Zawne are forced to step down. Or worse, they could be planning an invasion of the Gaard continent and global war."

"They'd never," I said. I was aghast. Not only was a deadly virus on the loose, but now I had enemies, and they were mobilizing. They could be coming after me and my husband. I had never even wanted to be the stupid queen. It was supposed to have been Lordin's job!

"They might," Raad said. "And there's another issue. The Protectors. Their armor plating is produced in—yup, you guessed it—Surrvul. They've been stockpiling the phosphorus we need to manufacture the armor, and the mines in Shondur are almost all dried up. There's nothing left. If Surrvul has been giving anti-Protector weaponry to the rebels, and the rebels start to win the fight, we won't be able to build any more Protectors. It'll be like ancient times. It'll be war like the world hasn't seen in five hundred years. The streets will run red with the blood of our people."

"Unacceptable," I said. "All of this. It's all unacceptable. We need to put an end to the referendum in Nurlie before they start a war. We need to start restricting Surrvul's access to our precious minerals. We need to take away the Gurnots' weapons. We need to put a stop to whoever is burning down half the world, before they reach Gaard and burn down the palace. And we need to find a cure for this disease before it wipes out everyone in Geniverd."

"All in forty-eight hours," Raad said with a hollow, hopeless laugh.

I thanked him for the information and ended the call. I was at my wits' end. Where did I go from here? I had to save the world, but how? I couldn't even get my own husband to look me in the eye!

---

13

*E*verything had spiraled out of control. It was about time I made it back to Shiol. By the time I ended the call with Raad, it was only four in the afternoon, but I recalled that the Crown of Crowns had told me I could take an emergency nap if I ever needed to speak with them. Well, if this wasn't an emergency, I didn't know what was.

I lay on the sofa, let fatigue overtake me ...

And Zawne called me. My visin bleeped, and I saw his name on the display. "Oh, great," I said. "Here we go. Hello, Zawne," I said, sitting upright so we could talk face-to-face.

He looked upset. I could tell he was emotional. He said, "I'm sorry," and I was taken aback. Really, Zawne was sorry? Sorry for what?

Then again, if Zawne wanted to make amends, I was okay with that. "I'm sorry too," I said. "I'm sorry I kept secrets from you. It was wrong, I know."

"And I'm sorry I was distant," he said. "I'm sorry I lashed out at you. It wasn't right. Our ex-lovers showed up as Min. We were both confused and conflicted, torn between two worlds. The fact is, Kaelyn, I love you. And we're both here in the real world. It took this whole KS3 fiasco for me to realize how important you are to me. The world's falling apart, and all I can think about is you."

Zawne had left me speechless. I moved my mouth, unable to make a sound. I wished he were beside me so I could reach out and touch him. Damn the blasted quarantine! "I … I love you too, Zawne."

We held each other's gaze for a full minute, peering through the visin's display into one another's eyes. It was romantic. I wanted to somehow slither through the screen and kiss him.

I eventually said, "It's nice talking to you like this. We've been at odds, and it sucks. I wish we could be a team in this terrible time."

"We are," he said. "You and me, king and queen for life. We're the best team in Geniverd."

I chuckled. "Yeah, and we're trapped in separate apartments for the next forty-eight hours. The world will be on fire by then."

"I've started to put the fire out," he said with a cocky smile. "I sent a delegation to Nurlie to try to calm the rebellion. There will be a meeting held later today between all parties to come to an agreement. If the fighting continues, we'll use force."

"Force … What do you mean?"

"The underwater weapons system," he said. "It's been dormant for hundreds of years. The clans have been at peace, so there hasn't been a need for it. But it's still there, waiting to be used. We have enough firepower to wipe out Nurlie, Surrvul—every continent except Gaard if we need to."

I was appalled. I had known there were weapons, but I hadn't known how powerful they were. Torio had planned to give me a tutorial but had never gotten around to it, because we had been so busy.

Zawne saw my shock. "What did you expect?" he asked. "Did you think the rulers of the world wouldn't have a fail-safe, a means to maintain power? People may have forgotten because generations have come and gone, but the Crown still has the power to wipe out ninety-five percent of Geniverd with the push of a button. We've come this far because of war. From the ashes of destruction, we built this peaceful civilization. I promise you, Kaelyn, there will not be an invasion of the capital."

"What about Decens-Lenitas?" I asked, frantically making up excuses. "What about the public? They would surely hate us for the next forty years if we unleashed weapons."

Zawne shook his head. "The public are not the ones in power; we are. In times of trouble, we must maintain our image before the other clan heads to keep their respect. That's what Decens-Lenitas is all about, Kaelyn, respecting the monarchy, the upper class, the system, obeying the orders of those in power. And do not be mistaken, even though we have councillors and *you-know-who* pulling the strings, we are the ones who rule the world. Our word is law. The people must obey."

"I don't care," I said. "I couldn't wipe out millions of human souls. Not ever. When did Decens-Lenitas become a means for retaining power within the upper echelon of society? Does it mean nothing for the rest of our people, for the ninety-nine percent who are at our mercy? It's not fair, Zawne. We can't butcher our own subjects just to save face with a handful of spoiled nobility."

"Would you prefer a long and bloody war?" Zawne asked. "The alternatives are worse, Kaelyn, much worse."

"I … I won't let it come to that," I insisted. "I refuse to resort to weapons! I will stop this before it goes too far."

"How?" Zawne asked. "We can't even leave our living quarters! We still don't know who's in charge of VBione Corp. We can't even catch the elusive Gurnot who's been torching our residences. There are almost no retreats left in Surrvul or Shondur for the wealthy to take vacations." Zawne snarled and furrowed his eyebrows in frustration. "It doesn't even matter. I just want to be with you, Kaelyn. We should be solving this mess together."

"I know," I said.

It was weird. As the apocalypse bloomed on the horizon, Zawne and I were finally coming into our own as a couple. The fights were behind us, the secrets, the betrayals. If only we could survive the next week. If only …

A message popped up in the corner of my screen. It was from Raad. While Zawne went on boasting about his love for me, I opened the message and read it.

KAELYN, *triangulated origin of signal. Boss of VBione Corp is Emell —Lordin's mother. En route to make arrest. Seek ex-queen for answers. Remember the story Mama told us when we were young, about the king and his mistress. Don't tell anyone. Trust no one.*

* * *

IT TOOK LONGER than I would have liked to get off the call with Zawne after reading Raad's message. Zawne kept babbling on about our union and our future together, which was sweet, but I had priorities. I had a mystery to solve. A whole new set of clues and misshaped puzzle pieces had fallen into my lap.

I sent a discreet message to the ex-queen, requesting a secret meeting in the evening, somewhere on VondRust grounds. I would have to be sneaky to get out of my quarantine and past the Protectors. I figured if I could do that, then I could sneak into Zawne's private apartment and spend the night with him, feel his strong, calloused hands, full lips, tight abs … Yeah, that was a good idea.

But first I had to get to Shiol. I had to start asking the important questions. Lordin, Emell, VBione Corp, KS3, Nurlie rebels, Gurnots, Surrvul's greed—was it all connected?

I lay back and closed my eyes. Before I knew it, I was standing in the spatial void with Riedel and Hanchell glittering before me.

"What gives?" I said. I was in no mood to screw around.

"What gives with what?" Riedel asked, his blob of light fluctuating. I had the sense he was being purposely coy.

"Oh," I said, rubbing my chin sarcastically. "I don't know. Maybe the fact that because of your recommendations regarding VBione Corp, and against my better judgment, the kingdom is now on the brink of war. Not to mention the thousands of people dying as we speak. All of Geniverd has gone to the dogs in the last twelve hours."

"Oh," Riedel said, "that. Yes. We have been watching."

"So?" I asked. I was on the verge of hysterics. "What's the deal? How could you not foresee this? Aren't you omniscient? Or did you know beforehand? Are you behind VBione Corp? Are you friends with Emell?" I sucked in a deep breath, looked between their flashing masses. "What gives?"

"Well," Hanchell said, "we can see the future, but not so well. Our capabilities are restricted to somewhere between twelve and twenty-four hours. We had no idea humanity would break out in disease or conflict. In fact, the whole reason we ruled in favor of VBione Corp was because one of our Min convinced us it was the smart move for Geniverd. She told us that by siding with VBione Corp, more potent and effective medicines would be put into mass production. She showed us convincing evidence, and we passed the order along to you. We take full responsibility for the poor recommendation. That was our bad."

"Your bad?" I was furious! The Crown of Crowns was not supposed to make mistakes.

"Let us remind you," Riedel said, "at the end of the day, our recommendations are just that: recommendations. We picked you as queen because of your wise mind and questioning heart. Had you felt strongly enough to disagree with our suggestion, it was your decision to make."

"Now you tell me," I said sourly. I felt deflated, as if the Crown of Crowns had just smooshed the air out of me. *My decision to make?* They were trying to blame the entire mess on me, say everything was my fault because I didn't listen to my gut! The Crown of Crowns was acting like a couple of cowards!

"We do apologize," Hanchell said. "And we wish we could fix it. However, we are unable to directly interfere with humanity. We have our Min working to keep the balance, but we oversee everything from the spirit dimension. The future of Geniverd is in your hands, Queen Kaelyn. There's nothing we can do."

"You're saying I'm on my own?" I asked.

"You have all the resources available to a queen," Hanchell said chipperly.

"But I need your help! Can you at least tell me why Emell has done all this? And who was the Min who gave you the suggestion to side with VBione Corp? Was it Lordin? If you could at least fill in some of the blanks, it would make it easier for me to save the world from my quarantined apartment."

Hanchell and Riedel both fizzled strangely. I thought they were uncomfortable, which was odd considering they were thousands of years old and had seen this sort of thing before, war and death and disease.

"We cannot divulge information about our Min," Hanchell said. She at least sounded sad about it. "We do want to help you, Queen Kaelyn, but we cannot give up the secrets of the Min to a human. Our bond is sacred and may not be broken. However, we can tell you that Emell is currently being taken into custody by your brother. She is the head of VBione Corp, and she is very angry at the seat of power and seeks vengeance. As for the Nurlie conflict and the virus, it's almost too late. Without the distribution of a full cure in the next thirty-six hours, the world will be consumed by disease."

"Great," I said, all hope sucked out of me. "The world is doomed, and there's nothing I can do about it."

"No," Riedel said, "not doomed. The world will not end; it will merely regrow, like a forest burned to the ground that takes a long time to grow back. Humanity will flourish once again."

"But four billion lives will be lost!" I screamed. "I can't have that. I must save my people. I must protect the six clans!"

"I have an idea," Hanchell said, her gaseous light brightening to a fantastic hue of yellow. "What about your friend Roki? He's a good Min. We may not be able to give you information, but he can. I suggest you seek out Roki. He may be your only hope."

* * *

THE CROWN of Crowns had proved more useless than I could have possibly imagined. I supposed they didn't care. I couldn't blame them. If ninety-five percent of humanity were wiped out, they would just watch and wait while society regrew and restructured itself. We were nothing to them, a kingdom of ants who could rebuild if our nest was destroyed. Time was irrelevant to such beings. Five hundred years went by in the blink of an eye.

I woke from my nap supremely exhausted, eyes red and bleary. I sat up and checked the news on my visin. Twenty thousand more deaths around the globe. It was already more death than anyone in my generation had seen. It was too much, too devastating. I had to stop it. But that meant ...

Roki.

What had the Crown of Crowns meant when they told me he was a good Min? What did that mean to them? So long as Roki did his job in Geniverd for them, he could be considered good. But I knew better. Roki was an evil womanizer. Yet lives were at stake. The world was at stake. It looked like I was going to have to swallow my pride and call out to him. I just had to promise myself it would be strictly business. Then, after we saved the world, I wouldn't speak with him anymore. I also had to promise myself that when I saw him again in the flesh, I would refrain from getting emotional. No matter how badly I wanted to, I could not touch him. Not even a friendly hug!

I got off the couch and stretched, almost too exhausted to think. It was a quarter past seven, the time sifting away from me like grains of sand. Only thirty-four hours left to free the world from disease.

I checked my messages while pacing in a circle, trying to get my energy back. Raad had left a message saying he was escorting Emell to the security compound outside NordHaven but that she insisted she was guilty of no wrongdoing. As if to spite her arrest, VBione Corp had finally issued antivirals that could slow down the effects of KS3, though they claimed the full cure was still in development.

There was a message from Torio saying the delegation to Nurlie had been involved in a fist fight, and another message five minutes later saying that war between the island and the mainland was now imminent.

Nnati had left messages asking to call him back; so had Tissa. But they didn't have information relating to the salvation of Geniverd. They just wanted to make sure I was okay.

"Sorry, guys," I said to myself. "We'll have to catch up later. I've got to save the world."

Then I saw my final message. It was from the ex-queen. She had agreed to meet me in a secluded corner of VondRust's southern gardens at eight o'clock, in forty-five minutes. I scrambled to find a disguise and get ready, snuck from my room, and slipped through the halls of my mansion, out into the heat of the night, then farther into the garden.

* * *

UNDER DIFFERENT CIRCUMSTANCES, the garden meeting with Zawne's mama, the ex-queen, would have been pleasant. Under the moonlight, the flowers appeared moist, the strong scent of jasmine and hyacinth filling my nostrils, the beautiful twilight of the atmospheric bubble around VondRust painting the night in deep blacks and blues, like a fairy-tale garden. But as it was, the meeting was grim.

The Queen Emerita emerged from the shadows, wearing a black robe, her face covered by a thick scarf. I myself wore a gardener's outfit with my hair hidden beneath a cap.

"Good evening, daughter-in-law. What can I do for you in the midst of this unfolding tragedy? You clearly didn't bring me here to talk about the flowers."

"Sadly not," I said. It sucked, because I would have preferred to welcome the ex-queen back home under better circumstances, with a grand feast and much wine and laughter. "I asked you here because the kingdom is under siege, and I have a feeling you're familiar with the attacker."

"Is that so?" She came close to me, and I felt right away how warm a woman she was, kind and gentle. "Tell me, child," she whispered. "Tell me of this attacker. I trust you took a nap today."

It was funny. We both knew of the Crown of Crowns yet were sworn to secrecy, even with each other. I had to choose my words carefully. "I did have a nap, but it was not useful. I woke up more confused than ever."

"That may happen from time to time," she said with a sad smile.

I paused, wondering how to bring up Emell. I thought of Raad's message, him reminding me of the story Mama used to tell. I was sure Emell was the mistress in the story and that the king was the King Emeritus, Mama the Gaard-Ma in the scenario. I just came out with it.

"I heard a story once," I said. "In the story was a mistress of pale skin and light eyes. She had the king's ear, and the king of the time was very greedy for the land of Gaard. Gaard-Ma beseeched the mistress for her aid but was shunned. As a result, Gaard-Ma started a rumor that eventually drove the mistress to be condemned and banished to the farthest corner of Gaard. I've recently discovered who these players were, their true identities."

The ex-queen smiled at me. "You're a clever girl. It's easy to see why my son fell for you. To answer your question, yes, I was reigning queen during this debacle. And yes, your mama was Gaard-Ma. And Lordin's mother was the banished mistress. Imagine my surprise when Lordin began to gain fame throughout the kingdom. I couldn't believe it when she ascended all the way to Zawne's bedchamber. He never did know the truth of her mother, and the king and I kept our mouths shut."

She regarded me curiously. "But considering the severity of the current plague and turmoil, why bring this to me now?"

"Because Emell is the owner of VBione Corp," I said. "Raad has arrested her on suspicion of genocide. I am merely trying to determine how involved she is in everything. I'm trying to find a motive. I also need to know if Lordin is involved. As I'm sure you know …" I had to remind myself to choose my words carefully. "She's dead, but not forgotten."

"Oh, I see." The ex-queen nodded, her face pinched in a contemplative expression. "That is troubling."

"It would help if you could explain what happened," I said. "My brother suspects this disaster was premeditated. If I can find motive, perhaps I can stop it."

"It was twenty-five years ago," she said, "but I will do my best to recall everything clearly."

She took a deep breath and told me the story.

"Emell was always a vindictive woman. She cared only for power, and the young king was drawn to her because of this. They wanted to rule the kingdom with an iron fist. The whole reason the king sought extra land from the Gaard farmers was to build a lavish estate for Emell, his whimsical mistress. Why do you think Emell refused to help Mama with her request to stop the land acquisition? Anyway, after the rumor began to circulate, the king was distraught. He held meetings with his councillors to try to fix it, but there was no way around Emell's banishment. It was the only way to save face with the other clan leaders, lest they try to oust him as king. He bid Emell farewell with a heavy heart, sending her to the frigid north of the continent, where she stayed.

"Yet Emell vowed to get her revenge against the Crown. Before she left, she cursed us. Emell was mad with hatred for the king, hatred for me, hatred for Gaard-Ma. She said, 'Your kingdom will collapse one day. Gaard-Ma will choke on her slanderous tongue. The king and queen will suffer horrible loss. And as for the kingdom ...' Emell cackled sickly, the Protectors dragging her from the palace. 'The kingdom will burn, and the people will vomit and die in the streets. I vow this with my life!'"

The ex-queen sighed. "I never took the curse seriously. Even with this virus sweeping the world, I never imagined Emell could be responsible. But you say it's true, daughter queen?"

"Sadly, yes." I had never heard that part of the story. I had never considered Lordin's mother to be a corrupt and jealous woman, cast aside and hungry for vengeance against the entire world. I was wondering about something now ... something I had wanted to know for a long time.

I asked, "Do you think it was Emell who poisoned Mama?"

Her face turned glum, and she put her arm around me. "I am sorry for your mama's death," she said. "Gaard-Ma was a good woman, a good friend." She bit her lip, deep emotion moistening her eyes. "As for Emell ... it is possible she was involved. Perhaps she poisoned her. Perhaps Emell has been plotting the destruction of Gaard and the rest of the world for the past twenty-five years."

I gasped, staggered backward through the grass. "Which could mean ..."

"Yes," the Queen Emerita said. "It could mean Lordin has been helping her since day one. With Lordin's death ..."

She couldn't say it, but I knew what the ex-queen was thinking. She wanted to imply that with Lordin's transformation into a Min, Lordin would have ultimate power throughout Geniverd. She'd be able to pull strings, push the pieces where she wanted, maybe even get Zawne and me elevated to the throne. That was when I remembered Hagan and her mannerisms, her confidence. In a split second, I knew it had been Lordin inside Hagan's body, controlling her, securing the deal for VBione Corp. Yet how could Emell interact with Hagan-Lordin without knowing the Great Secret? Could it be Lordin was helping her mother from beyond the grave, using the cover of a businesswoman from Gaard?

It suddenly felt like I was in the center of a great conspiracy, a family rivalry that had trickled down through the years and left me to suffer in its fallout. It wasn't fair. It didn't make sense. Lordin had been such a good person in her life, so noble. Could that have been the plan all along? Could Emell have twisted Lordin and made her impure?

"I thank you for your time, but I must leave," I told the ex-queen. "I need to get to the bottom of this."

I also needed to confront Emell. If she had killed Mama, I wanted to look her in the eyes and hear her confess. I wanted justice.

14

I was at a crossroads. To my left was the cobbled path to my mansion. To my right was the path to Zawne. I wanted more than anything to be cradled in his strong arms, to tell him everything I had discovered. I needed advice, and I needed it badly. I couldn't go to Nnati or Tissa, or even to Raad. I couldn't discuss the Great Secret with them, but I could discuss it with Zawne.

On the other hand, I was a little nervous of Zawne's allegiance. I was sure in my heart that he was fully unaware of Lordin's deception. Yet I couldn't risk it. I needed a mutual mind to help me. I needed ...

"Roki."

I whispered his name, standing in the dark between the two mansions. I was out of options. He was the only one who could help me, even if I did hate him for betraying my trust. "Roki," I said, "I need you now. I need your help. I have nowhere to turn. I'm alone in the world."

I dreaded the thought of him appearing in front of me. I could still see the images of him and those other women tangled in lustful embraces. It made me sick. Yet deep in my heart was a longing for Roki. I had to trust my instincts, that summoning him was in my best interest.

His scent came to me on a breeze. I closed my eyes and felt the wind stir. When I opened them, Roki stood before me. Unlike in the past, he wore no smile. He had a sad and beaten quality to him. There was blood on his shirt.

"Are you bleeding?" I immediately threw away all my hardened resolve to keep things impersonal and rushed to Roki. I lifted his shirt and looked for wounds. I was checking him all over, Roki sagging where he stood as if drained of energy.

"No." He took my hands and gently pushed them against my chest. "But thank you for the concern. I have been helping in Nurlie, dragging the wounded from the streets, trying to protect the innocent. It's insanity there right now. Reinforcements are on their way, but right now it is violent. With Surrvul in the mix, flaunting their money and providing weapons, things look grim. The Gurnots are trying to help, but there is only so much they can do."

"The Gurnots? I thought they were terrorists!"

"Hardly," Roki said. We began to walk along the left path, toward my mansion, through the sweet night air. It was dark and no one could see us. "The Gurnots fight for the people of Geniverd. They despise the way Decens-Lenitas imprisons the lower classes. Everything they do is for the liberation of humanity. Sometimes they must use violence or intimidation tactics. It's why they released the Dragon. Just look, Kaelyn. Look at what the greed of the clans can do!"

Roki activated his visin to show me an overhead view of the nighttime violence in Nurlie. Buildings aflame, laser beams zipping between the ruined towers, wounded and dead stuck between two walls of opposing soldiers. The soldiers weren't even soldiers. Not really. They were ordinary men and women fighting for their cause. It was horrendous, and in their hands were weapons.

"I can't believe it has come to this," I said. "And on top of it, the virus is spreading. Why fight in the streets when people would be safer inside?"

Roki said, "They believe in their cause. That's stronger than the fear of death."

I had never thought about it like that before. I had never truly understood how devoted people were to their clans. Not until I saw them fighting, losing their lives for their beliefs. Only now did I realize the power the upper class and the media had over the masses. Quite frankly, it made me sick.

In the video, words on the bottom of the screen read: *Surrvul Clan denies involvement in Nurlie war. Claims soldiers are rebels and not endorsed by Surrvul.*

They had said this to save face, I figured. The clan leaders needed to keep up appearances, keep up their moral standing in the eyes of Decens-Lenitas. It was all blindfold politics. It wasn't for the people. It was all an act for the other illustrious families!

On Roki's screen, a massive ship came from the sky above the Nurlie capital. The back hatch opened, and P5 Protectors spilled from the ship by the dozen and used their booster systems to hover toward the ground. They immediately started using their built-in supersonic artillery to push back the invading islanders. It was mayhem. People were blasted back into buildings, against flaming cars. I could hear the screams.

From the rooftop were blasts of light. "Oh no!" I said. "The rebels are using remote plasma cannons!"

"Yeah," Roki said.

We both watched the green particle beams launch off the rooftops and dissolve entire groups of P5 Protectors like they were made of butter. It was a barrage of laser fire back and forth. Human and robot, rebel and defender, Gurnot and Nurlie and Surrvul—they all fought and died in the ruined city, the P2 camera drones recording all the action for the people watching in their homes, one last bloody show before they died of the KS3 virus.

"The humanity," I said. "I can't watch it. Please, Roki. Please turn it off!"

He deactivated his visin. We were entering the mansion, and I said, "Can you mask our presence until we're in my apartment? I'm supposed to be under quarantine."

"I already am," he said, giving me his sweet smile. "I've been masking us since I heard your call and zipped across the world. I'm tuned in to your voice. If you say my name, I will always come."

"But—"

"Don't worry," he assured me. "I haven't been listening to your thoughts. I'm still not. I guess I don't really need to. I can tell what you're thinking without listening. I guess it's because of the bond between us."

"I guess so," I said. But I didn't want to fall back into our old ways. I was still mad. I couldn't let Roki's charms seduce me. I had to ask, "Is it possible for a Min to control a person to get what they want? I need to know if Lordin entered the body of a woman named Hagan. I also need to know if Lordin is conspiring with her mother. What I'm asking is, has Lordin used being a Min to bring about all this destruction to get her mother's revenge?"

Roki let out a sigh. We were in my room now, and he plunked himself down on my sofa while I sat on its arm, observing him. "Yes," he said. "It's what Min do best. They invade bodies to manipulate events. I've been a little busy these last few weeks and didn't really have my eye on Lordin, so I can't say for sure if she is involved. But it is possible. A Min can do pretty much anything."

An idea burst into my head like a bomb, shaking me to my core. *A Min can do anything. If I were a Min, I could save the world!*

It was a good thing Roki had stopped reading my thoughts. He would never have let me consider dying to become a Min. My friends, my family ... my husband. I would be abandoning them all. Yet how else could I stop the virus? If Lordin was the kingpin of this terrible design, I could never stop her in my useless human body.

"Thanks anyway," I said. "The Crown of Crowns is no help. I don't know if I can trust Zawne. I've recently found out Emell killed Mama. And now—"

A message blipped onto my visin. "Sorry," I said to Roki while I opened it. "It's from Raad. Oh no ..." I gasped. "Raad says they had to let Emell go free. There was no evidence to suggest she had designed and unleashed the virus, nor that she was withholding the proper medicine. He says an antiviral is in the works but won't be ready for approximately thirty hours. That means Emell is going to distribute the cure just in time to avert mass extinction."

"It's not enough," Roki said. "The virus is spreading too fast. Thirty hours will mean at least two million casualties." He buried his face in his hands. "I can't believe it. I thought humans had a handle on these viruses. How could one woman have done all this?"

"The scorn of a loved one," I said, catching Roki's eye. "It's amazing what a broken heart can do."

"Kaelyn ..." he said. I could see the yearning in his eyes. He wanted to touch me, to explain himself. I wasn't having any of it.

"Don't start," I said. "I saw the photos. I'm not blind." I

shook my head. "Thank you for being here, Roki, but I think I need to be alone now. I have a lot of decisions to make."

"I'll always be here," Roki said. And then he vanished. Not even his scent lingered when he was gone.

* * *

I HAD LIED TO ROKI. I only had one decision to make. I needed to decide. Was I going to give up my life to become a Min?

The first thing I did was call Raad.

"Brother," I said when he answered, "you've made a terrible mistake letting Emell go."

"I know," he said. "I could see the guilt in her eyes when we arrested her, but there was no physical evidence. Plus VBione Corp had already started to ship the inhibitor antivirals to slow the virus. They've promised a cure within thirty hours. We had to release her."

"Thirty hours is too long," I said. "That's two million human lives, Raad. I'm positive Emell is biding her time until the very last second. She must want maximum casualties to make Zawne and me look incompetent."

"I figure the same thing," Raad said. "But my troops searched the VBione Corp main lab and factory. There was nothing. Protectors searched Emell's home, her known places of affiliation. They didn't find a single thing."

"What about the reopened plant in Krug?" I asked.

Raad shook his head. "It was a dud. VBione Corp had the Medseet factory stripped. It would take at least two weeks to rebuild the proper systems and get new machines online."

"Darn," I hissed. Then I looked to Raad. If I was going to become a Min, I needed to be sure he would chase Emell to the far corners of the planet. I needed to know he would get justice for Mama. "Raad," I said, "I talked to the ex-queen, like you suggested. And, well, we both figure it must have been Emell who killed Mama. We think she's been planning her revenge for twenty-five years."

Raad's eyes grew huge in anger. "What!" he bellowed. "I had Emell in my flyrarc! I had her in custody. And now you tell me this? Had I known she was responsible for Mama's death, I would have … I would have …"

"I'm sorry," I said, "but I just found out. It turns out Emell has a vendetta against our family and Zawne's family. She's poisoned the world to rid the throne of us. She killed Mama to get revenge for being banished all those years ago."

"I knew she was the mistress in Mama's story," Raad said. "But I never suspected murder. I can't—"

"I'm sorry," I said, "but I have to go. There's something I need to do, and every second I stall means more lives lost. I love you, brother. Get justice for Mama. Find the truth."

I ended the call with tears in my eyes. How could I say goodbye to Raad for the last time? He would be so upset when my body was found. I was thinking about what the Crown of Crowns had told me: a painful and tragic death. It scared me, but I needed to be strong. Strong for Mama, for Gaard, for my friends.

My tears only worsened when I called Papa, Nnati, then Tissa. They all knew something was wrong, asking me a thousand questions.

"Is it Zawne?"

"Is it the virus?"

"Is it the images of war on the news?"

"Why are you crying?"

I wished I could tell them about Shiol, Min, my plan to save millions of lives. All I could do was thank them for their friendship and tell them I loved them. Then I sat in the dark and wept. Only one person left on my list.

"Hello, Zawne."

"You're still up too?" he asked.

"Yeah. I can't sleep with all this turmoil."

I struggled to hold back my emotion. Going through with becoming a Min meant I would probably never touch Zawne again, never taste his lips, never smell his musk. *Will he let me slip back into his life?* I wondered if it was how Lordin had felt, if she had felt anything. I still wasn't totally convinced she was evil. I asked Zawne, "Did you hear the news about Emell?"

He nodded, twisted his face in a grimace. "It's hard to believe my dead fiancée's mother was arrested on suspicion of planned genocide. I hope it's not true. I only met the woman once at Lordin's funeral, but she seemed okay. I can't believe someone like Lordin, someone so divine, would have been raised by a murderer."

I suddenly felt bad for doubting Zawne, thinking he was somehow involved in the KS3 mess. His eyes were too sincere to be lying. I knew in that instant he had nothing to do with Emell's plotting. It gave me hope that Lordin was innocent too.

"It's not important now," I said. "I just wanted to say good night."

Or goodbye, I thought. *Goodbye forever, my sweet king. I must make this ultimate sacrifice for the good of our people. It's what Mama would have done.*

"Good night, Kaelyn," he said. Zawne blew me a kiss through the screen. I caught it, and tears spilled down my face.

"I'm going to miss you in my dreams," I said. It felt like my heart was being ripped in half. I could feel shards of glass tearing through my body, wrecking me until I quivered and lost my breath. Things had been so much easier three years ago, following Roki blindly through the pretend market. Why did Geniverd's salvation have to fall on me? Why couldn't I just have my happy ending?

"I'll miss you too," Zawne said, and he ended the call. No one had any idea what I had planned.

* * *

IT WAS difficult to keep my eyes closed for all the tears spilling out of them. I didn't think I had cried so much in my life, yet this decision was immense. I had said goodbye to my friends, to everyone I had ever loved, and when I awoke, I would face a terrible demise. I took a deep breath, hugged my blanket tight, and spelled Shiol over my heart.

"Welcome, Kaelyn," Riedel said as I materialized in the void. "We have been waiting for you. We've listened to your heart, and we understand you have made the decision."

"To become a Min," Hanchell said, visibly excited from the way her light pulsed.

"I have no choice," I told them. "If I don't find the cure for the virus right away, over two million people will die. I can't let that happen. I will gladly forsake my human life to save the lives of others."

"Which is why we made you queen," Riedel said. He seemed cheerful for once. I thought he had a soft spot for me and was glad to see me doing the right thing, the truly right-eous thing.

"Do you suspect the cure is already made?" Hanchell asked.

"Yes." I nodded. "I'm sure Emell is waiting until the very last second to send it out. She probably had it made at the same time she engineered the virus. She must have it stored in a secret location. As a Min, I'll be able to read her thoughts and discover the location, thereby preventing millions of innocent deaths."

I thought Hanchell's electric light was smiling. "You are smart for a human," she said. "Now let me give you some prep before we do this. You will wake up to a horrible death. There is no way around it. Next, you will be a formless Min. You will experience an intense desire to occupy a human body, but be careful. There are two options for occupying bodies. You may either occupy the body for its entire life span, or just long enough to complete a task given to you by us. Upon completion of the task, you will exit the body, and they will have no idea you were ever there. The human thinks they are in control, but really, they're just on a very intense roller coaster. In the case of a long-term body possession, the human will take a kind of back seat in their own mind. It's like your friend Roki. His body's owner is dormant while Roki works missions for us and does whatever fun things Min do in Geniverd."

"You think you can handle that?" Riedel asked.

"Got it," I said. "What happens if I break the rules, like if I disobey a direct order or give away the Great Secret?"

"Death," Riedel said. "The Seeing Water will see to it personally."

"Who's the Seeing Wa—?"

"The universe does not deserve the mercy shown by the Seeing Water. We'll tell you more later," Hanchell said. "Time is of the essence. Go back to your bed. A Min will take possession of an undercover Gurnot working alongside you in the council. They will assassinate you upon waking."

"It's going to be brutal," Riedel said. "Prepare yourself. Pain is temporary. The sacrifice you're making is eternal."

* * *

IT HAPPENED FAST. I dissolved out of Shiol and opened my eyes to pitch-blackness. It must have been two in the morning. I figured I had twenty-six hours left to save the species. Realistically though, I only had another two hours before the death toll began to peak and spiral out of control. I briefly thought, *Wait, aren't I supposed to be murdered?*

I tried to get out of bed, and that was when I noticed Torio standing above me with a snarl. He wore all black and looked terrifyingly evil.

"Tori—oh!"

He had a rope around my neck and was strangling me. Torio had one foot on the edge of the bed for leverage, tugging the rope so its rough fibers chafed my skin. He was strangling me to death!

My instincts took over. I tried to pry the rope from around my throat, coughing and gagging as Torio shook me out of bed and threw me onto the floor. Then he stood over me as he screamed, "I've waited my whole life for this!" Torio was insane, bloodthirsty, and violent. "I want to look in your eyes as you die, Kaelyn!" He cackled, tightened the rope, and watched me squirm.

In that moment, I wished I could take it all back. I had never known such agony or fear. My eyes felt like balloons ready to pop, my teeth sank into my bloody tongue. And Torio, so crazed. His saliva dribbled onto my face as he strangled me.

"Not yet," he said. He got up, seemingly lost or confused. "No, not here. Not like this."

I managed to say, "Gur ... not."

"Yes," he said as he snatched me by the hair and dragged me toward the kitchen. I kicked and groaned but couldn't scream. My throat had been crushed, and I could hardly take a breath. How could someone hurt a person so brutishly?

"I have been a Gurnot my whole life," Torio said, dumping me on the floor by the stove. "I've been feeding my associates information ever since I became Head of Courtiers. I hate the establishment. And I hate you!"

There was a frying pan on the cooker. It was red hot. He picked it up, grabbed a hunk of my hair, and pressed the hot pan against the side of my face.

"Yeo-o-o-ow!"

It was like ice and fire all at once. It burned like nothing I had ever felt before, and I had to remember what the Crown of Crowns had said: *Pain is temporary.*

But it hurt! Tears pooled in my eyes, the smell of singed flesh, burnt hair, and Torio's maniacal laughter. He tossed aside the pan and let me drop to the floor, where I writhed in agony, my throat muscles crushed, half my face melted off. "E —" I tried. "End it."

Torio laughed. "Gladly."

He pulled a pistol from his waistband and shot me in the head.

I didn't want to hate Torio for what he had done, but it was hard not to hate someone who had just murdered me. I floated out of my body and lingered, ghostly, below the kitchen ceiling. There I lay, the back of my head busted open, with fragments of hair and brain splattered over the kitchen floor like broken eggs. And there was Torio, seething above my bloodied corpse.

Had he really wanted to kill me the whole time we had known each other? All the smiles, the good advice, the late-night talks of politics, and all the while, he had fantasized about murdering me. I was surprised when he put the gun to his temple and blew his brains out.

Torio's body slumped over mine. It was very much a murder-suicide.

It was then I realized I was floating. But I wasn't in a body. I didn't even really have eyes. It was difficult to comprehend. I appeared to be a shapeless cloud the color of fire, like a fist-sized ember. I looked like the auras of the spirits I'd once seen in Shiol. I felt hollow, weightless. I drifted listlessly, wondering how I hadn't realized Torio was a Gurnot. It seemed obvious now. Then some part of me, like a third, invisible arm, reached into Torio's fading brain to find the truth.

I didn't know how I did it, but I did. I had accessed a library of Torio's memories, and they were cascading in front of me: him as a child playing in the river, him as a teenager sulking through the halls of his high school, him in a vast complex I had never seen, surrounded by men I didn't know—Gurnots, perhaps—and his most recent memory, my own face seen through his eyes, ugly and frightened as he choked me.

"Bleak," I said, and rid myself of the images. I didn't want to watch my own death through the eyes of my murderer.

I figured memory snatching was my special gift. Roki had told me that every Min received one. I'd just seen Torio at different stages of his life too—his image, perceived character, height, and shape. That meant I might be able to witness some past events related to the memories I'd be viewing. *Pretty cool,* I thought. *It'll help me find the KS3 cure even faster.*

And that was when the urge shocked me. I felt an inexplicable desire to slip into a human shell. It was like an extreme thirst. I wanted to wriggle into my headless body, even into Torio's warm corpse, slither into it like it was a sleeping bag. I seriously considered it.

"It's dead," came a voice from behind me.

I whirled my fiery spirit cloud around and saw a thin woman standing, translucent, on the kitchen floor. She, too, had a small red cloud, only hers lived inside her chest. "What?" I asked her.

"I see you eyeing that dead body," she said. "Trust me, it's not nearly as fulfilling as a live human. Obviously, you're new. It's nice to see a baby Min!"

Oh no! It was my murderer! It was the Min sent to kill me.

Yet … she didn't strike me as evil. She seemed more aloof than anything. I asked her, "Why did you have to kill Torio too? He was innocent … kind of."

"Oh," she said, "I didn't. I had already detached myself from him. The poor Gurnot shot himself out of guilt. I guess he didn't hate you as much as he thought."

"You could have stopped him!"

She laughed. "Silly baby Min. I don't have time for that. Don't worry, you'll shed your human feelings with time. Give it a few hundred years."

If I'd had eyes, I would have glowered at the wicked Min. She came across as mindless, like a dopey spirit floating casually through existence. It wasn't at all how Roki was, even though Roki was five hundred years old. I poked around in her memories, curious how long she had been alive. I found a barrage of images dating way back, machines and cities I didn't even recognize.

"Hey," she said, "I can feel you poking around in there." Then she laughed. "What a cool talent."

"Sorry." I was embarrassed. I hadn't thought she'd feel it.

"No worries," she said. "You were just testing your new power. It was like a tickle in my brain. I didn't even realize at first. But it's cool. Actually, I'm kind of jealous."

"Why? What's your power?"

She shrugged. "It's kind of lame. Basically, I can turn into a cat whenever I want. Sometimes I become a cat, and I just lounge around in the sun for weeks. I've become … very catlike."

"Ah," I said. It explained her weird attitude. "Why can't I read your mind?" I asked. "I thought Min can read minds."

"Only the minds of humans," she told me. "Min are sheltered from being read by other Min. We can think all the naughty thoughts we want."

I willed my cloud into the shape of a thumbs-up and said, "Good to know." It meant Roki couldn't read my thoughts anymore.

And that was when it hit me for the first time. Roki and I were both Min. He was already five hundred years old, which meant we could theoretically be together for ... another five hundred years! That would be one heck of a relationship.

"Anyway," the Min said, "I've got to go."

"Wait!" I floated my burning cloud closer to her. "One more question. What am I? What is this cloud I am in?"

She giggled. "It's your Valer. Only Min have a Valer. It's how you'll be able to tell the difference between Min and humans."

"Wow," I said. "Thanks. That's incredible."

She waved and floated out of the room, and I called after her, "Thank you for killing me."

* * *

I SLIPPED through an open window and took to the skies. I moved faster than the fastest rocket known to man. Yet I couldn't concentrate. I had to stop in the middle of some fluffy white clouds and think about where I should go.

Emell's house felt like the safest bet. It was still the middle of the night, which was convenient, because I hoped to float over her body and suck out her memories while she slept, though I didn't understand how anyone could sleep while they deliberately killed thousands of people. I thought back to Lordin's funeral, remembering the exact location of the place. Then I was zipping across the bruised sky at lightning speed. I arrived at Emell's estate in less than a minute.

But now what? Could I float through the ceiling? Could I move through walls? I tried but it didn't work. I had to squeeze my fluffy cloud through a cracked window on the upper floor and then float slowly through the house. I followed the echo of voices to the ground floor, where I found Emell and Lordin—residing in Hagan's body—sitting in the study.

I knew it was Lordin, because I could see her red Valer suspended in Hagan's chest. Hagan even had a faint resemblance to Lordin—petite, cute, pale skin, and electric eyes. I flattened myself against the ceiling in the hallway and eavesdropped on their conversation.

"The death toll has reached three hundred thousand," Emell was saying. She looked very much like a supervillain in her smart black suit, her hands folded neatly on her mahogany desk. "Projections tell us it will have reached well over two million by the time we distribute the cure."

"It's a lot," Lordin said. She crinkled her eyebrows. "Is there nothing we can do to lessen the casualties? Wouldn't five hundred thousand, even six hundred thousand, be sufficient?"

Emell frowned at her. "You're sounding a lot like my daughter again. That's something Lordin would have said. She never did have the stomach for brutality. Lordin inherited too much of her father, his soft heart and his caring soul. Lordin did as she was told, but she did it with a corrupted conscience."

"Genocide is a serious business," Lordin said. "It would corrupt any person's conscience."

I didn't know if it was my newly heightened senses as a Min, but in that moment, I had a clear vision of the relationship between mother and daughter. I could sense Emell's untamed fury and Lordin's apprehensive nature. Lordin wasn't a heartless monster, but her mother sure was. I dreaded what I might find in either of their memory banks.

"It's not genocide, anyway," Emell said. "It's just a bit of culling. We're trimming the population, encouraging war, disrupting the seat of power, humiliating Kaelyn and Zawne. It's everything we've been working for."

Lordin nodded. She seemed unimpressed by the whole thing, as if it was beneath her. Then she said, "My informers have told me that Krug is considering siding with Nurlie against the islanders and the Surrvul rebels. If the fighting continues, Shondur will undoubtedly follow. They are still upset about the phosphorus situation. After Shondur, we can expect Lodden to send the elite Aska warriors into battle. The Gurnots will get involved. I predict a world war within two months. Every clan's secret ambitions will explode into the open. It will be all-out chaos."

"Excellent." Emell interlocked her fingers and leaned over the table, giving Lordin a death stare. "We just need to rid ourselves of the underwater weapons system. We must leave Gaard totally vulnerable while allowing them the illusion of power. When the world marches on the capital, I want Vond-Rust to burn for what they've done to me."

Did she mean for what the King Emeritus had done to her? Was Emell really that petty? I had a hard time believing she would secretly organize global warfare over such a thing. However, she had been banished to the north of Gaard for over half her life. Perhaps her anger and disdain had evolved over time in that frozen place, mutated into something toxic.

Then I thought, *What if Emell poisoned Lordin with her toxicity? Maybe Lordin isn't inherently evil. Maybe she was just corrupted by her own mama!*

Lordin said, "My technicians are working alongside some undercover Gurnots to disarm the underwater weapons system. Surrvul has provided funding. With all the money we've made from these mergers, we can now hire engineers to build our own weapons system. Gaard doesn't stand a chance."

Yes, they do, I thought. *I'll tell Zawne about your plan, and he'll put an end to this madness!*

"Excellent." Emell reclined in her chair, looking pleased with herself. "What about the cure? Why won't you tell me where you've hidden it, Hagan?"

"It's better you don't know," Lordin said, her eyes darting around the room as if she thought someone might be listening.

She was smart. I had to give her that. Lordin must have known no Min could read her mind, so even if a Min intervened and tried to stop the rampant deaths, they'd never discover the secret location of the cure.

"I will make the cure available for mass production the moment you give the word." Lordin hesitated, then said, "But the sooner the better."

"Hush!" Emell roared, face wrinkled in anger. Her eyes radiated hatred. "Stop it with your cowardice. You and Lordin would have been the best of pals. I've had to babysit you these past months like I had to babysit my daughter her whole life."

Lordin licked her lips and said nothing. Even I could see her anger mounting. It must have been hard to sit in front of her mama in a stranger's body and listen to such vile slander. How could Lordin stand it? What was her angle? I cringed when she bowed and said, "My apologies, Mistress Emell."

It was too wrenching to watch. Besides, I was wasting time. I needed to extract Lordin's memories and discover the location of the cure. It would be pointless to probe Emell. She knew nothing, only malice. Entering her head would be like plugging in to the mind of a murderous psychopath. I considered possessing her body. I could order Lordin to release the cure right away. But then I would be stuck in Emell's traitorous husk for the next forty or fifty years, and I didn't want that. I also didn't want VBione Corp to be labeled a hero for saving Geniverd from extinction. If anyone deserved to be labeled a hero, it was Raad or Zawne.

I let my new gift stretch away from me, like invisible tentacles, and reach into Lordin's memory bank. I was slightly worried Lordin would notice, but within seconds I was lost in a world of images and remembrances.

* * *

LORDIN WAS WRAPPED HEAVILY in furs. She was young, beautiful, just a girl. Her visage was as smooth as porcelain under her fur hood, squinting against the bright sun as she carried her suitcase across the snow-covered yard to the awaiting flyrarc.

"Wait!" Emell came running out of the house. "I must say goodbye, my daughter. This is a big opportunity for us. Through hard work and determination, you've been accepted to train under the Grucken. We won't see each other for a long time. Are you prepared?"

"Yes, Mama." Lordin nodded obediently. "I remember all your teachings. I will advance up the ranks until I've gained a reputation among the nobility of Geniverd."

"And you'll do this by publicizing your ascension through social media," Emell said. "Your story will rivet the masses. You'll be an inspiration to everyone who aspires to be more than a simple commoner. But above all ..."

"Keep my identity a secret," Lordin said. "I know, Mama. I can't let anyone know who I am. As far as the public is concerned, I am a nobody from Gaard. I am proficient in Decens-Lenitas, and through the Grucken's teachings, I will become revered."

"Exactly," Emell said. "We are not like the other upper-class dolts. Remember our hatred for the king and queen, for the rulers of Gaard. We work to destroy them. We must use Decens-Lenitas to our advantage, disguise our intent, and rise until we've taken over the throne. I am trusting you, daughter. I entrust you with my vengeance."

"I won't let you down," Lordin said. "I will mask my intent, cover the secret of my heart, and one day—"

"Topple the king and queen, and seize power!" Emell said, fist raised to the winter sky. She looked mad even then, bent on domination and ruin.

Lordin hugged her mama goodbye and boarded the flyrarc. She sat by the window and watched as they ascended above Gaard's northern Gilfoil Mountains, looking down at the rural estate Emell had been banished to all those years ago, a small outpost amid the frozen wilderness. Lordin looked down at Emell and smiled to herself.

And then she was gone, soaring over the rolling hills of snow to meet the Grucken.

* * *

LORDIN PEEKED through the stage curtain. It was a full house. The Grucken was onstage, giving his address to a batch of newly anointed Aska warriors. Jaken and Raad were among them, and in the front row of the crowd was Zawne.

"This is it," Emell said. She rubbed her hands together. There was no one except her and Lordin backstage during the Grucken's speech. "This is your chance to shine, daughter. All these years with the Grucken, and finally some face time in front of the nobility. And just at the right moment. I've begun acquiring small chemical companies and medicine manufacturers. I'm in negotiations with a lab technician and a gene specialist to begin preparation of the virus. No one has any clue what they're participating in. They think it's research."

"That's nice," Lordin said. "You've worked hard."

Emell scoffed, "Harder than you know, child. Anyway, who do you see out there in the crowd?"

"A lot of people," Lordin said. She was older than in the last memory, a beautiful young woman ripe in all the right places. "I see Prince Zawne, Heir Shirpo of Surrvul, Heir Raad of Gaard, Heir Zolo of Krug. There must be ten male heirs in the front row."

"And each for your taking," Emell said, still rubbing her palms deviously. "I suggest you focus on Zawne. He's ambitious, like his pigheaded papa. With Zawne, you might have a chance at the top. Even Jaken is a good choice, yet he is an Aska and strong willed. Zawne will be easier to control. The truth is, daughter, either of the king's children will do nicely. I want the former queen and the former king to feel pain beyond this world when we dispose of one of their sons. Then you will be on the throne with me by your side. They will grow sick from despair!"

"Yes, Mama."

Lordin still peeked through the curtain, her eyes on Zawne. Anyone could have seen his potential, his positive energy. No one would have suspected a hardened Aska warrior would grow out of him, then later a king.

* * *

LORDIN WAS AT LITHERN SHRINE, Zawne propelling himself down to her in his modified flyrarc like an action hero.

"You came," she said. "It's six in the morning. I wasn't sure you'd come this early."

"I couldn't resist," said Zawne, a fish-eating grin on his face.

"Now that you're here," Lordin said, "let's take a walk through the gardens and get to know each other."

The date sped by in blips and flashes, scenes of tea drinking and subtle flirting. Then they were in the hidden room at the back of Lithern Shrine, Lordin caressing the smooth varnish of the Grucken's piano. "Can you play?" she asked Zawne.

"Oh, yeah. Can you?"

"Yes." Lordin sat on the stool and lifted the lid of the keyboard. "Shall we compose a song together?"

Zawne beamed. "Yes, an original score that only the two of us will know." His excitement was palpable. By the glazed look in his eyes, the sparkling affection in Lordin's face, it was clear the two were already in love.

"I'll start." Lordin softly stroked the keys, beginning a gentle melody for Zawne to sing to.

"When I soar, we soar," he sang, the music trickling through the room.

Then Lordin came in. "I soar; we soar."

"I never yield; we never yield."

"We are forever one."

The music was reaching a crescendo, Lordin's tiny fingers flittering across the keys as Zawne sang, "I soar; we soar, my love. I never yield; we never yield, my love."

Lordin stopped playing, and the chamber fell silent. Zawne blinked at her. "Hey, what'd you do that for?"

"The lyrics," she said. "They're powerful. How did you think of them?"

"It's how I imagine we will be in the future," Zawne said. "Together we will soar above the masses as the rulers of Geniverd. We will never yield for any man or kingdom or army. We will reach the heavens with our power and our love."

Lordin's eyes grew wide. "Do you mean it?" She appeared dazzled by the idea, so excited she started to shake. "Do you really think we could rule the kingdom together?"

Zawne chuckled. "Of course," he said. "You are practically the new Grucken. The Crown of Crowns will surely pick you, no matter who your husband is. And I'm the son of the current rulers. My knowledge of politics and the six continents is greater than any of the other heirs'. We'd be unstoppable together."

Lordin wrapped her arms around Zawne, nearly choking him. "Then let us be together," she said, her facial muscles twitching as if two different emotions were battling for control. Her jaw trembled, lips quivered, and tears bubbled at the corners of her eyes. She looked elated and terrified all at once. "Let's be together," she repeated. "I want you, Zawne. I want to be your queen."

* * *

LORDIN'S MEMORIES fast-forwarded in a colorful blur, slowing and coming to a halt in Shiol, the axis of the universe.

Lordin was speaking with the light forms Hanchell and Riedel. The Crown of Crowns was telling her, "But you must make the decision soon. Either become queen alongside Zawne, or perish and become a Min."

Lordin looked more serious than in any of the other memories. She looked like a person who had just been told the universe was run by spirits. She asked them, "And you say Min are free to roam Geniverd and do as they please, that Min can possess bodies?"

"Yes," Riedel said, "but this isn't an invitation to become all-powerful. This is a serious choice you must make. Rule Geniverd with Zawne, or live a thousand years as a Min."

Lordin's jaw had dropped. She licked her lips. "Let me think about it." But judging by the look on her face, she had already decided.

"I'll tell you honestly, I'm not sure if Zawne has the heart to be king. I might have to refuse your offer to protect him from his own failure. I don't want to become a Min, but I may have to. I mean, it would suck to give up my short human existence to become a spirit with superpowers and live for a thousand years with complete and total power over Geniverd." She shrugged and shook her head sadly. "But I might have to do it."

"The choice is yours," Hanchell said. "You've scored the best out of anyone we've seen in a long time. And not only in Geniverd. We rule multiple universes, dimensions, realms … and you are one of the most virtuous and kindhearted creatures we have ever seen. In any case, you'd do well as a Min."

"And you mentioned something about an election," Lordin said. "Am I to believe there is a way to move up the universal ladder?"

"Yes," Hanchell said. She wasn't very intuitive for an omnipotent, universe-controlling spirit. Either that, or perhaps Lordin had used the Grucken's spiritual teachings to disguise the rotten part of her heart. Her intentions seemed pretty obvious. "Soon," Hanchell continued, "there will be a chance to become the next Crown of Crowns. It's only for Min with a partner."

Lordin nodded. "Okay, great. Good to know." She was nearly salivating at the thought of all that power, the chance to rule a limitless galaxy. "I'll give you my answer tomorrow," she said.

* * *

EVIL!

I paused the memory show and scowled at Lordin, hiding so shamelessly in Hagan's body. She had wanted power. She had killed herself to become a Min. I could see it now. I could see it so clearly. Lordin may have loved Zawne, but she loved power more. She had thirsted for it her whole life thanks to the influence of her wretched mama. And now she was tearing the world apart to help Emell exact her revenge. But why? What was her scheme? Surely Lordin wanted something of her own.

Then I heard Emell say, "And once you, Hagan, are savior of the world, we will blame the tragic loss of life on Kaelyn of Gaard. She'll be cast out like I was, leaving Zawne lonely and hurt. Zawne is weak. We'll pull some strings to get the Queen's Council disbanded, then maneuver you onto Zawne's new council using your well-earned title as Hero of Geniverd. It won't take much for you to seduce the heartbroken king once you're seeing him every day."

Emell laughed, spun her chair in a circle, and cried, "And then you will install me as your most loyal adviser!"

If I had been in possession of a body, I would have gasped. It all made sense. Emell had put the pieces together for me. Sure, Lordin had killed herself to become a powerful Min and chase after the Crown of Crowns' position. But in the meantime, she wanted to reclaim her place as Zawne's wife.

She really did love him, I supposed. She had fought her way from the frozen northlands to the capital, to Zawne's bedchamber, then died. Within two years of her death, Lordin had helped Emell organize a plan that would plunge the world into chaos, all so that she could find her way back to Zawne's bedchamber while at the same time securing her mama's approval. Her resolve was astounding. Lordin was diabolical!

I had to see more. I slipped back inside Lordin's memories …

And was instantly viewing the night of her murder. Lordin's body lay cold on the walkway outside VondRust Palace. Her Valer floated above the path, the murderer standing stunned below. He looked a lot like Torio had in the moments after he had murdered me: lost, confused, stricken by what he had done. A Min must have possessed Lordin's killer and then fled, leaving him vacant and afraid.

Something bizarre happened. Much as I had accidentally experimented with my new gift, so too did Lordin. She formed her Valer into a little flaming hand and reached for the killer. He shrieked, but she wasn't touching him. She merely pointed at him.

"Bees!" he screamed, gripping both sides of his head. "The bees are everywhere! The bees killed Lordin!"

The man ran off into the night, ranting about Ava-Surrvul Askas. I didn't get it. I had to seriously think for a minute before it came to me. *Oh*, I realized. *That's great. Lordin must have altered his reality, made him think bees had killed her, instead of letting him live with the awful truth of being a murderer.*

It was a nice gesture on her part to save the man the emotional anguish of being a killer. But how was I supposed to battle Lordin if she could distort reality? All I could do was view memories and some of their past!

I had been so distracted by my wandering thoughts that I hadn't noticed Lordin get up and move into the hallway, and now she was watching me. Lordin stood right under me, eyes fixed on my flaming Valer, cursing me silently with her wrathful stare.

16

I flew away. I zipped down the hall, squeezed under the front door, and took to the skies. My mind was racing. It seemed like every hour I was bombarded with new and disturbing information. Now I had Lordin's elaborate history to dwell on, the innocent girl twisted into a power-hungry lunatic. Plus she was still in love with my Zawne! There was Lordin's ability to twist reality to consider. If that was the case ...

The photos!

I stopped midflight, hovering somewhere above the ocean. If Lordin could change reality, it meant she could have shown me falsified photos of Roki with other women. It meant I had lashed out at him for no reason, calling him a creepy Min when he was anything but. It made sense now that I knew the whole story. I had been the queen after all, and Zawne's wife. Lordin couldn't have allowed me to continue consorting with a Min. It could have ruined her plan.

Worst of all, I was nowhere nearer to finding the cure for the virus. Lordin must have disguised her memory of its location as a fail-safe against memory thieves. She really was prepared, much more than I was.

I decided to fly to Nurlie. It was the only move I had left. My plan was to find Roki, beg for his forgiveness, and ask him to help me save the world. I could only hope that he would forgive me.

* * *

ROKI WAS EASY TO FIND. I could sense the other Min and see their fiery Valers from a substantial distance. They were like little red beacons, pulsing more brightly the closer I got. But even without the Valers, I could smell Roki's toffee odor. I followed it to the scene of a great battle, Tomenistin, the port town that connected mainland Nurlie to the island.

P5 Protectors had made a wall of armor against the rebel forces, blockading the government building against the mob of angry, laser-toting Gurnots, Surrvul rebels, and island forces. It was hard to believe the agitators had crossed the water and reached the mainland, and that Tomenistin was now under siege. The whole place was on fire. I wondered if the supposed Gurnot Dragon from the news reports was among the attackers.

"Roki," I said, flying down to where he had pulled a family from a smoking apartment building.

He turned at the sound of my voice, then gasped when he saw my Valer. "Kaelyn, you're a Min!"

"And you're a hero," I said. "How many people have you saved today?"

He sighed and said, "Not nearly enough."

The family Roki had saved were scampering off down the sidewalk. They hadn't even thanked him. All they wanted was to escape the fighting, the laser beams, the desperate cries of the injured.

"If you want to stop millions more from dying," I said, feeling out of breath even though I had no lungs, "I suggest you help me. I know Lordin's got the cure, but I don't know where she's hidden it. Will you help me search?"

Roki didn't so much as blink. "Of course," he said. "Let's start looking. We can go right now."

I had a sensation of crying—again, even though I had no eyes. I rammed my little fire cloud against Roki's, which lived in his chest, and reveled in the sensation of our two spirit bodies rubbing together. It was like a hug, only euphoric and titillating. It was two balls of electricity warming each other with ethereal static. I wanted to stay like that forever.

And that was when I cried to him, "I'm so sorry!" I couldn't help it. I felt even more emotional as a Min. "I'm sorry that I didn't believe you. I thought you were bad." And even without a face, I felt wet with tears. "You were always the best thing that ever happened to me, Roki. Even after I was a total jerk, you still agreed to help me without another thought. You truly are amazing."

Roki laughed, which was weird to see, because his face was sooty and everywhere around us the world was burning. "I always thought you might return. I never lied to you, Kaelyn, but I can understand where your anger came from. I learned about Lordin's gift shortly after our little incident in Shiol, so I knew why you had freaked out. I just figured I would respect your wishes and wait it out." Then he squinted at me. "But how did you find out about her gift?"

"Oh," I said, "I forgot to mention, I can siphon memories from people and Min alike."

"Whoa!" Roki's eyebrows raised in an arc. "That's so cool! And pretty convenient, don't you think?"

"What do you mean?"

"Well, you became a Min just in time to find a secret cure that can stop millions of deaths. Your power is to steal memories, which will help us to find the cure. And me, because of my power to mask presences, we can fly around the world unseen and look at memories without anyone knowing."

"It's almost as if ..."

"The Crown of Crowns has known all along," he finished. "You and I are destined to be a team."

"But that would mean they knew what was going to happen years and years and years ago."

"Yes," Roki said with a smile. "Those guys ... I don't know if we give them enough credit. They may seem kind of blank and robotic, but they know what's going on."

"Incredible." I was at a loss. I had thought the Crown of Crowns was half at fault for this whole mess. Could it be that they had designed everything, that it was all part of some grand scheme?

"We should go," Roki said. "People are dying by the second. We must find the cure."

"And I need to find a body," I told him. "I feel itchy all over. I feel hungry, thirsty, and in great need of a human host."

"We can do it in Gaard," Roki said. "We'll find someone who looks like you, the same age and everything."

"Okay, but I'd like to find someone who's about to die from the virus. That way, at least I'll be saving a life ... kind of."

"Deal," Roki said with a nod.

"One more thing, Roki. I'm ... I'm a little scared of Lordin. She caught me probing her mind. Do you think she'll come after me?"

"No," he said. "Lordin has fully occupied Hagan's body. It means if she uses her Valer to fly, people would be able to see a human soaring through the sky. It's too risky. I can move across space at huge speeds because of my ability to mask myself. I'm invisible when I choose it. But Lordin and the other Min occupying human bodies have to travel the same as ordinary humans. Flyrarcs, trains, buses, cars, boats. That is, unless they're certain that no human being can see them."

"Good to know," I said. I felt safer knowing Lordin couldn't easily show up unannounced and warp our realities.

"Now let's go get me a body!"

* * *

A YOUNG GIRL lay dying in her hospital bed. She was easy to find—the dead were everywhere. She was about twenty years old. She had a shade of skin like mine, and it was warm and soft. Roki and I hovered above her body, admiring her.

"What do you think?" he asked.

"It's sad," I said. "It's sad and horrific that these people are dying when a cure is being withheld. I hate that I have to do this, but I'd rather occupy a dying girl than a healthy one. Uh ... how do I do it?"

"Ease into her," he said. "Lower your Valer into her chest, wrap around her heart, then spread throughout her body. It'll just take a second."

I lowered myself into the girl's chest cavity, immediately feeling her weakness and closeness to death. I caressed her heart, let my spirit flow into her veins, spread into her limbs, into her mind. Then I felt life bloom anew. Her sickness shed, and I opened the girl's eyes.

"Wow!" I sat upright, checked out my new hands, touched my new legs. I leaped out of bed and ran to the bathroom mirror. I felt alive, totally electric. It was like being in the best mood ever, a little drunk, and on the verge of a great pleasure. "This is amazing," I said, poking myself in the face. It was insane to see through someone else's eyes, yet I felt like myself. I felt powerful.

"Do you like it?" Roki asked.

"I absolutely love it!" I turned to face him, Roki grinning in the doorway. He had washed most of the soot from his face and looked handsome, rugged, like a lean street fighter.

"Good." Roki came and put his arm around me. The sensation was a thousand jolts, and I leaned into him, rubbing my face against his cheek like a cat just to feel the tingly warmth. For a second, I forgot all about our mission. I wanted to explore my new sensations and my newly mended friendship with Roki.

But then I remembered. I broke away from Roki and shouted, "Now let's go save the world!"

* * *

"Lordin's a dead end," I said as we hovered above the hospital. "She can distort reality, which probably includes her memories. Plus she's dangerous. We need another way. We need to figure out where she would have hidden the cure."

"We need a clue," Roki said.

"Exactly. We need a clue, but from where?"

"What about Zawne?" Roki asked. "Could Lordin have told Zawne of a secret place, a place so special she would feel safe hiding the cure there?"

"It's worth a shot," I said. "And you don't mind going to see him? I mean, he was the other man. Uh, maybe you were the other man. Either way …"

Roki gently touched my shoulder. "I understand your love for Zawne. He was your husband, Kaelyn. Of course you will always have feelings for him. On the other hand, we have centuries to be together. I'm not jealous. Now come on, we have lives to save."

Roki led the way, the two of us streaking across the sky like comets. I kept thinking how lucky I was to have met Roki when I did. He was handsome, caring, unfazed by my craziness. He pulled people from burning buildings and fought to save lives. It was more than Zawne had ever done. Still, Zawne was my love too. Only, he was also Lordin's love. I was finding it a bit tricky to figure out who belonged to who.

I couldn't dwell on it. We arrived at VondRust and snuck in through the back door while Roki masked our presence. We found Zawne in his apartment. He was on a call with ... Raad!

"I understand your reasoning," Zawne said. His eyes were red and puffy. Raad's were too. It was five o'clock in the morning, and they must have just discovered my body. "It's just, I think that, as queen, she should be buried in the royal crypt behind VondRust."

"She should be buried next to our mother at her home," Raad said into the screen. He was more imposing than Zawne. Both were Aska warriors, but my brother had been a warrior even before the training. He was stern and unflinching before the king. "Should you take my sister's corpse from us, there will be consequences, Zawne."

"You can't threaten me," Zawne said. "I am your king!"

Raad laughed. "Not if the Gurnots tear you limb from limb. If the fighting keeps up, you know damn well there will be war. If you spit on Kaelyn's memory now, Gaard will remember. Gaard never forgets."

Zawne sighed. He seemed stripped of life, empty, like he had been after Lordin's death. It must have been a crushing blow for him. Both his loves had perished. Zawne was the only human left to carry the secret of Shiol.

"I loved your sister," Zawne said. "I loved her with all my soul. You and I will work out her burial. I'm sorry to snap at you. It's just ... it's just so devastating."

Raad softened. He looked to be holding back tears. "I understand," he said. "If it wasn't for my Aska training, I'd be in ruins. I'd be on the floor with a bottle of rum."

"Me too."

The two men lingered silently on each other's screens. The sorrow was full and sweaty, making them appear damp. Zawne surely knew I was a Min, that I wasn't gone for good. But Raad didn't. His heart was shattered to pieces.

"There's something you can do for her," Raad said to Zawne. "Emell, Lordin's mother, she murdered Mama. We need an investigation. We must check her alibi, do DNA samples, and review all P2 footage from that day and the previous week. We need proof for an arrest."

"I'll handle it," Zawne said with a sigh. He didn't seem shocked. I wondered why. Maybe Zawne was too defeated to care.

"I have to go," Raad said. "Papa is bleeping on the other line. This news will devastate him."

Oh no, I thought. *Not Papa. His heart can't take it! I feel like such a fool!*

Roki took hold of my arm. He had been right. Even without reading my mind, Roki knew my thoughts. "It'll be okay," he said. "We'll find a way to keep you in their lives."

"How?" I asked. Zawne had ended the call and was lying on his sofa, blinking at the ceiling like a zombie. "Tell me how, Roki. I can't leave them like this!"

"We'll have to figure it out later," he said. "I'm sorry, Kaelyn, but we have a mission to complete. You need to get inside Zawne's mind while I keep our presence masked. Rummage through his memories. Find the clue."

"All right," I said. But I was extremely distraught. Seeing Raad's teary eyes, hearing him talk about Papa, about my burial—it had jarred me.

I tried to relax. I took a deep breath, stretched out my gift, and drifted into Zawne's memories.

a lifetime flashed by, the life of a royal boy grown into a man. I couldn't slow to watch Zawne's younger memories. It was as if my instincts had control over my power. They guided me to a dusky night on the beach, Zawne standing before his commander as his Aska training began.

"This is not a physical test," boomed the authoritative voice of Zawne's commander, a hulk of a man nearly seven feet tall. "This is not an athletic sprint to the finish line. This is not a day at the beach. This, men, is the greatest battle you will ever wage against your minds."

The commander, a man named Thun, paused to let the gravity of his words wash over the two dozen men gathered on the dusky shore. "Your mind will tell you to stop. The pain will be severe. The stress, the fatigue, the agony—they will destroy you. Your mind will beg for release. Your body will beg for reprieve. You will have none. The desert will burn you. The starkness of the ocean will swallow you. The traitorous brain in your skull will trick you. There is no way to overcome. Here, there is only suffering. There is only pain. Should you balk beneath it, you will die."

Thun paused, massive black waves breaking against the shore behind the nervous recruits. The air smelled of seaweed and driftwood. Zawne listened to Thun impassively. He already looked dead, unfearful of any pain, for there could be no pain greater than the loss of love.

"There will be no special treatment here," Thun said. He was looking at Zawne, at the spoiled prince. "Should you choose to wade into these waters, you will either die or overcome. There is no rescue. Your visins have been deactivated. There will be no calling for help, no food being delivered, no paths to guide you. All you have is your team and your pain. I suggest you embrace them both. Value your teammates, for without them you will die. Value your pain, for if you cannot embrace it, you will die."

Thun paused, puffed out his chest, and stared into each of the twenty-four recruits' scared faces. "Some of you are boys. You will probably die. Some of you are men. You, too, will probably die. The sharks will rip you to shreds. The leopards will chew on your bones. The hyenas will laugh at you in the night when you feel most hopeless. Should you give up, you will die of starvation and be stripped bare by the desert winds. Should you somehow make it to Lodden, the training will likely break you."

"I can't do it!" screamed one of the men. He dropped to his knees and shrieked, "Let me go home. I don't want to die here!"

Thun walked to the boy, glared down at him as he groveled in the sand. "Go," Thun said. "Go home, child. Congratulations, you've just cost your team a man."

The boy ran, scuttled through the sand and vanished into the night.

"Anyone else?" Thun asked. Again he was looking at Zawne. "If anyone wishes to leave, now is the time. Once you set foot in the water, you are beyond my help. You are forsaken to the wild and its untamed dangers. You are stripped bare, nothing but your rags and your packs to carry with you, nothing but your bones and loose teeth to be lost to the sands. As everyone knows, the route to Lodden is a no-go zone. Tech doesn't work. Drones don't fly. Flyrarcs are prohibited. Only over the next few months will you understand the meaning of loneliness."

No one said a word. Zawne was pensive. He doubted Thun's words. Zawne was thinking he could never be more alone than he was in that moment.

"These are your maps." Thun walked along the line of recruits and handed every fourth man a paper map. "This is your guide. You have no technology, nothing but this map to point you toward Lodden. You will first cross the Ganga Sea. All twenty-three of you will share the small raft over there." Thun pointed to a rickety platform of logs bound together by rope, a limp cloth sail on its shoddy mast. It didn't look big enough for a group of four, never mind twenty-three. There were six thin wooden panels affixed to rings on the edges.

"Some of you will die before this raft reaches Surrvul. Without working together, you will all die. The sun, the salt water, the harsh cold of the night, the elements to ravage your body. If you slip your toes into the water, you will likely be eaten by a shark. You have no fire. You have no water. It's one week of paddling to reach Surrvul's shore and the small cache of water placed ahead of your arrival. It will be your only mercy."

The men glanced at each other nervously, then glanced at the raft. No one said it, but they were clearly terrified. Half of them had probably never been in the ocean before.

"When you reach Surrvul," Thun said, coming to a stop and folding his massive arms, "you must trek through the wasteland to the other side. This means the entire western portion of the Surrvul continent. There are no people. It's a no-man's-land. There are small rodents, snakes, sand scorpions, and antelope. You may eat what you catch, if you can catch anything. Upon making it to the channel that separates Surrvul and Lodden, you must push your weary bodies across its shark-infested depths. In Lodden, you will begin the real training."

Everyone kept quiet.

"Bolster your thoughts," Thun said. "Steady your focus. Harden yourself. Brace for pain. When the pain comes, let it fill you. That's what being an Aska is about, accepting pain and using it as a tool. Should you cross this treacherous course and complete your training, you will be the most formidable of men, able to carry any burden and weather any storm. You will be greatly honored in our society and have far-reaching opportunities."

Thun nodded. "That's it. Your boat awaits. Upon reaching Surrvul, you'll split into groups of four and work together to survive. Good luck, men."

No one moved. Thun watched them with his arms folded. He had finished his pep talk and would offer no further assistance. It was only when the silence deepened into an inescapable dread that Zawne left the line, determination black in his eyes, and started for the boat.

The other men followed.

* * *

WITH MORNING CAME heat and dehydration. Six men rowed the crummy raft, Zawne included. He grunted and rowed with his mouth pinched. The current was strong in the ocean, and seventeen men lay in a pile in the center of the raft, half-naked, with their shirts tied around their heads as they chopped through the waves. They were sullen and grumpy, twisted into ugly contortions for the lack of available space. Mouths smooshed against shoulders, legs tangled in knots of limbs. And then someone screamed.

"Sharks!"

All around the raft were gray shark fins like arrowheads cutting through the water. Zawne kept rowing, his dull expression unchanged. But one of the other rowers lost his mind. "They're going to come onto the boat!" He took the paddle and tried to whack one of the passing sharks. The paddle smacked the water, and the man lost his balance and fell in.

There was a soft splash. A few bubbles rushed to the surface, then blood. Blood frothed around the exposed shark fins, and the man was gone.

Zawne shouted, "Someone take his spot! Keep rowing!"

* * *

FOUR DAYS later the twenty men left on board were very thirsty. There was no water. The sun beat down on them with unrelenting fury sixteen hours a day. The salt water had their lips cracked and dry, split and caked in blood. Zawne was deathly pale. So were the others. They were thirsty and lethargic and near death. They did what they had to in order to drink and stay alive. It was ugly.

* * *

THEY WASHED up on Surrvul's southern shore in the night, nineteen alive and one dead. Two of the recruits dragged the boy's corpse up the bank and into a patch of stark grass. "We should bury him," someone said.

Zawne shook his head. "There's no time. Anyway, we can't bury him deep enough without tools. The scavengers will get him."

The men looked unsure, glancing at each other with unease. They had survived the brutal week on the raft, and now they had to leave the dead boy on the beach to be eaten by vultures. In most Geniverd traditions, not burying the dead was bad luck.

"I'm with the prince," said a bald man. He was wiry and young, probably from Shondur, like Zawne. He stepped through the men and said, "We don't have time. Let's find the water cache left for us, rehydrate, then start walking. It's better to walk in the night and sleep in the heat of the day."

"What's your name?" Zawne asked him.

"Nkem," he said, "but it doesn't matter. We're all nobodies here, food for sand fleas. Let's make our teams and get off this beach. I'll team up with the prince."

Another man came forward. "Me too. My name is Stingl, and I'd like to join the prince and Nkem. If the rest of you want to waste your time with burials, go ahead."

"This is rubbish!" a man shouted. He steamed out of the crowd and picked up the dead kid's body. "At least see him off to sea. I'll give him a worthy Nurlie burial, but I won't leave him in the sand."

He took the kid in his arms and waded waist-deep into the water. The others watched as he let the body drift away on the current. He gave a salute and uttered some half-forgotten hymn under his breath. Then he started shouting.

"Ow! Hey, get away from me. Ow! What the ...?"

He struggled to shore, no one daring to jump in the water and help. He started up the bank and collapsed, twitching with spasms in the sand. Zawne and the others ran to check on him, and in the light of the moon, they could see pink and purple sores where jellyfish had stung him. He foamed at the mouth, seized, mumbled something, and died. His body was pink, and his veins distended from the jellyfish poison.

"Anyone else want to paddle?" Zawne asked. He received only silence as an answer. "All right. Let's get into groups and find that water. The desert awaits."

* * *

"FIVE THOUSAND MILES," Nkem said. It was dawn, and they were still walking, Nkem, Stingl, and Zawne. The others were mirages in the distance behind them, like wavering shadows following through the awakening scrubland. "Coast to coast, I mean. Five thousand miles from here to the north coast. It'll take us maybe eight months."

Stingl laughed. "Yeah, only eight months."

"It is nothing compared to a lifetime of discipline," Zawne said. "I remember when my brother, Jaken, returned home from his Aska training. He was the same man, but different. His emotions had cooled. He was sharply aware of everything. He seemed like a stronger person, someone still capable of love yet capable of great horrors. I saw a secret truth in his eyes, and the possession of this truth strengthened him and gave him purpose. That's what I seek in this desert. I seek truth and purpose."

"Deep, man," Stingl said.

But Nkem wasn't convinced. "You'll get truth all right, Prince. You'll get truth in the way of pain and misery like you wouldn't believe. Let's talk again after you've been stuck inside your own head for two straight months. That's the real torment. You, your thoughts, your regrets, your secret truths. Your mind will haunt you until you've gone insane."

Then Nkem laughed, raised his hands to the great dust plain and said, "Welcome to your doom, Prince. Welcome to the infinite horrors of your psyche."

Zawne shrugged it off. His pace was fast, but Nkem and Stingl kept up well. All three were fit and lean, made for desert walking. "Nothing can compare to the recent horror I've faced," Zawne said, "my wife being decapitated by a crazy groundskeeper. Lordin had given the world so much. She had given me so much! And some lunatic took it all away. The pain of this desert is nothing to me. The memory of Lordin will carry me through."

"Let's hope," Nkem said, "for all our sakes."

* * *

THEY SLEPT at high noon in the scanty shade of a cactus, and when they woke five hours later, the sun was a flare of death on the horizon. Nkem cut open the cactus, and they drank its milk. It was the only cactus they had seen thus far.

"I hope there's more of these," Stingl said. "I'm not sure what we're going to do for food."

"Or water," Nkem said.

That night, as they marched, the scuffling of many feet could be heard circling them as nighttime predators stalked them in the blackness. Zawne, Stingl, and Nkem walked clustered tightly to dissuade attack. If there was food to be had, it was too dark to find it. The same went for water or cacti.

As dawn's first light began to warm the desert sands, Zawne said, "We should walk in the day. We can find no food at night. We also risk attacks from animals."

So they walked through the day under the hot wrath of the sun and didn't sleep. They were far ahead of the other groups. The only sound was their harsh breathing and the call of the wind. As darkness fell, they used what few tools they had in their packs to set traps. Each man had an empty tin can. They dug three holes in the sand and placed an empty can in each one. "The dried juice on the bottom of the cans will lure scorpions," Nkem said. "We'll check them in the morning."

They caught one scorpion during the night and ate it raw in the morning, sharing the paltry bit of meat between them. The next night, they used the small tarp provided to make a solar still. They dug a wide hole and stretched the tarp taut over the hole, and through the night, the moisture dripped from the tarp into one of their tin cans. It was just enough for a sip, just enough to stay alive.

* * *

IT WAS six months and roughly four thousand miles later when Nkem was explaining to Zawne and Stingl about the primal history of the Ava-Surrvul.

"See, they used to farm salt out in these flatlands. It was maybe a thousand years ago, so the salt has mostly dried up. The Ava-Surrvul worked all day in the sun without water or food, chopping salt out of the ground in huge chunks. They shaved it, strapped it to their camels, and marched back to civilization to sell it. The tradition lasted until the unification of Geniverd, even after the advent of cars and machines. The Surrvul have always been a hardy people. They thrive in this wasteland."

"It's interesting," Zawne said. "But what I want to know is how you can still be so chatty after four thousand miles of stark nothingness. We've come across human bones, sucked water out of mud gullies, eaten lizards and venomous scorpions, had our skin flayed by the sun, and been forced to do disgusting things to stay hydrated ... and still you yap!"

Stingl chuckled. "It's Nkem's charm. Imagine how boring this would have been without him. Not to mention we haven't seen another person since the beach. I wonder if—"

"Better if you didn't," Zawne said. "I'm sure they're—"

Zawne stopped in his tracks. Up ahead was a shallow crevice in the desert, one of the many dried-up riverbeds that cut through the land. Climbing onto its rim were three leopards.

"We're in trouble," Zawne said. "Ready yourselves, men. It's another test!"

The leopards moved toward them with silent, stealthy resolve. They were nearly invisible against the sand, their yellowish coats the perfect camouflage in the scrublands.

Nkem was pulling his pocketknife from his rucksack, but Zawne stopped him. "No, brother. It will prove our worth as warriors if we can defeat our enemy without killing them. It will show our mercy."

Nkem nodded. "Got it." He dropped his knife in the sand, and the men readied themselves. They firmed their stances as the leopards began to charge.

The leopards worked as a pack. One dashed straight at Zawne, and the others flanked to attack Nkem and Stingl. Zawne's leopard leaped into the air and pounced onto his chest with its heavy paws, knocking him down and trying to bite out his throat. Zawne caught it by the muzzle and yelled in its face, "Not today, beast!" He flung it off him. At the same time, Nkem and Stingl were fighting desperately on the desert floor.

Zawne clambered to his feet and ran at the leopard, catching its paws in midair and headbutting it on the top of its skull. It gargled and landed on its feet. Its hair stood on end as it snarled, hissed at Zawne, and made its second attack.

But Zawne was fast. He kicked the oversize cat in the snout and knocked it sideways, then stood astride it. He punched its face—once, twice, three times between the eyes— until the leopard groaned and backed away snarling, then dissolved into the heat of the desert.

Zawne stood powerfully in the sand, his shirt ripped by the claws of the leopard. A primitive look had possessed him during the fight. It was as though the warrior spirit had entered his body, as though the memory of Lordin's tragic demise had turned him into a savage. He looked at the sky and roared in triumph.

Stingl was on the ground not far from Zawne, struggling beneath the ferocious attack of another leopard. Zawne ran to help. He drove the animal off Stingl, man and beast rolling through the scrub. They spiraled in a mess of fangs and claws, spritzes of blood flying as the leopard tore off chunks of Zawne's chest. It ended with Zawne on his back and the leopard in his grip. Zawne had his arm wrapped around its throat, choking the cat as it flailed and hissed. Then it was unconscious. Zawne pushed the leopard off him and into the dirt.

"Stingl!" Zawne stood up and dusted himself off. "Are you all right?"

"Fine," Stingl said. He was dabbing at the blood weeping from a gash in his arm. "It's just a flesh wound. But where's Nkem?"

Zawne looked around. There was no sign of Nkem. "They must have rolled into the riverbed," he said. "Come on, let's go!"

They found Nkem slumped against the wall of the gully,

blood leaking down his face. He was panting, hands limp in his lap. The leopard was gone.

"What happened?" Zawne asked. He skidded down the loose wall of the riverbed and knelt by Nkem.

"It ran off," Nkem said. "I shoved my arm down its throat, and it ran off gagging, but not before it clamped its fangs down on my head." He gestured to the tooth marks on his scalp, chuckling as he said, "That's probably going to a leave a mark."

"You bet," Zawne said, cracking a smile. He took off his shirt and ripped off a long strip. "Here, let me bandage your head. You don't want the wound to get infected before we reach the coast."

Whatever animalistic spirit had invaded Zawne during the fight had gone with the leopards. He was normal again, even cheerful, as he bandaged Nkem's head. He used the rest of his shirt to wrap Nkem's chest and Stingl's arm.

Afterward the three friends sat against the wall of the dried-up riverbed and talked about their victories. Stingl was a little upset because he had not defeated his own leopard, but Zawne comforted him.

"It's all right, Stingl. You faced a leopard and lived. We worked as a team to overcome wild beasts. That's what the Aska training is all about: perseverance, mastering the mind, the value of life, the value of others."

"Yeah," Nkem said. "There was no way Zawne or I could have defeated all three leopards alone. We needed to be a team. The same as we need to be a team for these next thousand miles. After that, a quick swim across a shark-infested channel. It should be a piece of cake."

* * *

It wasn't.

They stood on the shoreline, looking across the strait to Lodden. "It's right over there," Nkem said. "Maybe twenty-five miles."

"Twenty hours of swimming, I reckon, with breaks," Stingl said. "It's not bad."

Zawne was nodding to himself. He looked across the water to where the continent of Lodden lay shrouded in fog. "Not bad at all, Stingl. Our wounds have healed. Our minds have been fortified. We could walk another four thousand miles in our sleep, probably in half the time."

"I reckon you're right," Nkem said. "It feels like even though we have been eating bugs and dirt, I've gained muscle mass. I bet we make it across in fifteen hours."

Zawne flashed him a smile. "I'll bet we do it in twelve."

"You're on!" And with that, Nkem jumped into the water.

* * *

It was exactly fifteen hours later when the shoreline came into view. It was less than two hundred yards away. "I can see it!" Nkem shouted over the waves. Then he laughed. "I thought there were supposed to be sharks."

As if to spite him, a huge mass appeared beneath the water, rising quickly below Nkem's feet. Zawne screamed, "Look out!" but it happened too fast. The shark exploded out of the water and caught Nkem in its mouth. There was a quick image of Nkem's body being crunched by the shark's serrated teeth. Then the beast was back underwater, swimming away with its meal. Nkem was gone, only an inky trail of blood in the water to suggest he had ever been there at all.

* * *

THERE WAS a welcoming party waiting for Zawne and Stingl as they trudged out of the water and collapsed on the pebbly beach, exhausted. They sat on the rocks and panted while the waves broke against them.

Thun came over with a horde of P2 drones hovering over his head. "Well, well, I'll be damned. I didn't think you had the guts, Prince Zawne, yet here you are, the first two men to reach Lodden. You must feel so relieved."

"Huh." Zawne huffed. "I didn't think I had it in me. But now I know I can be supreme as a human being. I just had to look at life's challenges differently. I embraced my pain." Zawne glanced at Stingl. "And I embraced my teammates. Aside from them, I just remembered Lordin. I kept thinking of our first date, at Lithern Shrine, when we sang together and played the piano. I let her strength and love, my pain and guilt for her passing, and my teammates' support get me to the end. I would never have made it here without them. But there is one challenge I'm still working on."

"What's that?"

Zawne was weeping. Thun waited patiently, but the prince didn't speak. He just gazed out at the water, where his friend had just lost his life.

"Well, Prince Zawne," Thun said glumly. "It seems you have learned the lesson of teamwork. You understand now the bitter truth of death, its inescapability. Judging by your wounds, I'd say you looked death in the face and overcame. You've defeated your mind's interpretations of sloth, pain, fear, and infirmity. You've learned that it's within your power to disable a foe's supremacy while still preserving its life. Well done, valiant comrade! I welcome you to your training in Lodden. This will be your home for the next year and a half. The physical and mental tasks we've prepared for you are

CLARA LOVEMAN

designed to solidify your learnings and to safeguard Geniverd, starting with the principles of Decens-Lenitas."

* * *

I SHOOK free of Zawne's memories with a deep sense of understanding. I had known the Aska trials were tough, but I had never imagined that the hardships Zawne and Raad had been forced to endure were so brutal. The deaths seemed pointless to me. I couldn't understand why anyone would subject themselves to such torture, though I supposed in Zawne's case, he would have been dead or at least hollow without his Aska training. The loss of Lordin had torn his soul asunder, and the great revelation of his training had mended it.

I took a second to marvel at Zawne's intense devotion to Lordin. Her memory had literally turned him superhuman, had him wrestling leopards and trudging through the searing heat of the desert for months on end. It made me doubt my own worth. Could I ever have inspired Zawne in such a way? Asking myself the question gave me the answer.

I loved Zawne and Zawne loved me, but he would always love Lordin more. She had been his first, his truest. If Zawne felt for Lordin what I had always, in the deepest chambers of my heart, felt for Roki, we would always be loved, yet loved in the back seat. Zawne and I were afterglows of other loves, ghosts of a feeling that could never be recreated.

18

I had become introspective and hadn't noticed Roki staring at me. "Well," he asked, "did you figure it out? Did you get a clue?"

I snapped out of my daydream and looked down at Zawne, the poor man asleep on his couch, all alone in the world with his warrior's heart fractured into pieces. "Yes," I told Roki. "The clue is love, indefinable and incorruptible love."

Roki blinked at me. "The cure is in love? I don't understand, Kaelyn."

I smiled, still gazing at Zawne. I was happy Roki couldn't hear my thoughts. Zawne was such a good man. He deserved the best, and if I truly loved him, I would leave him alone. I couldn't put another hole in his heart with my confused feelings. I couldn't be with him and Roki. I had to choose.

"The cure is at Lithern Shrine," I said. "It was the location of Zawne and Lordin's first date. I think it is the only place of love that Lordin has ever known. If she stored the cure to save humanity anywhere, it's going to be at Lithern Shrine."

I chuckled to myself. "It's funny, you know. For all Lordin's evil, she still loves Zawne. I can't help but think that whatever immoral path she is on now, she's still attached to her human feelings for him. I'm sure she's fumbling for purchase, trying to rise as a powerful Min while maintaining her relationship with Zawne. I can't help but wonder what she would have been like without Emell's corruption."

"We can wonder later," Roki said, taking me gently by the arm. "Right now we have a world to save. Let's get our butts to Lithern Shrine!"

* * *

SURE ENOUGH, Roki and I found the cure inside the piano's casing. It was a green substance in a small vial, wrapped neatly in cloth and tucked inside the guts of the piano.

"Got it," I said, holding up the vial.

Roki smiled. "Great. Now we just need to reproduce it and distribute it to the people."

I tucked the vial into my pocket, saying, "I have an idea. We'll go to my brother at NordHaven and introduce ourselves as defectors from VBione Corp. We'll say that the cure was already made, but Emell was withholding it. This pins the whole fiasco on her. They'll have no choice but to arrest her. Even if the investigation into Mama's death goes nowhere, at least Emell will be behind bars."

"I like your thinking," Roki said. "Let's get to it!"

We left Lithern Shrine feeling like the saviors of the world, holding hands as we soared across the sky toward Nord-Haven. Once there, Roki unmasked us. The butler announced us to the household, and Tissa arrived after fifteen minutes, Rein and Forschi in tow. The canines barked with excitement.

"Hello. We're in mourning and meant to be in quarantine, so this had better be good. How can I help you?" Tissa asked.

The dogs flopped down on the floor, their wee eyes watching me expectantly. Tissa looked like a whole new person. Had she always worn so much makeup? Her clothing seemed to be getting frillier and frillier each time I saw her.

Yes! I wanted to scream. *Yes, Tissa. You can give me a hug!*

But I had to keep my composure. I said, "My name is Cerna, and this is my associate Roki. We were the lead designers on the cure for the KS3 virus. We finished human trials yesterday, but the owner of the company, Emell, has refused to allow the cure to be released to the public. We think she's bent on world domination or something. So we reproduced the cure on our own and brought it straight here, hoping that Gaard-Ma and Gaard-Elder would help distribute it."

It was a lot. Tissa gaped at me, looking like I had just slapped her in the face. "You're serious?"

"We are," Roki said. "The queen herself tasked us with this before—"

"Then get in here right now! What are you doing dallying outside like a couple of salespeople?" Tissa gestured for us to enter, then shouted into her visin, "Raad, we have a cure. Forget the quarantine and get down here as soon as you can."

Tissa gave us a sad look. "Sorry, but as you know, Gaard-Elder's sister—you know, the queen of Geniverd—was killed last night. He's obviously not in the best shape."

"We understand," I said. I was overwhelmed by the wish to reveal myself. It was hard not to.

Tissa turned to Roki. "Funny, the late queen had a friend called Roki."

Luckily, Raad joined us in the parlor at that moment, and Roki didn't have to reply. When we handed over the cure to him, I wanted to hug my brother and erase the sadness from his eyes. I wanted to celebrate our triumph with my family and friends, but I couldn't. I had to sit before them as a stranger and give him all the gritty details of Emell's operation.

"And you'll sign a testimony saying Emell designed KS3, unleashed it on the people of Geniverd, then refused to release the cure?" Raad asked.

"We will," I said.

Raad didn't answer. He was in go mode. He held up his finger for silence as he called someone on his visin and started talking. "I need a team to meet me at the VBione Corp main factory to reproduce the cure for the KS3 virus ... Yes ... Yes, the cure. I also need a team to arrest Emell again. This time we're not letting her go. I'll be at the factory in fifteen minutes."

Raad ended the call, leaned forward, and squinted at me. "You remind me of my sister," he said. "Not your body or your face, but your eyes. Yeah, you have the same eyes. It's like ... I don't know how to explain it."

Raad shook his head, got up from the sofa, and said, "I'm sorry, Cerna, I'm grieving and acting weird. But I have to go now to deal with this cure situation. Thank you for bringing it to me. I'll have someone write a testimony for you to sign. Probably tomorrow. Emell will never see the light of day again for what she's done."

I was glad to hear it. Raad and Tissa left, the dogs following closely behind them. Roki and I lingered a moment in the empty parlor. "I'm happy we're finally getting justice for Mama," I said. "I'm also happy Raad will be the one to save the world, not Emell or Lordin."

"Me too," Roki said. "Can you imagine if they had gotten away with this? It would have been a travesty. Still ..." Roki sighed, clearly stressed out. "There is the war in Nurlie to deal with. Surrvul is throwing money around and operating from the shadows. We have a lot of loose ends about to catch fire. And speaking of fire, I need to see a friend of mine. I never did tell you I have a dragon for a friend. Anyway, I don't know what to do."

"Dragon … Do you mean the one from the news reports, the one burning down noble mansions and clan retreats all over the world?"

"It doesn't matter," Roki said with a half smile. "We have too much to figure out. My fire-starting friend can wait."

"Okay," I said, and took Roki by the hand. "We will figure it out together. Now that I'm a Min, there's nothing in the world that can stop us."

He smiled, took my other hand, and drew me to him. Our eyes met, and it was like an explosion in my heart. Then I realized, *Roki and I are finally together. There are no secrets. I'm a Min. I have hundreds of years to be with Roki.*

We were standing with our noses almost touching, the heat between us undeniable. Then Roki said in a soft voice, "We have five centuries to explore these feelings. But I was thinking …" He bit his lip, trying not to smirk. "I was thinking that when the selection comes around for the next Crown of Crowns, we should join as a team. It would mean …"

"Being together for three thousand years." My breath had caught in my throat, and I thought I would cry. "I can't even fathom it."

"Me neither," he said. "Five hundred years has gone by so slowly. I've seen so much. To live six times the amount I already have is mind blowing! But if I'm going to do it, I'll only do it with you."

"Wow," I said, squealing like a piglet. "Imagine you and me, rulers for three thousand years. But … it's a big deal. I need to think about that."

"Take your time. We should get a drink to celebrate," Roki said. "You know, like the first time we met."

"I'd love to."

But before we could go anywhere, a strange feeling enveloped me. Then two voices were in my head, saying, "This is Hanchell and Riedel. You must come to Shiol. We need you immediately."

I looked to Roki and he was nodding. "Yeah, I got the same message. They must be summoning all the Min. It sounds like an emergency."

"A Min emergency!" I cried. "That can't be good."

* * *

THE SHIOL ROKI and I arrived to was not the one I knew, the empty vacuum with its peaceful sky overhead. Rather, it was the bright and pulsing city Roki had shown me all that time ago. We were transported into a massive plaza, a place much like Coronation Square in Geniverd's capital. Around us were other Min in human bodies, and also creatures I could hardly comprehend. There were lizard people, humanoid beings with pointy ears and short limbs, winged creatures without legs, orange-skinned people over nine feet tall, limbless blobs, and countless other life-forms. I could hardly keep from staring.

"This is the real Shiol," Roki whispered to me. "This is where the Min from other dimensions, other planets, other realities all live in harmony. It's why the city looks so strange. It's an amalgamation of a thousand different cultures. When we have time, I'd like to explore it with you. Even after five hundred years, I still haven't scratched the surface of Shiol."

"I'd like that very much," I said. But really, I was overwhelmed. Where did a newly minted Min begin exploring such a grand and infinite city?

"And those are Riedel's and Hanchell's true forms." Roki gestured to the Crown of Crowns, who had just revealed themselves above us on the podium. I balked at their true forms. They were three-headed monsters with scaly gray flesh, yellow eyes, and webbed feet.

"Incredible!" I said. "I can't believe I've been talking to monsters this whole time."

"Not monsters," Roki said. "They are from Dimension Z8. They were chosen as the best among us three thousand years ago."

"They've lived for almost four thousand years … That's impressive."

I wanted to ask more questions, but the Crown of Crowns began to address the crowd.

"Hello," Hanchell said. Even as a three-headed monster, I thought she looked compassionate in her golden robes; there were twinkles of kindness in her six yellow eyes. "We have brought you here to announce that our tenure as Crown of Crowns is coming to an end. In approximately six months, the Seeing Water will pick our replacements. That means you clever Min have time to partner up and present your cases. Choose wisely. None of you will live long enough to have another shot at being orchestrators of our galaxy."

"The suitable candidates must not only be clever," Riedel said. "They must also be strong, wise, invested in the future of the universe, and willing to make the hard sacrifices to keep the balance."

I thought, *If trying to run Geniverd was stressful, what would running the galaxy be like? If we were selected, how would Roki and I cope?*

"If you'd like to be considered for the position, please present yourselves to us sooner rather than later," Hanchell said, her gray tail wagging. "For now, we bid you farewell."

Hanchell and Riedel sparkled like static and then were gone. And that was when I looked through the crowd and saw Lordin glaring at me.

* * *

THE CROWD of aliens and interdimensional beings was gone. The square was empty. Lordin and I stood alone with the eerie strangeness of Shiol's megalopolis looming in the distance.

"You stole my cure," she said. Lordin made no attempt to attack me. She simply stood glaring at me in Hagan's body. It was creepy and intimidating.

"You were killing people," I said. "What did you think I would do?"

Lordin shrugged. "I'm just surprised you found it. It's not like I can blame you for trying to save the world. I wasn't comfortable with the death toll either, but I was powerless to my mama's commands. I needed to gain status in this body."

"So that you could schmooze your way back into Zawne's life?"

"Something like that."

"I don't get it," I said. "You both know the Great Secret. Why not just reveal yourself?"

Lordin laughed, folded her arms, and shook her head at me. "You guys were married, Kaelyn! Don't you think I tried? Zawne's a noble man. When I came to him in Shiol, I altered his reality so that he would see me in my original body. He told me he loved me even beyond death, but that he was a king and would not fold his commitment to his new wife, Kaelyn of Gaard, the daughter of my mama's enemy."

"Oh ..." I said. It was starting to make sense. Zawne had been honest with me the whole time. He'd had no intentions of cheating, so Lordin had needed to maneuver me off the throne somehow.

I said, "You used Emell's lifelong thirst for vengeance to try to dispose of me because Zawne rejected you. So you hatched an insane plot to spiral the world into chaos and get me banished for being a bad queen. Then you were going to insert yourself in Zawne's council and make him fall for you in Hagan's body!"

"Well," Lordin said, "it was Mama's insane plot. The virus would have been unleashed with or without me. Yet by helping Mama, I kept my lifelong promise to get her revenge, while at the same time getting rid of you. There's only one thing you've got wrong, Kaelyn. There's one sticky detail you missed."

I crossed my arms and said nothing. I wished she couldn't alter reality. I wished everyone in the square could have heard Lordin's sick confession, though I had to remember she wasn't naturally sick. Emell had filled her with evil. Then Zawne had filled her with love, and the Crown of Crowns had fueled her desire for power. Lordin was trying to juggle all these personas, all these goals and aspirations. I had a feeling it was driving her to madness.

"I wasn't planning to become Zawne's queen," Lordin said. "Emell thought so, but she was wrong. See, I want to trick Zawne into sacrificing himself and becoming a Min. I need him to partner with me. I'm sure that together we can take over as the Crown of Crowns."

19

"*N*ever," I shouted, suddenly angry at how Lordin planned to manipulate Zawne. "Not in a million years! I know you have a good heart somewhere inside you, but it's cracked and broken. You'll never get the universal throne, Lordin."

"Maybe not," she said, shrugging with cool indifference, "but maybe I will. All I need is Zawne."

"And to eliminate the competition," I said, suddenly understanding everything. "That's why you broke up Roki and me. You were scared of our power together. You were worried that Roki and I could ascend the throne instead of you. You're still scared of us and our bond!"

Lordin's face went dark. She started toward me. "I"—lips twisted in a snarl—"am"—balling her hands into little fists—"scared of no one!"

She raised her arm and I flinched, squeezing my eyes shut. Without warning, she flitted upward and, in a flash, was on top of me, hanging from my head, and we were skidding in all directions.

"Thief!" Lordin screeched as she made several attempts to grab my Valer. I used all my strength to unhitch myself from her, my Valer instinctively jittering around my body, its natural defense mechanism.

I panted. "I can't believe how foolish I was to believe in you!"

As I spun, my eyes hunted for her, knowing that she could see me. But then, in a shot, she was swinging at me again, and she tossed me into the air. I crashed heavily into the buoyant space. It felt like I'd hit the ground as my whole body cramped or spasmed.

I mustn't give in, I told myself, thinking about all the people who'd died because of her. I steadied my Valer, using it as bait, and fine-tuned my senses. Instantly I felt Lordin's presence just before she was upon me, and I lunged at her head, sending her hurtling several feet away.

I caught my breath, surprised at my superhuman strength, and looked up to see several amused Min staring at me. I didn't know if I'd struck something that had ended Lordin's spell or if someone had interrupted us.

Roki was there with a concerned look. "You all right?" he asked. "You kind of gaped out there for a second."

* * *

I EXPLAINED it all to Roki: Lordin's twisted motives, Zawne's loyalty to me, the whole bloated mess. We had left Shiol and were lying on the rooftop of the tallest building in Geniverd's capital city, watching the clouds go by as we tried to make sense of it all.

"It's wild," Roki said. "I hope Lordin doesn't turn into one of those perverse serial-killer Min."

"Me too," I said. "I hope she's all right. Her mama's in jail now in Gaard. So that's one good thing that came out of this. I just wonder how having her mama locked up will bend her mind."

Roki turned to me, looking offended. "Only one good thing came out of this? What about us? We're together again because of what happened."

"Of course," I assured him. "It's only you and me now, Roki. I've vowed to myself to let Zawne live his life. I won't lie to you, though. I still love him in my own way, and if I hadn't become a Min, I never would have left him. But things have changed. The world moves on. Raad taught me that. We must grow and face the future. You and I will face it together."

At that moment, I remembered that I still didn't know the identity of the Seeing Water. I asked Roki, "Can you tell me what the Seeing Water is?"

"I've only heard from secondhand sources," he said. Apparently, it's an amalgamation of the spirits of all the billions of babies and children unjustly killed in the universe since the beginning of time. It is 'seeing' because it can see through anything and everything in the universe. The 'water' represents the children's tears. Tears from having their lives cut short prematurely. Tears for saving us again and again despite what the universe did to them. The Seeing Water wields more power every time it gains a new spirit."

"Hanchell said that it is merciful. What is the Seeing Water saving us from?"

"From ourselves. The Seeing Water can end all our lives in an instant. It can destroy planets in the blink of an eye. Instead, it chooses to apportion power to the Crown of Crowns to help us look after our galaxy. It oversees all the Crowns of Crowns in all the galaxies in our universe."

"So we can ask the Seeing Water to help us? I mean, to stop Lordin?"

Roki shook his head. "You don't understand. It may be merciful, but its wrath is in proportion to the evil in the universe, the unrighteousness. Three great personal sacrifices of its choosing would be required to even approach its presence."

Just then I felt the presence of someone behind us. I craned my head to see an enormous man watching us. He had curly gray hair down to his shoulders, ashy-white skin, stern eyes. He was the hugest person I had ever seen. He just stood there watching us like a giant creep. "Who are you?" I asked, scrambling to my feet. "Why did you sneak up on us?"

"Sire," he said, ignoring me and looking at Roki, "we have a problem."

Roki didn't get up. He continued to watch the clouds flow by while he talked to the man. They seemed to be acquainted.

"What is it, Neuge? Give me the scoop."

Neuge's voice was like cannon fire. "King Zawne has managed to cool the fighting for now," he said. "A shaky truce has been reached between mainland Nurlie and the shadow government on Nurlie Island. As of now, there will be no referendum. The Ava-Surrvul reinforcements have scattered without their allies. The bloodshed in the streets has ceased. The medical Protectors are administering first aid and handing out antivirals for the KS3 virus. Things are looking up."

"Surrvul will be back," Roki said. "They were testing the will of the new king, poking the bear to see which clan leaders did what. Next time, they'll come stronger and faster and meaner. The other clans aren't dumb. I'm sure everyone is preparing for a dastardly conflict."

Roki got up, brushed himself off, and regarded Neuge. Roki looked more severe than I had ever seen him. "But that's all good news," Roki said. "So, what's the problem?"

Neuge hesitated. I saw then that he was a Min. Neuge was so wide that I hadn't noticed the Valer floating in his core. I thought it was strange that he avoided Roki's eyes, as if he feared to look straight at him. It was ridiculous, because Neuge could have crushed Roki with one meaty fist. Yet he appeared nervous.

"The problem, sire, is that you've been absent for several days since the conflict began. Our people must be given direction. There's talk of marching even without our allies. The people are restless. Many have lost loved ones because of the virus outbreak. They need an address from their leader. Some are calling for more fires, only this time with casualties by the thousands."

Leader, I thought. *Leader of what? Just who exactly is Neuge, and what the heck is going on? And who is the dragon starting the fires? Is Roki really friends with this dragon character?*

I shifted my eyes from Neuge to Roki. "Would you care to explain this to me? I thought we were done with secrets."

Roki started laughing. "I'm so sorry," he said. "This is huge news for you. I totally forgot!" Then he said to Neuge, "Leave us. Gather the people, and I'll be there within the hour to give a speech."

Neuge bowed. Then he shot high into the clouds and flew away. I was left speechless and confused, glaring at Roki as he doubled over with laughter.

"It's not funny," I said. "Seriously, tell me what's going on. Are you the leader of a spiritual army?"

He took my hand and kissed it gently, his brilliant smile making me melt. "It's better if I show you. Come, Kaelyn. Should you choose to be with me for the next few centuries, you're going to need to know my secret job."

* * *

WE FLEW west across the ocean, farther and farther, until I could see Krug's coastline of sandy beaches.

Roki came to a dead stop fifty miles from land. He hadn't stopped grinning since the rooftop. "You're going to love this," he said. "Hold your breath."

"No, wait, what are we—?"

Roki took my arm and pulled me downward, laughing hysterically as we plummeted toward the water.

I screamed, "No! I don't want to get wet!"

But we didn't hit the water. We passed through it, plunging beneath the surface as if it were an illusion. Then we were hovering inside a hollow tube like a giant drainage pipe.

Roki explained, "I keep all the ports masked using my power. It's why I have a hard time keeping other things masked for long periods. I divert a ton of my energy to these secret ports. This one is my private entrance to the city. It's like a metal chimney sticking out of the water, but it's invisible to anyone who looks at it."

I had no idea what to say. *Secret tunnels? Hidden ports!*

"There are other entrances inland, on the beaches of other continents," he said, "other ports disguised as oil refineries, hatches, and pods that lead many miles below the surface of the ocean. Air locks and security systems. There are passenger trains in metro tunnels in major cities, all disguised by my power. It's quite high tech. Combined with my Min powers, it's superior to all else in Geniverd ..." He shrugged. "At least, all else that I know about."

"Where are you taking me?" I blurted. It was hard to keep my panic in check. "Are you trying to say there is an underground tunnel system connecting all six continents to an underwater city?"

Roki's grin could have eaten the planet. "Yes," he said, teasing me with his eyes. "Come on, let's go see it."

We flew a significant distance underground, gliding through the hollow tunnel until we reached an air lock. Roki hit a button and the door opened. We stood inside a small room while machines groaned.

"It's for water," Roki said. "This tank is meant to purge any water before I go into the city. You know, in case my tunnel floods. This tunnel isn't made for humans. It's meant just for me. I haven't even brought another Min into the city this way."

"So, you're saying I'm special?" I asked. It was my turn to smirk and tease Roki.

"More than you know," he said.

The purge system finished. Then the door opened. We walked into a bare, sort of musty hallway and continued until we reached a red-varnished door. Roki stopped with his hand on the knob. "Home sweet home. Welcome to my house, Kaelyn."

We were in an antechamber. Roki took my hand and said, "This way. Come on." He led me through his mansion of a house, old picture frames on the walls and dozens of closed rooms. He was saying, "It's lavish, I know. I'll give you a tour another time, but right now we have to get to the city square."

I couldn't believe it when we exited Roki's house onto his porch and I was staring down at an enormous underground city. There were houses, tall buildings, streets, huge complexes. I even saw flyrarcs hovering beneath the domed ceiling. It must have been half the size of the capital!

"Are we beneath Krug?" I asked.

"About a hundred yards beneath Krug. We started building this place roughly a century ago. The more people we recruit, the larger the city gets. We have many Min on our side, so we use our combined power and influence to keep it secret and to expand. We also have the best architects and engineers in Geniverd working for us."

"Us? We? Our side?" I blinked at him, ready to explode if I didn't get some answers. "Roki ... who are you?"

Roki exhaled deeply, steadied himself, and looked in my eyes. "I always wanted to tell you. It just never seemed like the right time. Kaelyn, I'm the leader of the so-called Gurnots. It's been my task to support them for the last hundred years, a direct order from the Crown of Crowns to keep the balance. Our proper name is Defiance. And now, as the leader of Defiance, I am serving my second year in office."

It felt like Roki had punched me in the gut. Leader of the Gurnots? The man I had fallen in love with was a Gurnot! How could that be?

"I want to show you more. Let's walk to the center. I want you to see my people. We're not evil, Kaelyn. We're just tired of the upper class. I mean, why should anyone be born superior? We're willing to fight to free the kingdom from the tyrannical rule of the clans. Our views are directly in line with yours. We want to restore the balance between rich and poor."

I had no words. This was the ultimate shock. After so many twists and turns, betrayals and revelations, to find out Roki was the leader of the Gurnots—it turned my perception of the world inside out.

I couldn't believe the things I saw as Roki led me through the city. There were markets, people selling meats and fruits, artisanal crafts—only this time it was all real! And women with large round bellies waddling through the streets. They were pregnant! I had forgotten that the Gurnots favored natural births. I supposed it was also a way to keep their children out of the system. But I thought the most fascinating part was how the city smelled. I was so used to the controlled atmosphere I'd spent my life inside that I had never experienced such a bombardment of different smells. There was the scent of fresh bread, of engine exhaust, of tangy human sweat. It was overwhelming.

"There are about six hundred thousand living in the city," Roki was saying as we went past a couple of kids playing with their dogs.

Dogs! I thought. *They're probably not even replicas!*

"But in the entire world, I'd say about a quarter are associated with Defiance. That means a billion people. When the time to rise above the clans is at hand, it will be an even fight. Yet we must pick our time to rebel carefully. It was unfortunate how much life was lost during the Nurlie Islanders' revolution, but it was a good test of our abilities. It may be the catalyst that will ignite global change."

"Where do I fit into all this?" I asked. We had reached the center of the city, a big stage and a huge throng of people waiting for Roki to speak. He must have had us masked, because we walked straight through them unimpeded.

"By my side," he said with a wink. "Only if you're happy. These people revered Lordin, and they can never know her truth, or they would be broken by it. As for you ..." He licked his lips, giving me an "uh-oh" look. "Well, many will hate you because of the pandemic—the decisions made through your council's process. They won't know the truth. But you're a Min now, and you're in a new body. No one knows who you are."

"Neuge did," I said, remembering how he had ignored me. Now that I thought about it, he had seemed perturbed to see Roki with me on the rooftop.

"Neuge is clever," Roki said as we climbed onto the stage. "You're new, and Kaelyn of Gaard is dead. I'm sure he put the pieces together. But Neuge is loyal and won't say anything. Even if the other Min find out, they can't defy me as the leader, nor can they reveal your identity to the people. Trust me, Kaelyn, you're safe with me, and I'll protect your loved ones."

I did trust Roki. I trusted him more than seemed appropriate. I couldn't help it. He had been my dream man from day one, and now I was standing by his side as he was about to address thousands of Gurnots in a secret underground city. I wasn't queen of Geniverd anymore, yet I felt more like a queen beside Roki than I ever had sitting in my council chamber. As a Min, I had energy and power beyond mortal grasp. I had forfeited my original body and found confidence in the skin of my host. I felt complete, smart, aware of who I was. More than anything, I felt valued. I felt ready to face the next trial.

"My people," Roki said, his voice echoing over the attentive crowd, "thank you for joining the battle in Nurlie. Thank you for fighting for our freedom and sacrificing your lives for the good of the world. It was not the first fight, and it won't be the last. We have hardships ahead of us, foes the world over, and seemingly impossible odds. Yet we will prevail!"

The crowd cheered. I crossed my arms humbly and looked them over.

"We have battled the system for many years," Roki continued, "and I say to you now, friends, we are almost home. The moment of reckoning is upon us, upon the world. For too long has the upper class pushed our faces in the muck, humiliated us, and stood righteously atop their precious Decens-Lenitas. Well, I say, no more! Our numbers have grown in pace with our strength. The time is right to strike the heads of the hydra. Nurlie was only a taste. Prepare yourselves, my friends, for the ultimate battle lies just over the horizon."

Roki raised his fist. "The titans shall fall!"

And the crowd roared, "The titans shall fall! The titans shall fall! The titans shall fall!"

I didn't know what I was doing. I had raised my fist and was echoing with the others, "The titans shall fall! The titans shall fall!"

The audience whooped with delight, and the wave of praise continued for the longest time. When the applause died down, someone shouted Lordin's name. And just like that, a new wave of cheers began, interspersed with a chant of "Lordin! Lordin! Lordin!"

And I thought that of course they loved her. I was once like them. I'd only just died, yet they still grieved for Lordin. I wanted to forgive them, because they didn't know her as I did now. And as I watched, filled with sadness, the livestream briefly caught someone who stood out because he wasn't clapping. Roki must have seen it too, on his display, because he interrupted the shouting and asked for the man to be given a microphone. Then the camera zoomed in on the person. I couldn't believe my eyes.

"Tell us your name and what's on your mind," Roki said most gently. "Why do you not cheer for Lordin?"

"My name is Nnati. I will never cheer for Lordin."

There were loud gasps, but Roki was unmoved.

Nnati continued boldly. "Can't you all see?" he said. "She bought into the system. She supported Decens-Lenitas. By the time she met her untimely death, she wasn't one of us. We don't know whether she would have treated us differently if she were queen. Yes, her murder was horrific, and I wouldn't wish that on anyone. But she did not die for our cause, yet many among us look on her as a beloved martyr. I tell you now, she died for nothing!"

There was disquiet and murmurs among the crowd.

I was still in such a shock that I didn't notice the tears

streaming down my flushing hot face. I had always known Nnati was defiant. Now I knew just how defiant. The sight of him made me smile. Perhaps I could still salvage something of my old life. Perhaps I could be Nnati's friend.

"Thank you, Nnati, for speaking your truth," said Roki. "No one should deny him that. He is not our adversary. The upper class, on the other hand, have become too powerful, too rich, too mighty. But observe around you what we've built right under their noses, for the powerful have grown weak and complacent in the long years without conflict. Trust me when I say we are strong and have a firm resolve. Our fight has only just begun, and our enemy is within our reach. They are crippled and slow with their pockets stuffed with money and their bellies bloated on our food. They've pushed us so deep into the dirt that they do not fear retaliation. But I promise you, brothers and sisters, they will fear us!"

By the time Roki finished his speech, I felt drawn to his cause, to the magic of his words. Roki's passion invigorated me. He was mine and I was his, and we were in the fight together. For the first time in my life, I had a purpose. I felt on top of the world. It no longer mattered what tomorrow may bring.

Roki and I walked off the stage, and I threw myself into his open arms, thinking it was crazy that I had to die to truly live. I was free and unassailable in that strange place and in Roki's arms. No one was going to take that away from me, nor would they punish me for being there, far from my home.

Because I was home.

GODLY SINS

CROWN OF CROWNS

GODLY
SINS

CLARA LOVEMAN

1

_____

*T*he clock struck ten, and the chime went off just as we landed under the moonless sky.

"Seven days to go," the Crown of Crowns said. "In the lead are Erda and Lithra from Spectrius Z8."

Relieved, I let out a long sigh, and Roki held out his hand. I clutched it and took a sharp breath before we stepped together onto the papery golden walkway. That Roki and I were in VondRust like this was almost too surreal to believe. It wasn't a problem to be in VondRust now that our twins were about to start high school. It was more that I felt undeserving of the hero's welcome. It was so strange to be back in the palace in another person's skin.

The lights shone so brightly in our faces that I could hardly see the distinguished royals lined up in front of us. All I could do was smile and look down at the delicate flooring, picking out the individual bodily scents from the lightly fragranced air that swirled around us. It was how I knew exactly who awaited us at the other end of the raised passageway, apart from Zawne and Lordin; I could smell the pheromones of each particular person. I felt Raad and Tissa's presence at the end of the line, solemn and reflective. Seeing them again without having to hide was the only thing that brought me any warmth. Next to them were Zawne's parents. Beyond them, inside the ballroom, the other guests chatted quietly among themselves.

The flyrarc rose behind us and took to the sky, and we sauntered quietly to the royals. We were dressed to match them, me in a gown of the finest silk with a satin bodice and Roki in his handsome velveteen suit. The thirty steps between us and them was far enough for the entire world to catch us from a hundred different angles with their visins. I didn't think too much about our audience. My concentration was fixed on Zawne and Lordin. When Roki and I reached them, we bowed low. How strange it felt to bow to my ex-husband in a different body—and with Lordin at his side!

It was the first time I'd seen Zawne face-to-face in my Min form. Even though I suspected that Lordin might have changed his memories for this occasion, I quickly downloaded his memories and scanned them. True to form, all I could find was a memory left on purpose, intended as a message. I watched the memory of Zawne talking to himself in the mirror, asking to see me at some point that night. How convenient.

"Please rise," Zawne said.

My eyes met Lordin's first. "Your Most Supreme Majesties," I said, looking from Lordin to Zawne.

"Welcome to VondRust Palace," Lordin replied. She was beautiful in Hagan's body, her jeweled evening dress glittering in the light. "Today Geniverd awards you both the highest honor of our land. All the clan leaders and heirs have joined us here to show the world our respect for you. Tell us, how was your journey?"

I tried to smile for the cameras, all the P2 drones floating overhead. I had to remind myself that the award was from the people, not from Lordin herself. Roki and I had been nominated by the clan leaders and the people of Geniverd for our part in saving the world, and that put Zawne and Lordin in an impossible position. Knowing it wasn't their choosing helped a little.

"Very secure," I said, trying to use the fewest words possible. I couldn't change the fact they were together or that I had to face them. An award like this had to be presented by the king and queen. It almost brought tears to my eyes that Lordin was leading my people. So much had changed in so little time, and almost none of it for the better.

It was only five months ago that Xerx and Vowkin had been born. At two days old, I'd wanted them to see the world they'd been born into, my world of Geniverd. We had gone traveling as a family, keeping a low profile to avoid being recognized. Being summoned to VondRust months later had presented the perfect opportunity for us to introduce the twins as our adopted children. The problem with Min children was that they grew too fast. Roki and I were teenagers ourselves, and it would have looked out of place for us to have teenagers of our own. I hated lying, but it had to be done. It was the rule set for us by the Crown of Crowns. We couldn't reveal their secret—not that I would have, anyway—and so we lived with the lie. These children were my responsibility. They were of my flesh, my blood, and my spirit.

The trip had been good for us as a family. As Min, we were able to explore every far-flung nook and cranny in Geniverd. It had been the breathing room I'd so desperately needed after all the excitement that had happened once I became a Min. Zawne's audacity to make Lordin his new queen had been too much for me to bear, never mind the way he'd done it.

"She means we're very grateful for the royal Protectors," Roki said on my behalf, flashing the handsome smile I loved so much. "As you know, we have our own people, and we could have made our own way just as easily. But we're grateful for the gesture. It was a safe flight."

Zawne chuckled. "We simply didn't want to ruin the surprise." His voice was deep and low, almost a hum. Lordin tucked her arm under his elbow and looked me in the face, smiling pleasantly. Even in her new form, she seemed too sweet to fully take in. But of course, this was all for the benefit of the billions of people who were watching at home. "As you can see," Zawne said, "we have Geniverd's finest people waiting to award you the Shield, our highest honor, for your efforts in the pandemic."

I raised my eyebrows and feigned surprise. We'd known about the accolade and the accompanying banquet for days through Roki's spy network of fellow Min. I did my best to act thrilled at receiving such a prestigious award, but inside I was dying. I just didn't understand why Zawne had taken Lordin back, and it was all I could think about. Most likely he didn't know the full story, and that was my fault. I had left him to deal with the aftermath of the pandemic and my death, and my absence had been the perfect opportunity for Lordin to pounce on him. At the time, I'd thought it was selfish of me to tell him how to live his life. I had no right after leaving him the way I did. And then everything happened so fast, the babies and their incredible growth. Now I felt like he was punishing me for my decision to leave him and join the spirit world.

"This evening is all for you," Lordin said, gesturing around us with her free hand. "Geniverd is most grateful."

Eight Protectors ushered Zawne and Lordin into the

palace, and we followed behind, ready to bow and greet each of the twelve clan leaders.

It wasn't long before we got to Zawne's parents. The King Emeritus and Queen Emerita were both friendly and chatty. They talked about the traditional Gaard wines the palace had ordered for the evening, saying they were sure we would love them. They even turned to Raad and Tissa to fully express their love for the winemaker.

As Raad and Tissa looked upon us kindly, I knew neither of them wanted to be there. Being a Min did have its perks—namely, allowing me to read the minds of humans. I knew Tissa was thinking that she would only stay for a maximum of two days and not one minute more. Two days would be enough not to slight the monarchs. There was no way she would stay for ten days at a lavish banquet thrown by the same people who'd treated me so despicably, her dear friend and sister-in-law. At the same time, Raad was thinking about when to find a private moment alone with Zawne so that he could condemn him for taking a new wife merely a week after I'd been buried. That was when I heard quiet barking. Rein and Forschi were perched at Tissa's feet, tongues lolling and tails wagging. They appeared to have grown fur coats that sparkled in the light.

I knew Raad and Tissa wouldn't engage in small talk with us in such a formal environment, but I didn't know if I would have any more time with them afterward. So, after we'd bowed, even though it was considered uncouth for a commoner to speak first, I said in a quiet voice, "You remember us, don't you? We came to you with the cure."

"Oh yes, of course," Tissa said. "That's the whole idea behind your award." Tissa's eyes lit up, and she managed a small laugh as her voice trailed off. All the while, she was thinking, *How can this nobody think I'd remember anything that happened? Kaelyn had just been murdered in cold blood. Some people are so hard to like!*

"You saved the world," Raad cut in, authority thick in his voice. He had grown even bolder from ruling Gaard. "Thank you for coming to us first and entrusting us with the cure."

Roki smiled and said, "Gaard-Elder, Gaard-Ma, it was your quick thinking and fast action that saved the world. You were grieving, but you still offered your time, which was instrumental in the whole process. It is entirely feasible that the other clan leaders wouldn't have believed us and the virus would have taken even more lives."

"Thank you," Raad and Tissa said simultaneously, tipping their heads as if to end the conversation and move us along.

The meeting pained me. If the next day weren't the first day of high school for the twins, I might have considered staying the night, if only to forge some kind of relationship with Raad and Tissa in my new life. But I also saw how hard it was for them to see us. The day I'd entered their world as Cerna had been the worst day of their lives. I needed to accept that they could never know who I was.

* * *

Raad and Tissa were ushered away from us to mingle with the other guests. A courtier informed us that we would be free to interact with everyone else following the award presentation, which was to happen within minutes. Everyone in the room was led to the adjoining ballroom, where Roki and I were asked to stand before Zawne and Lordin. The Grucken then appeared and, after a few words of welcome, invited Lordin to make a speech.

"We have no doubt that the Gurnots killed our late queen and started the pandemic," Lordin said to the room. "The king and I are aware of the rumors that Queen Kaelyn had a hand in the spread of the pandemic. Unfortunately, we can neither confirm nor deny these rumors." She winked at me, sending a shiver down my spine. What was she doing? If it weren't for the Crown of Crowns, she'd probably have revealed that I was Kaelyn! "In these times of aggression, we cannot forget that our continents stand united. The monarchs who came before us defeated every cancer and disease that threatened to blight our society, including any possible uprising. Along with our Askas, our Protectors, and our precious Decens-Lenitas, we will continue to prosper and hold our world together."

She took a breath, letting her eyes pass over those in the crowd. "Make no mistake, Gurnots are our biggest threat. Let that be absolutely clear. They killed millions of our people by unleashing the virus. King Zawne and I promise that we are going to pull the Gurnot vermin from their lairs and extermi-nate them. We are going to bring back some of the ancient punishments from hundreds of years ago to show how serious we are. We vow to burn the Gurnot leaders at the stake!"

Everyone clapped and cheered, the whole lot of savage rich people. It didn't surprise me that she was using this ceremony as an opportunity to attack Defiance, all the while presenting herself as the saint everyone thought she was. What kind of people clapped for such a brutal threat from their queen? This was the one time I wished Lordin could hear my thoughts, so she would know exactly what I thought of her.

"Let us not bog down such a magnificent ceremony, nor the thing that has brought us here in the first place," Lordin continued. "Before I present the awards, I want to make a special announcement. King Zawne and I have decided that everyone in Geniverd should have three days to celebrate this momentous achievement. We've all been through a very rough time. Our loved ones have been taken from us. Innocent people have been slaughtered in the streets of Nurlie. It is truly tragic what has happened. But we must look at the bigger picture. This pandemic could have obliterated mankind. It is thanks to these two individuals that we're still standing. We must be grateful our important moral code is still intact, and for that, we will celebrate for three full days. We've laid on food, drinks, street parties, costumes, decorations, and entertainment for all."

She held out her hand to a courtier, who gave her and Zawne our medals. I seethed as Lordin placed the award around my shoulders, Zawne doing the same for Roki. I was sure Lordin could see my blood boiling under my skin while everyone clapped.

After the short presentation, music was played while a courtier announced that the live broadcast had ended. We were now free to move between ten huge ballrooms, where we could enjoy food, drinks, and all kinds of royal entertainment for the next ten days. However, the 'we' did not extend to Roki and me, since we were not of the royal persuasion. We were permitted one night in the palace, and that was it, even if we had just saved the world. Some thanks. Not that I wanted to stay. The ordinary people had suffered the most and deserved so much more; three festive days were an insult in comparison to what the nobility had arranged for themselves.

Lordin and Zawne were being pulled in every direction by clan heads and other highborn people. Roki and I lingered at the fringes of the party, and that was when a bulky young man approached us. I knew right away he was a Min from the fiery Valer in his chest. He had long raven hair tied back, strong brows, and angular cheekbones. Roki greeted him, and the two men hugged. From over Roki's shoulder, the newcomer gazed at me warmly.

"Roki," he said in a rich, deep voice when he finally took his eyes off me. "How long will you stay at the party?"

"I'm afraid we're just here for a few hours. There is no need for us to spend the night. Oh, I don't think you've met my girlfriend, have you?"

The big guy shook his head, his gaze back on me, holding my eyes. "I think I would have remembered."

"Well," Roki said, and gestured to me, "Knotts, meet Cerna."

"An honor to finally meet you," he said, pulling closer. We exchanged kisses on both cheeks. "It's a shame that you're leaving so early. We could have used you to really beautify this palace."

Knotts had a natural charm about him. I couldn't help but smile and assume familiarity. But I worried that a comment like that might draw unwanted attention to me, especially as there were several people within earshot. "Shh," I whispered. "There's Queen Hagan here to do that."

"Don't worry," Knotts said, seeing my unease. "They won't suspect anything. Anyway, you're allowed to say that. I'm not, because I know how much it upsets you."

Who is this guy? I wondered, glancing at Roki. How much did Knotts really know?

"Before you go," he added, "have you tasted my wine yet?" He stopped a server holding a silver tray and grabbed some glasses for all of us. Then Knotts made a toast. "Here's to you," he said merrily, "the saviors of Geniverd." We all drank, then put our empty glasses back on the server's tray. "Cerna," Knotts said, "do you mind if I borrow Roki for a couple of minutes?"

"Not at all," I said.

The two men went off, and I was by myself in a room overcrowded with people talking in pairs. *Great, I thought, now*

I'm alone. Thanks, Knotts. Raad and Tissa were making their way to the next room, flanked by colorful nobles I didn't recognize. I wondered whether anyone would miss Roki and me if we left within the hour. I smoothed down my gown and tried to slow my breathing. That was when I felt the presence of someone I knew all too well approaching from behind.

"Did you get my message?"

Zawne wasn't one to waste time over pleasantries. I turned around and, after a slight bow, followed his lead. "I did. I don't know how much time we have, but I must tell you how shocked I am that you made Lordin queen only a week after—"

"It had to be done," he said, cutting me off. "It wasn't personal."

My heart thudded dully in my chest. "From where I'm sitting, it feels very personal, Zawne."

It was true that I didn't have romantic feelings for Zawne anymore. Still, I cared about him. There were so many women in the world he could have chosen to date, and he had picked Lordin. I just wanted what was best for him.

"Actually," he said, "Lordin told me she's the one who found the antiviral, and that after she found it, you stole it from her to try to impress me."

"No!" I said, my voice cracking with emotion. "After all this time, do you really think I'm that kind of person? Have you not figured out whose side I'm on yet, Zawne? Lordin was holding the cure hostage and working with her evil mother."

"I think you'll find she was working against Emell all along," Zawne said with his nose turned up at me, as if he hadn't heard a single word I'd said. "Lordin led us to Emell and we imprisoned her."

"No, you're mistaken," I said in an angry whisper.

He shook his head. I could see there wasn't anything I

could say that would change Zawne's mind. In any case, I didn't want to be the one to show him Lordin's wickedness. If he was going to be convinced, he needed to witness irrefutable proof firsthand. I hoped that one day he would see her for the evil witch she was.

"Besides, what is it to you that I'm back with Lordin?" he asked. "You're the one who changed and then disappeared for nearly six months. You know it bugged me that you sacrificed yourself. You had *everything*, Kaelyn, and I was fiercely loyal to you. You didn't have to save the world. There were people doing it for us. You think the Crown of Crowns would have let humanity die out?"

They nearly did! I wanted to scream. Yet it was no use arguing with Zawne. I wanted to tell him about the Geniverd he'd never seen, the naturally beautiful places I'd discovered while exploring with Xerx and Vowkin and avoiding the major cities. The untrodden deep caves in Krug, the serene Nurlie archipelagoes, the undisturbed blue lakes in Gaard. His royal head had no patience for any of that. I just wanted to have a normal conversation with Zawne, but he was clearly too stubborn.

"You know I couldn't just sit by and do nothing," I said, folding my arms and frowning.

He shook his head. I knew that Zawne thought I had become a Min to be with Roki, the ultimate betrayal of his trust and loyalty. There was nothing I could say to convince him otherwise, especially since he was with Lordin now and had her poisonous words leaking into his ears every day and night. I knew in that moment I had nothing more for Zawne. His judgment was blinded by love. This talk was futile. It was like telling someone who was lost to find their way on their own. I just had one question for Zawne.

"Do you love her?" I asked.

I could see that he did, even before he answered. His lips parted and he hesitated. I just wanted to hear it so that I could finally draw a line between my old life with Zawne and my new life with Roki. I needed to hear his words. I resisted the urge to read his mind and watched his eyes moving, calculating. Finally, he said it.

"I do. I love her."

That was when Roki joined us. It was time to go. We had to get back to the twins.

"If you ever want to speak to me," I told Zawne, "please ask the Crown of Crowns to relay the message."

Zawne nodded and walked away into the crowd. He never once looked at Roki.

In the heat of all this drama, it was great to have Roki back, even if he'd only been gone a few minutes. I treasured him so much. He was my rock, my lover, my partner. I grabbed his face and kissed him.

"Can we go now, Roki?" I asked, my fingers threading between his.

"Yeah," he said. "Let's go."

As we made our way out, I saw Lady Shiru and Aska Xi drinking wine and chatting. They were both part of the newly combined King and Queen's Council.

"They were—" I started to say.

"I know who they are," Roki interrupted, "and I know what they did to you. Forget about what people in this world once meant to you. It will only bring you pain. You'll now be fighting spiritual wars. Use them to protect the ones you love, but if you mix human emotions with everything else going on, we'll lose."

I thought he was right, that the only way forward was to fully move on. I had to be brutally honest with myself, even where it concerned my family. They would never know my real identity. I wasn't sure that I could extricate myself from their lives without some kind of slow transition. This wasn't like ripping off an adhesive bandage! Yet that was what I'd done to them, wasn't it? I had taken everything. They'd never even had a chance to say goodbye.

Talking to Zawne had made me start to doubt the decisions I'd made. Should I have let things remain as they were? I tightened my grip on Roki's fingers. I needed to be confident, now more than ever.

Just then the room quieted. On one of the screens high up on the wall, I saw Lordin was about to speak. She was somewhere else, in one of the other giant chambers. She held a hand to Zawne, and I heard him think, *Oh yes, the revelations!*

Revelations? What revelations? I couldn't leave until I'd heard what Lordin was about to say.

The lights dimmed and the music stopped. "We have saved the best for last," Lordin said, the thrill in her eyes unmistakable. "We are dying to show you that we're not resting on our laurels."

And then something unexpected happened. I watched as the cameras zoomed in on Zawne, and his eyes turned a fiery gold. He stood in the center of the stage while Lordin moved back off to the side. Two Protectors came and dropped a massive weight on the ground before Zawne. It must have weighed over four hundred pounds.

"Watch me!" Zawne said as he ripped off his shirt. He flexed, and his muscles bulged to a massive and clearly inhuman level, too big and veiny for even my liking. Zawne then lifted the huge weight over his head with both hands, grinning through his teeth. He wasn't even breaking a sweat! People gasped and shrieked, then began to applaud. After Zawne lowered the weight, he called five volunteers onto the stage. Together the five men couldn't budge it an inch, let alone lift it off the ground.

Lordin shouted at the top of her voice, "Imagine Aska warriors who are stronger than ever before." She sounded like a saleswoman. "Imagine these powerful Aska warriors quashing the Gurnot threat forever. Imagine enhanced bodies that will destroy the next superbug before it has a chance to take hold. Ladies and gentlemen, every man and woman in this room can now have superhuman strength and lifelong immunity from the ravages of deadly infections. That's right—all of you! The current ban on genetic engineering won't be lifted. However, we'll allow selective use and introduce aspects of our technology in a controlled way. Thanks to cutting-edge advancements in biotechnology, very soon, if you wish, you will be transhuman. No disease, no slaughter, no Gurnots, and eventually, no death. You will be one step away from immortal, so we'll call our therapy Immuno-Mort. IM!"

The cheering seemed to go on forever. After everyone had hushed, Zawne, whose eyes had returned to their normal brown color, said, "My friends, this is the only way to prevent another virus outbreak. This is the only way to put a stop to the tedious vaccines we must always administer to safeguard our bodies from disease. This is the only way we can conquer the universe as one united race of people!"

The vaccines were now being administered every month. All over the world, the masses were shaken and depressed, still rebuilding their lives after the pandemic. They needed to feel protected against superbugs.

Zawne smiled widely at the crowd. "But that's not all. We have one more surprise for you."

A server brought a basket to the front and held it up high. People craned their necks as something inside shifted, revealing a little face and little hands, little feet kicking its blanket.

"We've just had a baby girl," Zawne said, "and we've named her Arta. She is tiny but mighty. So precious." Zawne pulled in a deep, satisfied breath and held her up for everyone to see. She was as gorgeous as she was jolly.

"Everyone, meet our heir!" Lordin howled.

2

I was waiting outside Istvan High with my arms folded and my fingers drumming anxiously. Xerx and Vowkin would be finishing their first day of school any minute.

This was one of the major disadvantages of being a Min and living in Geniverd. I had to live by the rules of man, by physical laws, such as opening a door with my hand instead of slipping like a ghost through cracks and windows. I had to stand outside the school like an ordinary person and wait for the kids. It was also annoying to use my visin for communicating with people. I hated that. Worst of all was using a flyrarc to travel between continents instead of zipping across the sky like a bolt of fiery lightning.

Before I became a Min, I had thought humans were complex beings. Now I knew better. I could discern their thoughts and their actions, perceive their anxieties, heartaches, and struggles. It all seemed so redundant to me. Humans were really quite simple. Their fears and motivations were common and almost identical from person to person. It

266

was what people said or did, or didn't do, because of these things that made them seem complicated. The annoying part of having a direct line into people's thoughts was that I couldn't say anything to them when they were lying or holding something back. I just had to be patient.

One of the most shocking changes for me was that I no longer cared for man-made luxuries. I didn't care about palaces, expensive clothing, shoes, or fancy items. I cared only for freedom of my spirit. The saving graces were places like Istvan, the coastal town we'd adopted aboveground. Istvan had a wide, clear sky and white sandy beaches. There were perpetual sounds of rustling breezes and waves crashing ashore, interspersed with exotic birdcalls emanating from the woodland in the area.

Humans lived inside boundaries, every house and strip of land marked by a border. Over the last five months, I'd gone wherever I wanted and trespassed on every frontier. There were no more confines for me. I climbed to the tops of the tallest mountains, dived into abyssal craters in the deepest parts of the sea, and traipsed through the thickest forests. With Roki and the twins, I trekked, flew, and swam without a care in the world, no deadlines or obligations. Those were the real luxuries. The whole world was my playground, mine and Roki's. And the best part was that I had a thousand years to explore it, and more than a thousand planets to explore on.

Roki's voice surprised me as he whispered in my ear, "We'll have to go easy on the boys." I breathed in his sweet herbal scent, gentle against the humid and musty atmosphere of the coastal town.

Roki was hunched over behind me, smiling mischievously. When we had gotten back home from the banquet the night before, we had stayed up all night talking. Zawne and Lordin's baby news had taken us by surprise because it signified their unity and decisiveness. How could the Zawne I knew, so pure, so kind, and so sensible, fall for someone like Lordin and commit to her so? Scarier than that was Zawne's display of strength.

"This is a nice surprise," I said, letting Roki wrap his arms around me, smothering me in his scent. "I thought you'd be meeting the senate. There is so much to discuss given yesterday's events."

"This is the first day of school for our kids, Kaelyn. I wouldn't miss it for the world." Roki looked at the sky and smiled. "But I also come with great news for you. We think it's time that you joined the senate. Our meeting is in an hour."

I squeezed him against me. I knew it was time to get on with challenging Lordin. I only wondered where this news was coming from. I never assumed that I'd be invited to join Defiance's leadership. Out of all the people in the senate, I was only familiar with Neuge. He'd scared me a little at first, but I'd come to know him. As for the others, I had no idea what to expect. I would need to make a strong and firm impression with those who helped rule the Gurnots with Roki.

Roki sensed my nervousness. "Only two of them are Min. The other three are humans. Use your gift if you're unsure of anything."

It was true. I could examine their memories if I needed to.

"At least you've saved me from potential small talk with other parents," I told Roki. "As much as I want to be social, I don't want to lie about who I am or make up some elaborate story about why the twins had to start school in the middle of the term. If they ask me to join the parents' club or something, I am going to lose it!"

"A club might be fun for you, Kaelyn. Apart from Neuge, you've hardly made any friends since—"

"Nnati is worth a thousand friends," I cut in.

Being a member of Defiance was a secret that Nnati had harbored for a long time. Even Tissa had never known about it. When I'd asked Nnati to join the Queen's Council, he'd been conflicted. As one of the most high-profile people in Defiance, Nnati had wanted to do more for the secret organization, but the council and the Gaard-Ma Foundation had taken up all of his time. With me gone, Nnati finally had more time for the foundation and Defiance.

Roki had helped me fix Nnati up with Neuge so that I could see more of him, and five months had passed since they'd started dating. At first Roki had had to frequently invite Nnati over for various socials. He was nice to us but behaved very much like a guest—hesitant, polite, guarded. I had still been working at slotting into Nnati's life again without raising his suspicions, hardly speaking about our past or my family. When he hit it off with Neuge and they became an item, I was elated. We were finally able to double-date and spend more time together in Tsiser.

The kids were out of class and chatting in front of the building. They were easy to spot, surrounded by dozens of boys and girls. We'd kept the twins out of sight since their birth, and this was their first full day with humans. Xerx and Vowkin could teach all the classes themselves if they wanted to; they didn't need any tutoring. Our story, if anyone asked, was that we'd adopted the twins after the pandemic, since the incident had left so many children orphaned. Privately, we hoped that going to school would keep them busy and out of trouble. The kids kept begging us to go alone into Shiol, but we weren't ready for them to go there by themselves.

"You have to give credit to the boys for lasting so long with human teenagers," Roki said, pride thick in his voice.

I shook my head. "You know I was once a human kid too. Don't underestimate the human race."

He shrugged, a silly grin on his face that made me crack a smile. I turned my eyes back to the school gates. I could tell Xerx was enjoying all the attention. On the other hand, it was obvious that Vowkin couldn't wait to leave.

"These kids remind me of my teen years," I muttered. "Some full of plans, others still figuring out what to do with their lives. They're growing up too fast, literally."

"You do realize you're still a teenager," Roki said. "You're only eighteen." The way he said it made it seem as though only decades separated us—he was five hundred years older than me! Honestly, with everything that had happened, it was incredible that more time hadn't passed.

"You're barely an adult yourself," I said, and laughed, turning around and kicking his foot playfully. He chuckled before gently wrapping his arms around me and resting his chin on my shoulder. "I just wish Vowkin wouldn't make it so obvious how bored he is."

A pair of women walking by waved at us. They must have been trusted Defiance members who'd visited Tsiser. One of them kept stealing jealous glances at us. I couldn't blame her. I knew how lucky I was to be with Roki.

Roki huffed. "Vowkin feels restricted by his body, and on top of that, he's confined in school. I can understand the humdrum of their lives after everything they've been up to since they were born. We should consider letting them wander Shiol—with protection, of course."

"I'm not sure, Roki. Even with protection, anything could happen to them in Shiol or on other planets. You've told me before that in five hundred years, you have rarely come across Min kids roaming around on their own." This made me slightly jealous of Zawne and Lordin's human baby. It would have a normal life, a normal growth. "Tomorrow they'll meet Hanchell and Riedel. Then we'll know what to do."

"Yeah," Roki said, "you're right, just like always." He nuzzled his nose against my shoulder. I knew he was about to change the subject. "Hmm, you smell so good. I can't wait for us to be alone."

He smelled good too, and he felt good against me. I didn't want him to stop, but we were at the school. I pulled away gently. "That's what got me pregnant in the first place."

Roki shook his head. "Uh-uh. What got you pregnant was your decision to have your ovaries reimplanted." I felt his warm breath on my neck, and I squirmed. He was seducing me in public, teasing me. "We exchanged our vows, and then the contraception failed."

In my defense, I had wanted to preserve my eggs before the labs could destroy them, a standard procedure soon after a woman's death in Geniverd. I was attracted to the idea of experiencing pregnancy one day, but the experience turned out to be anything but normal. Instead of a gestation period of nine months, it had lasted six days. I hadn't been able to leave our house until the babies were born. I knew the twins would be different, but I hadn't expected them to form perfect sentences and to be brilliant at math at only four weeks old. Their curiosity about Shiol was already piqued, and I feared that I couldn't hold them back any longer.

Children were being chaperoned by Protectors into their flyrarcs, engines rumbling. I envied the friendships these kids were making, waving goodbye to their classmates and laughing. I had been homeschooled. My only friends growing up had been other nobles—that is, until Roki came along.

Vowkin approached us. "This is so embarrassing. You didn't have to pick us up."

"It's your first day," I said. "We wouldn't miss it for the world."

"You had fun though, didn't you?" Roki asked. "You've

made new friends, right? Those girls were all over you. They're still whispering."

We all turned to see the group of girls the boys had left behind. They were chatting excitedly and stealing glances at the twins.

"Ask Xerx," Vowkin said, looking unimpressed. "He's totally obsessed with this one girl."

There was a girl waving shyly at Xerx. She had a slim face and long, thick brown hair. I could see why Xerx was taken by her. She was beautiful. She walked to an awaiting vehicle, trailing behind the other kids.

"I'm not obsessed with Erwun," Xerx said as he came running up to us.

"Yeah, right," Vowkin said. "That's why you made Oliviria sick and made everyone think she was having one of the unwanted reactions." He turned to me and Roki. "She had such a bad tummy ache that she had to be carried out of the theater about two hours ago."

I was confused. "Unwanted reactions from what?"

Xerx's and Vowkin's eyes met briefly, looking at each other like I was nuts.

"Adverse reactions to IM therapy," Roki said calmly. "Over the last couple of hours, there have been reports of people having headaches, fever, dizziness. I'll tell you more later."

I shuddered. I'd expected some adverse reactions, so I wasn't too concerned about these. What surprised me was the speed at which Zawne and Lordin had terminated the vaccination program in favor of the IM. I'd been deliberately ignoring most announcements from VondRust in a childish sulk, and it had to stop.

"Xerx," I said, now cross. "I told you, no showing off or using your powers on humans. At least wait until you've met the Crown of Crowns to understand what you're dealing with."

"I wasn't showing off," Xerx said. "I was helping her. The whole school thing is so mundane otherwise."

"Okay, maybe Erwun isn't such a bad thing," Roki said. "It sounds like she makes school a bit more interesting for you, Xerx. Maybe we can help you with that, as long as you stay in school and act normal."

I widened my eyes at Roki. His reasoning was sound, but was he bribing Xerx with dating advice? He shot me a look that said, *Trust me, I know what I'm doing.*

"That's great for Xerx. What about me?" Vowkin said.

"Just stay positive and think creatively," Roki replied. "In time, you'll find something that interests you. We'll help both of you to stay focused." Roki narrowed his eyes as if something had just occurred to him. He folded his arms across his chest. "Did you say the IM is now also causing stomachache?"

"No, just in Oliviria's case," Vowkin said, rolling his eyes at Xerx.

"Okay." Roki patted Vowkin on the back. "We should get back to the house. Your mama and I have work to do."

3

*T*hirty minutes later we were back at our house in Tsiser with the twins. The twins immediately settled in front of the giant holo-screen in the parlor and began playing some video game that I didn't understand. I knew they played against other Min, constantly trying to beat the top score in Geniverd.

Roki retreated to the library, where I found him hunched over some papers at his desk. I now belonged to him even though Min didn't exactly marry. They were simply bonded in friendship, enchantment and deep love. I'd wanted more than that—a promise or a commitment that was intimate, meaningful, powerful yet simple. And so, we made vows. We pledged to forever treasure, respect and care for each other. To cheer each other on and protect each other forever. I cherished him and I didn't want to share him with anyone. Seeing him now, peaceful and undistracted, made me so happy. I slid my hands down his chest and kissed his neck.

"I know this meeting is important, Roki. I just hope it's

quick. I'd rather be here at home, cuddling with you, than doing any bureaucracy stuff."

Roki turned, breaking my grasp on him, and pressed his lips to mine. He was delicious, so very delicious and all mine. I wished we could stay like this forever. It was too bad we had so much work to do if we wanted to save our world.

Defiance had been stalled recently. Our members had been blighted by horrible depression. It didn't help that the majority of the upper class had come out unscathed from the pandemic. Now that Zawne had installed Hagan as his new queen, VondRust did nothing to quash stories that I was to blame for the virus. I wanted to use Defiance to hit back at them. I just didn't know how. There were just six days left before the new Crown of Crowns was to be announced, and Zawne and Lordin hadn't gained traction with their election campaign. It was hard to convince Min from all over the galaxy to vote for Zawne, since he was a human. It made sense that Zawne and Lordin's focus would turn fully to Geniverd. Still, I didn't think Lordin would give up a chance at ultimate power so easily.

Roki groaned. "I want to stay home too, Kaelyn. I forgot to mention that Knotts is joining us today. He doesn't usually join the meetings, because he's busy with other important work, like making sure we're manufacturing a sufficient number of Guardians and weapons and keeping up connections with royals and very influential nobles. Knotts is the reason our Guardians are more advanced than the Protectors are. That's why, as our main sponsor, he's also on the senate."

We hadn't discussed the mechanics of the senate meetings and members in great detail before today. He told me the other senators' names were Gorm, Marten, and Olorc.

"But you can end the meeting whenever you want." It was a

statement, but it came out like a question. "Just in case it's too much too soon for me and I can't handle it."

"Well, I'm the chair, so technically, yes, but I don't know if Knotts has something else planned. Come on, we need new ideas, new strategies. I can't see a better nomination than you."

I was still hesitant. I didn't completely know what my role in Defiance was. Not really. I wasn't sure about joining the senate. It seemed a poor time to go, since the main sponsor was attending.

"What about the fact that everyone thinks I caused the virus?" I asked. "I'm just not sure how much help I can be. I think it's more likely that I'll end up derailing any progress you've already made."

"Just come, for me," Roki said. "Now that Lordin is running the show in VondRust with Zawne as her puppet, your inside knowledge of Zawne could come in handy. We may need that information in the upcoming struggle."

I sighed. "Yeah, I guess that makes sense. I just wish we could tell everyone that Hagan is actually Lordin and that she's evil. That anyone thinks Hagan is some pure soul is beyond belief. I can't bring myself to call her our queen. If only they knew the truth. That's why I don't understand how Zawne returned to her. He does know the truth!"

Roki shrugged. "Maybe he refuses to see it."

"Maybe." I sighed again, crossed my arms, and said, "Okay, I'll come with you."

"Perfect! You'll need the snow gear that I got just for you. It's in the wardrobe. And we need to leave now or we'll be late. I've already told the boys that there's food for them in the fridge."

"Snow gear? Where are we going?"

"Capernort."

* * *

Roki masked us as we flew over Krug like a pair of fiery stars in the day sky, then over the sea. We landed in Capernort in the foothills of Mount Cap, located close to the northern-most point of Lodden. My face was wet, as heavy snowflakes blustered around us. Only now did I understand why Roki had gotten the winter gear for me. This place was a frozen nothingness, with only about fifty people gathered inside a lonely encampment.

"Aska trainees," Roki said. "This is one of their training camps. It's a fifteen-minute walk to the snow house. Neuge will join us at some point. He's currently running an errand for me."

"Okay," I said. It must've been twenty degrees below freezing. The walk would've been treacherous for me if I were human. I wondered how the trainees were coping with the frigid conditions and the beating snow.

"They come out in the snow for short periods to build up their endurance," Roki said. "We may be using these bodies, but we have some perks, thanks to being Min. It could be twice this cold, and we wouldn't experience any ill effects from it. Sure, we feel the cold, but there is no pain or chance of death by hypothermia."

"Don't you consider your body your own?" I asked. "I've been in this body for nearly six months, and I already consider it mine. Why call them 'these' bodies?"

"Your perspective shifts when you've had to change bodies several times," Roki said dryly.

I'd never thought about it like that before. I'd never really considered how many times Roki had changed bodies. I knew he'd done it a lot. He was a spirit that was over five hundred years old. All these months together, and we'd never discussed it. Now that I thought about it, there were a lot of things we'd never discussed.

"Long way for us to come for a senate meeting," I said, "especially when you could have held it in the study at home, like you usually do. Did you give everyone sufficient notice?"

"Yes. I wanted us all here in time. They may have gotten here before us, which is why we are staging this trek to the house. That way, if Gorm, Marten, or Olorc see us, they will assume we landed by the Aska training camp. Unlike Neuge and Knotts, the humans won't be able to see very far in the snow."

"Look," he said, pointing through the swirling mist, "you can see the trainee Askas." He pointed to the foot of Mount Cap, to a line of people huddled outside in the cold. One by one they were being jabbed in their arms. My eyesight was perfect even through the haze.

"Are they getting their IMs?" I said, shivering. Even though I was a Min and couldn't be harmed by extreme temperatures, it was still darn cold! The layers of wool around me did nothing to insulate my body. I hugged myself tight as my boots crunched the thick snow underfoot, my feet leaving a long trail in the snow next to Roki's.

Roki must have sensed me shivering. He wrapped one arm around me and squeezed tight.

"Thanks," I said. "I know it's just a few minutes' walk, but this must be the coldest place I've ever visited."

"What? Cold? Summer is just getting started!" He laughed. "This is mild compared to spring."

Just then a large flyrarc descended in front of us, next to the snow house we were heading to. It was a big log cabin nestled near the mountain. I matched Roki's quickened pace to meet the vehicle.

"Our human senators have arrived before us," he said. "Wait for me inside the snow house."

Two men and one woman disembarked. They were older than us in appearance; I estimated somewhere in their thirties. Gorm was tall, lean, and bald. Olorc was a bearded man with heavy jowls and a husky frame. Marten was a tall woman, her dark hair arranged into a short, no-nonsense style. Roki greeted them, and to my surprise, all four of them walked back into the flyrarc. I figured Roki wanted to tell them about Knotts's attendance or my attendance, or both. I waited at the doorway of the snow house, wondering if Neuge was close. I wondered how he and Nnati were doing.

I shuddered when I heard a voice in my ear. "Your first time in Capernort?"

I turned, and Knotts was staring at me with his sharp green eyes.

"Uh, yes. Actually, I've been to Lodden a couple of times, just not this far north. Is it that obvious?" My overly friendly voice made me cringe.

"A shame," he said, "we both had to visit the end of the world in the freezing snow just to be alone together. It's funny how life turns out. Only a year ago, there I was, hoping we'd be happily married by now. And now here we are, not married and standing in a blizzard."

"Married?" I barked a confused laugh, thinking it was a joke.

Knotts's expression was serious. "Before you chose Zawne, you received a marriage proposal from me. It was only fitting that a man like me propose to the most beautiful woman in the world, Kaelyn of Gaard."

I tried to recall the deluge of proposals I'd received and remembered that I hadn't taken any of them seriously. I hadn't even bothered to read any of them myself. It felt like a lifetime ago, yet a year had barely passed. I didn't want to offend Knotts by accessing his memories for further details.

"Then I saw Zawne announcing your engagement," he continued. "My heart was broken beyond repair."

"I'm sorry," I said, genuinely apologetic. "I had no idea. But honestly, you know how it is. I had no say in the matter. I never even saw any marriage proposals. I think it was my brother, Raad, who took care of them. Did you not hear from someone in the family?"

"You mean the polite, generic rejection from NordHaven after Zawne's declaration of his love for you?" Knotts scoffed. "Look, you don't have to apologize. It is what it is. I proposed to someone else after you rejected me. All for the better, anyway, since I'd already have been a widower if we'd married."

I wanted to throw some snow in this guy's face. He was being so smug to me! I glanced at Roki in the hope that he'd hurry up. He was exiting the flyrarc and laughing with the senators.

"I'm sorry that you didn't receive a personalized response." It was all I could come back with. My face was growing hot.

He didn't answer. Instead, Knotts smiled tightly and glared at me as if he was about to kill me. I desperately wanted to search his memories but I didn't know the extent of his Min powers, and I needed friends in my new world. I couldn't afford to offend Knotts and alienate him just because he was jealous of Roki and Zawne.

I asked him, "Are you here because you hate me?"

"No. I wouldn't be here if I hated you." Knotts looked past me, a weary expression on his face. "Anyway, it doesn't matter anymore. You chose him in the end."

Roki was finally approaching us, a big smile on his face.

Knotts whispered to me, "Do you even know why he was at the ball where you first met, Kaelyn?"

"No," I said, surprised at the question. Everything Knotts was saying surprised me, although I tried not to show it. "And I don't need to know," I added defiantly. "He's mine, and nothing else matters."

The truth was that I desperately wanted to know. Roki had never told me anything about his past, about his life before he'd met me. What secrets were locked in Knotts's thick skull?

"Okay," he said. "Suit yourself."

"I see you two have met again," Roki said as he appeared. He patted Knotts on the shoulder and ushered him toward the door, miming silently to me that he was sorry. What in the world had just happened?

* * *

The inside of the snow house was larger than I could have imagined. The walls were decorated with ice sculptures six feet tall, kept frozen inside pale blue streams of subzero air. A ripple in the air ushered into my nose the scents of woodsmoke and ice. It seemed the perfect location for a clandestine meeting with a secret senate. Still, it was my first time with these people, and something about the affair seemed incredibly odd to me. I didn't like the bear rug in the center of the wooden floor; it left me feeling unsettled.

Ever since I'd joined Defiance, all the senate meetings had taken place underground in Tsiser, the secret Gurnot city. Maybe that was why it felt weird to me. Or maybe I just didn't like it because I was cold and therefore cranky. Maybe I was too used to Gaard's tropical weather or the moderate sunshine of Krug.

"Please, sit." Roki motioned all of us to two benches while

he stood in the center of the room, looking self-satisfied. Our eyes locked, and his lips twisted into a mischievous smile.

"Thank you for inviting us here, Knotts," said Roki, gesturing to Knotts, who had taken off his beanie to reveal his slick black hair. Knotts had an overall visage that was glowing. "It's a nice change. My girlfriend, Cerna, joins us today. Please join me in welcoming her."

Knotts looked right at me. His face changed into a supercilious look that I didn't understand. It was irritating. I averted my eyes and focused on Roki, willing him to hurry up and get to business.

Roki started the meeting.

"We might as well admit it," he said. "We're losing followers to Queen Hagan. Her constant visin briefings have convinced many of our supporters that she's doing more on social injustice than we have ever done or could ever do. She says that she's transforming their fortunes behind the scenes. We haven't seen evidence of this. Every month, our people grow poorer and poorer. They have no major assets to speak of, whereas the rich keep growing just by virtue of their existence. And now, as we mentioned in our briefing, there's the rapid rollout of the IM, a substance we don't fully understand. For most people, the lure of becoming superhuman will be too great to question timescales. More recently, the queen's supporters are saying her name belongs alongside Lordin's."

Marten cleared her throat and said, "Saint Lordin."

"Uh, yes ... of course. Saint Lordin." I could feel the pain in Roki's throat as he corrected himself. After a brief pause, he said, "We're here because we urgently need new ideas. How are we getting on with the markets?"

Olorc's heart started to beat abnormally fast. I could hear it across the room with my Min senses. What was he so nervous about?

"Well," Olorc said. He had to exhale just to steady his voice. "We've had great successes in Krug and Surrvul. A record total of nine market days in a space of three weeks. Two of those days have been held in Szuc. And considering—"

"Considering we've never been to Szuc before ..." I interrupted. I knew what Olorc had been about to say, but I was beating him to it. Szuc was an unheard-of town in southern Surrvul, and I wanted the senators to think that our agenda had my full attention. "It means our work with the Ava-Surrvul has reached new heights."

"Yes," Gorm said. He sounded surprised. "To be fair, Knotts has been working on the Surrvul nobles for a while in order to get us the market approvals. How did you know we hadn't been to Szuc yet?"

"I do my homework," I said, smiling but feeling a tad guilty for using my Min powers this way. I remembered that Surrvul had been trying for centuries to get on the throne. It looked like more and more of them were feeling slighted by the monarchy and getting ready to join Defiance.

Olorc was beaming when he said, "More Defiance members are learning that they can carry babies and that it's not an unnatural or evil thing. The situation in Gaard, Shondur, Nurlie, and here in Lodden isn't improving. But given the death of Queen Kaelyn, it's amazing that our outcomes in Gaard are stable."

Gaard? I didn't expect Raad to understand the cultural importance of the markets to the people. *Then again, isn't Tissa helping him?*

"That's amazing news," Roki said. "The dummy markets are our main gateway to the people. Let's all keep up the good work. But we still need new ideas. Once our people discover they've been neglected and won't be receiving the same genetic privileges as the upper class, we need to show that we're on their side and ready to take action. We need to build anger on top of disappointment."

Everyone started talking at once, apart from Knotts and me. One person dared to suggest that we merge our efforts with Hagan. This went on for thirty minutes. While they bickered among themselves, I noticed that nobody contradicted anything Roki said. This was nothing new, but it was the first time it had hit me so blatantly: *Nobody argues with Roki. Period.* But something was changing. There was a shift of attitude in the air. I knew Roki had always been revered as the leader of Defiance, but I caught a few jabs being thrown at him subtly, even though nobody openly challenged him. And what was that business earlier about 'Saint Lordin' from Marten? Was Roki losing his power as the leader of the Gurnots? If he was, did Roki have me to blame?

I started questioning myself. I thought, *If I hadn't married Zawne, maybe Lordin wouldn't have killed all those people. Maybe she'd have released the antiviral sooner. Maybe she'd have gone about things differently to start with. Maybe ...*

I snapped out of it when I felt Knotts's hot gaze on me again. He was now standing quietly at Roki's side as he stared. I guessed, since he was the main sponsor, he was allowed some pull in the organization, but why had he remained so silent? And why was he always leering at me? He could have helped Roki's position or said a positive word about one of Roki's ideas. He hadn't. It was almost as if Knotts had called the meeting, not Roki, to try to throw my boyfriend's leadership off-balance. What was this guy's deal?

Neuge entered the snow house in a huff. He paused, bowed to Roki and Knotts, then whispered something in Roki's ear. Roki turned around and looked through the window at the Aska trainees while people prattled on to each other. After a few seconds, Roki clapped his hands to get everyone's attention.

"I'm very sorry," he said, somewhat hesitantly, "but I must end our meeting early. We'll reconvene soon."

Knotts was unmoved. He was still focused on me with a strange, stony smile. "No problem, Roki." But his eyes were on me as he spoke. "It was great to meet your girlfriend, Cerna. I hope we meet again soon."

* * *

Roki and I were home in minutes after the meeting, back in our house in Tsiser. "I need your help with something very important," Roki said after we'd shrugged out of our snow gear and established ourselves in the kitchen. I desperately wanted a hot mug of tea after such a strange and frigid day.

"Of course," I said, pouring myself a cup. "What is it?"

"It is the final blow to stop Lordin once and for all and to put an end to the wicked cycle of Decens-Lenitas for good. Thanks to the fires, nobles are scared of what we can do, but the time has come for us to fulfill our purpose. The final battle is upon us."

I remembered the mysterious fires I'd only ever heard about or seen from the safe distance of my visin, back before I knew about Roki's involvement in Defiance. I had always wondered how the supposed dragon had managed to destroy the materials, resources, and buildings that nobles cared about without anyone getting hurt. Was I finally going to meet Roki's supposed friend, the notorious Gurnot Dragon?

Roki continued. "And if we're not going for the Crown of Crowns position, then we'll have to do something special, something unprecedented."

"Theoretically," I said, swirling the tea gently in its mug, "we could still enter the race with several days to go." I shook my head. "But never mind. I don't think I want another throne. Geniverd was hard enough. I can't imagine trying to rule the galaxy."

"None of that is important right now," he said. I hadn't seen Roki so serious in a long time. "I'm talking about a major war targeting the upper class. This time it will be epic. I'm talking about real war. I don't like it, but I'm afraid it must be done. We have to move beyond fires and strike the monarchy where it hurts—in the capital."

I was stunned, my body unnaturally still. I was thinking about the potential loss of life, and people who could get hurt. "And ... but ... war? Really, war? What do you need me for?"

"I need you to instigate the war."

4

"*You* want me to instigate a war!"

I stood for a moment in shock, eyes wide, full of horror. I wouldn't have believed Roki if not for the grim expression on his face, his lips taut and his eyes cold. I'd never seen him so stern before. I knew he was serious. Still, I couldn't imagine it. "You're joking, right? Tell me you're joking, Roki!"

He said nothing.

I was under no illusion that the creation of an equal society in Geniverd was going to be straightforward but starting a war … that was not how I'd imagined my introduction to the senate was going to turn out. Maybe I'd been too naive in believing change could be achieved without violence or death. I'd been warned so many times about the Gurnots, but I'd trusted in Roki to persevere through love and peace. I barely recognized the man standing before me.

"How?" I asked.

"Gaard already wants a war," Roki said. "They just don't know it yet. We have intelligence that says they are already teaming up with Surrvul and Krug to show their solidarity after what Zawne and Lordin did to you. Surrvul has always been up for a war. We now have a huge opportunity to hasten Gaard's decision. If we have Gaard, we'll probably get Krug too. Defiance can't do this without your help."

I felt like Roki wasn't telling me everything, that there was something Neuge had told him in Capernort that had led to this.

"I'm still processing your words," I told him. "What is your justification for such a war?"

"You already know, Kaelyn. Right now, we are losing, thanks to Queen Hagan, aka Saint Lordin. More people are being swayed by the current system and are losing their faith in Defiance. Our agents are telling us—"

"You mean your spies," I snarled. My stomach was tense.

"Fine, our spies. Don't say it like it's a dirty thing. We need spies to operate efficiently. Look, Lordin has recruited Min in Geniverd to work for her, and two of them recently infiltrated our network. We caught them, and they won't be coming back. We can shape things before it's too late, but we need to act now."

I suddenly realized what this was about. Roki was vulnerable. He'd lost control of Defiance and the senate. Instead of connecting with others and looking for a sustainable way to deal with the problem, he was seeking control. This was just like how he had abandoned me after my mother had died, because there had been nothing he could do. I understood now. In times of trouble, Roki sought power. With Lordin in the lead, Roki needed to do something drastic to regain his control.

"We planted our own agents," he said. "What they discovered is unnerving."

"What did they find?"

"They found out that the IM is laced with something we haven't been able to identify yet, but we figure it's something sinister. That's what Neuge told me in Capernort. The people are being conditioned. We just don't know what for."

"Dosed! You mean we're being drugged?" It was hard to stomach. I didn't think Zawne had a single evil bone in his body. How could he condone such a thing? Then again, after seeing that brutish display at the party ... could he have changed so radically in such a short amount of time?

"Maybe people are just experiencing side effects," I said. "That's pretty normal."

"No." Roki shook his head. "We don't think so. Lordin may be trying to make the entire population transhuman, but something else is going on. Our investigations are only in the early stages, but we are fairly certain there are two different substances being administered. There is one for the common folk and one for the upper class. As of fifteen minutes ago, we learned that about one hundred Askas have been confidentially receiving the same dosage as Zawne, and they're all on track to reach the desired effects."

Roki sighed, made a fist, and said through his teeth, "It's just so hard to prove. The manufacturing process is tightly controlled, and there is nothing we can do about it. The times our people have accessed the manufacturing plants and gained some footing, it turned out even those at the highest level didn't have a clue what was going on. We suspect Lordin has a powerful Min, or maybe a few of them, supporting her cause."

"I could read people's memories," I said, "get to the bottom of it that way."

"I doubt it," Roki said. "I'm sure Lordin has thought about that already. Besides, ascertaining which Min are working for Lordin will be challenging, since our resources now need to be focused elsewhere. Anyway, here's what I know: A war like this will disrupt the IM supply. It will also test Lordin's resolve and force her to make mistakes. If we hit her hard and fast, it will also rattle her campaign for the spot of Crown of Crowns. I know she's not winning now, but that could change at any time in the next couple of days. I'm sure she hasn't given up."

Roki was making good points. If Lordin was truly mutating the entire human species with an unregulated substance, she definitely needed to be stopped. Still, the harder we hit Lordin, the harder the people would be affected.

I asked, "Has someone analyzed the IM yet?"

"Neuge has been testing random samples, but we've got nothing out of them."

I hated that Lordin was still up to her scheming ways. Just how evil could one person be? Could she really want to eliminate the entire human race—all of Geniverd?

Roki ran his fingers through his golden hair and sighed. "She may be using her power to distort things, distort our findings, distort the chemical compounds in the IM. It's impossible to say. Whatever is in the IM can't be good though, right? Otherwise, she wouldn't have to hide it."

"Yes," I said, not wanting Roki to think I didn't trust his judgment. Then I remembered what Knotts had said back at the snow house, about Roki's murky past. "Hey, why didn't you tell me who Knotts really is?" I asked him.

"Knotts?" Roki looked confused. "I did. Remember? I said he is our main sponsor."

"Sure, but you never told me he was once my suitor."

Roki's face slowly relaxed. Then he started laughing. "He was?"

"Apparently." Now I was laughing. "Another rebel high-ranking nobleman who fancied being king."

"Didn't you check his memories at the banquet? You can use your gift whenever you wish, remember?"

"I didn't want to be rude."

"His wife was a major supporter of ours. She got sick with the virus while assisting in the Nurlie Island revolt and died before we found the antiviral."

"Oh," I said, thinking this might explain why his behavior toward me had been so odd. "He seemed angry with me," I said. "I wonder if he believes it was my fault that his wife died. Surely he knows about Lordin."

"He does know."

I reached forward and took Roki's hand in mine, then lowered my voice. "Let's say I can help somehow with the war, like you want. What about my family? How do we shield them from this?"

"I will protect them," Roki said. "I made a promise to you, and I will not go back on that promise. If anything, they will be better off standing with us rather than standing against us."

"With us or against us?" I let go of his hand. "Where are you going with this?"

"This is where you come in, Kaelyn. I need you to get Raad to lay the foundation for war."

I laughed, a bit too loudly for my own liking. "I'm sorry, Roki, but not even I am fully convinced. Raad will never go for it. Decens-Lenitas and all that. It's against the code."

"That was before," he said. "Raad loved you a lot, and we know he's angry at Zawne for disrespecting your memory. The code hasn't seemed quite so important to him since your death, and Raad won't be alone in feeling this way. We only need him to ally with us. Krug will only join the effort if Gaard is with us. Then, with our links to the Ava-Surrvul gained through Knotts, we can push the war into full swing. But it needs to be justified first simply by using strength of numbers, and for that we need Gaard. You, Kaelyn, are our only way in."

"It won't happen," I said. "Raad may be angry, but he won't consider a full-blown war. It's just too extreme." I paused, remembering what Knotts had said. "Is that why you invited me to Capernort? Are you using me as a tool in your little war effort?"

"What! No way. Come on, Kaelyn. Do you really think I would do that to you?"

"Okay, then tell me what brought you to the ball in the first place, when we met for the first time. Why were you there?"

Roki's face went tight. "Not now," he said, little more than a whisper. "I'll tell you. I promise that I will. Just not now."

I narrowed my eyes at him. Something about this was wrong. Roki, Knotts, war—what was happening here?

"Does Knotts know about your proposed war plan?" I asked.

"No, not yet. I received the IM intel from Neuge at the senate meeting. I haven't had time to discuss anything with anyone."

"I see." It sounded to me like Roki was desperate and this was more of a bid for power than for world peace. "Give it a few days, Roki. Let's see if there is anything else that we can do."

"Like what?" Roki's face was going red. "You want to have a peaceful protest? You want to have a conference call with the clan leaders? They would never give us the time of day, Kaelyn. They can't even comprehend the danger they are in. All that the clans are interested in is maintaining their power. No one would dare challenge the monarchs, apart from the Surrvul, without our backing and approval."

"But isn't war an automatic death sentence for Defiance

and its followers?" I asked. "We can't match Geniverd's weapons."

Roki's expression got deadly serious. "Actually, we can. We have been building our weapons inside royal factories and smuggling them out for the last four years. We now have double the number of weapons that Geniverd has, and we have twice as many Guardians as they have Protectors. All these units are just waiting to be activated. I masked the whole operation so that nobody knows. And by the way, you can't reveal anything about the IM to anyone. Not yet."

"Why not?"

"Because Lordin can't find out what we know about the IM. If she does, she'll have time to prepare. She might poison everyone seriously with the next batch. Our first attack must be a surprise."

"And in the meantime?" I asked. "You will just say nothing and let the population be slowly dosed?"

"That's your decision," he said. "If you say yes to the war, we can stop IM administration immediately. It's up to you, Kaelyn. Talking to Lordin or the clan heads will do nothing. The only solution is war. And we don't have much time. We need to attack soon, before the next dose is handed out. That means we only have a couple of weeks."

Before I could reply, the chime went off. The voices of Hanchell and Riedel boomed around us. "Six days to go. Still in the lead, from Spectrius Z8, are Erda and Lithra!"

* * *

There were times when I wanted to be with Tissa and Nnati so badly that I secretly watched them when they were together. I hated doing it, because it felt wrong, but I did it anyway, because I was desperate for their friendship. I had the whole world at my disposal, and yet I craved my old human connections. It was funny in a way, maybe ironic. I had invited Neuge and Nnati to the house several times before they had finally accepted, and it lifted my spirits greatly to see Nnati in the flesh. That was over two months ago. Now Nnati and Neuge were coming to the house at the behest of Roki. They were coming to speak of war. Still, at least I would get to see Nnati.

Xerx and Vowkin had just put on their school uniforms. Roki was going over their homework quickly to help them decide what to get wrong on purpose to maintain their normal teenage appearances. I stood over them with my arms folded across my chest. "Will I see you boys when you get back from school?"

"I have a thing with Erwun after school," Xerx said. "I probably won't get back until very late."

"A date? I can't believe it, Xerx. You've only just met this girl."

He shrugged, indifferent.

"Okay," I said, "but I want you to take your brother with you."

"What?" Xerx blurted out. "Why? They are just humans. Besides, Vowkin has his own plans."

"Yeah," Vowkin said. "I'm going with the other boys for a keinball match after school. I'm trying to get on the team, but the coach has it in for me for some reason. After the match, I might go to a street party."

Roki came over with their schoolbags. "You've only been in this world for six months," he said. "Your mother just wants to make sure you make no mistakes. Otherwise, you could get into trouble with the Crown of Crowns before you turn one year old. Do your things but come home together, okay?"

"Yeah, yeah," the twins said in unison as they took their bags.

I kissed them both on the head and then watched them scuttle out the door.

"I hope they'll be all right," I said to Roki once they were gone.

"They'll be fine," he said. "They've got our blood, after all."

We moved through the house, which Roki had renovated after I moved in a few months ago. Downstairs it was incredibly homey, painted in soft tones of vanilla and gray, and decorated with modern artwork. We walked through the twins' game room, with their equipment scattered on the carpet, through the expansive sitting room, and to the rear entrance, where Nnati and Neuge were being escorted inside by a pair of brass-armored Guardians. Roki and I leaned against the marble support column and watched them enter. They were so busy with each other that neither of them noticed us.

"I might as well move to Tsiser," Nnati was mumbling. "I'm always here, anyway."

From his thoughts, dreams, and memories, I knew that Nnati was deeply in love with Neuge, which was astonishing considering how contrasting their personalities were. Nnati was warm and gentle, while Neuge was firm and gruff, although I guessed it didn't matter. It warmed my heart to see them together, especially coming into the home I'd made with Roki.

Neuge and Nnati were paused in the foyer. Nnati cupped Neuge's face. "I think it would be better for me to live here. Here is where you are, and I always want to be with you, so it only makes sense."

"Is that right?" Neuge said dryly, unenthusiastically. I was surprised when he planted a firm kiss on Nnati's lips, then ran his fingers through his dark hair. "Maybe you can give up your work at the Gaard-Ma Foundation," Neuge said. "That way you can spend all of your free time with me. They won't miss you aboveground anymore. You can stay … with me."

"No," Nnati and I both said at the same time. I had said it by accident and instantly stepped forward, while Nnati and Neuge whirled to gape at me. Neuge quickly let go of Nnati and took a step back.

"We didn't see you two there," Neuge said, smiling, looking like he was up to something.

I wanted to defend what I'd said—I had reacted out of instinct. I didn't want anyone other than Nnati to care for the GMAF. It belonged to Nnati now, and I would always trust him to uphold the memory of my mother, the former Gaard-Ma. Rather than explain myself, I walked over and gave Neuge a big welcoming hug, then I gave one to Nnati. "You know, Neuge," I said, stepping back to look between them, "you can't ask Nnati to cut himself off from the thing most dear to him. That's shameful. It's just plain mean."

Then I said to Nnati, "And you, don't listen to a word he says. I heard you were in the front row at the woman's funeral with the Gaard-Elder and the new Gaard-Ma. You must have meant a great deal to the family. They might not take it kindly if you quit the foundation out of the blue."

"It will be fine," Neuge said with a dismissive wave of his hand. "Raad and Tissa will understand. I'm sure if Kaelyn were alive, she, too, would understand." He said this while looking straight into my eyes, piercing my Min soul.

"I just can't do it," Nnati said. "Cerna is right. Kaelyn trusted me with the foundation, and I believe in it. I can't just give up all my responsibilities and move underground like a troll. Everyone will be suspicious. The Protectors will look for me, and the monarchs will be terrified of me spilling their secrets. Also, the foundation links the former Gaard-Ma's legacy to the, uh ... to beloved Lordin's."

Nnati was looking at me carefully. I could see he didn't trust me yet. The Nnati who'd once publicly spoken out against Lordin during a speech given by Roki, and among her greatest supporters no less, was censoring himself, succumbing to the disease of referring to Lordin as saintly or beloved, lest it peeved me in some way. If only he knew that he didn't need to worry. I wanted to tell him who I was so badly that it hurt!

"Not only that, Nnati," I said, "but just because you are in Defiance and clearly in love, that does not mean you have to give up the rest of your life. You still have to live for you and what you enjoy, and I can see in your eyes that you love helping people through the foundation."

"True," he said. Nnati turned to Neuge. "Well, there you have it. I think I'll have to stay aboveground. At least for now."

Neuge sighed, somehow looking bored and concerned at the same time. "I was never going to win that argument, was I?" he said.

Nnati smiled playfully. "Not in a million years."

"Okay, okay," Roki said, stepping from the shadow of the column. "That's enough lovey-doveyness for now. Neuge, I need you in the library right away." Roki looked at me. "Cerna, can you entertain Nnati while Neuge and I have a little chat?"

"Sure," I said, smiling genuinely between the three men. This was it. After so many months, I would finally have Nnati all to myself! "It's no problem. Come with me, Nnati. I'll fix us something to drink."

* * *

There was so much I wanted to tell Nnati. There was so

little I was allowed to tell him. I could reveal literally nothing of what had happened in the past six months, unless I wanted us both to face an ultimate death. I had to grit my teeth and treat Nnati like a semi-stranger, like a new friend, some guy who was dating my boyfriend's friend. I supposed it was okay. He was still the same Nnati I'd always loved. Only, I was beginning to wonder … was I still Kaelyn of Gaard?

I took Nnati into the sitting room, decorated in the worldly aesthetics of an explorer. I had one of the Guardian defense robots fetch us cups of tea as we sat on beige sofas and faced each other.

"It's refreshing, this place," Nnati said, looking absently out the window at the waterfall cascading in the distance. "Even though we are underground, it feels like we're immersed in nature. The wooden paneling is soft and natural. The stones in the ceiling make it feel like we're under the overhang of a big boulder or cliff. And I love the virtual scenery in the windows—the forest, beaches, and deserts. Tsiser sometimes feels more natural than the world aboveground."

"Yeah," I said. I had to keep in mind that Nnati thought I was an orphaned scientist from Gaard, and that my backstory was that I had met and fallen in love with Roki completely by accident. "Roki is the architect and the designer of this place. He's so wonderful at creating a cozy environment. I always feel very at peace here."

"Well," Nnati said, "he is gifted. He is also humble and using his wealth to help our members. You obviously barely use these rooms. I can tell because everything looks new. The carpets, the furniture—none of it has a worn appearance to it. You must have other homes, right? Probably aboveground."

I was not surprised that Nnati was speaking his mind. It was one of the things I enjoyed most about him. He was right. We hardly used the rooms in the house. Most of our time was spent doing Min activities. I only needed to briefly rest my body to keep it from withering, but I was able to do that in any place, and I preferred to sleep beside rivers and waterfalls. Other than our 'fake' house in Istvan, which we used to keep up appearances, we had no need for other homes.

"We don't, actually," I told Nnati. "We are just very busy. Not much time to lounge around the house."

"That makes sense," he said. "What's it like, anyway? How does it feel to be the boss's girlfriend, Cerna? You are both so young, yet Roki is the leader of Defiance, and you have already adopted orphans. It must feel like a whirlwind."

"It does," I answered immediately. Nnati was thinking about money, and I needed to maintain my cover. "I was just a lowly scientist in Gaard before I met Roki. I never expected to have all of this comfort. As for the kids, well, they keep me grounded. Plus, it was the least Roki and I could do after the pandemic took away so many parents. I love them and I love Roki. Everything else is superficial. You may feel the same way, that material things are not important."

I could tell by Nnati's expression that he was baffled and maybe a little bit skeptical. After all, lots of well-off people claimed they weren't in it for the money. I tried to explain myself better. "This is completely different from what you probably experienced as Queen Kaelyn's right-hand man. You saw everything she did, the enormous palace with hundreds of rooms, the countless Protectors, the unimaginable acres of land. By anyone's standards, she had it all. And yet, could you say she was truly happy?"

"I'd like to think she found happiness in me, in her family, and in her friends, especially the new Gaard-Ma. But to be completely honest, who knows if she was happy? She seemed genuinely happy with the king, but it's impossible to know what was inside her heart."

Nnati seemed sullen. He got up and walked over to a large silver sculpture standing at the opposite end of the room, then tilted his head as if asking for permission to touch the piece.

"Go for it," I said, and Nnati slowly glided two fingers across it.

I could see that talking about his dearly departed friend—me—to a person he thought he barely knew—even though it was still me—was a kind of betrayal in his mind. Still, he seemed curious about my intentions. He wanted to know why I had suddenly joined Defiance and what I planned to get out of it. I hated having to lie to him. I hated him treating me like a suspicious stranger.

"So, you have given up your work as a scientist?" he asked a few seconds later, but it was more of a statement. He was trying to dissect me and my motives.

"Yes," I said. "The pandemic took everything out of me. I was happy about my achievements, of course. As a scientist, all I ever wanted was to innovate and promote health. Before we found the cure, I saw people on the brink of death, people dying by the thousands as the virus disproportionately killed the poor. It just wasn't right. So, I became interested in fairness, which isn't something I could have directly influenced at that point. Roki was in the thick of the conflict in Nurlie at the time, rescuing people." I chuckled, hoping Nnati was more at ease now. "Catching the virus was the least of his concerns. I couldn't help but fall in love with such a selfless man."

"I'm sorry I asked you something so personal," Nnati said, but I knew he wasn't sorry. It was Nnati's nature to pry and to question.

"How about you?" I said, trying to turn the tables. "I can see you're in love with Neuge."

"Is it that obvious?"

"As a matter of fact, yes, Nnati—yes, it is! You declared as much when you announced your desire to move to Tsiser."

He blushed, glanced at the exits to see if anyone was coming, then, with springy steps, walked back to me and sat down.

"I've never felt like this about anyone," he whispered, on the edge of his seat with excitement. "Neuge makes me feel so useful. And to be honest, I'm incredibly grateful not to be on the royal council anymore. I loved Queen Kaelyn and she was my closest friend. She had all the power to do everything we'd set out to achieve with the foundation. Yet she hardly heeded my advice. I felt so useless to her. The decisions she made were alien to the real Kaelyn I knew. I was scratching my head, thinking, 'Why does she need me here?'"

"Maybe she needed a familiar face," I said, "to make things seem less daunting. She may not have wanted all that responsibility, and it overwhelmed her."

"Maybe," he said. "We'll never know for sure. She's gone now."

"Why do you think she ignored the advice of the council?" I asked, curious to understand what Nnati's thoughts had been at the time.

"I didn't say that," he said. "I only told you that she hardly heeded *my* advice." Nnati lowered his voice and leaned forward in his chair. "You know, I haven't talked this openly with anyone since Kaelyn's death, not even with Neuge. I don't know why I'm so comfortable speaking to you. But I am. That's why I feel safe in telling you something. At one point, I knew she needed me. I could hear it in her voice. The truth is, Cerna, I think something awful happened to Kaelyn. I don't know what it was. Not power or obsession. She never wanted that stuff. Yet there was something that changed her. Something ..."

Nnati slammed back into his chair and started shaking his head. "I'm sorry. I've said too much." Nnati's eyes glinted in the light; he looked close to crying. I briefly listened to his thoughts and understood that he was reflecting on when I had first met Zawne, thinking that it had been the beginning of the end. I wished so badly I could tell him who I was. I at least wanted to hug him. The very minimum I could do was offer a stranger's condolences.

"I'm so sorry about what you've gone through." It was the only thing I could think of to say.

I got up and went to him, bent over, and was pleasantly surprised when Nnati opened his arms to me. We stayed like that for a long time, hugging in the quiet parlor of Roki's house.

* * *

Shiol, the great shining city of interdimensional gateways, towers of glittering silver and gold, and a sky like a shattered rainbow of swirling stardust, never failed to impress me when I gazed upon its vista. Unclothed spirits and indescribable life-forms floated here and there, slinked along the ground, and buzzed through the sky in strange vehicles I'd never seen before and would soon forget. This was the nexus of Min life, a place where we could rent bodies, trade precious gifts, and travel between dimensions and planets. Roki, Xerx, Vowkin, and I looked small here in our human bodies, much weaker and more fragile than the other creatures. We had fewer limbs too.

"What took you guys so long to get here?" I asked. I had been waiting for my family for at least ten standard minutes. "We can't keep them waiting!" I took Xerx's hand in my left and Vowkin's hand in my right, then hurried them along.

"This is your first time here. We are all at the mercy of the Crown of Crowns. You'd best learn that now, children."

"If we get into trouble," Vowkin said as he gave his brother a dirty look, "then it is Xerx's fault."

"What? Who said anything about trouble?"

"No time for that now," I said, clenching my jaw. "Here they come."

Hanchell and Riedel appeared before us in their true forms, three-headed monsters with scaly gray flesh. It was strange that only their middle heads had mouths.

"Hello," Hanchell said, chipper as always.

Hanchell blinked several times as she inspected our children. "Darn these eyes," she said. "Four thousand years does a number on you."

"I hear that," Riedel said.

It was funny. These three-headed dragon-type lizard monsters were four thousand years old and still brimming with love for one another. I wondered if such a thing were possible for humans.

"We'd best take a seat, Hanchell," Riedel said. "We don't want to wear out our old bones."

Two thrones materialized behind the Crown of Crowns. They were massive, colorless, and totally liquid, like two floating chairs of the purest water. Only they weren't shaped like chairs, they were shaped like crowns. Hanchell and Riedel floated into their fluid thrones and relaxed, both of them sighing and stretching out their scaly webbed feet like they were at the beach.

"Is your throne made out of water?" Vowkin asked. I was glad he had, because I couldn't figure it out either.

"It is," said Riedel, smiling at him. "It's made out of bits of all the different water molecules in our galaxy. This is the seat of true omniscience, crafted by the All-Knowing One for the

Crown of Crowns. By 'All-Knowing One,' I of course mean the Seeing Water, that which grants us our ultimate powers. Perhaps one day you youngsters will sit in these very thrones."

"Thank you," Roki said for the twins, who wouldn't stop gawking. "That would be quite something. As for Kaelyn and me running for the Crown of Crowns, we won't be doing that. We have a lot of business to take care of on Geniverd."

"That's a crying shame," Hanchell said. "We see huge potential in this family. We know that you criticize us sometimes, which means that you could probably do our jobs better than we can. And even though you are conflicted about the Crown of Crowns' role in the universe, there is no denying that you would be perfect for the job. This is a great opportunity. Were it to be handed to you, Kaelyn and Roki, I hope you would do the right thing and accept." Hanchell's six eyes swept over us, eerily sublime. "Anyway, I think Riedel has something to say."

Riedel cleared his throat. "Yes, um ..." He looked to Xerx. "I need to clear one thing up right away. No one is getting in trouble. When we are gone, Hanchell and I would like to be remembered for our love and lenience. Now, do you have any questions before we begin?"

Xerx quirked an eyebrow. "I have a question!"

Riedel nodded. "Speak, my child."

"You are spirits, like us. Couldn't you just get new bodies if your current ones have aged and your eyes are starting to suck?"

"It's true," Riedel explained, "we are allowed new bodies when our bodies die, just like Min. For example, most Min in Geniverd allow their bodies to reach a natural end at around one hundred and ten years. However, in Spectrius Z8, the average life span is one hundred and fifty years, and we are close to that. But our spirit lives are nearly over, anyway, and we've never had bodies age so much. We've always managed to unintentionally get rid of them somehow. Now that I think about it, I believe the oldest we have ever gotten was only one hundred years. It makes sense for us to have natural deaths and for these to be our last bodies, especially now that our four thousand years is up."

"Old age is exhilarating for us," Hanchell added. "We've lived for so long and had all sorts of experiences. We might as well experience this too, old age and death. But enough of that. Can we get down to business? We have other matters to attend to. Time is no longer on our side."

"Yes, of course," Roki said. "We know you're busy. We don't want to take up any more of your time."

"Great," Hanchell said, rubbing her hands excitedly. "This is the fun part. We know that Xerx and Vowkin have already been testing their powers at their young age. That's because we have given them strong, unique powers. It's only natural that they are itching to experiment with them. We've limited what they can do for the next couple of days, while we're still alive. During this time, we'll personally train them. They will be our apprentices. We'll find opportunities to speak to them during the days and nights, to show them what to do. I'll let Riedel explain the magnificent details."

Riedel beckoned the children closer to him and lowered his throne, hovering just above the ground. "Xerx," he said, "you will have dominion over pleasure and pain in the universe. Vowkin, you will be a warlock, able to use supernatural forces. There are no other Min like you, Vowkin, because being a Min warlock is the ultimate power a Min can have, and sometimes it's more power than the Crown of Crowns can control. The Seeing Water has given us express permission to bestow upon you the powers of a warlock. There are dark days ahead, children. After we're gone, no matter who sits on our throne, it may be up to this extraordinary family to maintain the universal balance."

"Oh," Riedel said, "and I almost forgot. From this point forward, only the Seeing Water can take away your powers."

Roki and I were both floored. We gaped at each other, at our children, at the three-headed monsters that were the Crown of Crowns. Were they suggesting that Lordin was going to win her campaign? Dark days ... Could it be that Lordin was only days away from plunging Shiol into chaos? And my sweet babies, were they now the saviors of Shiol with their fantastic powers? I was so confused. Hanchell stood up.

"Look at that," she said. "It's time for our announcement."

Together she and Riedel said, "Five days to go. In the lead, from Spectrius Z8, are Erda and Lithra!"

5

*W*e all woke up late the next day, feeling utterly exhausted. Even the kids were wiped out.

"This is exactly how I felt the first time I was summoned to Shiol," I told the twins over breakfast, "only it was ten times worse because I had no Min strength to support me."

Vowkin was sulking. "I didn't want to leave that place," he said. "It was incredible to see Min from all over the galaxy in strange bodies. The whole city was incredible. Do we really have to go through with this ridiculous school charade for the next year?"

"Unfortunately, yes," Roki said. "I know it sucks, but you must do it to keep up normal appearances."

"Besides," I added, "it's only for a year. Then you have nearly infinite time to do whatever you want." I paused while I spread fruit preserve over my bread, then said, "Shiol is magnificent, I agree. Still, it doesn't feel quite real to me. It's a place where Min have meetings and then report back to their homes or their adopted planets. It's completely alien to me, but I can see why you two don't feel strongly for Geniverd.

You've only been here for a few months, and there's a whole galaxy out there for you to explore."

"Vowkin can have Shiol," Xerx said, "but I'm staying in school!"

"Is this about Erwun?" Vowkin said. "Can't we have one conversation as a family without you bringing her up?"

"That's uncalled for, Vowkin," Roki said. "You should be nicer to your brother." Then he looked at Xerx and smiled. "Maybe we should invite Erwun to supper with us. Your Mama and I would really like to meet her."

"Only if you want to, though," I said. I thought it might not be easy to invite a human he cared about over for dinner with four Min.

"I will think about it," Xerx said.

Roki looked like he'd been waiting to talk. In the brief moment of silence, he blurted out, "Let's talk about your powers! You guys have been given some amazing gifts. I just wish we could hurry up and use them against Lordin. How do you guys feel?"

"The training has already begun," said Xerx. "It's so much fun. Vowkin and I are getting instructions and helpful reminders periodically. The Crown of Crowns even taught us how to do tricks. You should have seen Vowkin transform the flyrarc into a giant butterfly with the wave of his hand, then back into the flyrarc."

"Wow," Roki said. "That is impressive."

"Who's Lordin?" Vowkin asked. "And why do you wish her harm?"

"Lordin is Queen Hagan," I said. I was sure the twins could feel the revulsion spilling off my tongue. I spoke Lordin's name with venom. Anyway, it was about time I told them the truth, especially since Defiance was kicking into gear and there was a possible war on the horizon. "Queen Hagan used to be a human, like me, who followed the teachings of Decens-Lenitas," I said. "Because she was considered a commoner and had managed to catch the attention of the most eligible bachelor at the time, Prince Zawne, she became a huge celebrity. She and Zawne dated, were engaged, but before they got married, Lordin was killed. She refused the role of queen, and so the Crown of Crowns killed her, and she became a Min. A while later, after I was running the Gaard-Ma Foundation and Zawne had become an Aska ..." I laughed to myself. "Well, Zawne came back a changed person."

"And you married him?" Xerx asked.

"I did, yes. It was weird, because I had never dated a man like him. I'd always wanted your father. But hey, how did you know we got married?"

"Isn't that your motivation for hating Lordin?" Vowkin asked.

"Well," I said, "it's more complicated than that."

Roki then explained to the kids that my real name was Kaelyn of Gaard and that I had been chosen by the Crown of Crowns to become queen. He told them the whole story, beginning to end, finishing with the outbreak of the virus and up to today. He ended by saying, "And now Lordin is trying to become the next Crown of Crowns."

"She can't!" Vowkin said, enraged by the story. "Surely the Seeing Water won't allow it."

We were quiet for a moment. Then I said, "Hopefully, you're right ... hopefully."

"So, if Zawne is a human," Xerx said, "and Lordin is a Min, and they are king and queen ... that means I can date Erwun!"

"I guess it does," Roki said with a laugh.

Vowkin was a little more serious. "Why don't you guys run for the ultimate throne? It seems like the best way to stop

Lordin. And you heard what the Crown of Crowns said. You would be great for the role."

"I don't think so," Roki said. "We have too much on our plate as it is, your mama and I. The only reason we would run for the Crown of Crowns would be to stop their interference in human affairs. For that matter, the affairs of all the other worlds too. I know that the Crown of Crowns has been mostly good for the galaxy, but sometimes I feel like they have meddled enough. Still, your Mama and I decided that we didn't want to get involved.

"Please try to contain your new powers for the time being. We don't want you to risk falling foul of the Crown of Crowns' rules. We also can't risk humans being killed for finding out about your powers by accident, just because you couldn't control yourselves."

Xerx was legitimately confused. "Then what's the point of having powers?" he asked. "Why have all these great abilities if I can't use them?"

"You have to use them in secret," Roki said. "It's the rules. Humans can never know about us. It would be a disaster."

"I see." Xerx shrugged. "I guess that makes sense."

Vowkin asked, "Who gets to vote for the next Crown of Crowns, anyway? Like, who decides who wins?"

Xerx's eyes glowed. "Min have fifty percent of the vote, and the Seeing Water has the other fifty percent. So technically, the couple in second place could win, but the Seeing Water rarely goes against the Min outcome."

"How do you know that?" I asked. I was sure Roki and I had never discussed the election rules with the twins.

Xerx beamed at me. "I talked to a Min who was at the school yesterday."

Roki nearly spat his breakfast onto the table. "What was a Min doing at your school?"

"I don't know." Xerx shrugged. "It was during the first recess, and at first I thought he was a teacher or something. He just approached me. Then I saw his Valer and we started talking. I didn't understand half of what he was saying."

Roki was immediately on his visin. "Neuge, I need you to investigate if there are any Min teachers at Istvan High. Someone approached Xerx yesterday at school."

I could hear Neuge saying through the visin, "Yes, sire. Right away."

Roki leaned over the table and looked between the twins. "Boys," he said, "this is very important. You must listen carefully. If a Min ever approaches you, find a way to make them leave and immediately call me or your mama. Some Min are extremely dangerous and may be working against us."

Roki sat back, folded his arms over his chest, and narrowed his eyes at me. I knew exactly what he was thinking.

"It's now or never, Kaelyn. We need to start this thing."

* * *

Thirty minutes later, Neuge arrived at the house. He was alone, and I was disappointed that Nnati wasn't with him. I desperately needed to talk to someone other than Roki about his war. Neuge obviously agreed with Roki, so that wasn't going to work. I needed a third opinion before I made a final decision. This was my world we were talking about destroying through war. My people, my countrymen, my birthright. Geniverd was where my friends and family lived, and war had the potential to destroy their lives.

The three of us were in the senate boardroom upstairs. Neuge was saying, "It's as you suspected. Lordin is using her network of Min comrades to get at the twins."

"Damn," Roki hissed. "What about her campaign for the

Crown of Crowns? Do you know if it has any momentum yet?"

"I don't think so."

"Is she trying to get my sons to vote for her?" I jumped in.

"Probably," Neuge said. "It's the only thing that makes sense. Your sons are not involved in Defiance, so I see no other reason to approach them."

"I feel violated," I said. And I did. What right did Lordin have to try to manipulate my children? It wasn't as if I would approach her baby! How selfish was she? I asked Neuge, "How can we protect them from now on? It's not like I can follow them around all day. They wouldn't appreciate that much."

"I can shield them," Neuge said. "I am able to distort the senses of Min. I can create a force field around Xerx and Vowkin that will activate when Min who are strangers get too close to them. The approaching Min will immediately be made incredibly ill and confused. It will work for a while, but at some point, Lordin will figure it out."

"Thank you," I said. "I would really appreciate it. We can figure out a more permanent solution later."

"I need to tell Knotts," Roki said. He was barely listening to us. "I need the Dragon to start more fires."

"Is Knotts the dragon keeper?" I asked.

Roki squinted and cocked his head. Neuge just smiled at me.

I gaped at Roki. "You mean Knotts is the Dragon? He's the one who has been starting the fires?"

"Knotts and I," Neuge said, "but mostly Knotts. Roki gives the command for which sites to burn. I ensure the place is completely empty, so that no innocent people will get hurt. Then Knotts goes in the middle of the night and burns the location to cinders. I also create one of my shields, if necessary, making sure the fire doesn't spread to a secondary location."

"Wow …" All this time, and Knotts was the infamous Dragon. "Wait," I said. "Is Knotts really a dragon? I mean, does he turn into a literal fire-breathing dragon?"

Roki and Neuge burst out laughing. "Kind of," Roki said. "We call him the Dragon because he exhales fire. In his original form, he is a flying reptile creature."

Hearing this blew my mind. I had always wondered how nobody had died in the dozens of fires started by the Gurnot Dragon. Now I understood. I also understood why Roki needed Knotts so badly. Not only was Knotts their biggest sponsor, he was practically a fire-breathing dragon. Roki needed to keep Knotts fighting for Defiance. He was too powerful. If Knotts defected to the other side, he would be one tough adversary.

"Listen, Kaelyn …" Roki had his hand on my shoulder. "I know this is a lot. Lordin, the Dragon, the war, but I need you to make a decision. I don't want to put pressure on you, my love, but you really must—"

"I know, I know," I snapped, backing away from him. "This is not an easy decision for me. If I say yes, it's something that will leave me anguished for the rest of my life."

"I think you'll find that what Lordin is about to do will make you feel even worse for the rest of your life," Roki said, "especially if you choose to do nothing about it. The guilt will eat you alive."

I shook my head, not knowing what to say. I was so mad at Roki for putting me in this brutal position.

The good thing was that Neuge stepped forward and changed the subject. "Knotts is waiting for us in Capernort, at his snow house," the big guy said. "We should get going." I wondered if he could feel my annoyance.

"Again?" I asked, a little surprised. "Why doesn't Knotts come here, Roki? I thought you were the leader of Defiance."

"We need to keep him happy," Roki said through clenched teeth. I could tell he didn't like his authority being questioned. "He has all the Ava-Surrvul and Ava-Krug connections that we need to win this war. And he's a fire-breathing Min. Come on, Kaelyn. Let's go."

We left the house, and Roki masked our presence as we took to the artificial sky above Tsiser, its streets surprisingly quiet. We flew up and through a hidden port, then burst into the real atmosphere.

As we streaked across the sky, I was thinking, *Knotts has the connections to Surrvul and Krug ... and I have the Gaard connections that will seal the deal with Krug. Knotts is an intricate part of Roki's plan ... and so am I.*

* * *

We landed at Capernort to find Knotts waiting for us outside the entrance to his snow house. I could see why he liked it there. Other than the few Askas training below in the encampment, there was no human life. Some bears, elk, reindeer, and wolves wandered the snowfields. Knotts must have felt right at home.

He kissed me on the cheeks in greeting, then tried to say something to me, but I avoided his eyes and walked past him into the house. I wondered again if Knotts was the one putting pressure on Roki to start a war and Roki wouldn't admit it. Or maybe they were equally to blame. The two men greeted each other like the oldest of friends, shaking hands and patting one another on the back. I hated how friendly Roki was with Knotts, especially since he knew how I felt about him. The only saving grace of this meeting was Neuge. He felt like an extension of Nnati.

Once we were seated by the hearth, talk of business began.

Knotts said, "I completed a huge batch of fires just before dawn. Twenty luxurious homes in Krug, Surrvul, and Cara are now melted down to atoms. The nobles are in an uproar. Even the Grucken is concerned. He urged the clans and nobility to stay clear of their properties and to add massive new security measures to keep themselves safe. It doesn't matter to me. Even Zawne's public statement urging the people to stay calm —it is nothing to me. I can burn the entire continent back into primordial dust."

I was currently in a very strange predicament. As much as I despised Knotts, I found myself watching him from across the room with a sort of interest. There was no denying how beautiful he was, even if he had been born a hundred years ago as a flying lizard monster. I had to remind myself that he was a smug jerk.

"Out of those twenty homes," I said, my lips curved into a tight smile, "how many of those were yours? Did you burn down any of your own properties?"

"As a matter of fact," Knotts said, returning my arrogant smile, "I did burn down some of my own. I need to keep up appearances. But what does it matter to you? I can just acquire new ones tomorrow. Don't look down on me as if you didn't grow up in luxury, Kaelyn of Gaard, even while operating your incredibly biased and privileged foundation. And don't act like your human family hasn't committed countless horrors in Gaard. You're lucky I haven't swooped over to NordHaven and breathed my terrible fire all over it. I'm dying to do it."

I couldn't believe this guy. He'd sent me a letter asking to marry me a lifetime ago and was still angry I had never answered. It was childish and borderline psychotic. What did he have against my family? I hated how he slandered my family as if they all disgusted him. What did my unintentional rejection have to do with Gaard or NordHaven? He was a monster from another planet. How invested could he have possibly been in the fate of Geniverd? I wished Roki would strike him down right there in his own house! Instead, Roki patted my leg and smiled weakly at me. Then the conversation steered back to business.

"The timeline of the next round of IM injections has been moved up," Knotts said, "but I don't have the exact dates. We need to decide what we're going to do about this war."

"Here's the thing," Roki said. "We are still discussing the specifics." He had turned his entire body so that he couldn't see me, though I was sure he could feel my angry gaze on his neck. "The reason we wanted to come here, Knotts, is because Lordin contacted Xerx using a spy. She must be up to something. I suggest you keep a sharp eye on Lordin when you're at the banquet. Please report back to me instantly if you see something suspicious."

"No problem." Knotts nodded, looking straight at me. "I will do anything for you two. However, I said it before: Lordin is always up to something. I need this war, Roki. We need to initiate the final act so I can finally leave this terrible planet. The enemy will line up their Protectors, their tanks, their silly metal weapons—and I will destroy them all using the full potential of my power. I highly recommend you take advantage of my powers while they are still at your disposal, Roki. Don't wait until it's too late."

"I know," Roki said, "and we are getting close. We just need an airtight justification for starting a war. We have to involve the third clan. Trust me, we are moving forward with the plan."

"Okay ..." Knotts didn't sound very convinced. "Just don't take too long. Every minute that goes by without a plan is another moment Lordin is implementing one of her own. Don't forget that."

The meeting was finished. Roki, Neuge, and I got up, said our goodbyes, then walked out of the snow house and into a blizzard. Just as I passed the threshold and the snow lashed my face, a mysterious force pulled me backward. I found myself standing face-to-face with Knotts, completely alone.

Before I could even react, Knotts was speaking. "I'm sorry for what I said back there. I was just heated. I'm also sorry for snatching you like this. But hear me out. It will only take a second for me to explain."

Knotts took a deep breath, then leveled his oddly handsome gaze at me. "I don't want you to think I hate you, Kaelyn. That's not the case at all. It's just that the people of this world sicken me, both the rich and the poor. They have ruined every good thing about Geniverd, from its natural resources to its natural beauty. Everyone is guilty, the rich and the poor alike. Some people think they could heal the world if given a throne, but it's never the case. Humans deserve nothing but misery, since they don't know a good thing when it is right there in their hands. I can't wait to finish this job and get out of here. I'm only doing this because I owe Roki.

"Do you forgive me?"

I stood there blinking at Knotts. He had just shown me his soul and had somehow inched so close that I could feel his breath on my face. It smelled sweet, like fruit tea. I didn't believe what he'd said about humans. Something about his passion for Defiance made me think he cared enough to help Geniverd regardless of his debt to Roki. I wanted to ask what he thought about Min and the Crown of Crowns, whether they were, in his opinion, superior. Instead, I was simply nodding and gazing deep into his green eyes.

I opened my mouth to speak, or at least that was what I thought I wanted to do—then I turned and ran. "I have to go!" I called over my shoulder.

I burst through the front door and grabbed Roki. "What was that?" he asked.

"Knotts wanted to apologize for his behavior," I told him. My whole body was shaking. "He says he owes you and that's why he's helping us."

Roki was about to answer when I heard a bloodcurdling scream tear through my bones. Roki heard it too. It came again.

"Mama, Papa, help! Please help!"

6

*W*e were back in Krug within minutes and scouring the forest around Istvan High, where we'd estimated Xerx and Vowkin's last known location using their scents and pitch. We couldn't find them. We yelled their names, used our Min senses, but there was no trace of the twins. We stopped near a ravine at the edge of the forest, the place where their trail seemed to evaporate. There was a girl lying on the ground under a tree on the other side of the ravine. She was crying.

I started across the ravine, but Roki said, "It might be a trap. I'll mask our presence just in case."

The girl was in her school uniform. She lay on the ground, staring blankly ahead, her eyes swollen from crying. When we got close, I realized it was Erwun, the girl the twins had mentioned a few times. I read her thoughts and projected her memories so that Roki and Neuge could watch them too. Her last memory was of kissing Xerx underneath the tree. They were interrupted by Vowkin, who emerged from the forest with both hands tied behind his back as if he were a prisoner. He looked terrified.

We heard Vowkin screaming at Xerx, "Do something, Xerx! Come on, use everything you've got!"

Erwun was clearly confused. Before Xerx could comprehend his brother's words, an invisible force lifted him up, along with Vowkin. Whatever it was, it must have somehow been immune to Neuge's shield, and it had been too fast for Erwun to comprehend what had happened. The twins began calling for Roki and me. Erwun called for Protectors using her visin and then collapsed, and that was when we had found her sobbing in the dirt.

"Who were those Min?" I asked Roki.

"Don't know," he said.

Neuge added, "I have never seen them before."

It turned out these evil Min had scents that were untraceable. They were protected by a special shield of their own, one that not even Neuge could break through. "This is crazy," Neuge said. "I'll be right back. I need to look into something." Without waiting for an answer, Neuge dissolved into thin air.

I was shaking in anger. I had no idea why or how, but I knew Lordin was responsible for the twins' abduction. I screamed in fury, kicked the dirt, and started to pace around Erwun. Roki just stood there, slouched, looking devastated. That was when a pair of Protectors arrived to investigate. They spoke to Erwun, who transferred the data from her visin to them, with video proof of what had happened, and then a flyrarc came crashing through the canopy.

"Come with us," said the Protectors in their electronic voices. Scared and crying, Erwun reluctantly followed the Protectors onto the flyrarc.

"We need to go with her," I told Roki. "We need to make sure Xerx's girlfriend is okay."

"Fine by me," he said. "I'd like to see where this field trip is heading."

Neuge returned just in time to climb aboard the flyrarc with us. We crowded into a corner, our presence still masked thanks to Roki. Erwun sat on a metal bench with the Protectors looming silently above her.

"Something's happening," Neuge said, his muscles tense. "Your boys have been abducted, but they are not the only ones. I went to Shiol, and the entire city is in chaos. Over five hundred children have gone missing in the past twenty-four hours in Geniverd, and that's not all. There are tens of thousands of missing kids all across the galaxy. Someone just stole thousands of children!"

* * *

I was completely frozen as the flyrarc rose into the sky. It felt like someone had ripped my heart out of my body. My babies ... someone had stolen my babies!

Neuge explained to us that there had been a whole line of Min waiting to speak with the Crown of Crowns when he'd teleported to Shiol. The situation had been getting worse for the past twenty hours or so, since the vanishings had begun. There was absolutely zero trace of the abductors, either on Geniverd or on the other planets. This was a relief in the sense that other people were sharing our ordeal, but it was troubling that none of the Min had been able to get a lead. Whoever had pulled this off was powerful enough to deceive the entirety of Shiol.

"It's all my fault," Roki said. He was holding me while I sobbed against his chest. "I should have done more to protect them. I should have asked them to stay out of school."

"No, it's neither of your faults," Neuge said. "If we're going to find your boys, we need to stay strong. We should plan our next move. I've already scheduled an appointment for us ... uh, for you two to see the Crown of Crowns."

"Do you think this was Lordin?" I asked, wiping tears from my cheeks.

"It's hard to say." Roki scrunched up his nose. "I doubt Lordin has the resources to pull off a stunt like this. It's too big and beyond her control. She has a grudge against us but not the entire galaxy. I can't imagine Lordin stealing thousands of children. I'll need to investigate."

"Yeah." I sniffed, trying not to break down sobbing again. "So long as we can reach them before something awful happens. Once we make sure this girl is safe, I think we should go and confront Lordin right away."

"Speaking of this girl," Roki said, "something feels fishy." He was watching the Protectors as they interrogated Erwun.

She had recorded the events in the woods using a livestream on her visin and was telling the Protectors, "We were only dating for a day or two. I just ... I thought I would record our first kiss together."

"Doesn't that seem awfully convenient?" Roki said. "What kind of teenager livestreams and records making out with their new boyfriend?"

"The twins were super popular, right?" Neuge asked. "Maybe she wanted to brag about making out with Xerx to her friends. Besides, teenagers livestream all the time. It's pretty common with this generation."

"I don't know," I said. "How could they have been emotionally attached after just a couple of days? It doesn't feel right. And how could Xerx and Vowkin have gotten so popular in their first week of school? Although ... I guess they are Min."

That was when the flyrarc landed. We watched Erwun and the Protectors walk down the ramp and vanish behind some tall fencing on their way into the building. It looked like a detainment center. The three of us gathered outside the flyrarc, and Roki took my hand. "Don't worry, Kaelyn. Lordin's no match for us. If she is behind this, she won't get away with it. I've been at this game a lot longer than she has, and I have much more powerful friends. Lordin will regret ever messing with our kids."

"It's just so much," I moaned, wanting to fall on my face and stay there for the next twenty years. "We still have to worry about IM administrations. We have a possible war. Our children have been abducted. Lordin is scheming after the seat of ultimate power. We're burdened by so much!"

"We'll manage," Roki said. He wrapped his arms around me, whispering in my ear, "We will get through this together."

"Guys!" Neuge was standing beside us, looking surprised. "You have just been granted your audience with the Crown of Crowns. Hopefully, they can help solve this case for you."

"I hope so," Roki said, furrowing his brow. He looked so serious, so strong. He looked me dead in the eye and said, "You saved the world from the pandemic. Now it's my turn. I will find our boys and save them."

I believed in Roki. I really did. And honestly, I didn't have any other option. He knew the spirit world and the other planets much better than I did. Still, I felt guilty. I had thought putting the twins in school was the best decision. It turned out they should never have gone. We should have protected our children better. I just hoped nobody had stolen them to try to exploit their gifts. I really hoped this wasn't another one of Lordin's evil schemes.

Roki said to Neuge, "We may need more Min to help us, both here and in Shiol."

"I'm on it." Neuge bowed and then backed away. "There are

enough Min in this galaxy who owe both of us a favor. I'll gather the forces."

I wanted to cry at this point. I had to shut my eyes and swallow my emotions. We were so lucky to have Neuge as our friend and our helper. I felt I didn't deserve him. All I ever wanted was to get rid of the class system, of Decens-Lenitas. Yet I'd blindly followed the recommendations of the Crown of Crowns, which had led to millions of human lives lost in the pandemic. And now I'd managed to lose my sons. I muttered, "That's really very kind of you. I'm not familiar with the other planets. I wouldn't know where to start." I felt that I'd lost my voice.

"You have nothing to fear," Neuge said. "I've known Roki for a long time. I know he's going to find them. As for the other planets, I'll ask around, see what I can find out, and then report back to you. I'm at your service, because I owe Roki my life."

Roki gave Neuge a wan smile. I could tell he was grateful, just horribly wrecked by this newest trauma. It occurred to me that everyone seemed to have an extremely deep history with Roki, and I had barely learned anything about him in the three years since we'd met. But we had too much to deal with right now. The mystery of Roki's past would have to wait.

* * *

We only had to wait thirty minutes to see the Crown of Crowns once we got to Shiol. It was obvious we'd been bumped up the queue. There was an increased presence of Min, all desperate for time with Hanchell and Riedel. Roki said that in all his years, he had never seen it so chaotic in Shiol. Neither had I. It was like a panicked beehive.

Hanchell and Riedel appeared before us, and a bubble formed around us. This was it, our private meeting.

"We know you have many questions, just like everyone else," Riedel said. "But first we'd like to assure you that your twins are alive."

I exhaled a massive sigh of relief and squeezed Roki's hand. I wanted to celebrate, but Hanchell's demeanor was unusually subdued. Something was still wrong. All I wanted was a look of hope from Hanchell's six lizard eyes, something to tell me everything was going to be okay.

"We know they're still alive, because somehow they're still receiving our training," Hanchell said. "We preauthorized the unlocking of new modules once skills have been mastered. Because of this, we can tell that the new modules are being uploaded into the twins' Valers; they must be alive. However, we don't know about the fate of the other missing children. They were all abducted, like yours."

"I feel a 'but' coming on," Roki said, his shoulders tensed. Roki looked ready to snap in half.

Riedel sighed. "Unfortunately, we can't see them or hear them, and we don't know who's holding them."

"What does that mean?" I asked. "Surely you're more powerful than all the Min combined. How can you not know what's going on?"

"We're just as baffled as you about the whole situation," Riedel said. "There is only one possibility. Whoever is doing this must have gotten their unique power from the Seeing Water."

"Impossible," Roki muttered. "How do you know that?"

"Because," Riedel said, "it's simple. Nobody can override our powers unless they have been given permission by us or the Seeing Water. Basically, the Seeing Water has given someone powers that not even ours can match. We can do nothing but sit here and accept it."

"But the training channel is still open to our boys, right?" I asked. "Can't you create a new training module to establish a communication line? Maybe that can give us some answers."

"We have considered it," Riedel said, "but it's dangerous. If their captor finds out they are in contact with the Crown of Crowns … Well, you get the idea. We still do not know if the captor is aware of the training modules continuously feeding information to your sons. It could be that the captor, or captors, is recording everything the boys are learning."

"What if we create one module that can only be accessed by Vowkin?" Hanchell asked. "That way, we cut the risk in half."

"We need to be certain first," Roki said. "It could backfire on us. How frequently are the boys accessing their new modules?"

"Quite frequently," Hanchell said. "Before they were abducted, they were completing a module every three hours or so. Now they're completing a new one every thirty minutes."

"They're bored," I said, a big bright light bulb going off in my mind. "The boys are bored. They have nothing to do, so they are learning. They must be in a place where there are literally zero distractions." I paused, remembering how the Crown of Crowns had been complicit in Lordin's previous treachery. "But wait," I said. "How do we know you are trustworthy this time?"

"I'm glad you asked," Riedel said. "We really want you to trust us. It's a simple matter, at this point, of securing our legacy. We have ruled for three thousand years and want to leave a positive impact when we are gone. We want our names to live on in glory forever. We do not want the end of our rule to be known for the massive loss of youth. Our galaxy is under attack only days away from our permanent retirement. It's not a good look for our everlasting images."

"We're in shambles!" Hanchell cried. She'd been silent most of the time, and now I saw why. Hanchell was hysterical. Her six eyes were darting all over the place, and she was fidgeting with her scaly gray fingers.

"I believe you," I said. I had never seen the Crown of Crowns look so weak or unsure of themselves. "Can you tell us which Min have been to meet with the Seeing Water recently? That will definitely give us a solid list of suspects to hunt down."

Riedel's gaze flitted around us, never settling on any of us for long. "Unfortunately, the whole business of visiting the Seeing Water is very secretive," he said. "Anyone in Shiol may request an audience with them, but we are shielded from knowing who goes through with it. Even though we don't have the exact figures, we are pretty sure not many Min have dared the journey in our three thousand years of service. Visiting the Seeing Water is a risky move."

"Even we only get fifty minutes of visiting time each standard year with the Seeing Water," Hanchell said, still fidgety and anxious. "We have a few minutes left. Maybe we can ask how many Min have been through in the past few years. If the number is small enough, you and Roki can hunt them down one by one and get to the bottom of this whole mess. You'll be searching for a Min who's given up a seat of power, either current or future, a Min who's given a non-Min sacrifice and given up a great love. Without these three sacrifices, it is impossible to have an audience with the Seeing Water."

"Wow," I said. "This is totally something Lordin is capable of. She would sell her soul in a heartbeat to get what she wants."

It occurred to me that Lordin might have inadvertently sacrificed her original human body, the throne of Geniverd, and her relationship with Zawne; she'd had three things readily available to give up for the Seeing Water. She had then regained them in a different life. But did that still count as a sacrifice? In any case, there was no way Lordin could have been planning such a complex deception from the beginning. She was definitely playing the game on a knife edge, adjusting to the new rules as they emerged.

"I see what you're thinking," Riedel said to me. "The truth is that Lordin pestered us mercilessly about the Seeing Water when she was first brought to Shiol. She bothered us so much that we got annoyed and answered all her questions. So yes, she definitely could have planned this far ahead. However, if she was planning to give up love and power only to regain them later, the Seeing Water would have seen straight through her soul and denied her an audience."

"I see," I said. I was still a little confused.

"When you go to the Seeing Water," Roki said, "you only need to look back on the last three years. Whoever did this went to the Seeing Water recently. If it was Lordin, which we know it probably was, then she would have been to them in the last year or so."

"Are you certain?" Riedel asked. "It might not be her. The galaxy is huge. It could be someone from another planet behind this catastrophe. It might be better if—"

"There is only one person this evil," I said, cutting off the Crown of Crowns. "Only Lordin would be capable of this. I wanted to believe that she had changed her ways, that she still had some good left in her heart, but I know now that I was wrong. Look back three years in the record. Only then will we have our truth."

* * *

I was inconsolable when we left Shiol. Even though Roki and I knew the boys were still alive, we had no idea how to find them, and I was distraught. I didn't want to go home, not back to our house in Tsiser. I felt so useless. As we soared slowly over Krug, I cried tears of misery. I cried for my lost babies.

"We should go back to our pretend house," Roki said to me, trying to wipe the tears from my cheeks as we hovered in the clouds.

"Okay," I said. "Okay."

We lowered ourselves into Krug, masked by Roki's power. Even through the tears in my eyes, I could tell that something was wrong. There were not enough people in the streets. Some sat hunched on the pavement with their heads in their hands. Others lay sprawled in their yards. I feared something awful had happened, but I was quickly distracted by the flyrarc filled with Protectors parked at the front of our house. Roki and I landed stealthily in the backyard, crept through the house, then opened the front door to see what the Protectors wanted.

I couldn't help crying again when the Protectors delivered the news about Xerx and Vowkin's abduction. They promised they were doing everything within their power to find them. When I asked about Erwun, the Protectors told me that she was still being interviewed and they would let me know when the time was right to contact her.

We left our house in Krug after that and returned to our home in Tsiser, where we found Knotts pacing angrily outside. Roki had been masking us to avoid being spied on by Lordin while we investigated the abduction.

"Where the hell have you been?" Knotts said. "The IM has

been administered again, and the entire population is suffering nasty side effects. People have migraines; they are hearing voices in their heads—the whole planet is sick! Except for the nobles, of course."

"Oh no," I said. "This whole thing was a distraction! Lordin kidnapped our children just so that we would forget about the IM. It's diabolical!"

"The twins have been abducted?" Knotts asked.

Roki sighed. "Yeah, Knotts. They've been taken somewhere, and not even the Crown of Crowns can help us."

"That's it!" I stepped between the two men, my fists clenched into tight knots and my blood boiling. "It's time for action. Roki, I need you to confront Lordin. Keep her distracted for now while I get the war started. Taking my children was the last straw. If it takes a war to get them back, so be it."

Roki and Knotts were shocked. They glanced at each other, speechless, then looked back to me.

I asked them, "Do either of you know a Min who has a power that involves water and pressure?"

Knotts nodded. "I do, yeah."

"Good," I said. "We're in luck, because Gaard is in the middle of its rainy season. We're going to sweep away our enemies in Cara using water, the most powerful element."

Roki took my hands and whispered, "I know I said I'd be the one to do it, but I can't. You must be the one to protect your family. Get your papa, Raad, and Tissa, and bring them here."

"I will," I said.

"But … how are you going to use water to start a war without revealing Min to the humans?"

"The moons," I said. "We can tell everyone that we have developed a new technology that can move our moons, causing the tides to rise dramatically. Just let me worry about the specifics. Roki, I think you should warn the other senate members and start rounding up the rest of the Defiance members to Tsiser. I'll pick up Nnati, and we will make our case to Raad. Knotts will handle Surrvul and Krug. You must both be ready when I make the call. You wanted me to start a war. Well, now you've got it. But it's not your war, Roki; it's mine."

7

*T*he Gaard-Ma Foundation in Cara now occupied a 110-story building in the downtown core. Nnati's office was on the eighty-ninth floor. Suffice to say, he was surprised to see me.

"Cerna, what are you doing in my office? Where's Neuge? Is he okay?"

"Neuge is fine," I said. "But your secretary looks like she's in trouble." Nnati's secretary was doubled over in her chair, drooling and perhaps close to slipping into a coma. She looked nearly dead.

"Everyone ..." Nnati's face was twisted in disgust. "My whole staff seems sick, some worse than others. I already called for help."

"That's kind of why I'm here," I said, and then I blurted it all out. "Our boys have gone missing. The world is secretly under attack. Defiance is about to go to war. I need your help, Nnati. You and I are going to Gaard to get them on our side. That will position Gaard, Surrvul, Krug, and Defiance against the rest of Geniverd. We can't lose."

Nnati was oddly quiet. He got up from his desk and faced the long window that overlooked central Cara. "So, the time has finally come. I knew it would. I have been waiting my whole life for this moment."

"Me too," I said. "I just never knew it until the moment came. Are you ready to go, Nnati?"

"Yes. I've never been more ready than I am now."

Nnati was rubbing at the bandage on his wrist where he'd gotten the IM earlier that day. I'd forgotten until just then that Nnati was considered a noble because of his previous position on the Queen's Council. Nnati wouldn't get sick, which I was infinitely grateful for. However, there was a chance he would turn transhuman. I supposed that wasn't a bad thing. At least Nnati was on my side.

* * *

The scent of summer flowers inside NordHaven's atmospheric bubble brought back intense childhood memories. I couldn't help but feel nostalgic. The sky went from cloudy to clear as we passed through the force field. I remembered the first fifteen sunny years of my life without a drop of rain except for when Papa was in a gloomy mood and changed the program. It was sad I didn't have the time to go for a stroll around the garden with Nnati.

The Gaard Protectors ushered us from our flyrarc and into the foyer, and from there Nnati and I found our way into the greeting parlor to wait for Raad and Tissa. There were very few helpers in the house; the majority of them must have been sick. Thanks to my powerful Min senses, I could hear Raad upstairs on the treadmill. I could also smell Tissa's expensive perfume as she moved through the halls like a peach-scented phantom.

I wanted to chat casually with Nnati, but the mood was too tense. We sat in silence, awkwardly, until Raad entered the room in blue shorts and a sweat-soaked vest that clung to his chest. His muscles were bigger than I'd ever seen them before. I knew right away that he must have been a volunteer in one of Lordin's genetic-engineering experiments, just like Zawne.

Tissa entered behind Raad, coming into the parlor on a cloud of peachy goodness. She wore a fabulous dress and a feathered hat, her two smart dogs, Rein and Forschi, padding along behind her. Tissa sat on the sofa and smiled at Nnati while Raad stood in the middle of the room, his sweat already drying. He didn't even stink like someone who had just completed a workout. I wondered if Lordin's product made him odorless.

"Thanks for coming to see us," Raad said. "We always welcome a visit from you, Nnati. But coming with Cerna is quite unexpected. How do you two even know each other? Aren't you a scientist, Cerna? Are you working with Nnati and the foundation for something?"

"Actually," I said, "Nnati and I have come to save you. Gaard is in big trouble."

"Trouble?" Raad took a seat on the sofa next to Tissa, his expression changing from happy to serious in an instant. "It can't be another pandemic. Not so soon. The populace has barely started to recover."

"It could be worse than that," I said. "Geniverd is about to go to war. Nnati and I know this because we are some of the highest-ranking members of Defiance."

"What!" Raad nearly rocketed out of his seat. "Nnati, you have been a friend to this family for years. Since when do you associate with Gurnots?" He turned to Tissa before Nnati could answer. "Tiss, honey, do you know anything about this?"

Tissa shook her head absently, not looking at Nnati or Raad. I knew by reading her thoughts that she had been aware of Nnati's allegiance for a long time. She may have grown preppy and spoiled living in luxury, but she still had her honor. "I had no idea, Raad. This is news to me."

"We'd like you to come with us," I said, seeing how feverish Raad's face was getting. "You could be caught up in the war, otherwise. We want you to be safe. Also, we want you to announce to the whole world that you stand with Defiance."

Raad gasped. "Are you insane?" He stood up and came toward me, looking like he was going to throw me out the window. Defiance stood against all of Raad's principles, his entire system of Decens-Lenitas. I sympathized, of course, since we had been brought up with the same beliefs. It was crazy to think how far we had drifted apart, my brother and I.

"Just think about it," I pleaded. "All you need to do is look at how the king and queen have treated the memory of your sister, the late Queen Kaelyn, ever since her unfortunate demise. They have disrespected this family repeatedly, while at the same time mocking the Ava-Gaard. The Crown cares only about their own people, the upper class and the rich. They don't care about Gaard anymore. You can thank Queen Hagan for that."

Raad was silent. He looked at Tissa, wondering in his mind why she was so quiet, sitting very relaxed while staring at her smart dogs, ignoring everyone in the room. He must have thought Tissa was acting extremely suspiciously.

"Defiance is not a terrorist organization," I said, trying to get Raad's attention. "We are fighting for the good of the common people. Deep in your heart, you must know this is true."

"Let's say we decided to come with you," Raad said, half

laughing. "Gaard won't fight alone against any of the clans, let alone against Geniverd."

"You won't be alone," I told him. "Surrvul and Krug are aligned with us."

Raad was thinking now. I could tell his mind was on the brink of agreeing with me. "You can't fight Geniverd or the Protectors, no matter what kind of weapons you think you have," he said.

I was hoping Raad would say that. "Watch this," I said, then called to one of the Protectors in the hallway. "Protector, come in here." The Protector stomped into the room with its strong metal legs. "Gaard-Elder, command the machine to do something for you."

Raad pointed straight at me. "Protector, kill this anarchist."

Nnati and Tissa gasped but I just smiled. I knew Raad wasn't going to have me killed—I could read his thoughts and his motives. And besides, the Protector didn't move. Raad called two more Protectors into the room and ordered them to attack me as well, but nothing happened. They wouldn't listen to him.

"What did you do to them?" Raad asked.

I thought about what Roki had told me in the fake market all those years ago and half smiled. "They're just machines, Gaard-Elder. I can turn them off whenever I want. We built them, and we can control and destroy them."

"Okay, okay," Raad said, "we get it. You're a scientist and you have some programming abilities. That doesn't mean you can win the war."

"Have you forgotten about the fires?" I asked. "Not one of your government agencies or your trusted Protectors have been able to catch us, and we are still burning down your world one property at a time, always one step ahead of you. If we had wanted to burn all of Geniverd to ashes, we could have already done it. But that's not what Defiance wants. We want to free the people and liberate the world, allowing choice and freedom for the masses. We want a rebirth of individuality and artistic expression. We want peace. And for peace, we will go to war." I chuckled, feeling like a mastermind. "However, the people will not know there is a war. This war will come and go very quickly. We would prefer there to be minimal deaths."

"If you have so much power, why save us?" Raad asked. "I'm as culpable as a born-and-raised monarch. What makes Tissa and me so special?"

"The fact that Gaard gives us legitimacy," I said. But I wanted to say, "The fact that I love you guys!"

He scoffed, "And you'll ascend to power when this is over, I imagine. What about my family? What happens to our assets?"

"I will not be ascending to anything," I told my brother. "Neither will my partner, Roki. We don't have the details worked out yet, but I expect the current system will be disassembled and the fate of the clans will be negotiated. Nobody will be left in the cold. It will be a fair process. There is enough wealth to look after everybody in Geniverd. I sincerely hope that you'll join us, Gaard-Elder. However, the war will proceed with or without you, and you'll be on the wrong side of history if you don't agree. Also, you'll be under attack."

I didn't mean the last sentence. Obviously, I would find a way to protect my family and friends. I just desperately wanted Raad to come willingly.

"I must speak to my wife in private," Raad said. He took Tissa and their smart dogs and left the room. Nnati and I waited in tense silence. I searched Nnati's thoughts to find that he was worried this would be the last time he ever saw Tissa.

Raad and Tissa came back a few minutes later, and my heart leaped with joy when I heard Tissa thinking about her dogs, worrying that she wouldn't be able to bring them with her; she wondered how many outfits were appropriate to take on the run. She sat back on the sofa and urged the dogs onto her lap, then petted them lovingly.

"You can bring them," I said to Tissa, playing off her clear emotions. "If you are worried about leaving your dogs behind, don't be. You can bring them with you."

For the first time that day, Tissa looked up at me and smiled. It warmed my heart. "Really, you mean it?"

"Of course," I said. "You can bring anything, Gaard-Ma. Any friend of Nnati's is a friend of mine."

* * *

After some working out of logistics, Raad agreed to come to Tsiser. He brought Tissa, my father, and the two smart dogs.

"This place is shocking," my father said as we flew over Tsiser in our flyrarc. "I'd never have expected that the Gurnots could build a place like this. The simulated daylight and skies make it seem as if we never came underground."

Raad was just as floored as Papa. He didn't say anything, though. Raad was trying to maintain his macho persona. Inside Raad's mind, he was putting together an escape plan in case things went sideways. I expected nothing less from his Aska training.

Our house, though spacious for Roki and me, was a lot smaller than what Papa, Raad, and Tissa were used to. I wanted to show them the rest of Defiance: the real markets, the playgrounds, the gardens, the spaces where people gathered for plays, films, and sports. But for their safety, I couldn't let them wander around Tsiser. Some of our members wouldn't understand why the people who'd made their lives miserable for centuries were suddenly being given a safe haven. I allocated a room for Raad and Tissa, and another for my father. Gorm persuaded Tissa's family and Nnati's family to join us, and so I procured apartments for them in other compounds, grateful that we hadn't run out of rooms in the wake of more and more trusted Defiance members arriving in preparation for war.

I wanted Xerx and Vowkin back. I also wanted to know if, in the face of war, Lordin had any demands before I set the wheels in motion. She was dangerous, and I worried that it was only a matter of time before Protectors noticed a significant number of known Defiance members missing. I hoped it wouldn't cause Lordin to do something rash.

With my family now safe and secure, I went upstairs to my private bathroom and called for Roki. He didn't answer. I tried a few more times, then after ten minutes decided to call for Neuge instead. Neuge said he hadn't heard from Roki since leaving Geniverd. With nobody left to call, I reluctantly decided to contact Knotts.

"I'm ready," I called out to him, reaching Knotts's ears all the way in Shiol. "But I can't reach Roki. I don't know where he is."

"It's only been an hour," Knotts said calmly. "Lordin is busy, and Roki is probably being forced to wait for her. She can't just leave her duties to see him. He may also be following up on another lead."

I heard Raad coming up the steps.

"Lordin is our only lead," I whispered. "Look, I have my family with me—"

"That must be a relief," he said. "That could have gone any number of ways."

"Yeah," I said. "I got lucky."

I paused and held my breath as two sets of footsteps disappeared down the hall. I could smell the old musk of my father as he headed downstairs with Raad—strange how my brother still lacked any kind of telltale scent. I waited for them to pass, then said to Knotts, "Are you ready to get started?"

"I was ready yesterday." His words were clear and firm. I was a bit worried about his blatant hatred of humanity, but I thought his anger could be useful. Hopefully, the war would be over quickly. "I have at least ten Min who can control water," he said. "Just say the word, Kaelyn."

* * *

I found my family gathered in the main sitting room, with the beautiful waterfall outside the window and the curious marble statues. Tissa had found a holographic photo album and was flicking through the pictures. She'd just started when I entered the room. Tissa, Raad, Papa, and Nnati were currently goggling at the first picture in the album. It was a photo of Xerx and Vowkin smiling happily on the southern ice field of Lodden.

"Are these your cousins, Cerna?" Tissa asked. "They are just too cute!"

"They're my sons," I said in a quiet voice. I knew how it looked, because the twins were already so much older in appearance. "Roki and I adopted them after their parents passed away in the pandemic. A lot of ..." I wanted to say, "A lot of poor people died, which the nobles didn't care about," but I kept my mouth shut. There was no need to provoke my family with such talk.

"Looks like you've bonded well in a short space of time,"

Tissa said. She went swiping through the rest of the album. It wasn't long before a picture of Roki and me appeared on the holo-screen. I was terrified that my father would recognize him as the 'lowborn scoundrel' who had tried to date his daughter a few years ago, but Papa wasn't paying attention. Neither Raad nor Tissa had ever met Roki, so I wasn't worried about them.

Tissa asked me, "Is that man your husband, the one who came to the award ceremony with you?"

We weren't officially married, but even if I were allowed to explain everything to Tissa, it would take too long, so I just said, "Yeah, that's him."

"Wow." She was looking at a photo of us standing above the Luminous Waterfall in Gaard, where the lichen glowed vividly blue beneath the cascading water. "It looks so romantic." She snapped at Raad, "Honey, why don't we ever go to waterfalls? I want a romantic photo like this!"

Nnati started laughing, while Raad bumbled, his tongue stuck in his mouth. "Well, um, the thing is …"

"You must make time for your beautiful wife," I said to Raad. "You may not find another one like her."

Raad was clearly embarrassed. Even Papa, who couldn't be bothered to look at the photo, was snickering at him.

"We can go there," Raad finally managed to say. "I promise, the second this whole ordeal is over, we will go to the waterfall."

"Can we bring the puppies?"

"Of course, dear."

With my family right next to me, I almost forgot I was wearing a different woman's skin, or that I was now a spirit that would outlive everyone I had ever loved by a full nine hundred years. And that was when my visin rang. Zawne was calling me.

"Excuse me," I said, and quickly scuttled out of the room to take the call in private.

"Zawne, what is it?" I asked, hunkered on the staircase out of earshot of my family.

Zawne's voice came out in garbled sobs. "Kaelyn, it's Roki. He … he killed my baby. Arta is dead."

8

"*W*hat? Arta is dead? Zawne, are you serious?"

My ex-husband, the king of Geniverd, was in a daze. He was distraught and inconsolable. He was raving mad. "I saw him," he said. "I saw Roki. I saw him do it. I saw him kill my baby!"

"Slow down, Zawne," I said. "There is no way Roki killed your baby."

Zawne kept on. "I saw him do it. I had just finished getting ready to continue hosting the banquet. I was asleep all afternoon because I hadn't gone to bed the night before, having drunk way too much. I wanted to say hello to Arta before I left."

Zawne stopped, struggling to keep his voice level enough to get everything out. "I thought someone would be feeding her or preparing her crib, but as I approached the nursery, I heard her crying really loudly. It was an unsettling cry, like a scream of pain. When I entered the nursery, I saw Roki standing over her crib. He was staring at the door as I entered, as if he had been waiting for me. That was when he pulled out a knife and killed my baby."

It was impossible. I told Zawne, "There's no way. Roki would never do that."

"Except that he did do it!" Zawne shouted at me. "He did it, Kaelyn! Roki killed my baby while staring me dead in the eye!"

"Lordin is playing tricks on you," I said. I needed some way to rationalize what Zawne was saying. "She distorted your reality with her powers. Roki would never harm, much less kill, a helpless child."

"You're not listening to me," Zawne said, getting angrier by the second. "It was Roki who did it. Hanchell and Riedel have no reason to lie to me."

"Wait. You have already been to see the Crown of Crowns?"

"Yes." Zawne's voice was flat. "I went to see them immediately after it happened. I wanted them to help me kill Roki. They wouldn't kill him for me, but they did confirm that what I had witnessed was real."

"What about Lordin?" I asked. "Where has she been during all of this?"

"Lordin is on the hunt. She's out searching for Roki with some of her associates. I couldn't sit by and do nothing while she was trying to avenge our baby, so I went to see the Crown of Crowns."

No way.

I needed to find proof that Roki hadn't murdered Zawne's baby. If only Roki would answer me. What in the name of Geniverd was he doing, anyway? This was the worst possible time for Roki to go rogue. I had no idea what to do, and I especially didn't know what to say to Zawne.

"I'm sorry," I squeaked. What else could I say? "I'm very sorry that Arta is dead. I want to help if you'll let me. Please,

Zawne, you must know that I have nothing to do with this. I have been trying to find Roki too, but I can't get hold of him. Just give me some time.

"But please," I added quickly. "Please be careful. Lordin has made a lot of enemies, and you may not be safe with her anymore. There is more going on than you know."

"I know enough," Zawne said, bitterness and anger thick in his voice. "And I don't need your help. I just wanted to call and tell you that I hate you. I don't know what you could possibly have gained from this. If killing a child adds anything to your new life ... well, I am truly sorry for you."

"Lordin kidnapped my babies," I blurted out, unable to control myself. I needed to have some kind of defense. "She stole Xerx and Vowkin, and she is holding them hostage. If something happened to your baby, it was Lordin who threw the first stone."

Zawne was silent for a moment, but his face was morphing from anger to total disgust. "I used to love you," he hissed. "I really did. You would never have been queen if it wasn't for me. I was loyal. I worshipped the ground you walked on. I wish I'd known how much trouble you were going to put me through, killing yourself to become a Min, upending my life, then murdering my baby with your scheming boyfriend. I promise you right now, Kaelyn, I will never forgive you for this."

"Zawne, wait."

He was gone. Zawne had left the call, and I was hunched over on the stairs, a heaviness in my chest. I immediately retreated to my room, leaving my family downstairs. I climbed into my bed, curled into a ball, and wept. After several minutes, I called for Knotts. He appeared a few minutes later, coming in through the window.

"Lordin's thirst for power is so great that she obviously

killed her own child," Knotts said after I'd told him what had happened. "Your twins are in grave danger, Kaelyn."

"I know, Knotts. That's why I called you. What should I do? I already ordered you to start the war, and Roki is nowhere to be found. I feel lost and alone."

"You're not alone," Knotts said.

He moved to me slowly. I made no attempt to stop him as he raised his fingers and wiped a stray tear from my cheek. I thought he was going to hug me; his face was so close to mine. But he did nothing. Knotts let his hand drop to his side and said, "You can do this without Roki. You are strong, Kaelyn. You didn't become a Min to do nothing. I know you may not need me to, but I am going to help you until Roki gets back."

"Why?" I asked.

"Why what?"

"Why are you helping me, Knotts? I don't understand. Why are you being so nice?"

He got a stubborn look on his face. "I'm doing this for Roki. Like I said before, I owe him a favor."

"If you are doing all this for Roki, why did you make him go to Capernort for the senate meetings? Why disrespect his authority like that?"

"Authority?" Knotts clutched his sides and laughed. "What authority? In case you hadn't noticed, support for Roki has been dwindling. You guys disappeared for five months. I know it was for a good reason, but it cost him a lot of support in Defiance. The rest of the senate wants me to take charge. I've been fighting for Roki to remain as our leader. Without me, Roki would have been voted out. Having our meetings in Capernort was a small price to pay for him to maintain power."

"Oh."

I understood it now. Roki had wanted the war to keep his

control. Now I had no choice but to help him reach his goal, because of my babies. Knotts was the only one I could depend on right now while I waited for Roki to explain himself. Why was my life such an insane whirlwind? I had to get rid of Lordin, or at least push her out of Geniverd. She was obviously the cause of all this pain. But Knotts's continued interest in Defiance meant that he cared for the people of Geniverd. He was helping them because he wanted to, even when Roki didn't require it.

"Okay," I said. "We'll start this thing together. I know we have Surrvul and Krug, but have we tried asking for support from Lodden and Nurlie? What about Shondur?"

"They're all staunch supporters of Decens-Lenitas," Knotts said. "They wouldn't even give us an audience. Shondur is obviously out of the question because Shondur-Elder is the king's brother."

"Of course," I said, feeling stupid, then sighed. "Okay, here's what we're going to do. You bring the Krug and Surrvul leaders here. I'd like the three clan leaders to make a joint live broadcast to the people of Geniverd, and I'll need you to help me write their address."

"Not a problem."

"By the way, how are your preparations going?"

"Great," he said. "My friends Tharva and Justein are in Cara already. Tharva is turning the rain into a storm. As soon as they have your word, Justein will bring in a tsunami from the Ecrah Ocean."

"Thank you, Knotts. Hopefully, we can avoid mass casualties. Keep up the good work. Get back here ASAP."

Knotts left through the window, and an instant later Hanchell was calling to me. She told me that the twins were still alive and learning a lot, thanks to the educational training modules. Relief brought tears to my eyes. Hanchell also told me that the Seeing Water had indeed received one visitor in the past three years, which felt like a huge weight off my chest. It surely must have been Lordin who had visited them. Last, Hanchell had a message from Roki. He wanted me to know he was alive and well in Shiol but was dealing with something urgent. Roki said he loved me and would see me soon.

I didn't know what to believe.

* * *

I paced my room, totally frustrated by the day's events. It was difficult for me to stay put, since I wanted to go straight to Shiol and confront either Lordin or Roki. But I couldn't leave Tsiser. Not only did I need to keep Raad, Tissa, Nnati, and my papa safe, but I needed Raad's compliance in the worldwide address I had planned. That was my main focus. I stopped briefly in the downstairs sitting room, told my family to make themselves at home while I took care of some important Defiance business, then went to the library to write the speeches for the leaders of Krug and Surrvul.

Darkness had fallen by the time Knotts returned with the Krug and Surrvul clan leaders in tow. The artificial darkness of Tsiser was like a shroud of shadow over the underground city. They descended onto a landing pad in their flyrarc, its many lights cutting across the brick courtyard, and I received them at the front door. Nnati was at my side. He had been trying to reach Neuge all night on his visin, but there was never any answer. Nnati had been hoping that Neuge would arrive with Knotts and the others, but that wasn't the case, as I knew Neuge was probably in Shiol. I could feel Nnati's disappointment as we invited everyone inside.

Dinner had been prepared by our robotic Guardians. I sat at the head of the table, with Raad and the rest of my family on one side and the other clan leaders on the other. It was tense even without words. Everyone was uncertain—uncertain of the future, uncertain of the outcome of the war. There were no jokes being told, no light conversation, and barely anything above a pleasantry. We were strangers from different continents stuffed into an uncomfortable situation in a secret underground city. It was only natural that everyone was a little awkward. Nobody knew whether the battle for Geniverd would take days or years. We were all a little on edge. We drank beverages and silently ate thinly sliced Nurlie roast meat, but the atmosphere was heavy.

Roki's chair remained empty at the other end of the long table. I had no excuse for his absence, which didn't sit well with the clan leaders, who had come to start a war and parley with the leader of Defiance. I had to reassure them that Roki was taking care of very urgent business and that the war was set to start at any minute; the gears were spinning and the stage was set. Of course, none of the humans had any idea we were fighting a spiritual war just as much as a physical one.

I was most thankful for the rich Gaard wine, which managed to lighten the mood after everyone's third glass. People began to relax, and before long, there were a lot of cross-cultural jokes being exchanged across the table, since we all hailed from different parts of the planet. It was strange to see Krug-Elder and Papa laughing about a royal banquet seven years ago, when Krug-Elder's father had mistaken Gaard-Ma for his wife. I'd never seen Papa laugh so openly with another clan leader. Everyone was scared, and the wine was providing liquid courage.

At some point during the evening, Knotts signaled for me to go upstairs. I then felt a new presence enter the house. I knew at once it was Neuge. I was so used to his scent that I could smell him coming from three miles away. I excused myself from the table, went upstairs, and found Neuge brooding in my bedroom. He was unshaved and a little disheveled. Something was visibly wrong.

"I came to say goodbye," Neuge said. His eyes were hard as stone, his voice unnaturally hollow.

"What?" I took a few steps closer. "What do you mean, Neuge? I don't understand."

"There's nothing to understand, Kaelyn. This is goodbye. The Crown of Crowns has assigned me and some other Min a new mission. We are to leave the war effort and investigate the missing children throughout the galaxy."

"No," I whispered, more to myself than to him. "That can't be. I need you here, Neuge. You are my friend, my only true Min friend. I don't even know where Roki is. He's just vanished."

Neuge shifted uncomfortably. I could tell he hated being a messenger. "Roki says he can't face you. He's ashamed."

"Ashamed of what? You don't mean to say he really did murder Zawne's baby, do you?"

"All I know is what Roki told me," Neuge said. "I saw him about ten minutes ago, and he gave me a list of things to tell you before my new mission starts. First, Roki wants you to know that things are not as they appear. He can't give you a full explanation right now, but he wants you to understand that things are not as they seem. He also wants you to know that he is trying to secure the release of your boys. Roki says that no matter what happens, he isn't stopping until Xerx and Vowkin are safe."

Neuge let out a big sigh, his huge arms folded over his chest. Saying goodbye seemed to make Neuge physically distressed. "Last," he said, "Roki said that he is extremely proud of you for going ahead with the war. He says you are stronger than you give yourself credit for. He doesn't want you to worry. While he is out saving your children, he trusts you with all his heart to stay in Geniverd and save the world by commencing the war."

"Wow," I said. It sounded like Roki had found the twins and was fighting to get them back. It actually made me proud. I felt a flare of love for him in that moment. Then I remembered Nnati. "Oh no," I said to Neuge. "Nnati! He is going to be devastated. How long will you be gone?"

"Don't know." Neuge shrugged. I thought he was trying to mask his emotions. "When this whole thing is over, I might not come back at all."

That was when it clicked. Neuge had come to say goodbye to Nnati through me. I understood all at once—Neuge's mannerisms, his behavior around Nnati, being sweet but gruff and distant. Neuge hadn't wanted to commit to Nnati. He had wanted to break up with him, and the Crown of Crowns had just given Neuge the perfect excuse to do it.

"He's going to be crushed," I said, my friendly tone completely gone. "How dare you do this to my best friend, Neuge! Nnati at least deserves a goodbye and an explanation. You will be tearing his heart out. Don't you see that? Don't you care?"

Neuge scowled. "No. I have lived too long to care."

I didn't believe him. I was sure that given ten more minutes, Neuge would crack. Maybe he didn't want to commit to Nnati—I believed that much—but I was sure he still loved him in his own selfish way.

"I am changing bodies," Neuge said. "After I leave here, I will appear to die in a flyrarc accident. Nnati must find out that way. If I say goodbye to him now, he will be suspicious. You know the rules, Kaelyn. My hands are tied."

"But you made the request, didn't you? You asked the Crown of Crowns if you could kill your body."

Neuge was so ashamed I could practically feel the guilt radiating off him. He didn't say a word.

"Answer me!" I screamed. "Tell me, Neuge, did you do this on purpose?"

Without another word, Neuge was climbing out the window. Then he was gone. Neuge was gone, and Nnati would be absolutely destroyed.

* * *

Later, once Knotts had edited the clan leaders' speeches, Knotts, Tharva, Justein, and I floated above Cara, abreast in the dark night sky. We couldn't have looked like anything more than the shadows of large birds in the downpour of rain. From there we could see it all, the clustered concrete ghettos that housed the workers, the domed hives of Protector stations dotted about the city, the great Bask River flowing along the fringe of Delta Zone, where the skyscrapers of glass and neon pulsated in the rain, VondRust Palace rising from the heart of the city. The palace looked like a fortress with its tall ramparts and gardens. It was nearly as big as Cara itself, sheltered by the opaque atmospheric bubble that shielded them from the elements and from tonight's rain. Those inside the palace were dry while the city drowned.

Seeing the city like this made me furious. Seeing the massive structure with *GMAF* displayed at the top of the building in big bright letters made me suddenly understand how futile my efforts as Kaelyn of Gaard had been. All that time with the foundation, and I had never once threatened the nobles, the Grucken, or the palace. It was no wonder they had let me carry on. I realized now the GMAF was nothing more than a rich little girl's therapy session.

I let the fire fill me. "Lordin!" I called to the night, howling her name like a wolf.

After about a minute, she appeared across from us, hovering in the rough gusting wind, her sweet strawberry-blonde hair already wet from the rain. She looked so innocent, beaming at me with a pure smile as she said, "You must be so happy, Kaelyn. Are you here to gloat?"

"Give me back my twins, and tell me what's in the IM," I said, almost growling.

"This again." Lordin exhaled, seemingly annoyed. "I don't have your twins. All I know is that my Arta is gone and she's not coming back. You're evil, Kaelyn. You are an evil creature. The only thing that keeps me going is the knowledge that I will soon be the new Crown of Crowns alongside Zawne. Together we will design a new galaxy, one that you will not be a part of. You and Roki do not deserve to live in this world."

Lordin laughed, put one hand on her hip, and sneered at my companions. "What is this? Your army of Min? Have you come to destroy me?"

Knotts floated forward. "We're here to give you notice," he said. There was no room for debate in his powerful voice. "In fifteen minutes, your rule will be over, Lordin. VondRust will be the first to go."

"You think this is news?" Lordin scoffed. "I anticipated this. You think you're far ahead of me, but in fact, you are very far behind. There are four of you and only one of me. Bring all your powers and might. Let's see if Kaelyn's conscience will allow her to finish what she's started."

I laughed. "I have no problem finishing you. Good luck finding a new body and a cute new face. Let's see if you'll deceive the people of Geniverd again. I very much doubt they'll keep Zawne on the throne after this."

"That's not how you win," Lordin said. "The people of

Geniverd are too dependent on Decens-Lenitas, and most of them don't work. After we give them money, do you think they'll go to work?"

"Time is up," I said. "No more arguing. Unless you plan to return my boys, abandon your campaign to become the Crown of Crowns, give up your dominion over Geniverd, and tell us what's in the IM, you'd better get back to your hiding place and watch the news with the king."

"I'll give you some advice for free," Lordin said angrily. "Stop chasing the moral high ground and stop striving for the betterment of the people. Leave the sleeping lions alone." With that, Lordin dissolved into thin air.

I shook my head. "You'll see." Then I turned to Knotts. "Go ahead. Publish the speeches."

Knotts opened his visin, widened the display, chuckled to himself, "Stupid human technology," and initiated the video stream. "The video is live in three, two, one ..."

We watched along with the rest of Geniverd.

Raad was the first to speak. His face appeared against a neutral background.

"As you can see, I'm here today with my wife, Tissa, and your leaders from Krug and Surrvul. For centuries, Decens-Lenitas has been hailed as the moral guide for Geniverd. It's been praised as the basis for our economic progress, standard of living, security, and peace."

Then Surrvul-Ma's face appeared. "But as the upper class, we lifted and protected ourselves using Decens-Lenitas as a shield. We became monsters, not human beings. We progressed our lives at the expense of the human race."

The camera shifted to Krug-Elder. "Today, on behalf of our forefathers and ourselves, we admit our wrongdoing and our extreme shame, and we beg for your forgiveness. We're proudly aligning ourselves with Defiance." A photo of Roki and me flashed onto the screen. "Under the leadership of Roki and Cerna, who you may be familiar with as the recipients of the Shield for saving the human race from the pandemic, we will work to undo our sins. Even as we wage war against the noble houses that refused to join our cause, we will try to ensure that no harm comes to anyone else."

"Yet we cannot prevent every scenario," Surrvul-Ma added. "Inevitably, some of you may be caught in the line of fire and lose your lives. But we will win for you and restore real democracy in the world. Stay in your homes, and do not leave for any reason until the time comes for you to join us in celebrating victory and freedom."

"VondRust, Lecon, Meallver, RiverRer," Raad said, "we are coming for you. You cannot hide. No longer!"

The transmission ended and was almost instantly replaced by a live broadcast from Lordin and Zawne. Lordin looked like she had been crying all day. Her hair was disheveled, her eyes bloodshot. Zawne held her in his arms as they addressed the world. From the sunny background, I guessed they weren't in Cara anymore. They must have been hiding in Nurlie or Lodden.

"My people, as you know, since taking over as your queen, I have been fighting for your safety and freedom. In the short span of six months, since the evil Queen Kaelyn's deserved death, you've seen the progress we have made. It's the reason so many of you have defected from the Gurnots. And now they can't handle the loss. Because we've not joined their secret society, they want to take our lives."

"Let's not forget who the Gurnots are," Zawne said. A picture of Roki and me flashed up in the corner of the projection. "The Gurnots are terrorists. We didn't know who the leaders were until an hour ago. Now we must admit that even though we gave them medals of honor, we are positive they created the pandemic only so that they could be the ones to stop it. Millions of deaths were only a ploy. They were tricking the world. They do not want you to live in peace and happiness. Not only have they declared war on the world, but they have killed our innocent child. They killed baby Arta."

Zawne rubbed Lordin's back as she sobbed. "An innocent child," she moaned. "What did a baby only one week old have to do with their war?"

"If that's what they call being human," Zawne said, "I do not want any part of it, and neither should you. We will fight this proposed war, if only to keep the rest of Geniverd's children safe from harm."

The broadcast ended.

Our Aska warriors and leagues of Guardian robots advanced on Cara. The city below us erupted in a dazzling light show of laser pulses and explosions. The war was on. Protectors and Guardians battled in the streets, and the cries of men could be heard even in the roaring storm in the clouds. Tharva and Justein used their combined powers and caused a massive tsunami to break the shore. A forty-foot wave rose in the darkness and crashed into the city, funneling between skyscrapers as it surged toward VondRust, where the massive wave broke asunder the atmospheric bubble and washed away the palace like it was nothing more than a flimsy sandcastle. Then the wave diminished before it could drown any more civilians.

Big explosions detonated in the distance, one to the west and one to the north. Lordin and Zawne had just bombed NordHaven in Gaard and Thalpha Palace in Surrvul. Everyone had been evacuated. It didn't matter. All we'd managed to do was destroy each other's toy houses.

Dawn broke, and with it came a sense of quiet. The rain continued to fall, putting out most of the violent fires before they could spread. Then something strange happened. Flyrarcs descended on the city. Doors opened, and people emerged from the ghettos and from apartment complexes by the thousands. They took to the streets, camping in the middle of the road, gathering in parks, going into the upscale neighborhoods and gathering on the lawns. They were at the Grucken's residence, along the river, around the GMAF building. They were everywhere! A quick look at my visin showed the same scene in every major city on every continent.

"It looks like they don't want a war," Knotts said. "Someone must be coordinating this. It's the biggest sit-in in human history."

Lordin's voice came from behind. She was laughing. "Oh, Kaelyn, you're not going to drown all these poor humans, are you? Zawne and I can't wait to see how you plan to finish the war you've started."

"Are you mad, Lordin? You're putting these people at risk!"

"*I'm* not," she said. "You are. If you choose to continue this charade, *you* are putting their lives at risk, not me. In spiritual warfare, Kaelyn, it is the humans who always bear the toll. You would do well to remember that."

Lordin once again vanished into thin air.

"Darn!" I hissed. "What do we do now, Knotts?"

"I don't know," he said. "It's so strange. How did she get them to come to these places? There hasn't been any communication issued to the people since her broadcast, and yet they are using themselves as shields."

"I don't know," I said, "but I'm not giving up so easily. Let's keep the rain pouring down hard. These people can't stay outside forever. Maybe they'll come to their senses."

notts and I returned to chaos and hysteria in Tsiser. We found thousands of our members at the main station, demanding to leave. It was a free-for-all. They were screaming and shouting to be let on the trains and allowed back to the surface. Olorc and Marten were standing on a dais in front of the gates, addressing the crowds over loudspeakers, trying to soothe the rioting mass of people. No one was listening. Knotts and I pushed our way through the throng and climbed onto the raised platform, which was surrounded by armed Guardians.

"What's going on?" I yelled in Marten's ear. It was so loud. Everyone was screaming.

"I don't know," she said. "It was like a stampede at the start. Everyone is frantic to get out of here and go back to the surface. We have no idea why. There have been no communications through their visins. It makes no sense. Our people are panicked and senseless. They are like zombies."

"What about another broadcast?" Knotts suggested. "It may reassure them."

"You can try," Marten said. "At this rate, I doubt they'll check their visins."

"We'll put something through on the Defiance channel," I said. "But let's keep it short and sweet. These people are acting like wild animals, and I doubt they will listen to reason. Knotts, we need to get back to my place. We must find Roki."

I desperately hoped that Roki would have some good news about our twins, the war, the Crown of Crowns—about anything!

As Knotts and I retreated through the multitude of people, he said to me, "Lordin may be right, you know. It may be better to leave sleeping lions alone. Your insatiable hunger to make the world a better place is in vain. What has the world given you such that it deserves all your attention? All they've done is hate you. In fact, they'll never stop hating you. You're not obligated to do anything for these pesky humans."

"What does it matter to you?" I said. "This is nothing to you. You're not even invested. Helping me is just a favor for Roki." My words weren't fair because I knew he cared about Geniverd's fate. My anger stemmed from Lordin's audacity to take my twins.

"Sure, but I have always liked you. That's why I'm trying so hard to help. And you know what, Kaelyn? I will keep helping for as long as you need me."

"Whatever," I said. "You can't understand. Geniverd is my home, and I have an obligation to the people. If those in power don't use their power for good, then what is the point? I can save Geniverd and still have another nine hundred years of freedom to enjoy life and have fun. I can't just leave my own people high and dry under a tyrannical and unfair rule. I can't leave them with Lordin. She's a psychopath!"

"You got that right," Knotts said. He rubbed his eyes with the palms of his hands as if he was considering what I'd said.

"Okay. If you want to defeat Lordin, show her your resolve. Don't balk. Fight until the bitter end."

"I plan to," I said, feeling hardened by Knotts's words. Then I remembered Erwun. She was still in Krug. I hoped she wasn't in the rain, getting hypothermia. Xerx would have wanted me to protect her.

I grabbed Knotts by the arm. "Knotts, do you remember that poor Erwun girl? I need you to find her and bring her here. The girl's family too. My son would have wanted it."

"No problem."

Knotts gave me a look, his top lip curled in something that might have almost been a smile. Then he was gone to fetch Erwun.

* * *

Back inside my house, I found Raad, Tissa, and Papa in the library, demanding an update from Gorm. They could all see what was happening in Geniverd through their visins.

"Are we about to give up?" Raad asked me when I entered the room.

"No," I said. "There is no way we will give up."

"But you're not going to blast all those civilians, right?" Tissa said. Her voice squeaked at an insane pitch that made me want to cover my ears. I was beginning to understand what Knotts continually said about humans. They were irate, quick to panic, and often insensible. And they could be weak and helpless. It made me feel ashamed, but I knew in that moment that I was drifting farther from humanity with each passing day.

"Calm down," I said to Tissa. "Everybody calm down. The king and queen are somehow using the entire population as a shield. It can't last forever. The rain is coming down hard, and it's not going to stop anytime soon. They can't stay outside forever. We will win this fight."

Raad lowered his voice and said, "You may want to go upstairs. Nnati is distraught."

Oh no! I had forgotten about Neuge's fake death. He was supposed to have died in a flyrarc accident when the war began. Nnati was sure to be crushed by the news of it. I tried to stay calm in front of my brother so I didn't give anything away. "Okay," I said. "I'll go check on Nnati. I'm sure he's emotional, like the rest of us."

I left the library and went upstairs. I was surprised to find a makeshift hospital room set up in one of the spare bedrooms. Nnati sat in a chair beside the bed, surrounded by humming machines. On the bed was a massive shape concealed by a thin white blanket, tubes hooked up to the body's veins, and an oxygen mask strapped to its face. It was Neuge. He was on life support!

"He's in a coma," Nnati said. He didn't look at me. He was holding Neuge's hand, staring at the big man's chest as it slowly rose and fell. His vitals were barely enough to keep him alive. If it weren't for the machines, Neuge's body would have been dead. His soul, however, had already occupied another body, I knew, and was somewhere on another planet. I wondered if Neuge had left his human body behind just in case he changed his mind about Nnati. That way, he'd have a vessel to return to. At least, that was my hope.

"His flyrarc crashed as the war began," Nnati said. "His body is running on machine power. But inside ... inside Neuge is hollow. The doctor said he's dead inside. There is no brain activity."

It didn't take my special Min power to see that Nnati was heartbroken. That much was obvious. But then I heard one of his thoughts come through: Nnati was planning to kill himself the moment he left the bedroom. He didn't want to live without Neuge. My stomach churned. "First my dear friend Kaelyn, and now my lover Neuge. I'm cursed. I'm cursed!"

"I'm so sorry," I said, feeling overheated. "You don't deserve this. It's all my fault." I approached him slowly, then very carefully put my hand on Nnati's shoulder. I hoped the warm gesture would ease a small portion of his pain, letting him know that he was not alone.

"It's not your fault," he said. "Just please tell me we won, or that we're winning. Just tell me Neuge's death was worth something."

"We're going to win. I promise, Nnati, Neuge's death will not be for nothing. But tell me, what did you mean when you said you're cursed?"

Nnati sighed. "It's always been this way. In high school, there was someone very close to me. Then one day he left. He disappeared and I never saw him again. Everyone I get too near to vanishes or dies. I'm cursed, Cerna. I don't want to live in this world anymore. I don't want to be alone."

Nnati started to cry, to really cry. He slumped in his chair and sobbed. All I could do was rub his back. I wished I could tell Nnati that Neuge hadn't loved him in return, and that Neuge was not worth anyone's life.

"I still have no news about the twins," I said. I thought it would help just to hear a voice. "Roki isn't back. I only hope that I don't suffer further pain. I can't take more. My family in Gaard died; now my children and husband are missing." I said the next part softly. "You are not the only one with losses, Nnati. We must keep moving. We must stay strong. There is nothing for us in death. Death is the end. We should focus away from death, to the goodness of life."

He turned to look at me, eyes red, face strained. I heard his thoughts and realized I had made a terrible mistake. What I'd said was exactly what Nnati wanted. He craved an end. He wanted the nothingness that only death could provide.

"What are you thinking?" I asked in a soft voice.

"I'm thinking … darkness. My thoughts are dark, Cerna. I don't wish to burden you with them." He stood abruptly, brushed himself off, and wiped the wet streaks from his nose and cheeks. "He wouldn't want to be kept alive like this. Neuge was too strong to be kept as a brain-dead vegetable."

I wanted to scream, "No! He might come back! You may yet see him!"—even if it was a slim chance. But I couldn't give anything away. I was helpless as Nnati reached for the machine. "Can't you wait a little longer?" I asked, tapping a loose fist against my lips. "Do you really want to shut him off so quickly? Just give it another few hours. Please, Nnati. Wait until the end of the day. Then we can do it together. Just give yourself some time to think."

Nnati collapsed back into his chair. "Okay. I don't know why, but I trust you. I'll wait, and we can do it together. But after that … I don't know. I just hate this world."

* * *

I hated leaving Nnati alone in his miserable depression. Had I done the right thing when I'd fixed him up with Neuge? What had I done? I couldn't lose him—I just couldn't! But the war was still ongoing. Things needed to be done. Plus, Knotts had arrived with Erwun. I greeted them at the door, feeling light-headed. "Welcome, Erwun. Come inside."

The girl was speechless and confused. She saw me, the leaders of Krug, Surrvul, and Raad all staring openmouthed at her from the doorway of the parlor. "What …" she stuttered, "what am I doing here?"

"I told you," Knotts said. I could hear in his tone that he

was annoyed after their journey together. "You are here to meet Xerx's mother."

"Hi," I said. I didn't know what else to say. I could hear her thoughts bouncing around like crazy inside her skull: *Have these people kidnapped me? Isn't she the leader of the Gurnots? Where is Xerx? What is happening?*

"It can't be," she said. "You ... you are ..."

"I am Xerx's mother," I said. "And yes, I am one of the leaders of Defiance. Xerx and Vowkin are still missing. The war has started. These are all the leaders of the rebellion. I do wish we had met under different circumstances."

Erwun looked like she was going to faint. I took her gently by the hand. "I promise you, no harm will come to you in my presence. I brought you here because I want to keep you safe during these difficult times. Come, let's get you something warm to drink."

I got Erwun a hot tea from the kitchen and then took her into the library, accompanied by Knotts. We sat down on the sofas, and I immediately downloaded all of Erwun's memories for later inspection.

After a second of silence, she surprised me by asking, "How did you get so many people to follow you? You look so young."

I chuckled. "That's a story for another time. What other questions do you have for me? I don't have much time. As you can imagine, I am pretty busy right now." But mostly I was concerned about Nnati. I didn't want him to commit suicide while I was talking to my son's girlfriend.

"How is this place possible?" she asked. "How did you make such a huge underground city?"

"Well, Erwun, when people believe in a cause strongly enough, I think you will find they can be extremely resourceful. This place is the result of centuries of hope and hard work. Tsiser is a haven for anyone who believes in change. This city was designed and built for people who believe in a better world, without class discrimination, a world where we are all equal."

"I see," Erwun said. She was only fifteen, and such a conversation was overwhelming for someone so young, I knew. She respected my answer but was still trying to process everything. Then she asked what she really wanted to know. "Do you think they'll find Xerx and Vowkin?"

"Yes," I answered. "Roki is out looking for them now. He's a good person, not at all like the monster the media portrays him to be. Roki is strong and clever, and he will find the boys. I promise you that."

Before she could ask another question, Knotts cleared his throat to get my attention. His eyes were fixed on his visin. "Kae—um, Cerna, something's come up. It can't wait."

Great, I thought, *more bad news.* I stood up and said to Erwun, "I will come see you as soon as I can, but now I have to go. I'm glad you're here and that you're safe. Don't worry, Xerx will be home before you know it."

Out in the hallway, Knotts delivered the bad news. He told me people were falling sick in the streets. "They're vomiting," he said, "spitting up blood, getting sick, keeling over, and seizing. We have no idea what's going on. It's not the rain. Rain wouldn't make people sick like that after two hours."

"Maybe if they get sick, they will go home," I said, a little surprised by my sudden lack of empathy. "I'm still determined to destroy Lecon, Meallver, and RiverRer. You know what, Knotts? I think it's time to see the Crown of Crowns again. Could you watch Erwun and Nnati for me? Please make sure that Nnati doesn't do anything impulsive. That should be your number-one focus right now. If he tries to do something to himself, stop him."

"Got it," Knotts said. "I'm happy to be of service."

* * *

I barricaded myself in my private chamber, far from where the guests were congregated. Nobody would be able to hear me. I then called for Roki, but of course, he didn't answer. No surprise there. When I called for Hanchell and Riedel with the intention of requesting a meeting, they scared the pants off me by materializing right in front of me. Right in my room! They had never come to Geniverd to speak with me before.

"What is it, Kaelyn?" Hanchell said in her sweet voice. "We are here for you, and making house calls now."

"Thank you so much," I said. I wanted to drop to my knees and cry at Hanchell's gray webbed feet. "I'm sorry to call you like this, but I have emergencies, and they can't wait."

"What is it?" Riedel asked. "The situation is crazy right now, but we will do everything to try to help you. Xerx and Vowkin are our top priority."

"Is there any word on their whereabouts?"

"Nothing," Riedel said. "We know Roki is looking into it. However, we are unable to see exactly what he's doing. He's totally off the grid. Something strange is going on, blocking our usual powers."

"Great," I said. "Just great. When it rains, it really pours, huh?"

"It sure does," Hanchell said sadly.

"Anyway, I have a favor to ask of you."

"We know," they both said. "And it's okay. We will allow you to do it."

I was a little surprised they had agreed so easily. "Really?" I asked. "You're sure? I mean, I have never heard of any Min doing this before."

"All things considered," Hanchell said, "we will allow it. But this is only temporary until your twins are found. We don't see how this could possibly help your missing children, your global war with millions of lives at stake, or your fight against Lordin—but go for it."

"Wow, thank you. I don't know how I can ever repay you."

"No need to repay us," Hanchell said. "We just hope you know what you're doing. It won't be easy."

10

---

*B*efore becoming a Min, I would never have imagined there would be a day when the world rioted against me. Everything I was doing was for them. I didn't deserve such hatred. As I sat on a bathroom floor in my house in Tsiser, everything barreled down upon me, and I felt overwhelmed. I needed a break. The Protectors were out feeding the people, and the entire war effort was a mess. I searched my mind for Erwun's memories. At least I could see my boys again through the young girl's eyes. I found the day when she'd first met the twins, sat back against the wall, and closed my eyes.

* * *

Erwun's alarm woke her up at five in the morning, an hour and a half earlier than usual. She hit the snooze button and rolled out of bed, hitting the floor with a hard thud. She lay for a moment, groggy and exhausted. It was so early! She eventually managed to get herself up and to the bathroom, where she splashed cold water on her face. Then she was reciting lines in the mirror from her school play.

Erwun was the firstborn child of three, which was rare, because most commoners only had one or two children. Also unusual about Erwun was that she went to a school where the kids were keen to reach high levels of achievement, as opposed to most of the schools in Geniverd, which were more of a fad or a rite of passage for the children. Because of this, Erwun was primed to reach her full potential. She had the highest grades in all her classes and the unyielding pride of her mother and father, setting a positive example for her younger siblings. Erwun was perfect in every class, and she was the moderator of the debate club.

Erwun was happy to be such a prominent student and an important member of the debate club. Still, she often thought of herself as an impersonator. She was not the moderator because of her debating skills. Far from it. Erwun was not confrontational in the least. She was levelheaded and fair, and she would need to remain that way if she was going to earn an apprenticeship from the school. There were over sixty million fifteen-year-old students competing for only eighteen thousand apprenticeships, three thousand of which were in Krug. Without an apprenticeship, Erwun would be looking at a lifetime of handouts. She hoped to be the first one in her family to break the ugly cycle of joblessness.

Erwun had tried all the extracurricular activities available at her school, including language, sports, writing, and programming. She had never fallen in love with any of them. She wanted to find a hobby or activity she truly loved doing. That way, she could rise to the top of that field. Debate club wasn't really the most stimulating, since politics was generally reserved for royals. Erwun figured she'd try her luck with drama. If she could entertain nobles successfully, Erwun could raise her profile. She just had to get a really important part in the school play coming up in ten days. She hoped she'd be called on. There had been endless fighting and arguing going on in the rehearsals.

She practiced her lines in the bathroom mirror for another hour, then continued practicing in the shower. Erwun got dressed in a yellow tunic, fastened her brown hair with a silk ribbon, then got her bag and went to catch the flyrarc to school.

* * *

Erwun went straight for the bulletin board to check if the casting had been posted yet for the play.

"Oh!" she yelped to herself. Erwun's name was listed next to Oliviria, meaning Erwun was to be her standby. Maybe today was finally Erwun's day.

Erwun entered geography class, her digital notebook and holograph cards tucked under her arm. The class was a mess. The eight boys who attended her class were gathered around one desk, howling with laughter and cheering. She heard one of them say, "Amazing, you're nearly there. Go for it."

Oliviria and the other four girls in Erwun's class came in just as Erwun was sitting down and updating the holographic lesson module connected to her desk with last night's homework. Erwun watched as Oliviria stiffly crossed her arms, pursed her lips, and stared judgmentally at the boys howling like a clutch of prehistoric apes. Then Oliviria and her friends went to go see what all the fuss was about.

As the girls crowded around the boys, Erwun watched from her desk. There was a big fuss, everyone talking loudly, and then Erwun saw a boy through a gap in the students. Their eyes met, and Erwun felt her whole face flush. The boy had dark, perfect hair and glowing blue eyes. The most thrilling part was that the boy looked straight at Erwun, past Oliviria and her friends.

Someone said, "Watch out!"

There was a series of disappointed groans from the crowd of boys around the desk. Then everyone started clapping. "That must be the highest score in the history of Askagar! You could have gotten a perfect score. And in record time no less!"

Erwun realized they were watching the handsome boy play a video game. The teacher came into class and the students dispersed, but Erwun and the strange boy at his desk continued stealing glances at each other, even as the boy was tucking the game key away in his backpack. She thought he looked intrigued by her, which surprised her. He was a new student, and a new student had never looked at Erwun like that before. There was another boy beside him, also new, almost identical, with the same handsome features but darker eyes and a slightly broodier demeanor.

The teacher addressed the children as they quieted in their seats. "Students, we have two new boys joining our class. Their names are Xerx and Vowkin. They will be with us in class from now on. Please show them the ropes."

The kids mumbled among each other, and then the class started. There was an interactive video about the dangers of multi-tectonic shifting and superimposed flare charges from within the third crustal cavity of Geniverd. Half the kids were asleep. Erwun took notes on her holo-pad. Then there was a test. She finished first and reviewed her notes quietly. She always sat at the front of the class, closest to the teacher and farthest away from the rambunctious students.

The bell rang and it was time for recess. On Erwun's way out of geography class, someone tapped her on the shoulder. She was darn surprised to turn around and see the cute boy from before, the one the teacher had called Xerx, smiling at her with straight white teeth and eyes like blue oceans. "Hi," he said.

Erwun was struck. She didn't know what to say. She needed to hurry and go to her private place in the theater to practice her lines, but she could no longer think. The boy was so cute, and he was staring right at her!

"Aren't you going to say something? Maybe you could tell me your name."

"My …" Erwun was flustered. "Erwun. My name's Erwun. Sorry, that was rude of me. Please, welcome to class. It looks like you already feel very welcome."

Xerx chuckled. "I do feel welcome, thanks. Actually, I like the look of your face. I was wondering if you could show me around."

Erwun peeked past Xerx. The other kids in the class were crowded around Vowkin and chatting. Oliviria and her friends were stealing glances at Xerx, whispering to each other and glaring at Erwun. They must have been shocked that the cute new boy wanted to spend time with Erwun and not them. She didn't understand it either. She also didn't know what she was going to do. She needed to practice her lines. Would she really risk her place in the play for a cute boy?

"I would love to show you around," she said, "but I have a thing."

"What thing?" Xerx asked.

"It's the school play. I need to use my recess to go over my lines."

"Wow," Xerx said, looking truly interested in what she was doing. "That's amazing. Why don't you rehearse your lines with me? I would really enjoy helping you out."

Erwun was stunned again. She usually avoided boys, but

for some reason, she couldn't pull herself away from Xerx. Then he activated his visin. "Send your script to me. Come on, I'll read as we walk."

* * *

Erwun was intimidated by Xerx's confidence. He walked with his chest out and his hands in his pockets, as if he didn't have a care in the world.

"I have to clear something up," she said, feeling nervous just speaking to him. "I'm not exactly in the play."

"I know," he said. "You're Oliviria's understudy. She has the lead role of the cruel princess."

"How do you know that?"

"I checked the bulletin board this morning." He took his hand out of his pocket and tapped a finger to his temple. "I have an awesome memory. And I'm great with names."

"Wow," Erwun said. "I'm impressed. It's true that I'm her understudy, but it's more like I'm her standby. I don't think I have a chance at the part, to be honest. Still, with all the drama going on between the cast members, who knows what could happen? I need to be ready."

Erwun stopped Xerx as he walked past the entrance to the theater. "We're here," she said.

"Oops." Xerx chuckled. "I guess I don't know the school layout yet."

"You'll figure it out," Erwun told him, giving Xerx an awkward smile. "Let's hurry. We only have fifteen minutes."

Erwun climbed onto the stage, and Xerx sat below her in the front row. There was nobody else in the theater, and Erwun's heart was beating in her ears. She couldn't believe how charming he was, just sitting there quietly, one arm thrown over the chair beside him and his legs crossed. "Are you ready?" he asked.

Erwun knelt on the stage, thinking this new boy was so captivating. She felt under his spell. How would she focus on her lines? "I'll start," she said. "Come forth, master—"

"Louder," Xerx demanded. "Take a deep breath; suck in from your gut, then project your voice to the whole room."

Erwun's face was flushed. She took a deep breath, sucking it in from her gut, then belted loudly, "Come forth, master. I will avenge your blood. I have sworn, for my torn heart bleeds at your coronet. This is my plea. Make me powerful, master, for I will avenge your death."

There was a slow clapping from the theater entrance, then giggling. Standing on the threshold was Oliviria with a cocky look on her face. "You're amazing," she said.

"Thank you," Erwun replied, feeling a little embarrassed. She hadn't expected a compliment from Oliviria.

But then Oliviria said, "Not you," and she looked sweetly at Xerx. "I was talking to him. He makes a great director. We could use him during our rehearsals. Are you available to help, new kid?"

That hurt. It felt like Oliviria had just punched Erwun right in the gut. She suddenly regretted bringing Xerx into the theater. It had been trouble from the beginning, no matter how cute he was.

Xerx was smiling at Oliviria, and Erwun desperately hoped he'd refuse her offer. Instead, Xerx said, "Of course. I'm happy to help. When can we start?"

Erwun was scrambling to leave. She was mortified.

Before she could get out the door, Oliviria blocked her path. "What do you think you're doing, you little twerp? Erwun, do you honestly think people will be happy to see you up on that stage instead of me? Just think about it—they'll want their money back."

Erwun had no response. She was on the verge of crying. "Leave me alone," she said, and shouldered past Oliviria into the hallway. She heard Xerx calling after her, but it didn't matter. She put her cordless nubs in her ears and turned on her favorite playlist on her visin, drowning the world in music.

* * *

Erwun spent the rest of the day trying not to think about Xerx. But then, after her last class, he appeared at her desk. "Erwun, are you avoiding me?"

She stood up and walked right past him, saying, "Why would I avoid you? I don't even know you."

"Okay, that's fair," Xerx said. "But are you going to the play rehearsals?"

Erwun shook her head. "Nope."

"Why not?"

"Because I'm the standby. I don't need to be there." Erwun turned around. "What do you care, anyway?"

"I thought you wanted the lead role," Xerx said, following her out of the classroom.

"Yeah, I do." She didn't want to talk to him.

They had stopped in the hall and were quiet as a group of boys walked past. Then Xerx said, "So try to get the main role from Oliviria. Show them how badly you want it."

"But ..."

"But you're worried about Oliviria?" Xerx chuckled and shook his head. "Don't let her get to you. I agreed to attend practice so I'll be able to help you get the part. Forget about Oliviria."

"How are you going to do that?" she asked. "Why are we even having this conversation?"

Vowkin then appeared with a group of boys. "Come on, Xerx," Vowkin said. He smiled briefly at Erwun. "We're going to the game. Aren't you coming?"

"Not today," Xerx said. "I'm helping to direct the school play. I need to help Erwun."

Vowkin shrugged. "All right. See you later." He departed with the rest of the boys, leaving Xerx and Erwun alone again in the school hall.

"You know," Xerx said, "I only said yes to Oliviria because I needed an excuse to see you again."

"Really?" As much as she hated it, Erwun could feel her face getting hot. She looked down, unable to meet his eyes.

Xerx smiled. "Yes, really."

Erwun was speechless. Had she overreacted? Maybe Xerx wasn't that bad after all. "Fine, let's go," she said. And they walked together to the theater.

When they got there, Xerx sat near the front, and Erwun sat in the back. Rehearsal was in full swing. Xerx directed, literally taking over the job of the teacher. Erwun watched as all the problems that were in the play were fixed by Xerx's supreme direction. Everyone was getting along, and there were no mistakes at all. If things kept going so well, Erwun would never have a shot at the part. There would be no need for a standby. Even the stage manager was impressed by Xerx's ability.

"Wow, he's good for a new student," the stage manager said as he took a seat beside Erwun. The manager's name was Lewell.

"Yeah, he's okay."

"Anyway," Lewell said, "have you been practicing?"

"I have, yes." Erwun couldn't keep the disappointment

from her voice. "I have been going over all my lines in case I'm needed for the part. Of course, it looks like that won't be happening anytime soon."

"Don't lose hope," Lewell said. "You are equally as capable on that stage as Oliviria, maybe even more so. If I were you, I would be hoping for my chance to get in the play, no matter how it happened."

Erwun remembered how Lewell had praised her acting skills during the auditions. She was pretty sure Oliviria had only gotten the number-one role because the school liked her more than they liked Erwun, not because Oliviria performed better. It was favoritism and Erwun knew it. Life wasn't fair. School wasn't fair. Not even the teachers were fair!

The double doors opened, and four Protectors marched into the theater. Erwun had forgotten it was IM administration day.

While the Protectors began injecting the students on stage and the other people in the theater were lining up, Xerx appeared at Erwun's side. "Are you okay?" he asked.

"Fine," she said. "You certainly look like you're having fun."

"It wasn't hard at all, because they all need validation," he said, chuckling to himself. "But trust me, the last thing I'm going to do is dedicate my life to entertaining royals. No way."

"That's because a boy like you has options," Erwun said. The Protectors had finished vaccinating the people on the stage and were now working their way through the room.

"What do you mean, a boy like me?"

Erwun shrugged. "You're obviously intelligent, charismatic, and able. You seem to make an impression on people. It looks like you can even influence them. After all, you got me here. Plus, you have been bossing around a whole stage of pretentious kids for the past hour. You even took the job from the teacher." Erwun stood abruptly; the Protectors were nearly finished with the rest of the room. "Now, if you'll excuse me, Xerx, I don't want to miss my shot."

Erwun waved over one of the Protectors and rolled up her sleeve. "Excuse me, Protector. I haven't gotten my shot."

The Protector scanned her and made a loud beeping sound. Then it said, "You've already had your injection. Sit back down."

Erwun opened her mouth to argue, but Xerx grabbed her by the elbow. "Don't," he said. "Trust me, it's better this way."

That was when Oliviria screamed. Erwun gaped at the stage as Oliviria dropped and began to moan, clutching her stomach. Two of the Protectors quickly transmuted their arms into an uncomfortable-looking stretcher with a hard, thin bottom, scooped Oliviria onto it, and boosted out of the room using their propulsion feet. It happened so fast that nobody could fully comprehend what was happening. Erwun was in shock.

"Looks like your opportunity has come," Xerx said quietly. He had his hands shoved in his pockets, looking quite pleased with himself.

"Did she just have an adverse reaction to the IM?" Erwun asked. "And what about mine? Xerx, why did you stop me from getting my IM? What's going on here?"

"You don't need it," he said nonchalantly. "The king and queen were previously just giving people dummy vaccines to keep up morale, and this new substance, the IM, hasn't been approved by the regulatory authorities. I think the real reason for IM therapy is because the entire population is being dosed with something."

"How could you possibly know that?" Erwun asked, staring at Xerx like he was an idiot. "That's a crazy conspiracy theory."

"Call it whatever you want," Xerx said with a smile, "but I'd call it fate. Look, Oliviria is gone. Your opportunity is here. Quickly, Erwun, get on the stage. They need you for the play."

* * *

"No, it can't be!"

I struggled off the floor, swiping Erwun's memories back into my internal storage. It all made sense now. Could it really have been fate? Erwun, the massive crowds of people, the flocks of Gurnots trying to flee Tsiser. What I had seen in Erwun's memories made it all fit into place. Everything was suddenly crystal clear.

I rushed to the library, where I found Knotts staring absently out the window at a nameless beach somewhere in Krug, the waves lapping the sandy shore. He looked like he was daydreaming. Erwun was on the sofa, playing on her visin. I completely ignored Knotts as he turned to me and opened his mouth, and I hurried across the room to Erwun. I was so frantic that I nearly shook the girl by her scruff. "Erwun," I said, my voice high-pitched, "where did you say your family was? Where are they right now?"

Erwun was shocked. "In Krug," she said, blinking rapidly. "They are camped outside the Lukaurus Mansion."

"Why didn't you go with them?"

"I didn't want to," she said. "I told them to stay in the house with me because of the war, but they weren't listening. It was like someone had turned their brains off, and they'd gone deaf. My mother chanted, 'Lukaurus, Lukaurus.' Then she went completely quiet, and my entire family followed her outside. I had never seen them act like that before. Nobody even said goodbye to me as I stood in the doorway, calling after them. A bit later your big friend there"—she pointed at Knotts—"came and picked me up in the flyrarc."

379

"I see," I said, nodding dumbly. It was just as I'd thought. Erwun had managed to avoid the last doses of the IM thanks to Xerx, but the rest of her family hadn't been so lucky. They'd all been dosed. So, when the war had started, Erwun had been the only one in her family not completely drugged by the IM. It was why she wasn't under the influence of the IM.

"Knotts," I said, suddenly feeling so weak I could barely stand, "I understand it now. The IM ... Queen Hagan has been slowly linking everyone's mind to her own. She's brainwashed four billion people!"

I kept Erwun confined to the library and informed the clan leaders, Raad, Papa, and Tissa of everything I'd just discovered. They had a hard time believing me, but I convinced them by saying a confidential informant on the ground had provided solid proof. By 'informant,' I meant Erwun. Five minutes later we were all pacing the main parlor while on our visins, trying to figure out what to do. Knotts leaned on the hearth and stared into the flames. Papa just kept watching the footage of NordHaven as it smoldered from the blast that had reduced it to rubble. It was hard for him to accept that his family's seat of power for hundreds of years was now nothing but crumbled brick and singed curtains.

Tissa covered her mouth as she yawned. "If the king and queen have all this power," she said, "why would they want to control only the commoners? Do you think they can control us too, and we just don't know it yet? Can they listen to what we're saying? Can they control what we're thinking?"

"I don't know," I said with a shrug. "We'll have to wait and see. It was the last dose that activated whatever formula the queen has been injecting into the people. We know this because of our agents. Olorc, Gorm, and Marten are not under the queen's control—they didn't take the last dose of the IM. All I know for certain is that if we hadn't decided to start the war, we would never have known about this."

Surrvul-Ma cleared her throat. "Well, the king and queen are grieving over the loss of their child. It may be the anger that's making them react like this."

"The royal heir died after the last injection was administered," Knotts said. "I know it seems far-fetched, but my theory is that the queen killed Arta herself to gain the sympathy of the other clans."

The room went quiet, the leaders looking shocked. They thought it was a very unfair accusation.

"You all need to get your heads around this," Knotts continued, his tone harsh and unforgiving. "Queen Hagan may seem harmless, but we can't trust her. The woman is dangerous."

"I keep hearing people say this," Surrvul-Ma said, "but what about the king? Where does King Zawne stand in all this? We blamed Queen Kaelyn for the last pandemic, and now we're blaming Queen Hagan for the mass manipulation of the world."

"Just trust us," I said. I let my eyes pass over everyone in the room. "We aren't absolving the king of guilt, but we are saying that Queen Hagan is the mastermind behind everything."

* * *

Everyone retired for the night. We had all been awake for almost twenty-four hours and needed rest. I let Erwun sleep in Xerx's room—I thought he would have wanted it that way

—and went to see Nnati. There wasn't any time left before he was supposed to turn off Neuge's life-support machines.

I found him passed out in the chair beside Neuge's bed. I lightly draped a throw blanket over his shoulders and stroked his cheek. I felt so sorry for him, devastated to the point where he wanted to kill himself. That was when Knotts walked into the room.

"Are you okay?" he said quietly, moving slowly into the dark room. The only light was from the twin moons outside the window, the nightly simulation that played in my house's windows.

"Yeah," I said. "It's just been a long day."

I walked to the door, eager to get away from Knotts. I needed him to leave and go meet with Tharva and Justein. That way, I could slip back into the room alone.

"I just wish Roki and the twins were here, you know?" I slipped onto the threshold, hoping Knotts would follow after me. "I don't know what Lordin is planning to do with all those poor people. How long is she going to force them to act like this? I could never have anticipated a mass brainwashing with her engineering experiments. There's no way I could have known. Anyway, I'm going to call Roki and see if he finally answers. You should go meet with Tharva and Justein. I'll be there soon, and we will confront Lordin together."

Knotts had moved into the doorframe and was blocking my exit. We were so close that I could feel his breath on my face, smelling oddly sweet for such a strong and brutish man. He looked at me silently, his deep-green eyes mystifying. I thought he knew I was trying to get rid of him. Then he surprised me by stepping out into the hall, putting his back against the wall, and sliding down onto his butt. "Come," he said, and patted the floor beside him.

I stepped over Knotts's legs, then sat next to him.

"What a night," I said. "Maybe I do need a break for a minute."

"What you need is some seriously gutsy move," he said. "People like Lordin don't listen to weakness or hesitancy. They only respond to bold actions. We need to come up with a fierce plan to throw Lordin off her game. Obviously, the attack on Cara wasn't enough."

"You're probably right," I said. "But I have no fresh ideas. Lordin's audacity has caught me off guard. I don't know what to do."

Knotts was studying my face. "It's a shame," he said, and shook his head.

"What do you mean? Why are you looking at me like that?"

"Hypocrisy," he said. "Kaelyn, you're fighting for everyone to have the right to the same things you had before you were killed. You were a sixteen-year-old girl who set up a foundation. It was an extremely privileged thing to do. You had some great achievements, but you were no better than the other nobles. The only thing you're fighting for now is to bring privilege to more people, not equality or fairness."

"What?" I was shocked and offended. "Are you crazy? How dare you judge me like that! You don't know anything about me, my people, or even my world."

Knotts laughed like he didn't care. "Don't deflect this onto me, Kaelyn. I'm just saying, how many kids could have done what you did?"

"That's not fair," I said. "I didn't know about the world I was born into. I was shielded as a child, slowly indoctrinated into a cult of power and wealth. When I understood what was happening, I tried to do the right thing. It's all I have ever tried to do."

"Okay, but what do you think is going to happen after you 'save' the people, Kaelyn? Do you expect everyone to become suddenly prosperous? Do you think everyone who survives this war will just start living exceptional lives?"

"I think it will take time for everything to balance itself," I said, a harsh edge in my voice. "But it needs to be done. Someone needs to rescue the world. I never thought of myself as the savior of Geniverd. I don't want to be revered." I pushed off the wall and stood up, suddenly furious. "Anyway, if you don't agree with what we're doing, then why are you helping us? I'm not going to sit here defending myself to the likes of you."

Knotts looked up at me, blinking his long black lashes. He was so adorable. It was hard to be mad. "I'm not attacking you," he said. "Sorry. I don't mean to be a jerk. I just don't know if Min should be out here trying to rescue humans. What makes us any different from the Min who interfere with human affairs for their own gains?"

I said nothing. I folded my arms and stared down at him. "I don't have time for this, Knotts. You need to get back to the other Min. I have work to do."

"Okay, okay," he said, sucking his teeth. He seemed upset that his words weren't having more of an effect on me. What was he trying to pull? "I apologize. Sit back down with me. Let's talk. Maybe we can figure out a new strategy."

Knotts held out his hand as if I would take it. "Yeah, right," I said, and swatted his hand away. "I'll sit down, but only because we do need a new strategy. Don't you dare touch me."

"Fine," he said, raising his hands in defense.

I sat back down against the wall, keeping enough distance between us that our shoulders weren't touching. I remembered a few important questions I'd been meaning to ask him. It seemed as good a time as any. "I think you owe me a few answers," I told Knotts. "Especially after what you just put me through."

"That's fair," he said. "Shoot. I'll answer whatever you want."

"I'm curious," I said. "I know your wife died for our cause, and I'm sorry to hear that. Could you tell me about her?"

Knotts threw his head back. "Argh. Why?"

"Because you're helping me," I said. "I'd like to understand who you are. You know everything about my life, and yet I know nothing about yours."

"Well, what is there to say? I guess you and she were very much alike, except you outranked her. She was desperate to save the world. She was one of our highest-profile members. A lot of her views were the same as yours."

"Do you miss her?"

"Not really."

"No?"

"It was a marriage of convenience."

"Aren't most high-profile marriages born from convenience?"

"I guess."

"She gave you access to royalty, right? That's why you needed her?"

Knotts laughed, although there was no humor in it. "Actually, she didn't. I already had contact with the royals through my vineyards and other enterprises. I met many of the royal members by selling my super-expensive wines. You know how royalty is when it comes to luxurious things."

"I sure do. They're all trying to one-up each other. It's one big feeding frenzy between those people."

"That's right," Knotts said. "I banked on it. I supplied wine to some of the most exclusive parties in Geniverd. I made friends and contacts all over the world who ended up helping us with the current war. After you turned down my marriage proposal, I chose to marry Rhienne. Rhienne was kind to me and sympathetic to our cause. I loved her ..." He shook his head, looking guilty. "But the thing was, Kaelyn, I wasn't in love with her. And she wasn't in love with me. Still, with her, I fully pledged to support Roki and Defiance. She helped me orchestrate a lot of the fires that caused so many nobles to scramble for shelter, disrupting their rule. Rhienne introduced me to Gorm, Olorc, and Marten. The rest is history. We got Roki elected as Defiance's leader, and now here we are."

"Wow," I said. "You did all this work as a favor to Roki? That's one big favor."

"Yes, and I'd do it again in a human heartbeat."

"Why?" I asked. "I don't understand. Why do you owe him such a huge favor?"

"Roki saved me from my evil sister," Knotts told me. "Her name was Soren, and I was terrified of her. She was a monster to me as a little boy and all the way into adulthood, then grew even worse when we became Min. It was right after we got our powers. My fire-breathing talent was just developing. Whereas I was intrigued by her gift, she coveted mine and became jealous. She tried to drown me in a lake."

"Your own sister tried to kill you? Poor little Knotts."

"She had some power over water. She could control it masterfully, using it for all kinds of incredible things. She also had a mean streak of jealousy.

"Back then, Soren was dating Roki. Roki didn't know we were Min at the time. He had no idea that if something happened to me, I could just come back in a new body. He saw Soren drowning me one day in the lake behind our house and dived in to save me. Soren stopped him with an invisible barrier, and Roki fought to break through it. I saw right then that he was a bold, fearless, and honorable man. Soren eventually realized her insanity and let down the barrier, at which point Roki swam deeper into the lake and dragged me to safety.

"Because of the rules of the Crown of Crowns, I knew Roki would be killed for learning our secret, since he had witnessed Soren using her powers. I also knew that Soren would be killed for displaying her power in front of a mortal. As such, I begged on my hands and knees for the Crown of Crowns to show mercy. They must have been in a good mood, because they allowed Roki to become a Min."

"What about Soren?" I asked.

Knotts shook his head sadly. "They sentenced her to live the rest of her Min life in prison at the edge of the galaxy. She was eighteen. She'd just been transformed into a Min."

"Eighteen ..." I was shocked. "That's a sentence of nine hundred and eighty-two years. I can't imagine being locked in prison for almost a thousand years, and only with the mind of an eighteen-year-old girl. That must have been brutal on her, no matter how jealous or crazy she was."

"I didn't care," Knotts said. "That may seem cruel to you, but she tortured me relentlessly my whole life. I was elated when the Crown of Crowns put her away. So, yeah, Roki's intervention ended with a new friend and the eternal imprisonment of my biggest tormentor. I will owe him for the rest of my existence. If it wasn't for him, Soren would have killed me."

Knotts turned his eyes on me; my heart skipped a beat. "The things we do out of jealousy can cost us in the long run," I said, breaking eye contact. "They can be stupid. Thanks for sharing your story."

"You're welcome."

Time was slipping by. Still, I didn't want to leave Knotts. I felt we were bonding, that I was beginning to see the real soul underneath his hardened exterior. I decided to ask him more questions. "So, on a lighter note," I said, "where do you live when you're not in Geniverd?"

"I live on Ikuwl," he said, "a beautiful planet at the edge of the Oasa solar system. We have two moons and many strange, alluring creatures."

"Is that why you have a base in Capernort?" I asked. "Does it remind you of Ikuwl?"

Knotts laughed. "Capernort doesn't come close to Ikuwl. But maybe it is a little more similar to it than the other continents. The natural beauty, low population density, and many of us in Ikuwl are related to each other."

"Do you mind showing me pictures?" I asked. "I'd like to explore other planets when I'm done here on Geniverd."

"Sure." Knotts projected pictures he'd stored in his memory onto the wall in front of us. They were truly beautiful landscapes of plains, mountains, streams, tall trees, and plenty of snow. It actually did look a lot like Capernort, only with odd seven-legged creatures possessing long noses and no eyes, slithering weirdly through the snowy plains. The cities looked weird too, with domed ceilings half-buried underground, like submerged igloos.

"I can see why you like it," I said after seeing a few images. "It's absolutely amazing."

"Yeah?" Knotts gave me a sly look. "Maybe you can visit sometime. Would you like that?"

"Yeah, maybe I would," I said, surprising myself with the answer. I suddenly realized how much time I'd been spending with Knotts lately. He really wasn't a bad guy, not as bad as I'd first thought. He seemed considerate, loyal, and even kind. He was just bitter. But who wouldn't be at his age?

"Anyway," I said, "I really must go. We have a lot of work to do."

I stood up and moved to the doorway to check on Nnati

again. I really did need to leave. There was no time to sit around talking. Nnati could wake up at any moment. But as I moved to the door, Knotts stood and tripped over his own shoes, reached for the doorknob to steady himself, and we somehow ended up crashing into the doorjamb together. Our lips brushed, and I grabbed his shoulders for support. Heat rushed through me in a wave, flushing my cheeks and making my spine tingle. His hand went to my face on instinct, just as our lips separated, and from the shock of it, I jumped backward out of his grip. Then we were standing in the doorway, staring each other in the eyes, my heart racing like a runaway horse. My gaze kept dipping from Knotts's eyes to his lips.

Stop it, Kaelyn! What are you doing?

"I'm sorry," he said softly. "I tripped. I didn't mean to."

"You sure about that?" I snapped. Could he have done it on purpose? Why did I feel such a primitive heat inside my body? Why couldn't I stop staring at his full, soft lips?

"I'm sorry," he repeated. "I'll go now."

"Wait!" I touched his arm softly. "I … I'm sorry. I know it was an accident. Listen, go meet the other Min, and I'll be with you soon."

"When is soon?" he asked. I heard it in his voice, how much he wanted to stay with me—to not be too long without me.

I needed to move, but it was like time had stopped. "I just need to freshen up, come back, and check on Nnati, and if I get a few minutes, I might eat something. I'm also going to try to reach Roki again. I shouldn't be more than thirty minutes, one hour max."

"Okay," he said, and turned, then walked down the hallway.

I pressed a finger against my trembling lips and lingered a moment on the threshold of Neuge's sickroom, trying to catch my breath. My heart was still beating like a drum.

* * *

I HAD a quick shower and then changed into a sleeveless top, long pants, and a smart jacket. This was in case I needed to do another live broadcast. Then I lay down on my bed, stretched out my legs, and willed myself from my body.

It was only one of a handful of times I had left my body since occupying it, and the sensation was odd. It felt like I had just lost one hundred pounds and all my nerves had stopped working. I was weightless, almost without feeling, yet somehow fully alert. I hated it. In anticipation of what was about to happen, I suddenly became strangely euphoric as I zipped down the hallway and into Neuge's sickroom, where Nnati was still slouched asleep in the chair. I hovered an inch above Neuge's chest, remembering the first time I had occupied a new body. Slowly I lowered my Valer into his chest, wrapped around Neuge's heart, and allowed myself to spread throughout. There was a trickle of warmth, then sensation. It was like water flowing over an ice tray, my soul filling each individual portion until Neuge was full and brimming with life. His heart—my heart—kicked, and I opened my eyes.

This body was bigger than I was used to. I felt a sudden rush of strength and power. I'd never had muscles like this before, though I'd have been lying if I'd said I hadn't imagined how much fun it would be to occupy the body of a muscle-bound man, to feel the swollen pecs, the washboard abs, and every other bit that came along with it. However, my current experience was not as expected. I felt like my whole body was inflamed. I turned my stiff neck to see Nnati gaping at me. The transfer of energy must have woken him.

"You're awake," he said, softly at first. Then he exploded. "Oh my, Neuge, you're back!"

"Yup," I said, unsure what to expect from my voice. It

sounded strange in my head when I spoke. Internally my voice was the same, but aloud it sounded hoarse and gruff, just as Neuge's always had. "I'm back. Hi, Nnati."

"Baby, I thought you were gone for good. How ...?"

"What happened?" I asked. Now I needed to be an actor.

"Don't worry about it," Nnati said. His hands were all over me, touching my face, my arms, my hands. It was such a strange sensation. But at least I had saved Nnati from taking his own life. "You were in an accident," he told me. "Everything is going to be okay."

"Thank you," I croaked, trying to act as sick as possible. I wanted to leave Neuge's body before things got weird. All I had wanted was to give Nnati hope so that he wouldn't do something rash, and now I had achieved that objective. "I feel tired," I wheezed, then fake coughed a few times. "I think I will go back to sleep. Wait for me, Nnati. Don't unplug me ..."

I shut my eyes and immediately slipped free of the body, making sure to leave behind enough traces of energy so the husk remained warm and alive.

Nnati was cheering, stroking the body of what was, essentially, a costume. "Sleep, baby. Sleep now. We will talk later."

I felt a little bad for tricking him and giving Nnati false hope. It dawned on me that what I had just done might end up causing Nnati even more pain in the future. But that was a problem for later. One of many problems for later. I was now leading a triple life.

12

I was back in my body moments later. The difference was startling. It was as if gravity's pull had lessened by fifty percent. I felt lighter without all that muscle weighing me down like a suit of armor, though I kind of missed the sense of power and toughness, as if I could squash someone just by stepping on them. No wonder Neuge was so curt and broody. He must have felt powerful and gigantic every day.

I went quickly to Nnati's room, muffling a shout of glee. He'd sent me an emergency message on my visin. When I entered, Nnati was beaming with excitement. "Cerna!" he called, nearly squealing with delight. He rushed across the room and embraced me in a tight hug. "He's back. He woke up just a few minutes ago. It's not the end after all."

"I'm happy for you," I said, but mostly I was happy to have a little part of my Nnati back. He clearly trusted me and valued my company, and that felt good.

"I came so close to losing him," Nnati said, now stricken by emotion and waving his hand in front of his face. "You don't know how much this moment means to me. I think when Neuge wakes up, I will ask him to marry me."

"Whoa! Slow down, Nnati. Take it easy. You're emotional and impulsive. Wait for Neuge to wake up before you start getting ahead of yourself. You still need to get to know him better. You don't want to jump straight into marriage. Who knows what could happen?"

He sighed, then sat down heavily in the chair beside Neuge's bed and began to run his fingers up and down Neuge's exposed forearm. "Maybe you're right," he said. "I'm just so excited. What do you think I should do?"

"Wait it out," I said. "See if he's the real deal. Don't throw yourself at him—he might think you're desperate."

Nnati was nodding along with me, but I could tell he wasn't fully absorbing my advice. It was selfish advice on my part, anyway. I just needed Nnati to take it easy and not get too excited while I worked out how to go about my triple life. I needed Nnati to be let down gently. He couldn't go getting himself worked up over marriage when it was an impossibility. I wasn't about to marry my best friend!

I quickly changed the subject, since I had to meet Knotts soon. "Have you eaten yet?" I asked.

"No." Nnati paused and sniffed his armpits, then wrinkled his nose. "But I do need a shower."

I laughed. "Okay, Nnati. Go take a shower. I'm going to a meeting in Cara. While you were with Neuge, we discovered that the queen has modified everyone's genetic material, except for the nobles, to be under her control. Like zombies, Nnati. Mind-controlled zombies. She and Zawne have everyone out in protest on the properties of the upper class that we had targeted for destruction. We're currently stuck on what we can do. Plus, Roki is still looking for the twins."

"Oh no," Nnati said, his face sagging. "I hope you find the

boys soon. I miss seeing them around. I also saw what happened to VondRust. That's a pretty huge achievement, Cerna. What will you do now?"

"Face the king and queen soon, I hope. I don't think they can keep so many people outside much longer in these harsh weather conditions. The rain is coming down in sheets, and it is freezing out there. Anyway, I doubt the Grucken will be happy with whatever Queen Hagan thinks she's doing. Mental slavery goes against every tenet of Decens-Lenitas."

Nnati was shaking his head. "This is really crazy. It's gone too far."

Discussing politics was working to take his mind off Neuge. I thought I would try to lighten the mood even more. "I know this is random," I said with a silly grin, "since we aren't really that close. But you'll never believe what happened to me before I came here."

Nnati's eyes went wide and sparkled. "Are you talking gossip in the middle of a war? Spill it! What happened?"

My knees went weak. "Knotts and I accidentally kissed. He tripped and I fell, and we kind of … well, we hit the wall with our lips touching."

"And then what? Did you kiss for real? Do you even like him in that way? What about Roki?"

This was better. This was the old Nnati I remembered. It was almost as if I were Kaelyn again—almost but not quite.

"I actually don't like him in that way at all," I said with a laugh. "It just kind of happened."

Nnati smiled mischievously. "I bet he likes you."

I opened my mouth to speak, then stopped. I hadn't considered whether Knotts liked me in that way. The kiss had only been an accident. Knotts was friends with Roki. Considering he was working so hard to pay off his life debt to Roki, would Knotts really try to smooch his friend's girlfriend? I was thinking about how he kept looking at me. Was there more going on behind Knotts's deep-green eyes?

"No," I said, as much to Nnati as to my own inner monologue. "I don't think so. Anyway, it doesn't matter if he does or not. I'm with Roki and I am a loyal woman."

Nnati shrugged. "All right. Then maybe it was just a silly accident. But I still bet you felt something when your lips touched."

"Why do you say that?"

"Your eyes," Nnati said. "You told me the story with such excitement in your eyes that I would have thought you were telling me about your crush."

I gasped and held my hand to my breast. "What! No. Really?"

"Second," he continued, having way too much fun, "if it didn't matter to you, then you would never have said anything to me. We hardly know each other. But it was important enough that you had to spill it to someone, even a stranger. For all you know, I could start a rumor."

"I didn't think of that," I said, then laughed nervously. "Please don't tell anyone. Honestly, I only mentioned it to you because it was a silly, awkward experience. I would have told Roki if he were here."

"Relax," Nnati said. "I'm just teasing you."

"Oh." I sighed. "That's good to know. I hope you feel like you can trust me the same way I trust you. I hope we are becoming closer friends."

"I think we are," he said. "In fact, I formally declare that we are closer friends than we were before." Nnati paused, his face darkening and getting serious. He stared me right in the eyes. "Just be careful around him. Don't be naive. Roki is away; you are a beautiful woman, extremely vulnerable, and perhaps in a position where someone as powerful as Knotts would be happy to take advantage."

"Maybe," I said. "But I refuse to be emotionally unfaithful to Roki. I won't let Knotts get too close, even if there is some small amount of feeling somewhere inside me. You are Neuge's man and I am Roki's girl, and that's that. Let's keep looking out for each other like this. I've enjoyed talking to you this morning."

"I have enjoyed it too," Nnati said. "It's hard to believe we can go from chatting about the men in our lives to you facing off against the queen and the world. You remind me of ..."

"Of the late queen?" I finished.

"Yes. I'm sorry if that makes you uncomfortable."

"Not at all. I'm just glad you like me, and maybe it's not such a bad thing to have a person who reminds you of a dear friend who has passed on. You should keep her memory alive inside your mind."

"Thanks," Nnati said. I could tell he was a little ashamed for comparing me to the late queen, to the old Kaelyn. "I really do like you," he said. "Is there anything I can do for you while you go to Cara?"

"Actually, yes. Please keep the royals happy, as well as you can. Treat this home like it's yours. And Xerx's girlfriend is here. Her name is Erwun. Please try to keep her safe and sound."

* * *

I smelled Roki's toffee scent the moment I walked out of Neuge's sickroom. I raced through the house, following his delicious scent all the way to our bedroom. I flung open the door, and there he was, my handsome Roki, standing at the foot of our bed, waiting for me.

CLARA LOVEMAN

"Sorry," he said.

He didn't get out another word. I jumped across the room and hugged Roki fiercely, nuzzling my face into his chest. I was weeping tears of joy. I stood up and looked into his bright gray eyes, stroked his golden stubbly chin, and squeezed his big, muscly arms. "I've missed you," I said. "But where are the twins?"

"Not here," he said, "but they are alive. Listen, Kaelyn, I'm sorry I couldn't come to see you sooner—"

I interrupted his words with a kiss, and then we were spinning. My legs were wrapped around Roki's waist, and his tongue was sliding across my lips. We hit the bed, and he was on top of me, already breathing heavily. He was ready to devour me.

"How long have you been here?" I suddenly asked. I was concerned he may have overheard my conversation with Nnati. After all, Roki was the master of concealment.

"Just now," he said, and rolled onto his side. He propped his chin up on his knuckles, his face hovering a few inches above mine. "And I can't stay for long, so I don't think we are going to have time for this."

"Later," I said, smiling playfully. Then I got serious. "But where are the boys? Tell me what happened."

"I know where they are, although they're not completely safe," he said. "I'm hoping they will be freed when I go back. Honestly, I can't tell you anything more than that."

"Why not?" I demanded, recoiling in dismay. "What kind of sick game is going on here? Is Lordin forcing you to act against your will?"

"I can't say anything," Roki said. We were both crawling off the bed now, deadly serious. The mood was ruined. We stood up, and Roki said, "I only have ten minutes here. You have to trust me."

I sighed. "Always. But if we only have ten minutes, then we need to make this quick."

I summarized everything in a few short sentences: how Zawne had said Roki had murdered Arta, Lordin's announcements to the world, Erwun's memories, and the sinister secret behind Lordin's IM and her genetic-engineering program. All the while, Roki's expression grew more and more worried. By the time I'd finished, his head was hanging in disappointment. I knew there was no way he could have killed Arta. His shock and concern were too genuine.

"I was supposed to stop that damn IM, and I failed," he said, angry at himself for not preventing the mass mind control.

"It's not your fault," I said, gently holding Roki's hand. "Don't let any of this get to you. Right now, Roki, your only focus should be finding Xerx and Vowkin."

Then he asked me something strange. "Did you finish watching Erwun's memories?"

"No," I said. "Why do you ask?"

"Just finish watching them. Trust me."

"Okay, but what about the war, Roki? What am I supposed to do?"

He smiled and kissed me. "Don't worry, I know you'll make the right decisions. I know it sucks that you have to lead the main battle without me, and I am sorry for that. But you are a strong and capable woman and also a powerful Min. Not to mention, Knotts is here to help you. Use him if you need to. For now, I must leave. I need to make sure the twins are safe."

Roki held my hand to his lips, kissed it gently, then pushed back strands of my hair with his other hand and gave me a passionate kiss on the lips, sucking my bottom lip until it was tender.

"Remember," he said, his body disintegrating like so much dust in a gentle wind, "the memories. It's important ..."

* * *

I was glad the twins were still alive, but Roki had left me with more questions than answers. Why couldn't he tell me what he knew? And how much more was I supposed to discover in Erwun's memories? It was all too much, and I could only deal with one thing at a time. The first thing I needed to do was take care of the situation in Cara, so I left Tsiser to meet with Knotts.

I found him with Tharva and Justein in the clouds above Cara. After thanking the two Min for their help and support, they vanished to take care of some other business. Then I was alone with Knotts in the moody sky. I couldn't escape his piercing stare. My plan was to unleash the news on the world about 'Queen Hagan's' engineering scheme, but then Knotts said, "You took forever."

"Yeah, sorry. I was chatting with Nnati."

"You were with Roki," he said calmly. It was as if he could see right through me. Knotts must have smelled Roki on my clothes. His scent was so strong, as if he had marked me.

"Yes." I couldn't look straight at him, so I found myself staring past his face and into the lights of Cara below. It was still night, and the rain was falling heavily. "I saw him briefly. Roki told me to go through Erwun's memories and then left again. I have no idea what he's doing."

"Did he kiss you?"

"Excuse me?" Now I did look at Knotts. I scowled at him. "What does that have to do with you? Roki is my boyfriend. Of course, we kissed. It's none of your business."

What happened next caught me completely by surprise.

Knotts floated to me and lifted my chin. I got a whiff of his delicious breath. Then his lips were on mine. He kissed me softly, and my eyes grew wide, staring straight into his. It felt like fireworks were bursting inside my oversensitive Min body. I wanted to push him away, but instead, I gave in. He had me by the hips with his strong hands, pulling me tightly against his muscled frame, and somewhere in the heat, my eyes closed and I opened my mouth, taking in the warmth and wetness of his tongue. I was consumed by an uncontrollable force. I couldn't stop.

I had no thoughts. My hands were tucked under his long hair, pulling him into me by the neck. Our bodies were pressed together so tightly that I could feel his pecs firm against my chest. He stopped kissing me, and I pushed off him —it had all happened so fast—and I was hovering in the clouds, panting. My face felt like it was on fire.

"Did I hurt you?" he asked, Knotts's voice unusually soft and caring.

"No."

"Then why are you crying?"

I hadn't even realized I was crying, but I was. Tears streaked my face. "Because ..." I said. "Because ... No! Why did you kiss me?"

"Because I know you have feelings for me. I can feel it in your heart, Kaelyn. You have intense feelings for me, and it's killing you inside."

"You're wrong," I said. "You're crazy."

He was on me again, one hand on the small of my back while he kissed the tears from my cheeks, my nose, my lips. We were kissing all over again, and I didn't want to stop. He was so tender with me, so gentle and sensual.

"Sorry to interrupt such a lovely kiss."

I broke away from Knotts, thrust myself backward through

the air, and spun around to see Lordin smiling at me from the clouds.

"Having fun?" she asked. "That's nice. Good for you, Kaelyn. But if you don't mind, we're in the middle of a war. Can you cheat on your boyfriend some other time?"

I tried to answer, to defend myself—how could I have been caught cheating on Roki by Lordin? It was so humiliating—but she kept talking.

"I always knew you were a slut. I'm never wrong about these things. It's good to see you haven't changed. You're the same slut who tried to steal my husband from me."

"It's not what it looks like," I said. Lordin sounded bitter about me getting together with Zawne after she'd died, but that was nothing like this. This was much worse. For the first time, I was actually cheating on my partner, physically and mentally. I had no excuse.

"Don't try to rationalize your garbage behavior to me," she said, looking truly disgusted. Lordin pointed through the clouds. "The people of Geniverd need some justification for participating in this ludicrous war. They deserve an explanation from their dearly departed queen."

Knotts moved forward to defend me. "Tell the people to go home," he said. He was far more commanding than I'd have been capable of.

Lordin crossed her arms. "I'll do that as soon as you end this stupid temper tantrum. I get it, you know. I do. Kaelyn wishes she was still the queen. She wants the people to understand she ended the pandemic. She wants the fame. Obviously"—she looked straight at me—"the highest honor we gave to you and Roki was not enough. It was the best we could offer, but apparently not good enough for you. Roki and his cheating girlfriend had to start a war, all because they were jealous. Well, I suggest you avoid humiliating yourself further and give up now while you still have lungs to breathe."

"Are you threatening me?" I was so mad. My blood was boiling. "That's it, Lordin. I'm done messing around."

I made a dive for the city. I streaked through the night sky and landed in an abandoned alley. Of course, Lordin and Knotts were right behind me. They landed in the alley just as I was activating my visin to make a global address. I cleared my throat and then spoke to the whole world while Lordin watched, snickering as if there was nothing I could do to harm her.

"My people, you have all been deceived," I said with great authority. "You think that you are protesting against Defiance to stop the war, but in fact, you are only tools being used by the monarchy. You see, you are not protesting of your own free will. You have been summoned by forces beyond your control, ordered at the behest of your queen."

"Stop this right now," Lordin snarled. "Don't you dare."

I ignored her, completely unfazed. I was recording Lordin on my visin for the whole world to see, dripping wet and maddened as she screamed at me to stop.

"As you can see, people of Geniverd, the queen is begging me not to tell you the truth. But the truth cannot be silenced. The bold fact is that your genetic material has been engineered to obey Hagan's commands. This deception happened through the IM you've received. She betrayed your trust. She has injected you day after day with a secret formula that makes you obey her every command. You are only there to protect the nobles, those who hide behind their fences, their atmospheric bubbles, and their metal gates. Please, go back home so that we can finish this war."

I was watching the screen, the feed showing me seven different mass gatherings throughout Geniverd. Nobody was moving. That was when I noticed Lordin smiling at me through the projection. "Come on," I said. "Move. Go home. You're all being used."

Nothing happened. Lordin started to cackle.

"You're evil," I said. My heartbeat raced, causing pain my chest. "What did you do?"

"What are you talking about?" she said, feigning innocence. "I didn't do anything. The people simply love me. Tell her, everyone. Tell her you love me."

As if by command, a massive chant rose up all over Geniverd, on every one of my screens: "We love Hagan. We love the queen. We love Zawne. We love the king." The chorus reverberated all around the city and the world.

I killed the broadcast. It was pointless. Whatever Lordin had done was enough to completely melt the brains of all the people of Geniverd, making them stupid and obedient. They were quite obviously her toys.

Lordin raised her hands in a gesture of helplessness. "Oops," she said. "Looks like I've won. Your little stunt is over."

"Don't push me," I said. I had a sensation that things were moving too quickly for me to process. There was no way this was the end. I hadn't become a Min to be intimidated and bullied by an evil woman. I was so furious that I balled my hands into fists.

"Come again?" Lordin leaned forward and touched her ears. "I can't hear you over the chant of my people. Just admit your defeat, Kaelyn. I have everything and you have nothing. These people will never be yours. Geniverd is mine. Haven't you learned by now to leave well enough alone? But I guess you haven't. You're just like your mother. Neither of you could ever leave well enough alone. Now look at you both."

"Don't you dare mention my mother!" I screamed into Lordin's face, spittle flying from my lips. I didn't care anymore. I didn't care about anything. A shudder swept through my entire body. "You think you've won? You underestimate what I can do. I have power, Lordin—more power than you'll ever know!"

My face pinched, I looked to the sky and screamed with all my might. "Tharva! Justein! Destroy it! Destroy it all! Wipe out the targets! Wipe out the cities! Destroy! Destroy! Destroy!"

Knotts grabbed hold of me. "What are you doing? Are you insane?"

My thoughts froze, and then it was too late. I heard the crashing of the waves, the great titanic tsunami as it broke over Cara, over the entire city like a shattered dam washing away a village. There weren't any screams. All I could hear was the sound of rushing water, a great cacophony of destruction, and then I was hovering above a submerged city. Bodies floated around the tops of skyscrapers like discarded dolls bobbing around flagpoles. The entire city had drowned in a flash of water. Then the wave slowly receded, and with it, nearly a billion bodies were dragged into the ocean like so much broken flotsam.

And then I was staring but not seeing.

"What have I done ...?" Tears fell from my eyes, and I began to pound my fists into Knotts's chest. "What have I done? Knotts, what have I done?"

13

"Sh-sh-she made me do it," I said to Knotts through my tears. I was still shaking from the anger.

"I know." He rubbed my back. "I know she did."

"She cornered me," I said stubbornly. "What did she expect? I shouldn't even be crying. We won. Defiance has finally won. Lordin thought I didn't have it in me, Knotts, but she was wrong. Now she knows better than to mess with me. If she keeps pushing, Lordin will have no kingdom left to rule."

I knew I'd committed the worst crime ever and that I would hate myself for it. Soren had been jailed for life for much less, so I deserved far worse. But the gravity of the situation hadn't truly sunk in yet. Inexplicably, I was still in warmode.

"You're right," Knotts said. "Still, it is totally natural that you feel guilt for the loss of life. Cry it out. Then we will pick up the pieces. But what's the next step? What will we do now?"

I took a deep breath to try and regain control of my emotions. "Well," I said, talking slowly to diffuse the moment,

GODLY SINS

"I can't actually claim victory. This whole deal needs to look like a natural disaster. Mind you, the most brutal natural disaster in the history of Geniverd. We can only hope that Lordin will concede defeat and then issue an apology to the world."

"That only works if she stops controlling their minds," Knotts said.

"Right. We need to find a way to force her hand. We need to sever Lordin's link between herself and the population. And I want my twins back. She should be thinking now that if she doesn't deliver Xerx and Vowkin soon, there is going to be much more devastation from me."

I couldn't focus, and my chest felt like it was caving in. I wanted to forget everything I'd just done. Then I found myself wondering if I should talk about the kiss, if I should say something to Knotts. I knew it had been a terrible mistake. I had betrayed Roki, and I felt horrible about it.

I was thankful when Knotts said, "Let's not talk about what happened. We can deal with us after we deal with this current mess." Then he picked me up and swung me in a circle, ending by hugging me tightly and whispering in my ear, "Don't worry, I'm not going to kiss you again. I just want to celebrate your victory."

I giggled, feeling both sad and relieved. What was wrong with me? What did I want?

"So, can we finally leave this planet?" he asked. "I'm dying to show you mine."

"Definitely not yet. Geniverd needs a strong plan for the future, and I still need to get my twins back. I should start by reviewing Erwun's memories again, like Roki suggested."

"I understand." Knotts released me and stepped back. "Do you want me to stay with you?"

"No." I shook my head. "Thanks, but no. You should get

back to Tharva and Justein, then return to Tsiser. I need you to get a message to the Surrvul clan leaders to boost the production of Protectors. This is going to be one big mess to clean up."

"Got it," he said. "Call for me when you're done."

I turned to leave and Knotts called back to me. "And, Kaelyn ... um ..." He was acting like a schoolboy. "Never mind," he said, pinching his bottom lip. "I'll see you soon."

* * *

I flew to Krug, where I found a shallow cave mouth on a remote section of coastline and sat down on the wet sand to finish viewing Erwun's memories. It was warm with a muggy, tropical heat, and I was very comfortable there. It was peaceful and exotic. I rested my back against the smooth rock of the wall just as the sun peeked above the ocean far away on the horizon. Then I opened Erwun's memories.

* * *

Oliviria didn't show up for school the day after she'd fallen ill, and so Erwun's role as the cruel princess was solidified. There wasn't enough time left before opening night to be switching back and forth between actresses. It helped that Lewell and the other kids in the play were all extremely pleased with her performance. It helped even more that Xerx was especially supportive. He arrived halfway through the second day of Erwun's rehearsal as the cruel princess and helped Lewell direct from the front row, clapping and smiling and cheering Erwun on. Whenever Xerx and Erwun locked eyes, a whole kaleidoscope of butterflies fluttered in the young girl's belly.

It was the day after the second rehearsal, and Erwun was going over her homework in class. The teacher hadn't come in yet. Xerx and Vowkin played video games, and the rest of the class was crowded around their desks, shouting and whooping. Then Oliviria walked in.

Erwun's heart hammered against her ribs, then dropped into her stomach with an icy splash. It was clear Oliviria hadn't recovered. She had dark circles around her eyes, and her cheeks were gaunt. She looked terribly ill. But that didn't stop Erwun's sudden fear that Oliviria, even though she was one layer of makeup away from being a ghoul, would demand her position back as the cruel princess.

"Hey," Erwun said as Oliviria half walked, half limped over to her desk. "I'm sorry you were unwell. I hope you feel better now. Let me know if there is anything I can do to help."

"Yeah, there sure is," Oliviria said. She was trying to be a snob, but her voice was scratchy and she sounded weak. "You can help by stepping aside as the cruel princess when we go to the theater today."

Erwun already knew that Lewell wasn't going to switch back to Oliviria, especially not with her in such rough shape. But Erwun didn't want to get into a confrontation before class had even started, so she smiled and nodded and let Oliviria find her seat. She'd wait until it was time to go to the theater. Let Oliviria find out from the teacher, Lewell. That was the safer bet.

A few hours later, at lunchtime, Erwun wanted to invite Xerx to eat with her in the cafeteria. She wanted to know what he thought about Oliviria coming back to school, and whether Xerx thought there was a chance she would lose her role as the cruel princess. The problem was that Xerx and Vowkin were too popular. The second the bell rang, the other kids bombarded them, trying to impress them. Troy wanted to show Xerx his *MonGPRX* cards. Stacy wanted to ask him for help with her math homework. Muller wanted to battle him in a game of *Merdfork Blip* on their visins. It was chaos. Erwun sat at her desk and watched Xerx as he was swarmed by a whole mob of kids. It was like Xerx was king of the school or something.

"Come on," she whispered to herself. Erwun had to dig deep and find her confidence. She stood up, packed up her stuff, then stormed across the room to Xerx just as the class was moving toward the door. To her surprise, Xerx pushed out of the crowd the moment Erwun approached. It was as if he knew she was coming. Erwun opened her mouth—then Oliviria appeared out of nowhere and cut her off, stepping in front of Erwun and batting her long eyelashes at Xerx.

"Um, Xerx, I'm sorry to bother you."

"Please," he said with a charming smile, "go right ahead and bother me."

Oliviria chuckled softly. It was an unappealing noise, since her voice was so hoarse and she sounded very sick. "Wow, Xerx. You are the sweetest. Would you like to join me for lunch today? I'm still a little bit sick from the other day and could use your kind, strong company."

Erwun wanted to scream and spit in Oliviria's face. Did she honestly think Xerx would agree to spend his lunchtime with her? Oliviria just wanted to steal Erwun's thunder.

"Sure," Xerx said, and Erwun gasped. "Would you like to go now?"

Oliviria's eyes briefly bulged in surprise. She quickly composed herself, smoothing her dress and smiling innocently. "That would be most kind, Xerx. In fact, that is the kindest thing anyone has done for me all day. Come, let's go."

Erwun was crushed. She could do nothing while Oliviria stole Xerx, and they left the classroom together. She felt ashamed. Oliviria was the most popular girl in class, so it made sense for her to date Xerx. She wished Xerx were her boyfriend. Then he would eat lunch with Erwun every single day. For now, she could only pout and feel sorry for herself.

Oh well, she thought. *Better to concentrate on my studies and my goals. Boys are stupid, anyway.*

* * *

Erwun ate lunch in the cafeteria at her usual spot, shouldered by the girls in her class. She hardly ate her food or listened to whatever the girls were yammering on about. She was focused on Xerx, sitting across the room at a table for two with Oliviria. He'd even been a gentleman and pulled out the girl's chair for her, treating Oliviria like some kind of princess. Xerx had also brought Oliviria her tray of food. He was now regaling her with some story or other, Oliviria laughing and laughing, Xerx giving her that charismatic smile that made butterflies blossom in Erwun's tummy.

The strangest part was that Oliviria appeared less sick than she had at the start of the day, as if Xerx were the cure for her illness. But what bothered Erwun the most was the simple fact that Xerx seemed to be enjoying himself. It wasn't fair. Oliviria was the type of girl who had her life delivered on a silver platter, her rise to the top facilitated since the day of her birth. Why should Oliviria get Xerx?

After lunch, Erwun arrived early for the final rehearsal of the play. She entered the theater to find Oliviria chatting with Lewell. Erwun stood on the threshold, seething, positive Oliviria was seducing her role back from Lewell. Then came Xerx's voice over her shoulder.

"Don't worry, she won't get it back."

Erwun whirled to face him. "How do you know?"

411

"I just do. I'm good at knowing things."

"Why do you care?"

"Because I like you."

Erwun couldn't believe her ears. "What?"

"I like you," he repeated, calm, serious, supremely confident. "I really, really like you. Not the same way I like everyone else, and everyone else includes Oliviria. She's all right, but I like you more. When a person likes someone else that way, they do nice things for them."

Erwun thought her mind was about to explode. Was Xerx playing games with her? What was his deal?

"I see you don't trust me," he said, smiling tenderly.

"You did just have lunch with Oliviria. What was that all about?"

He laughed. "That? Lunch? It was nothing! I was just being nice. Come on, she got sick and lost the leading role and asked me to lunch. Saying yes is what any good person would have done."

Now Erwun felt a little embarrassed. She'd been obsessing over Xerx and Oliviria all day and had never thought of him as just 'doing the right thing.' Erwun had thought for sure that he'd snubbed her. Now she was confused all over again.

"You still don't trust me," he said. "I can see it in your face. How can I convince you that I really, really like you? What can I do to reassure you? Do you want me to officially become your boyfriend? Would that make you happy?"

"Ha! Are you really just going to assume that I really, really like you too? Are you just assuming that I want to become your official girlfriend?" Erwun was talking in a way she never had before, since she'd never had a boyfriend in all her life and had never been the most confident or popular girl in school. She thought boys were a distraction. Xerx was definitely a distraction. Handsome, well-liked, intelligent, and oddly intuitive—definitely a distraction. And yet he was awakening something inside her, something that was making Erwun feel powerful and special, smart and capable of doing anything.

Before she could say another word, Xerx clenched his teeth and raised his hand. "Hold that thought," he said. "She's coming."

Oliviria was stomping toward them like an angry buffalo. She obviously hadn't gotten her place back in the play. She walked straight up to them and grabbed Xerx's arm as if she owned him, then sneered at Erwun. "You again. What do you want? Are you so jealous of me that you are trying to take everything that's mine? First my role and now my boyfriend."

"He's my boyfriend, actually," Erwun said in a tone that made her heart flutter and her face go hot. Where was this coming from? What was happening to Erwun's quiet personality? "Now take your hands off him."

Oliviria shook her head. "You're delusional too."

Xerx gently brushed Oliviria's hand from his elbow as if it were a piece of dirt that had fallen on him. "She's right." He stepped to Erwun and put his arm around her waist. "I am her boyfriend. Sorry for the confusion. I was just being nice by having lunch with you."

Oliviria looked like someone had just punched her in the stomach. She was stupefied. "You can both die!" she shouted abruptly. The girl was clearly psychotic when she didn't get her way. It wasn't something Oliviria was used to. "This isn't over. You will pay for this—both of you!"

Oliviria turned and stormed off, slamming the theater door behind her.

"I can't believe that just happened," Erwun said. She was not only proud of herself but extremely happy that Xerx had proved his loyalty. "I was a solitary, quiet person three days

413

ago," she said. "Then you joined my class, and my world flipped upside down. In a good way, of course. I feel like a whole new person. But, Xerx, why me?"

Xerx faced her directly. "Why not?" He took both her hands in his. "When I first saw you, I witnessed all your beauty, both inside and out. You are fearsome. More than anything, I want to be yours."

"Okay." Erwun took a deep breath. "Okay. You're my boyfriend. Xerx, you're my boyfriend!"

He smiled. "Yes, and you're my girlfriend. I can't wait for everyone in the universe to know."

* * *

Erwun was having a hard time paying attention in biology class. It was the day after Erwun and Xerx had announced themselves as boyfriend and girlfriend, and Erwun couldn't concentrate on cell division to save her life. All she could think about was Xerx; she could feel him stirring behind her in class, his eyes warm on the nape of her neck. The sensation of it made her shiver.

She let her eyelids get heavy and thought back to the day before, when Xerx and Vowkin had given her a lift back to her house after school in their fancy flyrarc. They'd argued about it first, Erwun had thought, the two boys waving their hands and whispering angrily outside the school as Erwun stood with her hands crossed and didn't know what to do. Then Xerx had smiled and waved her over, and she had been surprised by Vowkin's smile and cheery mood. She had been thinking their argument had been about her, but apparently not. Both boys were very welcoming. The three of them sat in the back of the flyrarc while Xerx and Erwun held hands awkwardly.

In truth, Erwun had been a little embarrassed by being dropped off at her outdated apartment in the residential building complexes of Krug's southern Kronk District, where the tenements rose and spiraled and fell into each other like great towers of brick and stone that had been weathered and partially melted by rain and time, the green spaces on the roofs burdened by clothes hanging to dry, along with makeshift antennae from a bygone age. It was where most of the Ava-Krug lived, in places like that, and Erwun desperately wanted to get out. She had hated being dropped off on the cracked and unkempt flyrarc pad by her new, obviously wealthy, boyfriend. The only silver lining had been when Xerx had kissed her softly on the lips and said goodbye.

She was thinking about that kiss now in biology class. It was making her feel warm and fuzzy all over again. She had no idea what was being taught. It was probably not the best idea to be so dreamily distracted by a kiss on the first day that the play was showing in the school. They would have to go on a tour of the major cities after today to perform in front of royals and wealthy aristocrats alike. It was finally her chance to secure a future career.

Erwun didn't hear the bell ring. She had been struck by a sudden imagining of an airy forest with calm, cool springs and orange falling leaves. She may have fallen asleep and started to dream because she was so at peace. She blinked, and the class was funneling into the hallway, and Xerx was at her desk.

"You okay?" he asked. "You seem distant."

"I'm just happy," she said softly. "I've never felt so fine in my whole life."

Xerx touched her on the elbow. "I feel the same, Erwun. Thank you. I feel like a whole new human!"

She didn't know what to say. Erwun just smiled at the cute boy standing at her desk, and the cute boy smiled back. He seemed a divine being to her, and she briefly wondered how long their sudden attraction would last. Time froze for a moment, and the youngsters were silent, simply enjoying the look of the other's face.

Then Vowkin yelled across the room, "Hey, Xerx. It's time to go."

"Oops." Xerx looked guilty. "Sorry, Erwun. I have to run."

"It's okay," she said. "I don't mind sharing you with the boys."

Xerx smiled. "Okay. Maybe we can spend lunch together and do whatever it is boyfriends and girlfriends do."

"Like you don't know," she said. "Don't act like you're from another planet, Xerx. Boyfriends and girlfriends make out, and you know it!"

"Great." Xerx beamed at her. "I'll see you at lunch so we can make out. Just tell me where."

Erwun was suddenly shy. She'd never made out with a boy before. What in the name of Geniverd was she doing? Before she could control herself, she blurted out, "Van Forest. That's where all the kids go to kiss. It's magical, almost enchanted."

"Isn't it forbidden?"

"Yeah," Erwun said, "but no one cares. It's near the edge of the school, and all the kids go there for … well, for girlfriend-and-boyfriend activities."

"Okay," Xerx said. "I'll bring my brother to play lookout. That way, we don't get caught."

"Cool. Smart thinking." Erwun's cheeks were hot to the touch. She knew her face must have been as red as a Surrvul apple. "I'll see you at lunch. I can't wait."

Xerx smiled. "Me neither."

* * *

At lunchtime, Vowkin was standing by the classroom door, waiting for Xerx and Erwun.

Seconds later, Erwun was sandwiched between the two most popular boys in school while they walked through the halls. She held Xerx's strong hand, their fingers interlocked. The other schoolboys hooted and hollered, throwing up high fives, while some girls looked on with jealousy, their lips pinched in bitter expressions as they leaned against their lockers. Erwun could vaguely hear their whispers. She knew what they were thinking, what they were saying, that she had no business being Xerx's girlfriend. But she was his girlfriend, and none of them were. They were just petty and jealous, and the fact that so many supposedly high-class girls were jealous made Erwun quite proud. Maybe she would be somebody after all. The lead in the school play, the cutest boy in school—things were looking up.

"How did Xerx convince you to keep watch?" she asked Vowkin once they were outside and moving across the cement playground toward the fence at the northern edge of the school. "You have so many other things you could be doing. You could bring your own girlfriend here if you wanted."

"That's true," Vowkin said. He seemed more easygoing than his brother, a lot more relaxed and introspective. "But I'm not interested in all that. This is a smart move, because now Xerx owes me big-time. There's something I need from him, and now he must do it for me."

"What's that?"

"Not important," Vowkin said dismissively. "It's just got to do with the keinball coach. I got in trouble for being too good at keinball. Can you believe that? I'm sure the guy just hates me because I'm faster than his son and my hand-eye coordination is unbeatable. He feels his dominance is threatened. I need Xerx to help straighten a few things out."

"You just need to play down your strengths and let him do his job," Xerx said.

Vowkin scowled at his brother. "I don't agree. Besides, I've already played it down enough. Without me, the team has no hope of making it to the second round of the tournament."

"True," Xerx said. "They definitely need your tricks if they want to win."

"Well, I'm sure your brother can help with it," Erwun said. "Xerx does have a subtle influence over people. He managed to get me the lead in the play somehow. I'm sure, without him, I would never have kept the role."

They were at the fence now, the edge of the forest just beyond. The mesh fence was cut discreetly, making it easy to pull a chunk aside while they shimmied through it. Then they were at the mouth of the woods.

"This place is beautiful," Xerx said. There were shafts of sunlight cutting through the tall pine trees. "I wonder why it's forbidden."

"Because the teachers know what the boys and girls do here," Erwun told him. "This is an extremely strict school. If kids get caught making out, they will be expelled. Plus, the forest is not secured."

"It looks big," Vowkin said. "You could easily get lost. I think it's best if you guys do your thing while I stay relatively close by. Not only do we not want to get Erwun in trouble, but we don't want to get her lost either."

"Deal," Xerx said. He smiled at Erwun, reaffirmed his grip on her hand, and they all started into the forest.

After about two minutes, they reached a spring, the cold water sloshing peacefully through the gully, little orange leaves carried along like lonely ships. "I'll leave you here," Vowkin said. "This looks like a nice place to make out. You have fifteen minutes before I come back."

Vowkin turned and trudged off through the woodland, probably to explore.

Now that they were alone, Xerx cupped Erwun's face, pushed back a lock of her hair, and leaned forward to kiss her gently. "I can't believe I'm here with you," he whispered, their lips brushing as he spoke. "I feel so lucky."

"I feel like I'm dreaming," she said with a giggle.

Xerx answered by smiling, kissing her again, and moving his hands down to the small of her back. That was when they were interrupted.

"Sorry, but we're going to have to break up your little session," a female voice said. Xerx pulled away from Erwun and whirled around, tucking her defensively behind him. Vowkin was standing in the trees. He was shaking; his eyes were red; and his hands were bound behind his back.

I was still unsure what Roki had wanted me to see in Erwun's memories. Had that sudden dream of a peaceful forest and a calm spring been meant to implant the idea of the forest into Erwun's mind, thus getting Xerx and Vowkin into the open? That was one possibility. Any Min could implant a dream into a human's brain. Maybe Roki had wanted me to see the kidnappers, but I hadn't. Whoever they were, they had managed to get past Neuge's protective barrier. They were probably friends of Lordin's ... powerful friends.

I left the beach cave I had taken shelter in around midday and went straight home to my place in Tsiser. Raad and Papa were in the dining room, having afternoon tea, when I walked in the front door. Later, when I went past them, they barely acknowledged me.

"Afternoon," I said, and they both nodded at me. It was hard to accept sometimes that I was no longer part of their family. I was just a warmongering stranger.

I left the dining room and followed the sounds of arguing voices into the library, where I found Tissa, Nnati, and Knotts in a heated argument. Nnati and Tissa sat on opposing chairs, facing each other, while Knotts stood to the side with his strong, sexy arms folded over his chest.

"What's going on here?" I asked as I burst into the room.

Tissa said nothing. She was pouting.

"They want to leave," Nnati said. "Tissa and Raad and the former Gaard-Elder."

"Why? I don't understand."

"Seriously?" Tissa gave me a look. "We were okay with starting a war. But come on, Cerna, there has been a natural disaster that just killed a billion people. There is an almost impossible amount of cleanup to do. Have you not seen the news? Do you not understand how serious one billion deaths are? Literally a quarter of the planet's population is floating around in the ocean for the sharks to eat. You, the queen, and the king should take responsibility for this. There's no time for war. We need unification and peace."

"What about the queen's mind control?" Nnati said to Tissa. It sounded like he had been pleading with her for a while. "Maybe all those people wouldn't have died if not for Queen Hagan. They wouldn't have been out in the streets. They could have taken shelter or at least predicted the freak tsunami."

"It doesn't matter," Tissa said. "There is no justification for continuing the war. We need to stop this immediately and help Geniverd. War at this point is utterly selfish."

"But we are so close," Nnati pressed. "So close. We need to dethrone Queen Hagan. What about the way she treated Kaelyn, our old friend? Hagan and Zawne have repeatedly spat on her memory and run her name through the dirt. That can't stand. Sure, a freak accident just killed a billion people, but there is nothing we can do about it now. Convince Raad to stay and finish this fight."

"What fight, Nnati?" Tissa activated her visin, displaying a grid of different views from around Geniverd. "If Queen Hagan really did brainwash everyone, she's stopped now. The streets are empty again. Everyone has gone home in the wake of the disaster."

They kept arguing. I had no idea what to do. "I can't let them go," I whispered to Knotts. "There's no way. I can't let them. They will expose our operation and our location. Nobody can leave Tsiser, or Lordin will come down on this place like a hammer strike. Everything we've been fighting for would be lost."

"We can leave," Knotts said casually. "You and I can go right now and leave all this nonsense behind."

I sighed, watching Nnati and Tissa go back and forth, arguing, sympathizing, Nnati flailing his arms and Tissa with the threat of tears in her eyes. "Not yet. I have to finish what I started. I will only leave Geniverd when it is a better place for everyone. I won't fail."

"Okay," Knotts said. He'd surely known my answer before he'd asked me to leave. "I'll support you no matter what. I'm here for you. But what do you want to do about your family? I can read all their minds from here. They've already come to their own decisions. The only one who wants to stay is Nnati."

"That's what makes this so hard," I said to Knotts. Then I spoke loud enough for Nnati and Tissa to hear me, stopping their argument in its tracks. "Tsiser is on lockdown," I said. "Nobody is coming in or going out. Sorry, Gaard-Ma. You're not leaving. This is for your own good. If you try to run, I'll be forced to call the Guardians and lock you and Raad in jail."

* * *

That was one of the hardest things I'd ever done. Watching

Tissa lose her mind and call me a psychotic dictator, then stomp out of the room with Nnati hot on her heels. Both my best friends furious and hating me for locking them up like common criminals felt like dying all over again. It was brutal. Knotts stayed behind to console me after they'd gone.

"I had to be decisive," I was saying. "I had to be firm. I had no choice. And now they hate me."

"Honestly," Knotts said, "I'm impressed. I can't believe you put your foot down like that. I was wrong about you in the beginning, Kaelyn. You were a great queen, and you still are."

He was trying to make me melt. The way Knotts complimented me and the way he gazed deep into my eyes were things I needed to ignore. I was scared he'd kiss me again, and now was no time to be flirting with another man. I had just murdered one billion people and trapped my best friends in an underground prison. The prison may have been my house, but to people like Raad and Tissa, it was surely a prison. I needed to stave off any advances from Knotts.

"I was wondering about something," Knotts said. I thought he saw the apprehension in my face.

"What is it, Knotts?"

"I heard that Neuge woke up for a few minutes last night. Care to tell me exactly how that happened?"

"Oh," I said, "that …"

Knotts had a funny look on his face. "Don't tell me you slipped into Neuge's empty body last night just to make your friend feel better. Are you serious?"

"I had to!" I cried. "Nnati would have killed himself if I hadn't done something. Besides, I asked the Crown of Crowns, and they said it was okay. It's just temporary."

"I should hope it's only temporary. How can you keep up such a charade in the middle of everything else that's going on?"

An idea came to me then. A smile slowly spread across my lips, taking over my face. "You know, Knotts, if you really wanted to be there for me, you could help me out with my little situation. Just for now. You would only need to wake up once in a while and say something nice to Nnati, then slip back into a coma and reenter your usual body. Just until I find a more permanent solution."

Knotts was backing away from me with his hands up. It was the first time I'd ever seen him look scared. "No way. I won't do it. I like girls way too much. All my years, and I have never kissed a male. Not in a human body and not in another body. Don't you think Nnati will try to kiss me when I—when Neuge wakes up?"

"Oh, calm down," I said softly. "You don't need to kiss him. You just need to keep his hope alive by waking up sometimes and showing signs of life. The entire point of this trick is to keep Nnati from killing himself. I can't let him do that."

"Here's a better idea," Knotts said. "Rather than me kissing Nnati, why don't you occupy Neuge's body and then break up with Nnati properly. That way, he won't be devastated and he won't kill himself. You can let him down gently."

"Huh …" That was actually a clever idea. Knotts continued to surprise me. "That's not a bad idea at all. You may be onto something."

"But what about us?" he asked, so abruptly it caught me by surprise. I had so many more important things to deal with, but I knew I was deferring the other situation staring us in the face. It was simpler to bury what had happened between us than try to move past it.

"There is no us," I said plainly.

"Kaelyn, can you please stop pretending that you don't have feelings for me?" He moved to me, towered over me, and put his hands on my waist. "You like kissing me, Kaelyn. I know you do. You like kissing me so much that you didn't even notice Lordin approaching us back there in the clouds."

"Yes," I said, "fine, I did like it. But, Knotts, this is neither the time nor the place. We have a lot of things to do. And besides, I love Roki. I don't know if I'm confused, or maybe it was just a moment of weakness at a time when I needed comfort."

"Hold on," he said, letting go of me and stepping back. "Are you saying that I took advantage of you in a moment of weakness?"

"I never said that. I just said that I was needing comfort. Maybe I wasn't thinking clearly."

But I had been thinking clearly, and I knew it. All it took was one long stare at Knotts's warm, velvety lips, and I was weak all over again. I knew I couldn't resist his charms. I had to put my hand out, and I staggered back until I hit the couch. "It doesn't matter," I said. "None of it matters. So what if I find you attractive? So what if I like the way you kiss me? I'm with Roki. We have to be realistic, Knotts, and the reality of this situation is that it can't work. Even if I wanted it to work, I have Roki and the twins to think about."

Knotts sighed. "Okay. Okay, Kaelyn, have it your way. We can put this discussion off for now because of how intense everything currently is, but we're not finished. I know this is more than just simple infatuation. You want me."

I said nothing. I had nothing to say. I stood away from Knotts with my arms crossed until I felt the heat leaving the room, both of us settling down.

He finally asked me, "So, did you get any leads after looking into Erwun's memories?"

"Yeah." I had to clear my throat because it had gotten so dry. "I, um ... Here." I played the voice I'd heard from Erwun's

CLARA LOVEMAN

memory. "One of the kidnappers. I didn't hear the voice the first time I watched the memories. Do you recognize it?"

"I don't think so," he said, rubbing his perfectly molded chin as he listened again and again to the recording. "Let me run it through my database. Every Min with a body from Geniverd is in the database, and I know every Min in Geniverd … but I don't know this one. This person must have gotten here in the last couple of days."

"Whoever did this," I said, "they got past Neuge's force field. They are bold enough to kidnap thousands of children. We can't underestimate them, Knotts. I won't ever underestimate my enemy again. I just wish I knew what Lordin was playing at."

"Isn't it obvious?" Knotts gave me a look suggesting I was being naive. "Lordin wants the position of Crown of Crowns. That's been her goal since the beginning."

"I know. But now I'm not fully convinced," I said. "Zawne isn't even a Min. It makes literally no sense that she could even be considered for the position with a human husband. They aren't even in the top one hundred contenders, and there are only three days left, or is it two? I've lost track during all this chaos."

"Yeah," he said, "but I wouldn't put it past her. Anything can change at the last minute."

"Maybe it's time to call Zawne," I said, "just to be sure. I want to hear an answer straight from my ex-husband's mouth. If Lordin is planning on a last-minute trick, I want to know about it."

Knotts chuckled. "Your ex? Do you think he'd want to help you?"

"I doubt it. He probably thinks I helped murder his daughter. Still, it's worth a chance. I have no other ideas at this point."

"Okay," he said. "I'll leave you to it while I go check on the rest of Tsiser, make sure nobody has gotten out to reveal our location. We'll meet up later."

* * *

I was nervous to call Zawne, but I saw no other choice. I rang him on my visin while I paced the library, so anxious. It rang and rang, and after the twelfth ring, I was about to hang up. Then he answered. He was in some nondescript location I didn't recognize, his arms crossed over his chest and a mean scowl on his face.

"What now?" he barked. "What do you want?"

"I know I'm the last person you want to see right now," I said, "but I'd like to help you with proof of Arta's real killer."

"I told you," Zawne said, his face stony. His voice was flat and lifeless. "I saw what happened with my own eyes. And even if I didn't, why would I want your help?"

"Because I care about you, Zawne. And I care about Geniverd. I want to help you discover the truth about what happened to Arta. I know you're a good person and that you would never have let Lordin control the masses if you'd known her plan from the start. But I need to know if she is trying to get into position to be the next Crown of Crowns."

Zawne was shaking his head and tsk-tsking me. "You don't get it, you stupid little girl. I don't care about anything you say. It's all lies. Lies, Kaelyn! Do you not see that I am the king who slept with a monster, then married a monster? Do me a favor and stay out of my life. Leave me alone. You're dead to me, and you're literally dead to Geniverd. We would appreciate it if you would stay that way. Stop interfering with human affairs and never ever contact me again."

427

"Lordin's dead too," I said, "and yet she is literally controlling humans."

"She is the queen!" he boomed in my ears.

I was starting to cry. Why was Zawne being so cruel to me? "I was queen first," I moaned pitifully. "I saved the world after Lordin tried to destroy it."

"Nobody believes that, Kaelyn. Just stop what you're doing. Not just for your own sake but for the sake of the world. You have no support. Even the Gurnots have turned their shifty allegiance from you and Roki. You're going to lose. The people left on this planet will never let you rule them. And I will never allow you to get away with the death of my daughter."

Zawne looked straight into the visin, through the screen, and deep into my eyes. What I saw was boundless, burning hatred. "Never contact me again."

The line went dead. That was the last time I ever spoke with Zawne.

awne's words hurt me. We had been close once, partners who had shared the same bed and the same throne. Now we were enemies. Still, his cruel words gave me some relief. He seemed to be solely focused on Geniverd, which meant he had no interest in ruling the galaxy.

I was too tired to think. I needed a nap.

When I woke, it was dark again. The twins still weren't back, and neither was Roki, and yet another entire day had gone by. I felt hopeless and alone, my arms stretched across an empty bed. I yawned and rolled flat on my back, and that was when I sensed Knotts at the other end of the room. He was watching me.

"How long have you been there?" I asked, not yet opening my eyes.

"I arrived just now," he said. "I came to wake you. Nnati's getting worried, since Neuge has gone a full day with very little brain activity."

"Nnati!" I had totally forgotten about my friend. I threw

the covers off me. "Is he okay?" I jumped out of the bed and rushed into the bathroom.

Knotts sauntered over and leaned against the doorframe, watching me splash water on my face. "He's okay for now, but you may want to act quickly. He's getting worried. Not to mention, Kaelyn, while you snoozed, the war pressed on. We're running out of Guardians, and Zawne is running out of Protectors. We're going to come to a standstill soon. Lordin won't concede."

I blinked at myself in the mirror, face red and puffy from sleep. A shower would have to wait. I'd slept too long. The world was moving on without me. "Give me one minute," I said, and pushed past Knotts. I grabbed a long, flowing dress from my closet. "Turn around and don't look." I had to trust that he wasn't peeking as I changed my underclothes and then slipped into the dress, cinched a skinny belt around my waist, and began digging for shoes.

"Okay," I said, seated on the edge of my bed and buckling up my shoes. I had to make a conscious effort not to be distracted by Knotts's rugged good looks as he stood near me, watching me like a hawk. "Here's the plan. I am going to see Nnati. Then I am going to see the midwife who delivered the twins."

Knotts was surprised. "Acuri the midwife? What for?"

"You know Acuri?" I asked.

"Of course." He chuckled. "I arranged the whole thing."

"Oh, I didn't know. Anyway, I know that Acuri has a lot of connections, both in the human world and in the Min world. I want to get her opinion on why the people are turning against me. Maybe she can create some publicity for us. I need to know what it will take to change the people's opinion of Defiance."

"Right."

"After that," I said, "I will go to see the Crown of Crowns to try to find out the identity of those two women. That must be why Roki wanted me to scan Erwun's memories. The Crown of Crowns should help me. After all, it's their fault that Lordin was unleashed on the world. They really made a monster. Whatever the case, we can't stop the war now. If we lose and Lordin regains total control, I'm positive she and Zawne will make life miserable for all our allies for the next one thousand years at least."

"You're probably right," Knotts said. "And in Geniverd, they would stifle the commoners to make sure another revolt like this could never happen."

"Exactly."

"Tell you what," Knotts said, that gentle kindness returning to his voice. "You go see Nnati, and I'll go talk to Acuri. That way, we save some time."

"You'd do that for me?"

"Of course." Knotts smiled, and I felt a punch in my guts. It was a good punch, warm, like an explosion of butterflies. It was how Erwun must have felt when she looked at Xerx.

"Thank you," I told him. "Thank you so much. Honestly, Knotts, I don't know if I would have survived this mess without you."

* * *

I found Nnati sitting beside Neuge's bed, twiddling his thumbs, waiting for his comatose boyfriend to wake up. Again, I slipped my Valer into Neuge's chest and wrapped around his heart, then spread throughout his body. I felt big and powerful once more, like I'd just strapped on a massive power suit. I opened my eyes and saw Nnati staring down at me. He looked ready to cry.

"Nnati …" I sat up groggily, straining my voice so I sounded exhausted. "Water. I need water."

"Yes. Hold on one second."

Nnati scrambled out of the room to get some water. I took the opportunity to explore this excellent body, flexing and squeezing my biceps, feeling up my pecs, tensing my thighs. Neuge had chosen a great body. I was one large mass of unyielding muscle.

When Nnati got back, I was sitting up in bed. "Thanks," I said, taking the water. I gulped it down and then put the glass on the table.

"You look so awake," Nnati said. "How do you feel? You've been in a coma for days. Aren't you exhausted?"

I swung my big, powerful legs off the bed, surprising Nnati as I stood up and stretched as if I had just woken from a nap; all the tubes that had been hooked up to my forearms snapped like broken elastic bands and fell onto the bed. "Actually, Nnati, I feel great. I feel refreshed. They must have pumped some serious regenerative drugs into my system. It feels like I had a really good night of sleep." I flexed my biceps again, stretching, feeling the incredible bulk and strength I now possessed. "Yeah, I feel amazing."

That was when he leaped onto me like a bear cub attaching itself to its mother. "I missed you so much," he said against my chest. It felt strange to be on the opposite side of this interaction. It felt strange to be so tall. I thought maybe I'd bump my head against something. "I was so worried," Nnati kept on. "The doctors said you were dead, that you'd never wake up."

"Well, they were wrong," I said, patting Nnati on the back. I was unsure how to behave. I just wanted to get the hard part over with before Nnati realized there was something wrong.

I started walking about the room to stretch my legs, and

the whole time, Nnati trailed behind me like a lovesick puppy. "How long have I been out?" I asked.

"You've been in a coma for two days," he said. "I've been here most of the time. I had to deal with something just once, but other than that, I haven't left your side."

"Whoa," I said, "slow down." Nnati was acting like an insecure teenager. I suddenly understood why Neuge had wanted to go away and never come back. Nnati was obsessive. He was surprisingly clingy in a way I'd never seen as his friend.

"Why don't you sit down, babe," he said. "Don't strain yourself. A lot has happened since your accident, and I think you probably want to hear it."

We sat in the loveseat by the window. Nnati nuzzled into my arm, and I tried not to crush him with my new, intense strength. Then he told me everything I already knew: the genetic engineering, the protest, the storm, the tsunami, how Cerna had locked down Tsiser. It was boring to hear it after I had just lived it, especially with so many of the important details missing.

"I'm out of action for a brief period, and suddenly we're the bad guys?" I said. "What a load of nonsense."

"Pretty much."

"Damn. Where's Roki?"

"Still vanished," Nnati said. "He's been looking for his twins, following up on important leads about the kidnapping."

"Poor Cerna," I said. "She must be having such a hard time. I hope everyone is okay." I lowered my deep voice, or at least I tried. "I want to say thank you, Nnati, for staying by my side throughout this ordeal. I hope you weren't too worried."

Nnati didn't answer.

"What's wrong?" I ruffled his short brown hair. I had no idea how to be Nnati's boyfriend. I only knew how to be a girlfriend!

"I was afraid of losing you," Nnati said. "I missed you so much."

I held his hands and kissed them. I was hoping to avoid a kiss on the mouth. "You can't torture yourself," I told him. "Life is too short to worry. I want you to know that if anything ever happens to me because of the war, you shouldn't wait around. Get out there and live your life."

"I'm sure nothing will happen again," he said cheerfully. "You're back with me for good. I'm never letting you out of my sight ever again."

"I'm serious, Nnati. I want you to be realistic."

"What?" Nnati looked confused, already hurt. "You realize I can't just go out and find a new boyfriend after you die, right? What are you saying? You want me to go kiss some other man if you are lying in a coma?"

"All I'm saying, Nnati, is that you need to be strong if something happens. So many people are dying, and more people will continue to die before the war is done. I can't have you worried sick or falling into a depression if I don't make it out of this thing alive. I love you, and I want you to be happy, and so would your late friend, Kaelyn. You are stronger than you think. You deserve the best."

We were silent for a long time. Nnati's fingers traced my arms, so small and thin they felt like pencils. Then he asked, "What do you think of the accusations against Roki? Do you think he really killed baby Arta?"

"Where did that come from?" I asked. "Do you think he did it?"

"No." Nnati shook his head, his scruff scratching my bicep. "But Geniverd does. That's why so many people are defecting from Defiance. They don't want to follow a child murderer."

"Pfft." I snorted. "Don't be so certain. I think genetic

manipulation has messed with their minds. I know Roki would never do such a thing. He's an honorable man."

"What about his girlfriend, Cerna?"

"You mean his loving partner?" I said, my voice booming inside the small room like a crack of thunder. "Absolutely not! Cerna would never ask him to do something like that. She, too, is an honorable person."

"Okay, okay. Relax. I was just speculating."

We fell quiet again. I felt weirder than ever with Nnati cuddled against me in awkward silence. I also felt stuck. I wanted to get off the sofa, but I needed an excuse. I also needed an excuse to finish what I had come to do. Then Knotts came to the rescue. I felt his presence behind us a second before he knocked on the door.

"Come in," I called, and immediately stood up, almost knocking Nnati off me in the process. I was a small girl in the body of a giant and didn't know how to properly carry myself. "I'm sorry," I said.

"Yikes," Nnati said, his brow furrowing. He took in a deep breath, and his voice cracked as he added, "It's okay. You're still recuperating."

We all gathered inside the room, Knotts grinning in a way I had never seen before. *Great*, I thought, *He's going to have some serious fun with this.*

"You look well, old friend," Knotts said, clapping me hard on the back. "And just in time too. Defiance has some serious issues going on. We need your help, brother. Strap on your boots—we're going on a mission."

"You can't!" Nnati screeched, his voice so high-pitched I almost recoiled. "He just woke up. No missions. He can't go on any missions!" Nnati stood between Knotts and me as if Knotts were a law enforcement Protector who'd come to haul me off to jail.

"Relax, Nnati. I feel great. I'm ready for action. This is part of my life. I thought you'd be used to it by now."

I could feel it coming. Now was my chance to end things with Nnati. But then Knotts decided to have a little fun. "Hop in the shower first, Neuge," he said. "You are still in your sick gown. Maybe you and Nnati can have a private goodbye while I wait in the hall."

"Good idea," Nnati said. I felt his little hand slip from the small of my back to my rock-hard buttock.

I burned Knotts alive with my eyes as he walked backward out of the room, smiling wickedly. When Knotts closed the door, I gently removed my friend's hand. "Not now," I said. "I'm not in the mood. I just woke up from a coma."

"At least let me shower with you," he begged. There was no other word to describe it—Nnati was begging. "Please, we don't have to do anything. I just want to be close to you."

"No," I said. "Not now. I have work to do."

I walked around Nnati, went into the bathroom, then slammed the door shut. I didn't really need a shower, since I wasn't planning on using Neuge's body much longer, but I kind of wanted to check it out more intimately before I went back into my female body. I got naked and then looked at myself in the mirror until the glass fogged. I thought to myself, *If I ever wanted to be a man, I'd get a body just like this one.* I felt a little obsessed. I let the hot water pour all over my long, curly gray hair and masculine body, and gently touched my body everywhere with my fingers.

Nnati had some clothes laid out for me when I emerged from the bathroom, dripping wet in a towel. He kept trying to touch me, and I kept having to push him off. "No, Nnati. Stop it. Why are you so clingy? I'm not in the mood."

And that was when it happened. I had gotten dressed. Knotts had come back into the room and told us it was time to go—I could have strangled him for the way he smiled at me, surely reading Nnati's mind and finding the whole situation hilarious—and then Nnati wanted a kiss. I saw the desperate longing in his eyes. "Won't you kiss me?" he asked. His lips were quivering. "Won't you at least kiss me before you go away?"

"No," I said. "I'm sorry. It wouldn't be right. We need to break up, Nnati. I'm not in love with you. I'm sorry that it took a coma for me to realize it. I'm sorry if this hurts you. The truth is, Nnati, I'm in love with Knotts."

Nnati's eyes grew to twice their normal size. So did Knotts's. I didn't know who looked more surprised.

"How dare you!" Nnati hissed. I hadn't expected him to get angry. I'd expected him to cry and fall into a lump on the floor, but not get angry. I could almost see the steam shooting out of his ears. "You're sorry? You're sorry for not loving me and for loving another man, after all I've done for you?"

"Yes," I said. "I'm sorry. I should have done this a long time ago."

Nnati lost his mind. He freaked out. "Go!" he shouted, and actually threw his shoe at me. "Get out! Get out of my room. Both of you, leave me alone. I never want to see your traitorous faces again!"

Knotts and I left the room. The door closed, and immediately there was a loud crash, followed by the clamor of a disgruntled bull. Nnati must have been having a fit, throwing glasses against the wall and flinging chairs. In my mind, it was a lot better than him killing himself. I didn't feel great about how brutal I'd just been by breaking Nnati's heart and plunging him into a psychotic breakdown, but it was definitely the lesser evil. At least he was still alive.

"You had to throw me to the wolves like that, didn't you?" Knotts said. "Why did you say you were in love with me?"

"Added effect," I told him, "for your little shower stunt. That was a serious situation, and you thought you'd have some fun with it. Well, so did I."

Knotts was about to speak, but then the chime went off. Hanchell and Riedel spoke in our minds.

"One day to go. In the lead are Queen Hagan and King Zawne of Geniverd."

16

*S*econds after the announcement, Riedel's sharp voice resounded in my head. "Kaelyn, we need your presence immediately."

Oh no. That sounded bad. It must have had something to do with Zawne and Lordin's lead for the ultimate throne in the galaxy. How could that have happened, and with only one day to go? Had that been Lordin's plan the entire time, to shock the galaxy by rising to first place the day before the choosing? If she and Zawne won, Roki and I would be finished. There was no telling what kind of horrors Lordin would unleash upon us.

I went to Shiol, where I found Hanchell and Riedel lounging on their water thrones. They seemed formal and distant, and I could tell right away they had bad news for me. I could also tell it wasn't about Lordin or Zawne.

"We have summoned you here," Riedel said, "because we have put you forward to have a meeting with the Seeing Water."

"What?" I blurted out, feeling a knot in my stomach. "How is that possible? Doesn't it require three great sacrifices?"

"That's right," Hanchell said. "A great power, a non-Min creature personally connected to you, and a great love."

"But I don't want to make those sacrifices. Why did you put me up to this? Is it because I killed all those people? Please don't make my loved ones pay for my crimes. Is Roki okay? Or is it my babies?"

"The twins are still alive," Hanchell said, trying to be sweet, but I could tell by her voice that she was agitated. "They have been making significant progress with their learning modules. However, there are more and more children missing by the hour, and this is causing some serious problems throughout the galaxy. We need you to meet with the Seeing Water to solve the issue of the missing children and the strangeness going on with the run for our positions."

"But why me?"

"Because out of all the Min in Shiol, we think you have the best chance of solving the case. Plus, the only way for you to see Roki and your twins again may be to solve this once and for all. We would have done it if possible, but we seem unable to progress even the slightest on these matters."

I was floored. I had always assumed the Crown of Crowns could solve any problem in the galaxy.

"We normally can," Hanchell said. She'd been listening to my thoughts. "But we cannot see the problem because the Min responsible is acting under the umbrella of the Seeing Water. Now you must act under those same powers to stop them, like how you first became a Min to stop Lordin."

"What if I say no?" I asked. "I don't want more deaths, or to give up love. What if I can solve it another way?"

"Impossible," Riedel said, leaning forward in his throne and looking at me with his googly lizard eyes. "The Seeing Water is already expecting you. It's too late. Neuge and the few hundred other Min have come up with no leads. We have no leads. The only lead, Kaelyn, is you. If not for your own sake, then do it for the sake of the galaxy."

"What about this Min?" I played the voice and images I'd taken from Erwun's memories.

"Yes, yes." Hanchell waved her hand. "We saw that already. The body was dead, and the Min hosting it was long dead. Think of that voice like a reanimated Min. Only the Seeing Water has the power to awaken a spirit like that."

"But what about Lordin playing with reality?" I asked, realizing I was starting to sound a lot like Nnati ten minutes ago, begging for a kiss.

"Maybe, maybe not," Riedel answered. "We can see through the gifts we give. You can't see through other Min's powers, but we can. We already told you, Kaelyn, the Min responsible got their powers from the Seeing Water. It's the only possibility. You must undo their wrong by getting powers of your own from the Seeing Water."

"And you must do it now," Hanchell said. She, too, sounded desperate. I guessed time was running out.

"Like, right now?" I asked.

Riedel leaned closer to me, almost spilling off his throne. "Like, right now. Go and meet with the Seeing Water. Save your twins."

"Okay." I took a deep breath, trying to steady myself against what was to come. "But first I need to know something. How did Zawne and Lordin move so quickly and so suddenly to the top of the polls? It looks like they will win."

"Yes," Hanchell said, "but you can still join the race. You may be far behind in the votes, but you can win if you have a compelling story."

"I don't want to win," I told them. "Even if I did want to

win, I'm too far behind. We only have today left, and I don't have time to start campaigning to billions of voters. I'd need Roki, and I don't even know where he is. But you didn't answer my question: How did Zawne and Lordin get to first place?"

"That's easy, dear," Hanchell said in her quiet voice. "They had a compelling story. It's all about the story. If you have a story, maybe you can turn the race around in the final hours."

"What story did they have?"

"Arta's death," Riedel told me. He was leaning back in his floating water throne and seemed bored while he picked at his fingernails. "The story had already been floating around in Shiol and beyond. Some Min have been suffering since children across the galaxy went missing, and many commiserated with Lordin and Zawne over the loss of their child. They also liked that Lordin was fighting for a cause, and because of it, someone killed Arta and one billion of her humans. Min really listened to that and took notice. They are giving them the sympathy vote."

"Oh no ..." I said aloud. I understood now. "The whole universe thinks Roki did it, right? They all think Roki killed Arta."

"There is nothing to prove otherwise," Hanchell said.

I had no words to exhibit my disgust. Nothing made any sense. How could Lordin possibly deceive the entire galaxy, and why didn't the Crown of Crowns do something about it? It wasn't fair. I felt a sudden crash of anxiety, and my eyes went kind of hazy. I swayed on my feet, feeling the blood rush from my brain down to my toes.

Then I fainted.

* * *

When I regained consciousness, I was at the center of a cosmic water vortex. The water spun around me in a dizzying maelstrom of froth and bubbles, and yet somehow I remained dry. I should have at least been disoriented. I was standing in the middle of the fastest-spinning typhoon I could have imagined. Then a great and imposing voice boomed around me.

"Your sacrifices first."

The voice had no gender. It was neutral and all-powerful. There was no doubt in my mind that I stood before the Seeing Water. It wanted a sacrifice, but I was unsure how to start.

"I've already lost everything that truly matters to me," I said quietly. "It's like I don't exist."

"Your presence here is an insult to Me and to everything I—"

"It doesn't matter," I cut in. I looked around for a face to speak to, but there was nothing. It was just a giant whirlpool with a voice that echoed from every corner. "The universe has conspired against me. I might as well be dead, but for real this time. I offer myself. Please, take me instead."

There was a loud rumbling, as if the whirlpool was angry. "Conspired? You speak of conspiracy! Who are you to insult Me? Do you even realize you're standing in My presence? I am the fiercest being in the universe. I can make your existence endless misery, and when you die, I could go after your family and friends. The Crown of Crowns exists and rules at My mercy. I can destroy every living thing in your galaxy just by willing it. Are you the one to contend with Me?"

I was so crippled by dread and terror that I was literally frozen. I couldn't cry or tremble. I stood wide-eyed, heart thrumming, staring into the swirling vortex of blue-white water.

"I don't want to fight," I managed after a long minute of

tension. "I didn't come here to disagree with you. I was volunteered."

"You mean to say that you are not up to the task," the voice said. "But it matters not. You owe Me your sacrifices for merely being in My presence. It matters not why or how you came to be here before Me, nor whether I bestow upon you a gift in return. If you will not give your sacrifices, I will search your heart and choose for you."

I remained silent. I had no idea what to say. Every time I opened my mouth, I only made the Seeing Water angrier.

"Coward!" it said. "Why did they send a coward before Me?

"Very well. Be condemned by your silence, foolish mortal. I do fear Hanchell and Riedel made a mistake sending you to Me. Yet I appointed them with confidence to rule over the existences birthed from My generosity, to carry on with wickedness and virtue at My pleasure. Yes, Hanchell and Riedel will be sumptuously rewarded for their service. Despite what you mindless Min may think, they were not appointed to please you or act on your behalf. They please Me. Your wishes do not matter. Your mercy does not matter. Your benevolence and deplorability do not matter. You are nothing. You will forever be nothing inside My universe."

"But what about justice?" I asked. It was a struggle just to get out the words. Never had I fathomed such a ferocious and imposing thing.

"Do not talk to Me of justice, Min. I am the definition of justice, and I am the screams of injustice. You think you have pain, but I represent the pains you have never suffered or seen. The burden of the pain I carry is so great that the Crown of Crowns must rule on My behalf. For without them, the universe would bow beneath My wrath, and it would be torn asunder!"

There was a pause. The water swirled angrily. Then the voice came again and said, "I have entertained you for too long. Choose your offerings, or I will choose them for you."

I knew at this point that I needed to tread carefully, and I needed to do it quickly, without thinking. "Please help me determine my next steps after our meeting. This might help me decide my sacrifices, thus saving your precious time, wise one."

"Very well," it said, much to my surprise. I went completely still. "I condescend to help you make your decision. Tell Me about your trivial problems."

"Well," I said, "I care a lot about the universe, your great creation."

"No," it boomed. "I did not say the universe is My creation. I am the caretaker of the universe, and My will is law."

"Right. My apologies. Please, the universe has never had a more generous or honorable caretaker, and I care a great deal about the universe."

"Go on."

"Well," I said, "my problem is twofold. The first part is that my twins have been abducted, and the second part is that tens of thousands of children across the galaxy have also gone missing. I believe the same abductor is the one who murdered Lordin's child and is holding Roki hostage somewhere. I also believe the abductor is Lordin herself. I want to free Roki and the children and put a stop to Lordin. I am worried that if Lordin ascends to our ultimate throne, she will destroy all the good things in the galaxy in her thirst for absolute power."

"Is that all?" asked the Seeing Water.

"Yes. That is all."

"Easy. The solution can be packed into one simple request. The rest will come with your sacrifices. First, I will return the missing children. Then, you must be the one to personally save your twins. When you succeed, you will gain your desire with little effort. To ensure you complete your task, I will upgrade your powers temporarily. You can now read the memories of the people within memories that you view."

"Wow," I said. I was wondering if I should bow to the Seeing Water, and if so, in which direction. I was surprised, grateful, and overwhelmed all at once. "Thank you," I said. "Thank you so much for helping me."

"We are not through," it said, the water cyclone quivering at the intensity of the voice. "We must discuss your sacrifices. They will be very painful, but you have no choice. You must choose now!"

The first sacrifice was easy. I'd already been thinking of it. I cleared my throat and said loudly, "I give up the seat of the Crown of Crowns." The truth was that I had never wanted it in the first place.

"Accepted," the Seeing Water boomed. "I would not have chosen you, anyway. No big loss."

The second sacrifice was one I had been eager to make. I found myself itching to say her name. "The non-Min connection I sacrifice is Emell of Gaard, Lordin's mother," I said. "She is the wretch who started this business, and while she is alive, nobody in my family will ever be safe. She murdered my mother, and now I will finally end her life with one command. This is for the millions of people dead in the pandemic, Emell. You pay now with your life."

"Please do not bore Me with speeches," the Seeing Water said. "I have no time for such nonsense. Anyway, your sacrifice is noted. Emell of Gaard will not see another day."

My third sacrifice was the toughest of all, but it had been made easier by a rather unpleasant conversation on my visin not too long ago. I felt terrible, but when it came down to the two men in my life who I had loved greatly, there was only one I was willing to sacrifice.

"For my great love, I sacrifice King Zawne."

"Wise move," the Seeing Water boomed. I thought it sounded happy. "Before the day is over, King Zawne will be put to death."

17

I opened my eyes to see Hanchell and Riedel staring at me like curious cats, only green and huge and with too many eyes for their strange faces. I must have been passed out like a drunk.

"Oh, wow," I said, rubbing my temples. "How long was I out?"

"Five hours," Riedel told me. "You have been curled in the fetal position and drooling. You probably feel exhausted, but it will go away. A lot has happened since your meeting with the Seeing Water, Kaelyn. The abductions have come to a stop, and many missing children have returned to their parents. Great job for making that happen."

"And what's the bad news?" I said, failing to stifle a yawn, so it came out "bad yews."

"Unfortunately," Hanchell said, "there is still no sign of Roki or your twins."

"Figures," I said. "That means I need to hurry." I dusted myself off and tried to shake the fatigue out of my bones, ruffling my hair and rubbing the sleep from my eyes. "I need to find Roki and the kids before the dramatic news breaks of what I've done. Once Lordin finds out, they won't be safe anywhere in the galaxy."

"Is there anything we can do to help?" Hanchell asked.

"Actually, yes. I need someone to assist me, preferably a Min who's well-connected and can search with me for what I need. Knotts is busy looking after Geniverd on my behalf, so I can't use him. Do you know anyone skilled who I can trust?"

"Neuge is back," Hanchell said. But she must have sensed my trepidation. "I mean, if you want Neuge to help."

I exhaled sharply. With all the craziness recently, I had forgotten all about Neuge. I wondered how he would feel about me pretending to be him and breaking up with Nnati. I was sure he didn't care about me squirming into his body, since it wasn't really his body, anyway. But I didn't know how he'd like me using his name, pretending to actually be him. It was better I kept my mouth shut, at least until Neuge helped me find Roki.

"It's okay," I told her. "I would appreciate it. Neuge is skilled and can be of great assistance."

"We will get him for you," Hanchell said. "Go to the main square in Shiol and wait for him there. You don't have to tell us what you asked of the Seeing Water, nor what you sacrificed to get it. All that information is blocked from our view, and we don't care, anyway. We are now a few short hours away from our final retirement. Our last action will be to see this thing through with you, Kaelyn. You have been a lot of fun. Now go. We will send Neuge to help you ASAP."

I couldn't have thanked the Crown of Crowns enough for their help. Even though I thought they were pretty incompetent sometimes, the Seeing Water had helped me view them in a more positive light. Hanchell and Riedel were creatures like the rest of us and had flaws like anybody else. I waved them goodbye, fully aware it might be the last time I ever saw the weird lizard monsters, and went back to the main square in Shiol.

I arrived just as Knotts was calling out to me.

"Yes?" I said, looking up at the colorful sky over the shimmering skyscrapers of Shiol as if looking straight at him. "What is it?"

"I've been trying to reach you for hours," he said. "Things are happening, Kaelyn. Lordin's mother, Emell, just killed herself in prison using a glass shard from a mirror in her cell. Lordin's a mess."

"Okay," I said. "Maybe it will keep her distracted until I can find Roki and the twins."

"Did you have something to do with it?" he asked. "You were gone for five hours. Did you see the Crown of Crowns? Did you somehow assassinate Emell?"

"I can't explain everything today," I said. It was in that moment that I realized how little time I had left. Emell was dead and Zawne was next. I had to hurry. I couldn't possibly predict how wild Lordin's fury would be after the death of her mother and her lover. "I need to go, Knotts," I said. Also, Neuge had just shown up in the square, back in his original Geniverd body. He was staring at me. I shivered, knowing I had been inside his skin.

"I miss you," Knotts said. Thankfully, he was using telepathy and Neuge couldn't hear him.

I said back, "When I find Roki, I am going to tell him what happened, Knotts. We can't be together. Okay? This thing, this heat we have between us, it's only heat. My love for Roki is real, and I am going to tell him what we did, even if he hates me for it. I won't live a lie. And I can't die without telling Roki how I betrayed him."

"I wouldn't worry about death," Knotts said, way too nonchalantly for my liking.

Neuge was now towering over me with his eyebrow cocked, waiting impatiently for me to finish my telepathic conversation.

"Why is that?" I asked. "Why shouldn't I worry about death?"

I could almost feel Knotts shrug, his lips turning up in a clever smile. "I just have a feeling that you'll be fine. That's all. I'm sure nothing will happen to you."

* * *

"Just some business in Geniverd with Knotts," I told Neuge. I could tell he was annoyed, both by having to wait for me and by having to be with me at all.

"It's fine," he said. "I wanted to thank you for preserving my Geniverd body. It's a pain in the neck to change sometimes. I'm used to this one."

I swallowed. Did Neuge already know what I'd done? Hadn't I left the body—?

"But why did I find it in a cave?" he asked. "Also, my body smells kind of girly, maybe a little feminine."

"I ... Shoot."

I was cornered. I hadn't expected Neuge to go back to Geniverd in search of his body, and so I had ditched it in the Krug cave, meaning to deal with it later. I had no choice but to tell him now. I really had no excuse for stuffing his body in a random cave. I told him right away what had happened, about Nnati's desire for suicide, how I had saved his life.

Neuge was surprisingly happy about the way things had turned out. When I was done, he said, "That's great. A lot of stress off my back. I hadn't known Nnati would want to kill himself in the wake of my death, or I would have broken up with him myself and avoided this whole mess. It was kind of you to do it for me, Kaelyn. I know I'm not in love with Nnati, but I still care about him as a person. You did the right thing. I'm not mad at all."

I was at a loss for words, a sudden lightness taking me over. It was a huge relief. Not only was Neuge okay with it, but he seemed a little friendlier with me than ever before. It made life easier as we dug into the investigation. Neuge established a cloaking shield around us that meant no one could come close to us or hear us, and I told him every last detail of what I had managed to uncover so far, except for the Seeing Water and my personal romantic life, of course. Then I showed him a new image I had captured from Erwun's memory.

"These are the two kidnappers," I said. "I have enhanced my ability, and now I can hack into memories within memories. Pretty cool, huh?"

"That is pretty cool. How did you do it?"

"A secret," I said with an unfocused smile. I had a sudden desire to be back in his body and feel Neuge's raw power and hard pecs. I had to take my mind off it. "Now watch," I said. "I'll display the memories from the girl on the left."

We instantly saw the woman's most relevant memory displayed on the inner curve of Neuge's privacy cloak. She was nodding to a shadowed figure whose face we couldn't see, looking like she'd just received instructions. There was no sound, and we couldn't read their thoughts. Everything was a little blurry as we viewed the memory within a memory; it must have been slightly weaker than a memory gained with my normal power. All we could tell was that they were in a big forest surrounded by tall trees and the strangest yellow grass over the entire forest floor.

"I'd recognize that grass anywhere," Neuge said. "They're on planetoid Cusper. It's the same place where I first met Roki, near the edge of the Kolbur system."

"Really? What was Roki doing there when you met him?"

Neuge chuckled and stroked his chin nostalgically. "That was a long time ago, back when Roki saved me from a lizard king. I haven't thought about those times in many years. He was there to imprison someone."

"Soren. You mean Knotts's sister?"

"Yeah. How did you know?"

"Long story," I said. "All I know is that she was evil and tried to drown Knotts. Then Roki stepped in and saved the day."

"That's right," Neuge said. "But we finished our investigations in Cusper just yesterday and found no sign of the missing children. And in any case, Soren would have a hard time kidnapping thousands of children from inside her prison. After the deadly incident with Roki and Knotts, after Roki was made a Min, Soren was imprisoned for life. Roki was tasked with the responsibility of hiding her cage somewhere on the planetoid. There's no way she could be roaming around the galaxy, causing trouble. She's been locked up for hundreds of years."

"Interesting," I said. My mind was racing. What if Soren somehow had a part to play in this sick game? She couldn't have visited the Seeing Water without making three sacrifices, and it wasn't as if she had much to sacrifice after being imprisoned for hundreds of years. Still, maybe it would be safest not to rule her out. If planetoid Cusper was the location of the memory, that was the best place to start looking for Roki and the twins.

"We should go there," I told Neuge. "Just to be safe, we should go pay Soren a visit in her prison."

"Sure," he said, "but we can't go like this. Cusper is a world of flying reptiles. We're going to need to get new bodies. And besides that, only Roki knows where her prison is."

"Leave that to me. Hold on ... Let me ..." I opened my most recent memory of Roki, then dug through Roki's memories until I found the exact location of Soren's prison. I wanted to look through the rest of his memories to figure out why he'd been so secretive and cryptic when I had last seen him, but there wasn't enough time. "Got it," I said, smiling wide at Neuge. "Now, let's go get some lizard bodies!"

* * *

Bodies were easy to come by in Shiol. We found a body rental shop with a storeroom of thousands of the oddest bodies I'd ever seen squished inside vacuum-sealed plastic, like costumes at the dry cleaners. I got myself a female flying dragon, and Neuge got his own male body, a muscly dragon with unnaturally thick biceps and a chunky tail. Then we teleported through the galaxy and materialized in the atmosphere of planetoid Cusper.

"This is so cool!" I shouted, soaring through the sky with my lizard wings. We must have looked like pterodactyls from prehistoric Geniverd. My dark green skin was soft and smooth, and each of my fingers ended in a sharp claw. I felt like a bat.

"This is the place," Neuge said. "Right there. Try not to crash."

We glided above the canopy of a great lush forest that looked as though no sentient creature had ever stepped foot there before. It was an expanse of cliffs and gullies, huge gorges dividing the land into segments, waterfalls splashing over the edges into massive rivers, and towering trees everywhere above the floor of yellow grass. We touched down in the middle of a moor, but the place was actually an entrance to a hidden cave.

"This is it," I said, projecting the coordinates of the cave from Roki's memories.

"He must still be using his power to mask it," Neuge said. "The lizards here live in underground caverns because many are nocturnal." We were walking deeper into the cave now; it smelled of wet rock. "If this cave weren't masked, it would make an excellent place to build a small underground city. The lizards love their underground cities. It's where Roki got the idea to build Tsiser."

After a few minutes of walking through the cave on my weird lizard feet, which I couldn't seem to get used to, we came upon Soren's prison. It was in a domed chamber with a rough ceiling and cold earthen walls. In the middle of the chamber's floor was a prison gate, barely large enough for Neuge or me to fit through with our wings.

We came to stand above the rusted bars worked into the dirt. "Hello?" I called down.

For a moment, my mind was restless and my body tingled with dread. What if I'd gotten it all wrong and there was nothing to find here? Then, just when I wished time would speed up, a very soft female voice answered like an echo. "Hello."

"Soren?"

"Yes."

"My name is Kaelyn. I'm Roki's girlfriend. Do you have our twins down there with you?"

"I do."

Could it really have been so easy?

"I will even give them back to you," Soren said, "because I have come to adore them. I see why you love these twins so much. I want them to have full, happy lives, and so I will return them to you. Kaelyn, you should feel very lucky."

Just then Xerx and Vowkin appeared beneath the bars. There was a click, the gate swung open, and my boys scrambled out of it. They were still in their human bodies. They rushed to me and I enfolded them in my lizard wings, ruffling their hair, rubbing my green skin against their dirty faces. It was lucky Xerx and Vowkin were Min, or they would have been terrified of their mother's new appearance.

"I've missed you so much," I said. My voice was nasal in this body.

"Thanks, Mama," Xerx said. "We've been so bored here."

"Yeah," Vowkin said, and pouted. "We are cut off from almost everything, so there is no connectivity for us to play our games."

"You can play your games soon enough," I said. "Wait with Neuge while I talk to Soren. Oh, and, Xerx, Erwun is safe at the house in Tsiser. Don't worry."

Xerx's countenance lifted. "Thanks!" He hugged me tightly. "You're the best Mama ever, even if you are a lizard now."

We all had a short laugh. Then Neuge took the boys outside the cave while I talked to Soren. I was unsure what to do with her, whether I should destroy her for messing with my babies or just leave her to rot in her dirt prison.

"Why did you do it?" I asked. "I thought it was Lordin who kidnapped all the children. How did you even pull this off?"

"It *was* Lordin," Soren said. She looked small and frail down in her dark hole, like a wisp of someone's soul slowly fading away. "She came to me to form an alliance. I would get revenge on Roki, while Lordin ascended to the Crown of Crowns. She promised to release me from prison once she took the throne, then give me another thousand years of life to make up for what was stolen from me by Hanchell and

Riedel. She somehow managed to unlock my cage—if I had to guess, I'd say it had something to do with the Seeing Water—then used it to store all the children. About a day ago, though, they all started vanishing, I guessed back to where they had come from. I assumed her campaign had worked. The children were never meant to be harmed. We only needed them so that Lordin and Zawne would win the throne, while at the same time distracting the other contenders."

"Pretty elaborate," I said. But I was wondering how the entire galaxy could be so stupid. I was also wondering why Soren was still down in her hole if the gate was open. It was lucky Roki had placed her somewhere with no large body of water, so if she still had her Min power, there was no way she could harm me. I heard Vowkin's voice in the back of my mind—"Papa!"—and instantly I knew my boyfriend was also in the hole.

"Give me back Roki too," I said. "He's mine. You can't have him."

"No," Soren said. "He's not coming out. He may never come out."

I shuffled back a step, my strange, hard muscles tightening. "Excuse me? What did you do with him? If you don't give him back right now, I will bring you all the harm you can handle! You don't want to mess with me, you—"

Roki called out of the dimness to me. "Kaelyn, don't do anything rash. I can't come back right now. I'm sorry. You will just need to forget about me. Take good care of the twins and move on with your life."

"What are you talking about?" I said, suddenly emotional and still tense. "What are you doing down there? Do you love Soren?"

"You wouldn't understand," he told me. I hated that Roki wouldn't even show me his face. It was like talking into a well.

"Trust me, it's better if you just go on without me." His voice was cracking, thick with emotion. Roki couldn't keep it together.

"We're not leaving without you," I said. "The twins are outside with Neuge. We're all waiting for you."

There were some hushed whispers from below. Soren and Roki were arguing.

I heard her say, "Tell her or I will."

Then Roki's voice came to me. "Kaelyn, you are going to hate me for this, but I need to be honest. After I tell you this secret, you must leave. I can't bear the shame."

"Just tell me, Roki. I love you." I took a big breath, regretting what I was about to say. "And I have a secret of my own. I might as well tell you now that I kissed Knotts. At first it was a complete accident, but when he came on to me, I gave in. I think it's because I missed you so much, but there is no excuse. I'm so sorry. I love you."

Roki was so emotional he was sniffling. "Do you remember the first time we met, when we were at the Ava-Nurlie noblewoman's ball?"

"Of course."

"Well, it wasn't meant to be me. It was supposed to be Knotts at that party. Knotts had been planning for a long time to burn down an estate. It was to be the first in a long campaign. Because the target was only empty on the night of the ball, Knotts asked me to go to the ball instead of him. The whole point of me being there was to make a connection to your mother and father so we could campaign for more market reenactments."

"So ... you were just with me for my parents ..."

"I'm sorry, Kaelyn," Roki said. "In the same way, you were only with me because I represented the change you wanted in your own life. I was something real and dangerous, and outside your scope of knowing."

I didn't think the comparison was fair, but I didn't want to argue with him.

"Our love was real," I said, "wasn't it? Isn't it? Don't we love each other?"

"Yes," he said. "The love was real. I grew to love you immediately. But what I'm about to say will cause me to lose your love forever. I know you think it was Lordin who killed her baby, but it was me. I did it. I killed baby Arta for revenge, and now Lordin and Zawne will be the new Crown of Crowns. I have doomed us all, murdered a child, and have nothing else to blame but my own bad intentions. I did it, Kaelyn. I'm a killer."

never even got a chance to reply. Roki closed the gate from the inside, and the hole went silent.

"Roki!" I shouted over and over until my voice was hoarse but he never answered. I could tell he was gone, or at least he'd masked his presence. There was nothing left for me to do. After waiting for an hour, I began to walk out of the cave. I wanted to cry, but my stupid lizard eyes had no tear ducts.

I couldn't believe Roki had killed Arta. Well, I believed his words were sincere. He did the crime. But I couldn't believe Roki was capable of such a beastly act. When had we turned into such vicious animals? I had killed a billion people with a tidal wave, and Roki had killed a baby with his bare hands. Oh, and Zawne was surely dead by now. I'd really mucked things up, and so had Roki. But he was no worse than me. We'd both turned out to be villains in the end. We had tried to do the right thing and only set the world on fire. We were beyond mercy.

Vowkin appeared before I reached the cave exit. I'd been so

deep in thought that I hadn't noticed him shuffling toward me. "Hey," I said. "Where's your brother?"

"He went to go find the tallest mountain on the planetoid. I was going to go with him, but I wanted to check and make sure you were okay. I left a copy of myself there. That way, Xerx doesn't know I'm gone. I can make short-living replicas, like very real clones that think, act, and speak just like me."

"That's amazing," I said. "Hanchell and Riedel were very generous to give you boys these awesome powers."

"I know. We have a lot of them, and each is different and cool in its own way. But really, Mama, are you okay? I still can't read your mind."

"Yeah, I'm okay. Thank you, sweetie. I appreciate it."

It was a little weird calling Vowkin sweetie, since he was not even a year old and already taller than me. We barely knew each other, and yet we had shared so many life-changing experiences. We had explored Geniverd together, climbed the tallest mountains, swum across the oceans, lounged with octopuses, and run with the wolves. *New and unique experiences have the power to bond souls, I thought. And it was true. We had bonded over the past six months thanks to our incredible experiences. This newest trial was different, more tragic, but we would bond through it as well.*

"Is Papa coming?" Vowkin asked.

He must have known by my expression that Roki was staying in the cave. "That's what I thought," he said. "Listen, Mama, I wanted a moment alone with you because I know things now that I didn't before. I know where your pain comes from, and I know how to make it stop."

"How's that?" I said.

"I mean that I know why you're helping Defiance."

"That's not a secret," I told him. "I've made it pretty clear to the world why I am helping Defiance."

Vowkin sighed and pinched the bridge of his nose. "That's not what I mean. What I'm trying to say is that you must accept your life. Accept that you have inflicted pain and that pain has been inflicted upon you. Only then can you break the cycle."

"I understand, Vowkin. Thank you, really, but it's not that simple."

"What if I told you that you and Papa aren't responsible for your sins? That an unseen force made you commit those murders?"

I shook my head slowly, my whole being numb with torment. Lordin might be resourceful, but I let myself down. I was the one that played with people's lives, and I killed them. I couldn't shift the blame onto someone else.

"Even then, I must be accountable for my deeds," I said. "The cycle of pain for Geniverd may be almost over, but mine is only just beginning. All this time I have been trying to save the world, and it has led me to this point, to this critical moment. We're hours away from stopping that cycle. If I stop now, Vowkin, we will surely be as good as dead. But I will never be free to roam the universe without any pain."

Vowkin stared at me—a resigned, peaceful gaze. He must have tried to do the same with Roki.

"Speaking of the dead," Vowkin said, "I met my grand-mother. I met your mama while down in Soren's jail."

"My mama?" My skin went ice-cold, and I almost fell to my knees. "How is that possible? Do you have access to dead spirits?"

"Not any more than anyone else. I don't have power over the dead. Min are able to access the dead the same as any other spirit or entity. The only difference between dead people and Min is that a Min is a living spirit and a dead person is a perished spirit. They are more invisible than anything, redundant in the physical world. The spirits of the lost are trapped in their ethereal realm, which overlaps with ours. In that sense, they are truly dead, in a sea of nothingness. They can affect nothing in our physical world, but their former consciousnesses, from their lives, can come to us—either by Min, human, or animal—if we are willing to allow them entry."

"My mind is blown," I told him. "You learned all this through the lessons the Crown of Crowns gave you?"

"Yes. It was so boring in the cave."

"And you spoke to my mama?"

"No."

"But ... what did you mean?"

"I saw her soul and her messages from her time on Geniverd. Her innermost thoughts and will for your life. She knew you had great courage. But if she were here now, she would've asked you to leave Geniverd be, allow it to work itself out. Let people ask for your help, and never impose it on them."

"But ..." I didn't understand why my mama would want that. It made no sense. Before I could finish asking Vowkin about it, Xerx and Neuge were coming into the cave. Xerx ran up and hugged me. He was usually taller than me, but not in my lizard body. He only managed to hug my lower half, and I brushed him with my wings. "Sorry, Xerx, but your papa isn't coming."

"I know." He was looking at the ground, kicking up clods of dirt with his shoes. "Papa promised Soren that he would stay with her until she died. That means he will be down there in her prison for a while. It was the only way she would let us leave—if Roki stayed with her to keep her company. Papa traded his life for our freedom. I could see it plainly on his face how much it hurt him to leave us and abandon you, the searing pain cutting his soul in half. Everything he did was for us, or to save someone other than himself. I understand that now, and I feel bad for him. I feel sad for you."

I was mad at Roki for making such a huge decision without consulting me. I just couldn't see where the future would go from here. But I wasn't about to give up, and I wanted Xerx to know that I was defiant.

I crossed my upper limbs and let out a little laugh. Maybe I looked a little crazy, because Xerx stumbled backward. "Your papa is commendable," I said, "but there is no need to be sad or feel sorry for us. He knows he won't be staying down in that jail. If he doesn't, then he clearly doesn't know who I am. Because after I get you boys to safety and deal with Lordin, I'll be coming back here to free Roki by any means necessary."

* * *

The four of us left planetoid Cusper and went back to Shiol. I left the kids with Hanchell and Riedel while Neuge and I went to trade our lizard skins for our Geniverd bodies at the body rental shop. Once we were changed and I didn't feel like a bat anymore, and Neuge seemed comfortable once more in his muscled form, he took me aside for a quick cup of tea at one of Shiol's amazing street cafés, where they sold teas from all over the galaxy.

"I wanted to talk to you about something," he said, cradling his mug of planet Olvic's rullien dark tea, made from rullien berries.

"What is it?"

"I've been thinking. I made a huge mistake by leaving Nnati. After my mission through the galaxy, going on the hunt for the lost children, then finding Soren, I have realized that I do love Nnati. I was just afraid. I've never known how to express myself. And truth be told, I've never experienced love like this. So, I ran away. I feel guilty as all heck. But I made a mistake and I want him back. I want Nnati in my life for good."

"You're serious ..." It wasn't a question. I could see the sincerity in his thoughts. "But how are we going to fix this after what I did? Nnati thinks you don't love him. And there's something else. When I told you what I did, I left something out."

"Oh no. What happened?"

I hesitated, took a slurp of my rullien tea—it tasted almost like the pinkberries back on Geniverd—then cleared my throat. "I kind of told Nnati that you are in love with Knotts."

"What!" He winced. "Why would you do that?"

"It was in the heat of the moment," I explained. "I'm so sorry. I just needed an excuse to get Nnati to break up with you. It was more important to me that Nnati didn't kill himself, and Knotts was standing right there. I didn't think you ever wanted to see him again."

Neuge burst out laughing. He threw his head back and howled. "Just my luck! It's so farcical. The man I want to be with thinks that I love the man who wants to be with you, all because you decided to steal my body. What a strange series of events."

"To say the least," I said. "But seriously, Neuge, what are you going to do? Nnati does love you. If you love him back, then you should be together."

He was awfully relaxed. Neuge just smiled and shook his head, took a sip of his dark tea, and told me, "It's not a big deal. I'll get him back. I'll get him back and turn him into a strong man. I'll toughen him up. He shouldn't be killing himself over anyone or anything. Period."

"But how?" I asked. "This whole situation is a mess."

"How else?" Neuge leaned forward and winked at me. "I'll seduce him. Nnati melts at the sight of me. I'll say I'm sorry and then seduce him. He'll never be able to resist."

"Let's hope you're right," I said. Then we were both laughing. It was a nice break from the chaos. We finished our drinks and got back to work. Time was almost up.

* * *

It was late afternoon when we got back to Tsiser. The air was tense. Papa and Raad glared at me like I was an evil menace when I walked in the door with Xerx and Vowkin. They'd been trapped in the house for days, and one quick reach into their thoughts confirmed that they hated me. Any chance I may have had of securing a nice relationship with my brother in this foreign body was gone. It was gone with Tissa too. They all thought they were on the wrong side of the war. They all thought they'd made a huge mistake by listening to me.

It was nice to see Xerx and Erwun reunite. How could a six-month-old Min be so romantic? Xerx took Erwun's hand and said, "I'm so glad you're okay. I missed you so much. Erwun, I need to tell you something." He paused, then looked her straight in the eyes. "I love you."

She squealed and wrapped her arms around him. "I love you too, Xerx. I feel like we've known each other for years. I was so worried about losing you after what happened in the forest."

They kissed, and that was my signal to get the heck out of the library. They were smooching like adults, Erwun on her tiptoes, her chest pressed against Xerx's body. I left the room and went upstairs, pausing in the hallway as Neuge and Nnati walked by me in a huff. They completely ignored me and headed into the room where Neuge had lain in a coma, then slammed the door shut behind them. Knotts appeared on the stairs.

"Listen." Knotts approached me, once more standing so close that his delicious breath tickled my nose. "I know you're waiting for Roki, but you should know that I am going to fight for you. Kaelyn, you are all that I think about."

"Okay. Well, you'll lose."

"You were supposed to fall in love with me, not him!" Knotts nearly put a hole in the wall. He crashed into it with both hands, heaving in frustration. "You were supposed to love me, not Roki. It's not fair!" He pounded the wall with his fist.

I was disgusted at this point. Jealousy and childish behavior were not the least bit attractive to me. "I'm not a tool," I said. "You guys used me in the first place, so your point is moot. If you want to talk about the kiss, save your breath. I know I'm weak when it comes to men, and I know it is not an excuse. But that kiss was a one-time mistake. I already told Roki what happened."

Knotts smiled, not at all worried. "Yeah? What did he say?"

"It doesn't matter what he said. Roki is currently the prisoner of your dear sister. When this is all done, I am going to find a way to free him."

"Have you considered that maybe he doesn't want to be saved? I've known Roki for a long time, Kaelyn, longer than you. Roki wants you to be happy, and he knows that your happiness is with me. I know it. Why can't you see it? Deny it all you want, Kaelyn, but I am your destiny."

I gawked at him, now leaning against the wall he'd just punched. I zeroed in on his parted lips, remembering how his teeth had playfully dragged at my lower lip the second time we'd kissed. Looking at him in that posture filled me with an overwhelming, tormenting desire for him. I desperately needed it to stop—I wanted to find a way to escape the situation. "How can someone as smart as you think smugness and overconfidence is going to win my heart? Your arrogance makes me want to reject you even more."

"I don't think so," he said, shrugging it off. "Don't waste your energy. The universe brought us together. My sister, the missing children, Lordin and this war, Roki's vanishment—all the motions brought us together. The only thing is that it should have happened earlier."

He laughed. "I was there, you know, at the party where you met Roki. I was there to make more contacts through my impressive wine vineyards. I saw you from across the room and lost my breath. Your beauty astounded me. I was on the move to approach when Roki swooped in. There was nothing I could do. I had to let the affair run its course. But honestly, Kaelyn, if I had approached you first, saying the same things about revolution and antiestablishmentarianism, offering you the dangerous side of life you had been craving, do you really think you would have rejected me?"

I looked Knotts up and down. He was insanely handsome. Just like Zawne. Just like Roki. I immediately saw a pattern. Knotts was right. When a hunky guy came up and offered me all the things in life I had been looking for, offering me a cause, a reason to exist, I couldn't say no. I hadn't said no to Knotts two days ago with my boyfriend and children missing; there was no way I could have refused him at fifteen.

"It doesn't matter what I would have done," I said. "This is the way it turned out. Anyway, if you had really been so crazy for me, then you could have pursued me. Even if I didn't answer your marriage proposal, I worked at the foundation in Cara for a long time and was always single. You could have approached me anywhere—on the street, at the office. You could have but you didn't."

"Because I didn't want to betray Roki," Knotts said.

"Oh, but you'll seduce me in the man's house, right? Not in the street before we even dated but right here in his own house." I turned from him.

"It's different now," he said, a hint of desperation seeping into his voice. He grabbed me by the shoulders and turned me to face him. "It's different now because Roki knows we are supposed to be together. Why do you think he brought you to Capernort? It was so you would meet me. Even if your heart is conflicted, I know your feelings for me are pure. I saw it the moment we locked eyes."

I thought back to the first time Roki had wanted to take me to Capernort, and his arguments for bringing me into the senate. I had a sinking feeling in my stomach. "That's nonsense," I said, my throat constricted. I added, "I don't believe Roki has been trying to set me up with you all along. Don't be ridiculous."

"He did not know what he was doing," Knotts said. His voice was cool, steady, and his face expressionless. "A seer told me about us. I didn't believe it, and I resisted it. Aside from betraying Roki, I think it was the reason I didn't chase you after your brother rejected my marriage proposal. Now I know we're fated to be together and we can't run from this even if we wanted to."

"The universe has somehow conspired for us to be together," I said, but I wasn't so sure. He made it seem like nobody could stay faithful for more than a minute, including me. That nobody had been faithful except for Zawne, and I had sentenced him to death. I suddenly felt terrible all over again. I couldn't deal with Knotts right now. But I was determined to fight our supposed fate.

"Enough," I said. But the truth of what I'd done, the horror of my willingness to rob Zawne of life after he had been the most loyal lover I'd ever had—it broke me, and I screamed.

I reordered my thoughts, avoiding his eyes.

"Enough! I've had enough, Knotts. Give me some space. If you truly want to be with me, give me some space, or I will snap. This is too much. There is a war going on."

Knotts was silent. For the first time, he kept his mouth shut. Then I was crying. The weight of all my burdens and all my pain broke against me, and I cried for all the life I'd stolen. Knotts took me in his arms and rocked me. He petted my hair.

"It's okay, Kaelyn. Everything is going to be okay."

No, it wasn't going to be okay. Because I would never forgive myself.

* * *

The news came all at once. I'd only just reapplied my face in the bathroom after crying streaks of mascara all down my nose and onto my lips, and I was standing in the parlor with a happily reunited Nnati and Neuge, a brooding Knotts, and a disgruntled trio who used to be my family. The leaders of Surrvul and Krug were sulking in the corner like scolded children. They all desperately wanted to leave Tsiser.

Then the news broke.

"No way," Nnati said. He was on his visin. "Quick, everyone. Quick, look!" He projected his visin onto the wall so that we could watch together.

"We've done it," I said. It felt like a giant boulder had been lifted off my shoulders, like I'd just lost a thousand pounds and could float through the ceiling. "We've done it. Lordin is conceding!"

All across the world, the white flag was being waved. The

Protector forces had retreated. The smoke was beginning to clear. Lordin claimed that a formal announcement would be made later to discuss surrender and the transfer of power. When she finished talking, she laid a splayed-out hand against her chest and her eyes filled with tears. I knew then for sure, even though she didn't say it, that the king had died. I had to clutch the doorframe to keep from collapsing again.

"I'm so happy we've won," Nnati said. "All that hard work, and we finally did it."

"The people didn't win," Knotts said coldly. I noticed Nnati was giving him the stink eye, probably jealous. I wondered what Neuge had said to him in private. "We may have won, but the people are out in the cold. It should be up to the people now to decide what direction the world goes in. This could easily crumble into a messy civil war. We may have just divided Geniverd back into warring clans. Without a capital of power, do you really think three billion people will agree on one idea, on one system of peaceful rule?"

Silence fell upon the room. I could hear Raad swallow dryly from all the way over at the window. Knotts was right. We had done all that we could do. The people would have to forge their own way forward, without Decens-Lenitas. I really hoped the people would come through.

Still, in the back of my mind, I wondered, *Did I just destroy the future of Geniverd to satiate my privileged need to come out on top? Could my reckless compassion truly have sentenced the world to death?*

Was I the harbinger of the apocalypse?

Or was I the savior of Geniverd?

19

<hr>

$\mathcal{T}$he final chime rang shortly after Knotts and I had excused ourselves from the parlor, after I'd informed Raad, Papa, Tissa, and the leaders of the Surrvul and Krug clans that they were free to leave Tsiser at any time. Knotts and I were downstairs in the library with the Min Tharva and Justein, the twins, and Erwun. And that was when we heard the final chime.

"Greetings," Hanchell and Riedel said. "The votes are in and we have the results. Congratulations to Xerx and Erwun, the happy new couple and the new Crown of Crowns. Get ready—you are now the rulers of the galaxy."

I was shocked but positively ecstatic. I remembered what the Seeing Water had said, *"The rest will come with your sacrifices ... You must be the one to personally save your twins. When you succeed, you will gain your desire with little effort."*

While I'd been busy with Knotts, Xerx had proposed to Erwun. He'd already gotten the blessing of the Crown of Crowns back in Shiol when Neuge and I were having tea, plus their express permission to reveal his true identity as a Min.

Erwun had happily agreed to rule the universe alongside Xerx once he'd told her about it, and they had been married by Hanchell and Riedel in a secret ceremony. The job of supreme judge of the galaxy was a huge upgrade from entertaining nobles as a theater performer, and Erwun couldn't have been happier. With Zawne dead and Lordin outed as the real kidnapper of the children, the Min of the galaxy had scrambled to put in their votes all over again. Knotts had used his connections to get the word out about Xerx and Erwun, while at the same time denouncing the rumors about Arta's death and replacing the old rumors with new ones that put Lordin in a grim light. The result was a last-minute overwhelming majority vote for Xerx and Erwun, the brave and fearless survivors of Lordin the Traitor, as she was now being called in Shiol.

The greatest part about Erwun becoming Min at the same time as she was sworn in as Crown of Crowns was that she didn't need to die in Geniverd and got to keep her original body. The transition was lightning fast, from human to Min with the snap of Riedel's green fingers. The sad part was that Hanchell and Riedel's time was at its end.

We were gathered in the massive square in Shiol not long after the announcement. The glittering interdimensional city sparkled red, purple, and gold because of the celebration, the final farewell to Hanchell and Riedel. It was like the entire city had been transformed into a rainbow. The buildings looked like multifaceted gemstones carved into pillars and skyscrapers. On the stage was Erwun, recently converted into a Min. She and Xerx were sitting in the floating water thrones while Hanchell and Riedel waved goodbye to Shiol, tears streaming from all six of Hanchell's eyes. Even Riedel was tearing up. I could hardly imagine what it must be like to say goodbye after three thousand years of rule.

Their departure was peaceful. In the midst of smiles, cheers, applause, and love showered upon Hanchell and Riedel from the thousands of loyal Min in attendance, some hovering or flapping in the air, other snaking along the ground, and many hundreds of humanoid creatures on their legs or stumps, Hanchell and Riedel simply faded away. It was beautiful. They were both smiling as they dissolved into sparkling dust and blew away on the breeze.

* * *

The party was crazy. There were at least ten thousand Min talking, dancing, and playing the wildest music. My brain could hardly comprehend the innumerable beats, melodies, dances, and weird drinks being passed around. Knotts and I were at the far corner of the square, where it wasn't too noisy. We'd brought bottles of soft drinks from Geniverd, and Knotts had just finished making a toast to my son and his wife, the new Crown of Crowns. Now we were basking in the insanity of Shiol.

"I thought she'd be here," I told him. "I was kind of hoping for a final goodbye, some kind of closure, even if we do hate each other."

"Lordin still might show," he said. Then Knotts laughed. "Man, I have never seen Shiol party this hard, not even after Draxineus 7 was saved from annihilation and the Draxinians brought enough blue-moon beer to get three thousand Min drunk for six days. This is wild."

I gave Knotts a weak smile. It was nice that the war was over, but I still wasn't in the mood to party. I was happy, sure. I was proud of Xerx. I'd found out that Zawne had died in his sleep, so that was the best outcome I could have hoped for. Our Guardians had found a way to get to him. I was glad

Zawne hadn't suffered. He didn't deserve any more pain, not even in death. Both Erwun and Xerx had agreed to attend school until the end of the year to learn more about humans, allowing them to govern better. That made me happy as well. Even if Xerx was omnipotent, it was still important he go to school.

In Geniverd, Lordin's genetic engineering was being reversed, as was her transhuman project with the Askas and the nobles. A senate was being put together by Marten, Olorc, and Gorm. All the clan leaders would be involved. Something they were calling the People's Direct Government, a form of immediate digital democracy, was being kicked around; the idea that every person would have a vote in Geniverd's big decisions, and the senate and clan leaders would be executors and figureheads. Hopefully, it would work this time. An empire had fallen. What would rise from its ashes was now no longer my concern. I had other plans.

I was half talking to myself. "She must be busy with the funeral preparations. She'll probably have to go into hiding after the service. She might move to an uninhabited planet or, if she can, another galaxy. Geniverd hates her for brainwashing them, and Shiol hates her for stealing their children and spitting out lies."

"No thanks to you," came Lordin's distinct voice from behind me.

I turned to see twin pools of gorgeous deep-blue eyes. Lordin had a black mourning dress on. My first thought was that she could be recognized and it would be the end of her. Then I understood we must have been in an alternate reality right there in the corner of the square.

"Why did you do it, Kaelyn? My love, my baby, my mama, my people, my seat of power. You took it all from me. If I wasn't fatherless, would you have taken my papa from me?"

I had been scared of Lordin for so long that it surprised me when I stood firm against her. Maybe it was the strength of Knotts standing so near to me. "You did it to yourself, Lordin. I am sorry for your losses, but you forced my hand. I never set out to hurt you or anybody else. All I ever wanted was what was right for Geniverd."

She crossed her arms, seemingly unmoved, but I knew she was hurting inside. "You can't justify bad behavior because you were trying to be good. That's not the truth. The truth is that you are cold and unkind. You used my people, spewing lies and propaganda so they would join your death cult. You and Roki glorified being Gurnots, magnifying every little difference between the classes until it grew into something toxic and unrealistic, when the truth was it didn't need to come to anarchy and mass murder to solve the problem. It could have been diplomatic."

"You're forgetting something, Lordin." I, too, crossed my arms and glared at her. "These are my people too, same as they are yours. Defiance is not a cult; it's a movement, an idea, and it was rampant far before I ever stepped into Tsiser or Shiol. Heck, before I was born. Everything I have done was for the people. I was queen and I died for them. I have killed for them. Just like you."

Knotts then came between us. "Stop this feud!" he said. "Neither of you is better than the other. Don't you see it?"

"He's right," I said. "We're all monsters. Roki and I are monsters. You, Lordin, are a monster, and so was your mother. Your mother murdered my mother, and I did the same to yours. You had the power to stop the virus that killed millions. Then our children went missing because of you, and in Roki's anger, he destroyed your child as revenge. Only monsters act like this. Only monsters kill millions and billions of people to reach their end. A true monster does it and still breathes. We thought we were gods. And yes, we may have fueled one another's inner monster in these recent months, bringing out the worst in each other. But there is no excuse for the things we've done, you and I both. From now on, we must leave humans alone."

"True," Lordin said, "but you could have been better. I know the members of Defiance have always loved me, and I have always loved them. I felt sorry for the Gurnots. I honestly never wanted it to come to this."

"But it did," I told her. "It went too far the moment you started injecting the population with genetic-altering formulas, turning the poor into slaves and the rich into superhuman soldiers. What did you think we would do, especially after you started kidnapping children? We had no choice but to stop you."

Lordin chuckled. "If only you knew the truth, it would destroy you. I knew human beings had reached a point of no return. Geniverd could never have saved itself from the exponential greed and sloth of the noble classes with a gentle push. My mother was greedy. I saw firsthand how greed consumes people. I figured that if I could control society as a whole, I could change the people for the better. But you!" She waved her finger at me. "You, Kaelyn of Gaard, destroyed and undid all my hard work."

"You should have told me your goals," I said. "Why would I have trusted you or thought you were a good person when all you did was work on clandestine plans in your secret factories? Come on."

I wasn't at all swayed by Lordin's blame throwing, nor did I care about the sappy history with her mother. "You have always known what Defiance stood for," I said, "and yet you warred with me rather than worked with me. If you had just communicated that you wanted the same thing as Defiance—

our mission statement is very clearly outlined in our demonstrations and in general knowledge—we would have reached a diplomatic solution to make the world a better place. To look back and think we were fighting for the same cause is absurd. It means everything was for nothing, and now we have destroyed ourselves in the process."

Lordin was silent. Then she whispered, "Passion is like love—cold to everything around its bubble. Love is stubborn and insensible to reason."

We were all silent then, the three of us. The party raged in the background but we were deaf to it. Lordin and I had been running the same race in different directions, and now we had come face-to-face at the finish line only to find neither of us the winner and the world in ruins. It would rebuild, of course, but we had wasted life. That was the real sin of it, all that wasted life and spoiled potential. Our crimes were heinous. Perhaps mine most of all. I felt ready to collapse from the weight of my sins.

"I have a proposal for you," Lordin said, her face hopeful. "You'll be pleased to hear that the people you thought you'd killed are waking up on beaches and in morgues. Every single one of them will live. And it's all thanks to my Immuno-Mort that their cells are firing up again. They're not yet immortal, but their cells are resilient."

I was confused. I glanced at Knotts who was blinking rapidly, and, like me, waiting impatiently for an explanation. If what she was saying was true—no, why would she lie to us about something like this—Lordin was a heroine. I was speechless.

But Lordin wasn't running a victory lap. "It's just that I can't save Zawne, Arta or my mother," she sobbed into her hands, her voice trembling. "Zawne stopped breathing. He had no pulse, and he was brain-dead. I waited and waited, but he

478

didn't come back to me. I built this amazing thing, and yet I couldn't save the most precious people in my life. So, I beg you ... give me Zawne's memories. His whole non-physical being."

That was when I understood—love was indeed stubborn. She wanted to clone him. I could've argued, should have said something about the ethics of it. The fact that she could never bring him back. But I was still coming to terms with everything she'd said and the disgraceful things I'd done. Now the drowned were alive again and they would never know I was the villain. I didn't deserve it.

Knotts came and took me under his arm.

"You were right this whole time," I told Knotts, looking up at him. "Min can't save the world. The world must save itself. That is the only way for change to last. The people must make it happen. It must be their decision, not mine, not Lordin's, not Min's, and not the Crown of Crowns'. The best we can do is remain helpful, kind, sympathetic, and good to the citizens of the world. Lordin and I sought victory on their behalf when we had no right. And even then we sought victory mostly on behalf of ourselves."

Knotts wiped my cheeks with his thumb. I was crying silent tears of despair for opportunities lost and knowledge gained too late.

"I'm sorry for all the pain I caused you," I told Lordin. "Let's end this here and now. I'll give you what you ask for."

Lordin nodded weakly and we shook hands and then hugged. There were tears streaking her perfect complexion. I was thinking, inside every person is the potential to be a monster. Was anyone free of this curse?

"We were just two women with too much love and too much anger," I said. "We made mistakes, and the world paid the price. Let's hope they pick up the pieces and build an even better world than the one we messed up."

* * *

All I could offer Lordin was forgiveness and friendship, and the knowledge that she wasn't alone in her suffering. I promised to deliver Zawne's memories to Xerx and Erwun. Lordin never told us where she would go. We watched her vanish, and I felt at the time that it was the end for us.

The party continued. Knotts and I stayed in our corner of the massive square, which was roughly seven of Cara's City Stadiums put together. Then, from the riotous crowd of indulgent Min, there came a familiar face. Two familiar faces. Roki came strolling over to us with Vowkin at his side. I had been planning to go back to get him but wasn't at all surprised that Roki had escaped Soren's prison. I wondered if Xerx had used his new powers as the Crown of Crowns.

"Kaelyn!" He ran and picked me up, then spun me in his arms and held me tight. "I'm sorry I was absent during your adventure, during the war, the strife. I was just trying to get our twins back."

"I know," I told him. "It's okay. After all that's happened, Roki, I just don't know what to do anymore."

Vowkin and Knotts had now pulled away from us, Vowkin chatting excitedly.

"I understand." Roki put his hand on my shoulder. "It's been a tough few days. You need to recalibrate and reenergize. Honestly, Kaelyn, I don't like the creature I've become. I have committed atrocities, and you have too. We should have guarded our thoughts and actions. I think it would be a good idea if we separated for a while. It would be wise if we spent some time apart. I don't think we deserve to be together after the horrors we have enacted. At least, not for now."

I wanted to start crying all over again; it was a shock that I maintained myself. I guessed I was getting stronger, hardening against the world and shedding my old, human emotions.

"I do understand," I said solemnly. "I don't deserve Geniverd and I don't deserve you. Or maybe it's like you say— we don't deserve each other. Whatever we deserve, I think you're right. We should take some time apart. I love you fiercely, but after all that's happened, maybe I need to go out alone and find myself. I still don't really know who I am. There must be more to me than an angsty eighteen-year-old girl who starts wars. Xerx is the Crown of Crowns, and Vowkin is fated to be one of the strongest Min in history. Maybe I can go away for a while. A trip around the cosmos. *I would explore the entire galaxy, one mountain, one beach, one planet at a time.*"

"That's a good idea," Roki said. He was holding my hands, looking into my eyes with all the love I had come to expect from him.

"Maybe we'll be together again one day," I said, "after I've explored the galaxy and come to terms with myself."

Roki smiled. "Yes, maybe."

"But one thing is for certain," I said. "We need to leave Geniverd alone. It's time to let humans live their lives without our toxic interference. We have given them a fresh start, and it's up to them now to forge a path."

"Agreed," he said. "Oh, and one more thing."

"Yeah?"

"Let Knotts in. I love you, and I know that you love me, but I'm not jealous. You're so young and we may not see each other for a long time, maybe double the normal human life span. You can let

CLARA LOVEMAN

Knotts in. Yes, you love easily but that's so much better than a miserable life. You are loveable, honest and kind. Allow him to look after you for our boys' sakes. Your happiness is mine."

"That's sweet of you to say," I said, passing a look to Knotts. He'd walked away with Vowkin to join Neuge and the other Min but was still eyeing me carefully. "But I'm not sure what I'll do. I don't deserve happiness. Like I said, Roki, I need to concentrate on myself. Whether that means six weeks or a century, who knows?"

It was quiet for a minute, like the ending of an era. The significance of our separation weighed heavy.

"What will you do with yourself?" I asked, shifting attention to him.

His eyes looked dark. "I'll find an enemy and ask them to sentence me to a punishment of their choosing."

"Aside from Lordin and potentially Soren, I don't believe you have enemies."

"You'd be surprised."

I raised my brows in disbelief, smiling tightly. Then I asked, "Well then. Given your family ties to the Crown of Crowns, I hope they won't be too harsh. What happens to Soren now?"

"Still in jail," Roki said. "That could change if Knotts decides to free her. And if that happens she'll likely be on probation. She's missed so much being locked underground. It saddens me because I know many Min who have committed much graver crimes than her."

"That's kind of you."

I dropped Roki's hands and took a step back, glanced at Knotts, then looked back at Roki. My day of reckoning was long overdue. "Maybe I will see you in the stars, Roki. Thank you for everything. Thank you for this life, for your undying devotion, and for your honesty. I do love you, Roki. And I think a part of me loves Knotts as well. Can you tell him for me? Can you tell him I said that?"

"Can't you tell him yourself?"

I smiled. "I can't. For now, I must say goodbye to you. See you around."

Knotts looked panicked as he realized I was leaving. He broke away from Neuge and started running toward me.

"And one more favor, Roki?"

"Sure."

"Can you mask my presence?"

* * *

From a peak in the Gilfoil Mountains, she could see down on Cara, the coastal capital city of Geniverd, on the continent of Gaard. She could see the buildings in development, the cleanup crews taking away the rubble, the mountains of Guardians and Protectors at the scrap heap, being recycled for parts.

The bodies were still being recovered from the sea using large boats, and nets had been set up to catch the bodies as they washed ashore.

The sky was filled with flyrarcs. The people were getting back to work. Not only had the richest and wealthiest organizations in the world been disassembled, their leaders long gone, but their physical buildings had all been engulfed in flames. Free enterprise would grow once more. The future would advance further into the stars.

The wounds of war would heal in time. The buildings would be repaired. The gardens would be replanted. Only time would tell if the new form of government lasted, those few senators gathered in the public square for all eyes to see and ears to hear.

NordHaven was a ruin. VondRust no more. One man spoke of rebuilding. "A more modest headquarters, perhaps?" he asked.

And others spoke of turning the rubble into farmland.

She left the Gilfoil Mountains and made a stop at Capernort. It was more for nostalgia than anything else. Nobody was home, and she walked through the few hallways, touched the artwork on the walls, stood before the cold fireplace and remembered its warmth.

Outside, the snow fell in a slow, soothing rhythm. She stood on the stoop and caught a snowflake on her tongue, then giggled at her own silliness. How grand life was when a person stopped to admire the world's natural beauty, the simple magic of falling snow.

She looked above, through the sheets of snow-laden clouds, beyond the twin moons of Geniverd, and to the stars.

Sign up to Clara's mailing list on ClaraLoveman.com/subscribe and be the first to hear news about her books.

Please consider leaving a review online if you enjoyed this story, even if it's only one or two lines. It will be a huge help.

ABOUT THE AUTHOR

Clara Loveman graduated from Liverpool John Moores University and has an MPH from the University of Sheffield. She lives in Maidenhead, UK, a riverside town not far from Windsor.

ACKNOWLEDGEMENTS

I owe an enormous debt of gratitude to many people who've supported my writing or played a role in shaping this story—particularly to Nick, Julie T, Leonora B, Lauren, Christine, Phebe, Phyllis, Jacquee, Helen L, Judith, Steve, Kate, Carol, Peggy, Branden, Keysha, Sean, Naveed, Lisa, Eva, Bernard, Kelly, Zion, James, Sally, Norah, Aaron, Arwen, Gareth, David T, Stefan, Monica, Szilvia, Ruth, Caroline, Rowena, Beth, Ruby, Boe, Lewis, Sophie, Ruth, Anna, Hetty and Liz.

A special thanks to Charlie and Chris who have put up with me at home, and a big thank you to my parents for giving me the best life possible.

I'm also sincerely grateful to my readers for joining me on this journey.

And finally to the God of heaven: words are not enough to express my profound gratitude for His unfailing grace and justice.